BREAKING THE RULES

THE TRISKELION SERIES
BOOK 1

JODI PAYNE

BA TORTUGA

BREAKING THE RULES

Saul Reynolds manages a busy bicycle shop in downtown Boulder, Colorado. A recent CU graduate, he's also a Dom, and has many friends his age in the scene. Saul's an old soul, and even at twenty-five, he's had enough experience to understand his own desires. He's had plenty of lovers and he's played the role of part-time Dom, but he's never found the perfect combination of lover and sub in one man.

Troy Finch lost his lover in a rodeo accident twenty years ago, moved to Boulder, and has worked as a line cook in his friend Carter's diner ever since. He's attended many parties at Carter's home with couples in the BDSM lifestyle and feels comfortable in a submissive role, but without a Dom of his own, Troy hasn't explored what that really means to him. He has needs he doesn't entirely understand and finds his only outlet at the hands of Carter's husband, Geoff, a tattoo artist who has used Troy's skin as a canvas for as long as they've known each other, covering Troy in colorful, intricate triskelia.

Troy doesn't know what he was thinking accepting a dinner invitation from a kid half his age, but everything feels right about their evening together, including Saul's Dominant side. The rules for a twenty-five year old gay cowboy from years ago, though, are totally different than for a twenty-five year old college grad in Boulder now, and despite Saul's confidence, Troy isn't sure whether they can make it work.

Saul and Troy manage to bend a good many rules in the name of caring and compromise, but in the name of love, there are some rules they're just going to have to break.

Note: This is a "true series" and should be read in order.

Breaking the Rules, The Triskelion Series, Book One
Copyright © 2020 by Jodi Payne & BA Tortuga

Editing by Sue Laybourn of No Stone Unturned Editing
http://nostoneunturnedediting.co.uk/

Cover illustration by AJ Corza
http://www.seeingstatic.com/
Cover content is for illustrative purposes only and any person depicted on the cover is a model.

ISBN: 978-1-7330076-3-4

Published by Tygerseye Publishing, LLC, September 2020
Printed in the USA

As always, to our wives.

1

S aul held the mountain bike like a lover, like it was
  something precious, babying the new paint job and
shiny chrome as he loaded it into the back of the pick-up
truck. He wrapped it in a blanket so it would stay spotless
on the drive and checked the tires for the third time.

Then he hopped out of the bed and shut the tailgate. All
good. That bike was some of his best work. Thank goodness
for Emma, he wanted to deliver this one personally and he
didn't have wheels of his own.

You got this.

It was another perfect spring day and downtown
Boulder was busy. He drove up Canyon Boulevard and
parked near the east end of the Pearl Street Mall, then
reversed the process with the bicycle, gingerly lowering it to
the ground. He got on it and took a lap of the parking lot,
fucking with the gears and brakes. Damn, this was a sweet
rebuild.

He walked the bike to Carter Lee's diner, which of course
he'd forgotten the name of, but he knew the one, he'd been
there a bunch of times. Best cup of coffee in town, crazy

good French toast. Small world, colliding with the man who owned that place.

He'd rebuilt the whole front end, put on new tires, a new chain, a new gear shift, replaced the scuffed-up pedals and the twisted handlebars, and had given the thing a new paint job. It sparkled like new, which was pretty much the least he could do after almost knocking out Carter's front teeth.

He pulled up outside the diner and peered through the window, trying to see if he could catch Carter's eye, but the place was hopping, and everyone was busy. He sighed and locked the bike up, making sure it was as far away from other bikes as possible, and headed inside.

"Just one?" The hostess grabbed a menu.

"Oh, I'm just... I was looking for..."

"This way, please."

He blinked, totally off-guard, and followed her to a small table. "I'm actually just here to see Carter."

"I'll let him know you're looking for him. Coffee?"

"Oh I, uh." She peered at him expectantly. "Sure. Sounds good."

"You take cream?" She handed him a menu, sighing as a group of mountain bikers showed up. "Ah, to-go orders. I'll be right back with your coffee."

"Yes," he called after her. He glanced over at the bikers, but he didn't know any of them. Must not be local. He knew a lot of the real enthusiasts in town from his shop.

He glanced at his watch. It was eleven-thirty and he'd been putting the finishing touches on the bike all morning. He supposed he could eat, but he really didn't need the menu. He wanted that French toast with the berries and the vanilla-maple syrup. He could almost taste it.

"Troy! Troy, I need seven more turkey sandwiches to go. All chips."

"On it, honey," a rough drawl answered her, the John Deere ball cap the only thing visible through the pass-through.

That was one of his favorite things, the way Carter's cook worked—steady, calm, fast and obviously damn good at his job.

He tried to think how long the guy had been working back there. Had to be forever, and in all that time he'd never heard the cook get ruffled. Just "On it," or "Yes, ma'am" with that deep tone. He liked the voice, and he was pretty sure he'd have recognized it anywhere.

"Hey, man, how goes it?" Carter came and sat, offering him a smile. "Run anyone over this week?"

He grinned and felt his cheeks burn, totally embarrassed. "Nope. I'm finding you a tough act to follow. I think I've hit a dry spell. You?"

"Busy as a one-armed paperhanger." Carter smiled for him, and, okay, he was totally glad he hadn't knocked those teeth out.

"I see that. I have to say I'm sorry again. Hopefully your bike will make up for the bruises. It's all done, I parked it outside. If you have any problems, you just let me know, I'll get it right for you." He smiled back, going for charming but not flirty. Carter was a handsome but married man.

"You rock, man. I mean it. Let me grab you a cup of coffee and...you're the French toast, right?"

"My favorite. Thanks so much." Carter was the coolest cat on the planet. He wasn't sure if he could be that chill if someone barreled into his path out of nowhere, sent him flying and mangled his handlebars. He'd like to think he could, he tried to be level-headed, and shit happens, right?

"Right on." Carter stood and went to pour his coffee.

"Troy, I need a French toast with berries and a side of bacon on the fly."

"On it, boss."

On it, boss. Saul smiled and leaned back in his chair. That drawl was something. He thanked Carter again for the coffee and his stomach growled as he picked it up to take a sip. Yeah, he could eat.

He drank his coffee and checked his phone while he waited. He answered an email from Emma about the supply order he'd placed the day before. Thank goodness Emma was as much of a workaholic as he was. The shop was demanding and busy.

He also made a cocktail hour appointment with Khloe, who said she needed a hand. He wasn't her Dom, but she didn't have one at the moment and she was a friend. If she needed him, he'd be there.

"Excuse me. You're the French toast?" Shocking green eyes stared at him. They seemed huge when paired with that bald head.

He stared right back and smiled, stunned by the handsome face that went with the drawl. "Actually, I'm Saul. But I'm having the French toast."

"Good deal." He got a smile, a nod as the plate was put in front of him. "Enjoy your breakfast, sir."

"I always do. You make amazing French toast." He boldly reached out and touched a triskelion tattoo on the cook's wrist with curious fingers, keeping the man there another second. "Great ink. What's your name?"

"Finch. Troy Finch. Pleased to meet you."

As his gaze traveled up, he discovered the triskelions climbing up Troy Finch's arm, some delicate and lacy, some violent and sharp-edged. It was fascinating, and he had all kinds of questions.

"I think the pleasure is really mine, Troy." As much as he wanted to keep this lovely man talking, he lifted his fingers away. "I know you're busy back there. Thank you for taking the time to run this out to me."

"You're welcome, sir. Boss is bad about letting his orders die in the window."

"Get your ass in the kitchen. I hear you, telling lies about me." Carter was barely holding his laughter back.

Troy snorted, but dropped him a wink. "Yes, sir. No smoke break for me?"

"Nope. Kitchen."

"Thanks again, Troy." Saul watched the guy take a few strolling steps toward the kitchen and then head back to work. He glanced up at Carter. "Interesting guy. Lots of pretty specific ink. Nice work." He picked up the little glass jug of syrup and covered his plate in it.

"It is. My husband, Geoff? He did all the work."

"Yeah? He must be pretty creative." Who knew there were so many different ways to draw a triskelion? He'd seen at least ten or twelve and he figured there had to be more going up that arm. He started in on his French toast. "Mm. So good." Like foodgasm good.

"Enjoy, huh? It's on the house." Carter grinned at him, dark eyes wrinkling with the power of his smile. "The bike looks great, man. Thank you."

"You're welcome. I'm glad you're happy with it. I thought it came out pretty sweet." Yeah, he could maybe be more humble. But he knew what his strengths were, and custom bikes was one of them. He was good at what he did. He smiled right back at Carter. "Try not to get in my way again, huh?"

"Yeah, yeah. Pay attention, and I'll do my best." The wink he got was pure mischief.

He laughed. "You're on. Listen, what are you doing Sunday? You want to ride? We could have a rematch."

"Sure. Sunday's my day off. Let me check with Geoff, but he'll be asleep. He works late on Saturdays."

"Perfect." He swallowed the big bite he had in his mouth. "Don't let me keep you, I get that it's busy. Thank you so much for the lunch."

"You're welcome. I'll text you." Then poof, Carter was off and running, greeting customers and bussing tables.

He knew Carter was going to like how he'd fixed up the bike. He knew it. Just like he was sure Troy's stunning green eyes had gotten a good look at his ring, the one bearing the symbol that matched the carpet of amazing ink on the cook's arm.

He finished his food and left a great big tip. Then he pulled out one of his business cards from the shop, flipped it over and wrote a quick note on the back before handing it to the hostess.

"Excuse me. Troy might need to reach me, so can you make sure he gets this?" He held the card out to her.

"Yeah, sure. Have a good day."

"Thanks much. You too." As he was leaving, he heard her calling back to Troy for more sandwiches to go.

2

_____

Troy sat in the back of the restaurant having his smoke break.

He didn't actually have a cigarette, because Geoff and Carter had made him a deal. Every cigarette-free day earned him five minutes under Geoff's machine.

It hadn't made quitting easy, but it had made it something shared.

Still, he wanted one.

Bad.

Troy took a deep, deep breath, and tried to just let the stress go.

"Oh. I didn't know you were out here, Troy." Charlie had a cigarette and a hot pink mini Bic in one hand. At one time they'd been smoking buddies; now they were just buddies. "I'm sorry. I'll come out later."

"You are a good man, but I'm cool. I need to finish cleaning up and get the hell out of here."

"All the same." Charlie walked about ten feet away before lighting up. "Crazy day. I bet you're beat."

"Yeah." Don't laugh. Don't laugh. Don't.

He cracked up, just tickled shitless. That pretty little French toast boy had come onto him. It made him feel a little embarrassed, a little less like an old man, a lot honored.

Oh, and surprised. Seriously. He hadn't ever expected anyone in Boulder to get his ink.

Charlie looked over one shoulder, then down. "Is my fly open?"

He peeked. "All zipped up. I'm just tired, man."

"You got tomorrow off?"

"Monday and Tuesday. They finally got me on a stable schedule with you and Juana." Juana was a single mom, so she worked the weekdays, and Charlie cooked on the weekends and whenever he could pull a shift doing anything.

"You better get some rest then, man. You're cracking up." Charlie made a swirly coo-coo gesture next to his ear with one finger and grinned.

"Is Troy still here?" Willow, the hostess, poked her head out the back door. Charlie pointed to him. "Oh, good. Some guy... uh. Young, friend of Carter's I think? He asked me to give this to you. I stuck it in my apron and forgot about it until now. I was afraid I'd missed you." She handed him a business card. "You're off, right? Have a good night, Troy."

"I'll be back in a second, Willow." Charlie puffed on his cigarette.

"Hope so." Willow disappeared back inside.

"Ooh. Y'all hooking up?" He did love a good romance.

He glanced at the card, Saul. What a great name. Seriously.

"Well, not yet." Charlie stomped out his cigarette. "She turned me down once. I don't think she really sees me yet, though. I have to come down some day when she's working and…well, I'm not, you know?"

"Yeah. Good deal." He sighed and stood, stretching tall. Then he caught sight of writing on the back.

In case you need me.

Whoa. Ballsy.

"We'll see, I guess. Have a good one." Charlie gave him a clap on the shoulder and headed inside.

Troy stopped in to grab his backpack and his to-go box with a patty melt and fries, then he started on his wander toward his condo.

In case you need me.

Lord, he was too old for that shit, but he sure liked that someone had made the offer.

3

"That was a hell of a ride."

Saul walked his bike up to the rack and locked it alongside Carter's. They'd met early that morning, found a trail and hit it hard until their legs were sore. Carter was great to ride with; safe, but gutsy and aggressive, just out to have some fun.

From what he could tell, Carter seemed happy with the bike's performance. Saul noticed him testing it out at the beginning, trying the brake response and playing with the balance, but not for long. Carter had trusted it quickly, and then they were off.

"It was. I tell you, I'm beginning to think the trails are getting steeper." Carter wiped his neck clean from the sweat.

"Yeah. That's gotta be it. It can't have anything to do with you getting old." He laughed, pulling off his helmet and running a hand through his damp hair.

"Shut up, kiddo, before I beat you." Carter snorted at him. "Look alive."

The water bottle flew at him.

"Whoa." He reached up with one hand and snatched it

out of the air. "Thanks." He smiled. That was a pretty slick catch, he'd always had good reflexes. He opened it and chugged most of it right down.

"Good catch." Carter sucked his own water down, Adam's apple bobbing. "Man, I'm so empty I can hear the water hitting my stomach and splashing. You want to come to the diner? I'll buy you breakfast."

"I will never turn down free food." He watched Carter swallow. Man, so handsome. Geoff was a lucky man. He sighed and finished the rest of his water, then grabbed a towel and tried to make himself presentable for the diner.

"No stress, man. We'll eat in the kitchen. Troy won't mind."

"Yeah? Awesome." He wouldn't mind Troy either. "That guy works his ass off, huh?"

"You know it. He's been working for me for...shit. Twenty years ago? Twenty-one? A while."

Saul had been in Boulder since he'd started at CU, probably came to the diner for the first time junior year when he was working and had a little money. But Troy had started at the diner when Saul was in Kindergarten. Maybe nursery school. He grinned. Crazy. "That's a long time. I guess you know him pretty well?"

"He and Geoff met when he won his first event. He was just a kid, coming in with his honey. It was great."

"Event?" *His honey*. Well, crap. Maybe he'd overstepped yesterday giving Troy his card.

"He was a rodeo cowboy. Him and Arnie both were." Carter rolled his eyes. "Talk about leather fantasies. Those two were stunning together."

"Wow. I bet. I knew a guy that did rodeo once, but I don't know much about it honestly. So what does Arnie do?" He tossed his towel and his helmet into the front seat.

"He was a bull rider. He died in Dallas a long time ago."

He stared at Carter. "Shit. I'm sorry." He sure put his foot in that one.

"Oh, it was twenty plus years ago, but thank you. It damn near destroyed Troy, but he survived it." Carter's lips quirked. "He remade himself."

Saul tried to put himself in that position for a minute and just couldn't, it seemed so sad. And he had no idea what remaking yourself meant. He was even more curious about Troy now, but he didn't want to ask for more details from Carter.

He was convinced that he was meant to hear the rest of the story from Troy himself.

"Man, I'm going to eat a stack of pancakes as big as my head." Carter started the engine. "You mind if I call Geoff to join us?"

He pulled on his seatbelt and lowered his window. "Not at all, I'd love to meet him. How did you two hook up? You don't look like a tattoo guy."

"I have some, but not many. We met in L.A." Carter looked at him squarely. "At a fairly kinky lifestyle convention." Oh. Damn, had he run over the right guy on that mountain or what? Carter watched him, and he could tell the man was trying to gauge his reaction, like this was a test.

"No way, really? I knew those existed, but I've never been to one. I'd like to one day though." That should clue Carter in a little. Saul hauled his bag from the floorboard and opened it up to pull out a clean T-shirt. "So... have you guys found other lifestyle people? Is there a scene in Boulder?" He unzipped his jersey and peeled it off to change.

"Everything's in Denver, really, but there are some good clubs in the city." Carter grinned, and Saul saw the way the man's shoulders relaxed. Carter plugged his phone in and hit speaker. "We have a group of ten or so that have parties, that sort of thing. I bet they have meetings at the university, though."

Sweet. His new goal was to get an invitation to one of Carter's parties. "I never found a real one. Doesn't mean it's not there, I guess. I was a late bloomer, I wasn't really playing in school."

He pulled on his T-shirt and slipped back under the seat belt.

"Yeah, I sort of had a wild ride until I found the diner. Then it was love at first sight. Story of my life."

Saul didn't have a story of his life yet. But he was really happy with this chapter. He stayed quiet as the phone started to ring.

"Hey, baby. You all done?" Carter's lover's voice was smooth and soft, and Saul could hear the affection.

"I am. Made it the whole way without either crashing or burning. You up and dressed?"

"The kid is learning! I am both. Need me?"

Carter chuckled softly. "Always. Come down for brunch? I promised Saul food."

"I would love that. I'm looking forward to meeting the man that tried to kill you."

"Ha." He grinned. "I saw Carter ride. It will take more than me to do him in."

Geoff gasped melodramatically, the tone sarcastic. "Oh my goodness. Are we on speaker phone?"

That just made him laugh harder.

"Would I do that, sugarbutt? Diner. Fifteen. Love you." Then Carter hung up with a grin.

"He's funny." Saul stretched and his stomach growled. "Oh, I can taste the French toast already."

"He's a hoot. I'm craving the green chile benedict, something with a little sting."

At this hour on a Sunday, it took them no time at all to make it downtown. He loved Carter's truck and was a little jealous of it. He didn't have wheels of his own, he biked everywhere or took the bus if he had to. He'd managed to get around just fine that way since his college years at CU.

"You're welcome to leave your bike up in the bed of the truck. I'll park back near the kitchen." Carter pulled up to the kitchen door, one of the cooks out there smoking.

"Thanks, I'll take you up on that." He jumped out of the truck and stretched, legs feeling stiff. "We pushed pretty hard, so I'm tightening up some."

"I got some Blue Emu salve in the backseat, if you want." Carter squinted at the guy. "Are you supposed to be smoking out here?"

"It's the smoking area, Carter. That's where you smoke."

"Man has a point."

"If I can con Troy into quitting, I can con anyone." Carter's eyes narrowed. "I just have to find what Charlie's soft spot is."

"Nothing soft about me, boss. Can't say the same about your man though." Charlie grinned and breathed out a long stream of smoke.

"Be good, Charles. My money's on Geoff, every time." There was a calm seriousness that made Saul's eyebrow arch. Impressive.

Also impressive was the way Charlie's eyes dropped to the blacktop. "Sorry, Carter. I was just playing. He's inside talking to Troy."

"No worries, kiddo." He clapped the guy on the back on the way by. "Busy day?"

"Swamped. It just let up about ten-fifteen minutes ago." Charlie nodded to him as he walked by.

Saul looked Charlie over as he passed. They were probably about the same age and he wouldn't say that was in "kiddo" range. He gave the guy a wink and they exchanged a soft laugh, then he followed Carter inside.

"Good morning, baby." The man who kept his distance and gave Carter a chaste kiss on the cheek had to be Geoff. "Ew. You're all sweaty."

Geoff was totally not the look he expected. Tattoo artists were supposed to wear metalhead T-shirts and be pierced and inked everywhere. This guy was...dapper. Clean-cut, coiffed, little button up shirt and khakis. Huh.

"I'd say it was totally my fault but that sounds so dirty." He gave Geoff a smile and offered a hand. "Saul Reynolds. Nice to meet you."

"Geoff Lee. You seem so young for attempted murder. Carter, you didn't tell me he was fifteen!"

"I didn't? I'm sure I told you a six-year-old hit me..."

Geoff laughed. "Maybe you did. Early senility and all. Troy, have you got a happy meal for junior?"

He rolled his eyes. This got old after a while, but he supposed having a baby face now meant he'd look young forever. "I'll let you all know when I need my diaper changed. Troy, man. Come to my rescue here?"

Troy glanced over at him, the smile pure wicked evil. "Now, look here. That is not my kink. In fact, you might have to go to Denver for that. French toast, right?"

Geoff practically squealed. "Troy! I'm so proud!"

"Yes, please." He laughed and crossed his arms as he leaned against the wall, playing at pouting. "Damn. This is a tough crowd."

"Consider it initiation." Carter grinned at him, and it felt good, like they were willing to let him in. "What do you want to drink? I'll grab it from the front."

"Grape soda, please."

Geoff blinked at him. "Oh my God, he *is* six."

Troy chuckled softly, cooking away. It was a bit like watching a machine—bread and bacon and sausage and eggs all working at the same time.

"Not six." He watched Troy move, so graceful and efficient, with total confidence. How much fun would it be to get this guy flustered? What would it take? How would Troy react to being thrown off-balance or forced out of his comfort zone?

Just look at the guy. How hot would that be? He was salivating over the promise of food, and the man doing the cooking.

"No, you're closer to twelve." Geoff cackled, but there wasn't meanness in it at all. "Seriously, thanks for helping with Carter's bike. That meant a lot to him."

Twelve. Ha. He wondered if Geoff was onto him. "Oh, God. It was the least I could do after sending Carter flying. My heart was pounding for real. I thought I'd really hurt him."

"I'm made of steel." Carter handed him his soda without a snarky comment.

Geoff. "Mm. Steel. For sure."

"Now who's twelve?" Saul snorted.

"Oh, honey. Carter's not for boys."

Troy's laugh filled the kitchen. "No?"

Geoff glared over. "Shut up, butthead."

"I mean, I don't..."

"Troy!"

"Hey. No worries, Geoff. Carter told me where you met." He grinned.

Oh, Geoff had the prettiest blush. How sweet.

"And Saul tells me he's had trouble finding a scene. I'm thinking he should come to one of our parties." Carter didn't even look up, just set a stack of plates out for Troy.

Score. *Please, oh please.*

"Oh?" Geoff was watching him differently now.

"Yes. In fact, we're having a get-together next Sunday night at our place, if you're interested."

"I would love to. Really. I'd love that. Thank you."

"We're not serving grape soda, Junior." Geoff winked at him.

"No worries. I'll bring a six pack to share." He grinned right back.

"Perfect. I'll text you the details. It's a relaxing evening." Carter smiled, looking like nothing more than a benevolent uncle. "Assuming no one's in the doghouse."

"Be nice, now." Both men chuckled together knowingly, then Geoff continued. "That's not Troy's kink either."

A plate clanged in front of him. "French toast with fruit."

Saul blinked at the food. The toast made the shape of a dog, with blueberries for eyes, a pineapple piece for a nose, and a strawberry tongue.

"Eggs benedict for you, boss, and an egg white omelet with spinach, mushroom, and tomato for Geoff."

"Oh my God, I got a dog! How cool!" Saul was totally sincere. The kid's menu shape was probably meant to be a joke but he loved it. "Really. Too cool, Troy. Thanks."

"You're welcome. Y'all enjoy." Troy winked at him before heading back to the line.

"Wow. Dog French toast. He must like you." Carter ducked when Geoff took a swing.

I hope so. He seemed to be a bit of a golden boy with these guys right now. They liked him, why not Troy too? He had to assume the hostess had given Troy his card, and Troy was still winking at him. He couldn't be that far off.

"Does Troy have... anyone?" He chose those words carefully, leaving Carter and Geoff to interpret what he was asking as they pleased. A lover, a Dom, family... whatever they wanted to tell him. Whatever they thought he should know.

"He has us." Carter sounded so sure.

"Not in a we're-a-threesome sort of way, though. Just in a we're-all-family-and-he's-a-doll-baby sort of way," Geoff added.

Okay. He could shoot straight then, right? "So... not in an I'd-be-totally-idiotic-to-ask-him-out kind of way?"

The guys shared a look, but it was Geoff who answered him. "I think it might be fun. He hasn't done a lot of dating."

Both of those statements were telling. They had no idea how Troy would respond to being asked out, which meant Troy hadn't said yes to too many people in the twenty-whatever years since his lover died.

He wasn't sure if he should take that as a warning or a challenge, but in the end, Saul decided not to even pay attention. He was curious about Troy, and he wanted to know more. Troy had to know he was attracted, maybe even felt it some too? He thought the man would say yes. Eventually. "Who doesn't want a little fun, right?"

Geoff smiled at him, genuinely. "Best of luck, Junior."

"Thanks." He dug into his doggie French toast. God, he was starving.

4

Mr. French Toast came in every day now, and every day Troy made French toast in different shapes—robots, cats, dogs.

Today he made a flower.

Carter looked at him when Angela picked up the order.

"What?"

"Seriously? A flower?"

"Shut up, boss."

Stupid, he knew, but... Shit, maybe he was flirting a little. What was the harm? It was French toast.

He hid his gaze under the brim of his ball cap and watched through the pass-through window as Angela delivered the flower to Saul, and a bright smile spread across the guy's face. It wasn't the goofy, cute smile from yesterday when he'd sent out the robot though, this one was warmer and seemed to settle over Saul like a blanket. Saul shared the moment with Angela, who laughed and poured out more coffee, but then suddenly, sharp, blue eyes flicked up from the plate and met his.

Oh, Saul made his mouth dry, which was not going to help with the teasing he was fixin' to get from Carter.

"Cradle robber."

"Shut up." He held Saul's gaze a second longer before he put a French dip together on a plate. "Don't make me hurt you, man."

"Promises promises."

They had the same kind of conversation eighty times a day, and it had a comfort to it, an ease.

"You do realize he's going to keep coming in here every morning until you talk to him, right? Are you making a point of how stubborn you are, or just waiting for him to hit three hundred pounds?"

"I don't know what to say. Hi. I'm old enough to be your father? That seems off-putting." Did he seriously just use the term off-putting? "Jesus, I've spent too much time with Geoff."

Carter laughed. "Sure. Go tell him you think you're too old for him. I dare you."

"Shut up." There was no way he could do that. No way. He wasn't rude by nature or raising. Still, he had permission to get off the line, so he gave Juana a nod and headed over to see if Mr. French Toast approved of his breakfast.

Saul saw him coming and stood, unfolding long legs and smiling at him. "Hi."

"Hey there. How was your breakfast?" *How are you so hot? Have I become a dirty old man?*

"It was perfect. Will you sit with me a minute?" Saul pulled out a chair for him.

"Thank you, sir." That made his cheeks heat, but he sat, didn't he? "I'm glad you enjoyed it."

"I've enjoyed it every morning this week. But it's not every day someone sends you flowers. I hope that means you'll let me take you out Friday night?" Saul seemed to be completely serious.

"Like a date?" How long had it been...had he ever been asked on a date? Ever?

Saul blinked at him. "Yeah. A date. With me."

"I-well, hell. Yes. Yes, I think I will." Huh.

Saul laughed, the sound pure joy. "Well good. I'm looking forward to it. What time and where should I meet you?"

He had to be back at work at five-thirty in the morning, so he needed to be home fairly early. "Five o'clock at my place?"

Saul nodded once. "I'll be there. You have my card still, I assume? My cell is on the front, text me your address."

"I can do that." Troy felt a bit like he'd been drinking— not enough to be drunk, but just a little tipsy.

"I better get to the shop." Saul emptied his coffee cup and stood again. "Thanks for finally coming out to talk to me."

He stood too, held out his hand. "Glad you liked your breakfast."

Saul caught his eyes and took it but didn't shake, just held on and gave it a squeeze. "The company was better."

He didn't shiver, but goosebumps popped up all over his skin. "Thank you, sir. You have a good day."

"You too." Saul let him go and dropped cash on the table, then gave him a smile and headed for the door. "Bye for now."

"See you." He grabbed the dishes and dropped them in the bus tub for Ang. He could see Carter, watching, waiting for a report. Fucker.

"You didn't tell him you were an old man, did you?" He'd say Carter was poking fun, the grin certainly made it look that way, but his boss was up to the elbows cooking in his place. Just stepped right in so he could have his five minutes with Saul.

"He asked me out on a date." He washed his hands and grabbed his hat. "I said yes."

"Sounds like fun, Troy." Carter smiled, gave him a nod, and then pointed to the griddle. "Sunny, scrambled well, Western no onion. Bacon light. He's a nice kid."

"Yeah." He'd see. He hoped so. He didn't want it to suck. "Got it. Thanks, boss."

He just needed to focus on getting through his shift. Then he could text his address, take a shower, and maybe jack off.

God knew he needed it.

5

Saul pulled into the bike lane and headed for the shop feeling a little high—on sunshine, on fresh air, on Troy. He wasn't trying to blow Troy's mind by asking the guy out, but he thought maybe he had. And he wasn't sure why that felt so good.

All he knew really was that those green eyes had stories to tell and he wanted to hear every one of them. Stories about ink, about kink, about how someone as genuine as Troy seemed could possibly be single all this time.

He smiled to himself all the way to work, so lost in his strange new obsession that he couldn't remember how he'd gotten there.

"Morning!" He ducked behind the counter and flipped open the orders book. "Sorry I'm a little late."

Emma looked up from the Yeti she was working on, her dreads bouncing like crazy. "I brought doughnuts."

"Maybe later, thanks. I ate." God, had he eaten. He'd eaten his own weight every morning for the last three days at that diner. Who the hell flirts over French toast? But it had worked, right? It so totally had. "He finally talked to me."

"No shit? Really? What did he say? Hell, what did the French toast look like today?"

"It was a flower." It was so sweet, but it sounded so ridiculous. He felt like a smitten little puppy all of a sudden. "He asked me how it was, and I asked him out."

"And he said?" Emma was a whore for a happy ending. Hell, she was all over a happy beginning.

This stupid smile was taking over his face. He had a feeling it was going to stay stuck there until Friday. "He said yes, of course. Who would turn me down? Get serious."

In fact, he'd been nervous about what Troy would say. Geoff said the guy hadn't dated much and Saul didn't really know how *not* to come on strong. He was worried Troy would say no. Even more worried Troy would say no for a real reason, not just because of nerves or something. It wouldn't have stopped him, he'd have asked again another day, but he was relieved it hadn't gone that way.

"Rock on, bud! Where are you going? What are you going to do?" Emma stood and stretched up tall—well, as far as her barely five feet tall could get her.

He stared at her. "Fuck. I have no idea. What do you think? I mean, he's not some college idiot, he's... well, you know, he's a man."

"Friday night, huh? If you were doing a day thing, I'd say Idaho Springs—you could do rafting and Beau Jo's—but staying here in town? Dinner and a movie?"

"Yeah, we have to stay in town this time. Dinner for sure. But a movie? You can't talk during a movie." Maybe dinner and an evening walk? He figured Troy wanted to get home early for work in the morning, why else set it for five o'clock? He could swing a nice dinner. "Catch the sunset maybe." He knew a spot.

"Oh, that's cool. Sunset and come back for a lazy coffee?"

"This is why I keep you around. I love lazy coffee." He reached under the counter and grabbed a doughnut. "I'm just going to eat my nerves."

"Fair enough. You want something to drink? I'm grabbing a tea." She wiped her hands off on the towel in her waistband. "And lazy coffee can last hours, right?"

"Yeah. Totally. I'll take a tea too, thanks." Lazy coffee was starting to sound like the best part of the date. "Speaking of dates... you had one last night, didn't you? And here I am talking about myself."

"I did. We're going rafting on Sunday. She's hot as hell, and? She has a Harley."

"You're a sucker for the tough girls, aren't you?"

This was good. Having someone he knew got it, someone he could confide in. He had this feeling that dating Troy was going to fuck with him a little. He'd never gotten this kind of vibe, felt a connection with anyone so quickly. Actually, he'd never gotten this kind of vibe from anyone at all. Ever.

"What should I wear?" He blinked. See? It was fucking with him already. He'd never given that kind of thing any thought, much less asked that question out loud.

"Jeans. Maybe that black shirt you bought in Aspen? The one with the barely there metallic threads?" She tossed him a bottle of iced tea.

He caught it and opened it right up. "Yes. Good idea. It's comfy too." He felt confident in that shirt. Oh, the things he'd learned in Aspen. His balls ached just thinking about that trip. He could almost smell the leather.

"It shows off your shoulders too, which is handy."

"Handy, huh?" He did have good shoulders, and he felt like strength was important. He wasn't short, but he wasn't one of those big guys who was imposing just by build. He needed to work for that image. He grinned. "I guess I need to work with what I've got."

"Don't we all." Emma stuck her tongue out at him, the piercing glinting in the lights. "Look alive. It's your favorite customer."

He fought his groan. Deb. The unhappily married, twenty-thousand dollar rack, perfectly coiffed Deb who thought Saul was the hottest thing since sliced bread.

She'd spent almost as much at the shop as she had on her boobs though, so he put on a smile as she walked in. "Good morning, Deb."

"Saul. My favorite person. I came to discuss a custom project. Something personalized."

This could be interesting. He loved custom builds. "Yeah? What are you looking for? A street bike? Mountain? Maybe a nice comfy cruiser for around town?"

"I'm thinking about something for around town. Something wonderful, maybe with a little sparkle?"

Sparkle. Oh God. He suddenly had a vision of Deb riding through town on a grownup version of a little girl's bike; pink glitter frame, white seat, white wall tires, silver Mylar streamers flowing from the handlebars.

And telling everyone he built it.

Oh, please God, no.

"A cruiser sounds great. We could look at some stock frames, see what you like." He pulled a book out from underneath the counter. "Mint green is really popular right now, blush, lavender, powder blue..."

"I love the idea of you making me blush, Saul darling."

Emma made a sound vaguely like a muppet being strangled by a vampiric duck.

He grinned at her. "Deb, I've met your husband. He's big enough that I know to respect him." In fact, Deb's husband had several inches and at least a hundred pounds on him, and Saul wasn't about to get on his bad side, no matter how much that rack cost.

And they'd had this discussion before.

"Mint, then?"

"Very en vogue," he said, and Emma nodded.

"Totally the hot color right now. Completely."

"Well, all right. Let me see." Deb came around the back side of the counter and stood close to him to flip the pages in his catalog.

He gave Emma big bug eyes and mouthed, "Really?"

She waved at him and blew him a kiss.

"How about a retro look. Like a 1950s Cadillac, you know? Mint frame, chrome fenders, white-wall tires?" It would cost her a pretty penny, but she had it.

By the time he got her spending money, he was back to planning his date. Friday couldn't come soon enough.

6

"I'm not doing this." Troy just couldn't. He was too old to date.

"Bullshit you're not." Carter was leaning on the doorframe of his bedroom while Geoff dug through his closet like a whirling dervish. Ninety percent of his admittedly limited wardrobe was on his bed. "Do you seriously make your bed every day?"

"Have you ever been in here when it wasn't made?"

"His bed is always made, but his closet is a disaster. When was the last time you went through this stuff, honey?" Geoff crossed the room with a pair of jeans in one hand and a button down in the other. "Do these jeans fit you?"

"Yeah..." Like a glove. "Maybe. They'll be a little snug, I bet."

"Oh, you have to show us." Carter didn't have to sound so friggin' amused.

"Try them on, please, Troy. Carter, make yourself useful please, and find the iron and ironing board?" Geoff started putting things back on hangers and rearranging them in his closet.

"You have an ironing board?" Carter raised an eyebrow at him.

He started to answer but Geoff cut him off. "He's Texan, baby. Of course he does."

"I do. It's set up in the guest room." He'd been ironing a pair of jeans dry this morning. They had come out of the dryer a little soppy and he hated having soggy balls.

"Oh, for fuck's sake. I'm going to...I don't know...make you and Geoff mud wrestle." Carter wandered by, muttering about insane assholes.

"Ick. Mud. What a mess. Let me see you in those jeans, honey. Turn around." Geoff watched him in uncomfortable ways as he modeled the jeans. "Oh, those fit just right, Troy. Your ass looks fantastic. Carter, come look at Troy's ass."

"Geoff, man, he doesn't have to—"

"Turn, boy, and let me see."

Troy turned, making sure to stick his tongue out at Carter on the way.

"Oh, honey, he's looking at your ass. He's not paying attention." Geoff's grin was absolutely evil.

"Hm." Carter hummed behind him. "Very nice."

Geoff seemed almost gleeful. "I told you."

"Y'all! Be good. I'm nervous enough without you hooligans talking about my butt."

"Look, you let me pierce your dick. I can talk about your butt." Geoff managed to appear affronted and amused all at once. "Are you going to shave or be scruffy?"

"I was thinking shaved, yeah?" He didn't think scruffy was good for a date.

"I think Junior will appreciate a shave, yes."

"I don't know what you're so nervous about, Troy. He asked you out. He's interested. It's not like you have to wonder." Carter glanced at the shirts Geoff had laid out on the bed.

"I know. I just..." *I've never done this, like this.* He picked up guys at the club in Denver a couple times a year or he prayed that someone at one of the parties was available and interested for a one-off. "I'm going to shave. Someone pick a shirt."

There was a short silence as he ducked into the bathroom, but he could hear them talking after he left.

"He'll be okay, baby. It's just... something new."

Troy sighed softly. Carter was right. He was being a dipshit. There was nothing to be worried about. This was a date—most likely supper and a movie at the theater. No big deal.

He shaved, making sure he took care in cleaning himself up, checking his scalp to make sure it was nice and smooth. Then he put on a little smell-good, deodorant, and his watch. Now he just needed his shirt.

"Y'all pick a shirt out for me yet?"

Geoff was leaning against Carter, and it was Carter who answered. "We like the gray or the pinstripe button downs. But any of those are fine."

"And roll the sleeves to show off your ink. Junior likes it." Geoff smiled at him.

"It's great ink." What wasn't to show off? "Soon we get to do more, hmm?" He grabbed the gray—it was comfortable, silky. Classy, in that redneck tuxedo sort of way.

"Maybe another week without cigarettes, right Carter?"

"Five days, in fact."

"You miss them still?" Carter asked

Troy nodded. "Every goddamn day." But he needed the release of the ink more than the nicotine.

"What time is it?" Geoff grabbed Carter's wrist to look at

the watch there. "Oh. Baby. We have to go. You don't want to be here when Junior gets here, do you?"

"No, you don't. Go on. Thanks for your help." He grabbed his summer straw off the hat stand.

"We're going." Geoff hugged him quickly and gave him a kiss on the cheek.

Carter stepped close and rested a hand on his shoulder. "It's just a date. It's not a contract. Relax and have some fun."

"I know. I got this." One way or the other, it was one hell of an ego boost, right? Right.

Troy let them out, waving before he closed the door. He put his hat on the pass-through, glancing at the front room. It looked great—the Pendleton blanket on the sofa bright and contrasting with the heavy dark leather of his sectional. He'd painted the room a deep navy, and it suited, making the furniture sink into the room and the framed photographs pop.

Not five minutes later he heard a horn beep and he saw Saul climbing out of an ancient, beat-to-shit Subaru. He raised an eyebrow. The car didn't seem to suit Saul at all, and in fact, he could tell by the way the guy frowned at it that it was someone else's wheels.

Saul headed up his walk, running fingers through wavy blond hair and tugging on a black button down to straighten it.

Pretty baby. Lord, he was a giant idiot for stressing. He just needed to go out, enjoy himself, and let it be.

The doorbell rang, and he opened it to find Saul smiling at him, blue eyes shining, completely at ease in that tanned skin. "Whoa! Do I have the wrong house? I'm here to pick up a guy in a greasy baseball hat and an apron, I wasn't expecting someone so handsome to answer the door."

"This is my secret identity. You have to promise not to

tell anyone. Would you like to come in?" Oh, go him! That was a quick comeback with a smile, and a good one at that.

"Not a word, I swear." Saul laughed, stepping inside and looking around. "Thanks. This is great."

"Thank you. It's mine, so I think I'll keep it." Okay, did he ask Saul if he wanted a drink or a seat? How did this work?

"I made reservations since it's Friday and all. If our table's not ready we could hang out at the... hey, the guys said you were a rodeo man. This is a great picture. Who is that?"

"Man named James Bridey. He was my roping partner while I was on the circuit." The man had beautiful hands and he'd been lucky to get some amazing shots.

"Did you take this?" Saul moved slowly through his living room examining his photographs. "Are these yours?"

"Yeah." He loved playing with his camera, seeing what he could see. It was easier now, with digital and sim cards, but sometimes he still shot film and developed it in his basement.

"You've got a good eye, Troy. I like them. How long have you been at it? Did you teach yourself?" So many questions.

"A long time. Thirty years, give or take." *Longer than you've been alive. Jesus, forgive me.* "My old man was into it. He was a sports photographer."

"Thirty years? Wow. That's forever. Very cool." Saul glanced at his watch. "We should head to dinner. I don't want to be late and lose the reservation."

"Sure. Sounds great." He almost offered to take his truck, but this was Saul's date, so he didn't. He just grabbed his hat, his wallet, and his keys. "I'm ready."

"Cool." Saul headed for the door. "I borrowed a car because I don't actually own one. It's not a fancy date car but it runs."

"Running is good. So, how did you decide to open a bike shop?" Saul seemed young for that, but what did he know.

"Oh, it's not mine. I just run it. Me and Emma. It belongs to this guy Chuck, he used to run it, now he's training with one of the Tour teams. And he's a dad. Busy guy."

Saul crossed in front of him and opened the passenger side door. "Climb on in."

"Thank you." He remembered training constantly, traveling. It had been a whole different life.

Saul closed his door and then slipped into the driver's seat beside him. "Emma was there before I was. She worked for Chuck and then she was trying to manage it on her own but really, she likes to get her hands dirty, you know? So she hired me, and we split up the management stuff so we both get to get hands on too. It works. And it pays the rent easy and then some, so I'm good."

The Subaru rattled along as Saul talked, and they headed for town when they left his neighborhood.

Troy liked the sound of Saul's voice—it was rich, a little musical, and easy to listen to. Even better, with very few prompts, Saul kept talking about bikes, about Boulder, about random bits of nothing. It was charming as all get out.

Saul parked the car in the garage at 11th and Spruce and shut off the engine. "We're going to walk up to Walnut, okay? It's just a couple of blocks."

"Sounds great. It's a gorgeous night. I love our seven seconds of summer." He remembered some endless summers in Texas, but here if you got warm, you just headed toward the mountains.

"Right? Enjoy it while we can." They went out to the street, which was busy on a perfect Friday night. "So you had me babbling all the way here. I don't mind, I can talk. I like to. It's not all that often I don't have something to say.

But at dinner, I'm listening. Fair warning." Saul smiled, walking alongside him, not close enough to be too familiar, but close enough to hint at more than just a friendly night out.

"I like listening." He hadn't used to. He'd been the guy who always had a story, a joke, something to say. Now he found that he loved listening to everything around him.

Saul turned the corner at Walnut and led him across the street. "You like Tapas, I hope? Mediterranean?"

"I have never met a food I didn't like." Small plates were so in right now, and there was something inherently sensual about sharing and tasting.

"Good. Me neither. This place is hopping on a Friday night. I made the reservation the day I asked you out, and it's a good thing we were on the early side. They're totally booked for later."

A gentleman in a suit greeted them as they came through the door. "Good evening, gentlemen. Welcome to Delmara."

Saul gave the guy a bright smile. "Hello. We have a reservation for six o'clock under Reynolds."

"Certainly. I'm Oscar, I'm managing tonight if you need any help. Barb up at the desk will see if your table is ready. Have a good evening."

"Thanks, Oscar." Saul spoke with Barb and she got them to their table, a nice one by the windows that looked out over the patio, and Saul pulled out his chair for him.

His cheeks heated, but he sat, murmuring his thanks. Was that wonderful or odd or embarrassing or just dear as fuck?

"Can I get you gentlemen something to drink?" Barb was adorable and tiny, and she had a tiny voice to go with it.

"Do you drink, Troy?" Saul pulled out the wine list.

"I have been known to have a beer or a glass of wine, even a Jack and Coke on occasion." He had a nice little collection of beers at his house and wine for Geoff. "How about you?"

"You know anyone that went to CU that doesn't drink?" Saul laughed. "I think I want a beer."

He nodded. That sounded good—not too much, but enough to ease the jitters. "I'll take a Fat Tire and a glass of water, please ma'am."

Saul put the bar menu down. "I'll have the same, please."

Barb smiled at him. "Sounds good. Can I see your ID, please?"

"Oh. Yeah." The kid's cheeks went pink, but Saul pulled out a bright green nylon wallet and showed her the ID in a clear plastic pocket on the outside.

She peered at it, looked at Saul and then nodded. "I'll be right back, guys."

Saul laughed softly and shook his head as he put the wallet away. "Every single time."

"Relish it. One day you'll be an old man like me." He put his hat on the empty seat, brim up.

"Old man." Saul snorted and tapped his temple. "Age is up here. You don't have to be old if you don't feel old."

Only a young man would say that.

Still, he grinned over and nodded. "Fair enough. Have you been here before?"

"I have. How hungry are you? We could start with some small plates and then maybe have an entree. Or even split one. The empanadas are good, the tuna tartare... what do you like? Oh, they have these crispy potato things... oh, so good."

"Mmm...crispy potatoes." He let himself make the

Homer Simpson noise, and it had a ring of truth to it. He ate one meal a day, as a rule, and he was starving.

"Oh, we're so getting those. What do you think about the grilled asparagus?"

He pretty much let Saul do the choosing and listened to him talk about the Environmental Studies program at CU, and the degree the kid clearly wasn't using. He was just glad when the food started to arrive.

"Carter says you've been working for him for ages, huh?" Saul pushed the plate of potatoes closer to him.

"Thank you, and yes, right at twenty years. He's a good man." A great friend and married to a wonderful, talented son of a bitch.

"He is. He seriously could have schooled me for being so clueless about where the two paths we were on intersected, but he was completely cool about it."

He watched the way Saul sat, the way the guy cut the potatoes with the side of a fork, the way Saul smiled almost constantly. So easy going, totally comfortable, didn't look the least bit guarded.

"Twenty years is a long time. You're from Texas originally, right? How did you decide on Boulder?"

"It is and I am. Carter and Arnie were buddies and when I came up to visit, I ended up staying." He'd been broken, and he'd brought Carter Arnie's buckles, intending to just disappear into the mountains. He'd ended up sobbing between Carter and Geoff, and then he'd simply stayed.

Saul reached out and touched his hand again, same as the other day, fingers steady and warm, and the eyes that held his as earnest as they were blue. "They told me a little about Arnie. You should probably know that. I mean, not details, just that you lost him. I can't imagine. I'm sorry."

"Thank you. I appreciate it. It was a whole lifetime ago."

Lord, Arnie would have been fifty years old this year. He wondered if they'd still be together, if they'd have come up here.

"Well, maybe you're ready for a new lifetime then." There was that smile again, it wasn't pity or kindness, it was just a kid looking to have some fun. Saul gave his hand a pat. "Come on, try those potatoes."

They were fabulous—golden and crispy, dusted with salt and paprika—and the sight made his stomach gnaw on his backbone.

Oh, crunchy, creamy potato goodness.

"So... orgasmic?"

When he opened his eyes again, Saul was staring at him, the expression as heated as any he'd ever seen.

Troy knew his cheeks were glowing, but he nodded. "Yes, sir. They're stunning."

"I'm glad you like them." Jesus, it didn't take Saul a second to go from chatty twenty-something to... this. Saul's look was knowing, and way beyond his years.

"You should try one." God, his voice was hoarse, husky —bedroom voice, Geoff would call it.

"You think so?" Saul slowly reached toward him and sank a fork into one of the potatoes, then made a show for him, closing hungry lips around the bite and chewing. "Mmm. So good."

"Turkey. They're still better than sex." He felt a little silly, really, but they were some of the best potatoes he'd had in a long time, and Saul was being good-natured with the tease.

Saul laughed. "Oh, no. They're not better than sex."

He let himself laugh along with Saul, because he could remember that feeling, very fondly. "Would you like a piece of the bread? It smells good."

"Sure, thanks. So, what's up with you and the guys? Are you like, a threesome? Is Carter your Dom?"

"What? No. No." His eyes damn near bugged out of his head. Not usually. Only in an emergency. "Geoff and Carter are just dear friends."

Hell, Geoff was the one who gave him what all he needed, helped him fly.

"Cool. Good." Saul took a bite of the bread. "Good. You want another beer?"

"I'm okay. I'll give it a minute or two." Because getting loose right now? Bad.

"Don't trust yourself around me huh? I understand. I get that a lot." Saul gave him a bullshitter's so-serious look.

"Totally. The last thing you need is a tipsy cook on your hands." He saved that for one Sunday night a month. Him, Geoff, sometimes Travis or Kris. They got stupid, watched movies, talked for hours because neither he nor Geoff worked Mondays.

"Mm. Such a good set up. You really have no idea the one-liners I've kept to myself during this conversation." Saul ate the last spear of asparagus and took the last sip of his beer.

"Uh-huh. That's my superpower—setting up those comebacks."

"Oh, so you want me to say I'd love to have you, tipsy or otherwise, on my hands?"

Troy chuckled, tickled as a man with a feather up his ass. "Lord have mercy. You are something else."

Saul watched him. "Maybe. I've never really been like everyone else."

He snorted. He had. In fact, he'd been three different people by the time he was twenty-five. "So, would you like to share an entree? Or just get more potatoes and something with protein?"

"I like the latter option I think. You like fish?"

Two plates of potatoes, shrimp, wee lamb chops, and a plate of seared tuna later, Saul waved down Barb for their check.

Fuck. Was he supposed to pay half? Was he not? Shit. He should have asked Geoff. "What's my half of the damage, man?"

"You paid your half. You subjected yourself to my babbling for a whole evening." Saul smiled. "It was my invitation, Troy. If you ask me out, you can treat then."

Saul pulled out his wallet and put cash into the little black folder before he could see the total. "You are really good dinner company."

"Thank you. You are too." He surprised himself by genuinely meaning it. "Would you like to go for a walk or something?"

"Yes." Oh, look at that smile. Sweet and young. "I had this idea and... well, there's somewhere I want to take you."

"A surprise? How cool. I'm in." He couldn't help but be curious about what would make Saul smile like that.

"Come on." Saul led him past a huge, brightly tiled fireplace and out through one of the patio doors into a gorgeous night. The sky was hinting at evening and the sun would be going down soon.

Damn, it was pretty out here, even if it would get chilly as the night fell.

"Do y'all stay open in the winter? At the bike shop, I mean?"

Saul was leading him back toward Spruce Street. "We do. It's slower, but people give bikes as gifts and stuff, and

Emma started building snow bikes last winter too. Neither of us work the hours we do this time of year though, and we close for a month after the holidays. Sometimes I get work in one of the ski shops."

"It's good to get a couple of weeks to rest, to get your head together." He was all over that. He liked to go on a cruise once a year, to get on the ocean and be anonymous and free.

"I usually go camping up in the mountains, sometimes I take my bike, sometimes I don't. I always like the idea of going by myself when I leave but then I come home when I'm sick of being alone." Saul snorted. "Which takes about three days. One year I pushed it to five, but I slept one whole day away."

"I go up about once a month and go fishing, but I come back to my own bed at night."

"You don't camp? Do you not like it?" Saul led him back into the parking garage and they headed for the car.

"I used to go constantly, but it's a lot of work for one person." And he wasn't interested in being cold and lonely in the dark.

"It is, right? And honestly? I get bored alone." Saul opened the car door for him.

"Thank you, sir. You have a lot of family?" Lots of people who got bored alone had all sorts of brothers and sisters.

"Yeah. I'm the youngest of four, and I grew up around cousins and all kinds of craziness." Saul climbed in his side. "They've scattered all over the place now, but we used to be pretty tight."

Saul pulled out of the parking space but went the wrong way. Instead of driving down toward the exit, they drove up.

Troy kept his questions to himself. Saul wanted to surprise him; it was up to him to allow it to happen.

They got to the top level and Saul parked in one corner. "One time in college I came up here to smoke up with some friends, just for the view." Saul got out of the car. "Come on."

"Coming." He slid out of the car and stretched. Too bad he wasn't still smoking.

Saul met him and steered him over to the low wall along the edge of the garage. "It turned out to be an awesome place to watch the sunset."

It was getting to be that time, too, and he realized that Saul had carefully orchestrated this, planned to be right here as the sun went down.

How damn wonderful was that? Thoughtful too. He settled, eyes on the Rockies and the pinks and oranges that colored everything.

Saul stood close for a long while, silently watching over his shoulder until the colors were deep and saturated and the sky started turning purple.

A gentle, steady hand rested on his hip. "Will you tell me about your ink?"

His mouth went dry, but he nodded. He wasn't ashamed —either of his need or his art. "What would you like to know?"

"Well, for starters, I don't want to assume, so tell me what the triskelion symbol means to you." Saul was close enough he could feel the warmth building between them.

"Balance, for the most part. Beauty. Need. The guys were there for the first one." He remembered that so clearly— safe, sane, and consensual, drilled into his skin. That was the beginning. Now, each one meant different things.

"Beauty. I love that. Like the sunset, it's a promise. The sun will rise, the sun will set, and your Dom will take care of you." Saul's hand left his hip and one settled on each of his shoulders, weighty and warm. "Why so many?"

Because nothing since Arnie had died let him sink into his subspace, and he needed it bad. "Isn't that what happens when your bud is an artist? I let him use me as a canvas." *And I use Geoff as a way to soar.*

"So they're all his designs? Or yours? Do you talk about each one before he does it? After?" Gentle fingers kneaded his shoulders.

"We don't talk about it much anymore; Geoff does his thing. Usually I sleep in the shop after so I don't have to get myself home."

Troy had a cot in the office. It was his whenever he needed it.

The sky was going from purple to deep blue as darkness fell around them. "That sounds great. I assume that's your outlet without a regular Dom? It's good you have that."

"It is." And it was good to be heard, to be understood. It felt... amazing, to be honest.

They both fell quiet after that, Saul's fingers working into his muscle without making anything awkward or too forward, just... kind. Friendly.

Caring.

"I should get you home, huh? I know you have to work early, so you need your rest."

"I do. Five to two." He liked opening the diner. It offered him an hour of peace before the regulars hit.

"Did you like the sunset? Isn't it crazy watching it from here?" Saul gave his shoulders one last squeeze.

"It was absolutely gorgeous." He checked his watch. "You interested in a cup of coffee? I've got a little while before my curfew."

He could just make out Saul's smile in the shadow of the garage lighting. "Yeah. That would be great."

"Excellent. I think so too." He leaned a little bit, then straightened. "Come on, I'll introduce you the best hazelnut caramel latte in Boulder."

"Are we walking or driving?" Saul hesitated by the car.

"Let's walk it. It's not far at all." And he was feeling pretty damned mellow for a guy on his first date ever.

"I'm in." Saul stepped in beside him, offered him an arm, and raised an eyebrow.

He grinned. Such chivalry. He loved that, dorky as it was. The only thing more dorky was Saul's adorable smile as he took the kid's arm.

"I'd have figured you for more of a macchiato kind of guy."

"I try new flavors all the time. Sue even invents stuff for me." He went three times a week—Monday night, Wednesday night, and Friday night, just like clockwork.

"Sue." Saul laughed. "Does Sue work Friday nights?"

"She does. Her daughter Alissa owns the place, and Sue works the weekday closing shift." Alissa and Brett came in with the baby a couple of times a week—veggie omelet and two eggs over easy with crispy bacon and home fries.

"Well, I look forward to meeting her." Saul tucked his hand in closer and let him lead the way.

"I've been here a lot of years. Believe it or not Alissa was in kindergarten when I moved here. She was a server at the diner through high school." He really did have an extended family here.

Saul looked at him. "That's... crazy. Wow. So she's... well, my age. Or thereabouts."

"Yeah. I'm old enough to be your father, no question about that." Okay, so that was a craptastic thought.

Saul sighed. "If you were wondering, I'm cool with that."

He wasn't sure he understood what Saul found intriguing about him, but this was their night, so he'd stress over that later. Right now he was going to enjoy their date. "Good deal."

"Is this the place? I've been past here a bunch of times, but I never stopped in." Saul pulled the door open for him.

"Troy! I was wondering if you were coming in. I have a drink to try out on you. Who's your friend? You look familiar..." Sue smiled across the counter, waving.

Big Bean, Little Bean had a handful of comfortable seats and low tables. Between the cozy little niches for conversation, the gaming area, and the counter stools, it was a great place to unwind.

"Hey, lady. This is Saul. He's at the bike shop."

Sue squinted at Saul. "Which one?"

"Up at the Cycle Rack. I think you came in with your son-in-law around Christmas... to find a new seat for his road bike, right?"

She pursed her lips, then grinned, just all of the sudden. "Ah, yes. You were very polite. So many times those shops can be so intimidating. What can I do you for?"

Saul looked honestly pleased. "That's a real compliment. Thank you. Um. Troy said I should try the hazelnut caramel latte, please."

"Oh, those are our most popular. You're getting white chocolate, mint, and peanut butter, Troy."

White chocolate, mint, and...oh, man.

Saul grinned but didn't say a word, just found them a comfy spot to sit while Sue got to work. The shop was half full, the buzz of conversation constant, familiar.

He paid, then he waited for the lattes. When he carried the cups over, the temptation to switch their drinks was huge, but he offered Saul the one he knew was good.

That didn't stop Saul from sniffing it first. "Thank you for the coffee. Good luck with yours." He could see the grin Saul was trying to hide behind a sip from that coffee cup.

"Yeah. I-Wow. Peanut butter." And white chocolate. And *mint*. In his coffee.

He sighed softly and took a sip. Sweet. Very sweet. And minty fresh.

"The look on your face... You're welcome to share mine." Saul laughed, watching him. "It's out of this world good. Wow."

"That one is the best, absolutely. They do an iced one too." He settled in, the sofa just perfect and cozy. "So you went to school here and stayed. I assume you like it?"

"I love it. Just... everything. It's a city but it has a small-town kind of feel. It's beautiful, busy, there's a shitload of things to do. It's pricey I guess, but it's worth it to me."

"Right? That's how I felt when I got here." He leaned over and put his coffee down. "I came here...at a bad time, and I fell in love."

Saul smiled. "I totally get that. Just the view alone is... inspiring. Good for the soul. I'm putting down roots here for sure."

"Where is home, originally?"

"Originally? Northeast Philadelphia. But almost everyone has moved on from there now." Saul shrugged. "Even my friends from home are all over."

"I get that." Although most of his old friends were still in Texas, he'd bet. He'd never gone back. Hell, he'd never looked back.

"We were all pretty free-spirited, got in trouble a lot. Nothing serious ever, just stupid kid shit, you know? Everyone was so ready to get out of there. My best friend Deitz—Johnny Deitz, but we used his last name because there were too damn many Johns—Deitz is in California. He went to LA, about as far from Philadelphia as you can get. But he comes to visit a lot. He keeps saying he might move."

"I liked Los Angeles." He'd ridden there a number of times and had loved the busy buzz of the city. He couldn't live like that, but he'd loved being there when he was riding.

"Yeah? I didn't care much for it, but the scene there is kind of amazing and the people I met were cool." Saul took another sip, smiling like he was really enjoying his coffee. "Where else have you been that you liked? Do you have somewhere you go on vacation or anything?"

"Oh, I like traveling. I like cruising, I've been to Cancun, Cozumel. I loved Hawaii. New Orleans. I love to visit sandy beach places and then come home to the Rockies." All his mad money was spent on his vacation fund, really. He loved to go.

"Wow, you get around, huh? I've never been on a cruise, but they seem like a ton of fun, and a great way to see things. And who doesn't love the beach? We used to go to the Jersey Shore a lot in high school." Saul grinned and that laugher was so carefree. "I'm an expert at getting a sunburn."

He glanced down at his arm — he had scars and ink and his tan. "I haven't had a bad one in a while. Probably since I started shaving my head. That first scalp burn was a stone-cold bitch."

"Oh man, I bet. Why did you decide to do that? How long ago?"

Oh God. That was a story. Troy felt his cheeks go red hot, and he reached for his coffee again. "A while. Eight-nine years, I guess?"

He wasn't sure he could tell that one. Although, why not, the man knew he was a submissive, so did he, there was nothing to be ashamed about.

Saul just nodded and didn't push him on the why. "A while, then. What color was your hair when you had it?"

"Bright red. Bright red and curly." It had been long too for a little while.

"Bright red! That's no fair. I spend all this time fighting the blond stereotype and you, a ginger who could attract anyone just by looks, shave it off." Saul put on a playful bedroom voice. "Although, I hear some really good things about you gingers."

"Did you now?" It felt good to flirt, surprisingly good.

"Very creative, I'm told. Typically uninhibited. Fun. Any of that true? More stereotypes, of course, I wouldn't know firsthand. I'm hoping to find out one day."

He gave that a little thought — a very little, if he was honest — and nodded. "You know it. I was a rodeo cowboy once upon a time."

"I know." The smile that spread across Saul's face said more than words. Eyes knowing and full of heat. "That might be another discussion entirely."

"Well, then you know I'm fun and unhinged—I mean, uninhibited." Troy winked. "I am a rare find, you know? The elusive ten-fingered roper."

"Mm. Rare and beautiful." Saul's eyes didn't leave his for a second, just as confident as anything.

Part of him really wanted to scoff, to say that no one had called him that in a long, long time. Maybe say 'my ink is gorgeous'. He hated that in other people, though, so he just blushed and smiled. "Thank you, Sir. That's good of you to say."

"You don't believe me." Saul smiled, and again it didn't feel like pity, just a statement. "Well, you are. But there's more to being beautiful than looks, right? I know how those stunning eyes of yours make me feel, and I'm enjoying getting to know the guy I'm finally spending time with. I'll make you believe it eventually. If you let me."

"You're something else. Honest to God." Troy'd never been wooed like this. "I have to tell you, I'm having a good time. It's been a great first date."

"Me too. Thanks for letting me take you out. Hopefully, you'll want a second one."

"I think I would. How are Sunday evenings for you?" He had plans this Sunday, and he thought maybe Saul did too, but next Sunday... "I have Mondays and Tuesdays off."

"The shop closes at three on Sunday and is closed on Monday, so that would be perfect. And I'm pretty flexible other than Saturdays. The shop needs both of us then. Otherwise Emma and I trade shifts around all the time, and we have hourly help too."

"Hooray tourists, right?" Troy rolled his eyes but laughed. "I have the monthly get-together this Sunday..." *Are you coming? I'd love to see you there.*

"Yeah, Geoff and Carter invited me. Their place, right? Is it all right with you if I go? I won't if you think it would be awkward, just be honest. It's your space."

"It's our space. I spend my time dozing on the sofa half the time, unless someone needs me." He was sort of the group peacemaker. Half the guys weren't sure how he fit in, so they just had to accept him at face value. "You're more than welcome."

"You're kidding!" Saul laughed. "Someone has to rescue you from the sofa. Consider yourself needed. I'll be there."

"Well, I will be too. Possibly with bells on."

"I'd like to see that." Saul pushed his chair back. "Let's walk. I've managed not to put my foot in anything tonight, I'd like to keep it that way."

"Sounds like a plan." He tossed the drink, shaking his head at Sue. "Too much mint."

7

B lack shirt?

No, he'd worn the black shirt on Friday night.

Gray sleeveless Tee...

Right. Sure, and look like he was twelve? He already looked like a baby, why make it worse?

Fuck it. Saul snarled, pulled out his phone and Face Timed Emma.

Friday night had been amazing. He'd never had a date that didn't end with sex before. Or at least mutual hand jobs. In fact, a lot of times he'd just skipped the date part entirely.

But Troy was... special. More mature. Gentle. Smooth, like a really nice wine. Someone you took your time with, someone you savored.

That sounded ridiculous maybe, but he thought it was a pretty damn good metaphor.

"Did you forget something? Whoa, put some clothes on!" Emma covered her eyes.

"You're a lesbian, Em. Please. I need your help."

Emma grinned at him. "The rubber goes on first. I know it's been a while, it's okay."

"Shut up. I'm serious, Em. I'm... almost a disaster. I mean I'm not, because a disaster would be more catastrophic than just an evening out and I'm really just nervous mostly but —help?"

"This is the party, right? So it's not just your guy, but a bunch? Is it casual?"

"It's casual, but it's a scene party. And I think it's possible Troy's going to... I mean I kind of said I'd take him on." Right? Isn't that what he meant when he said he'd get Troy off the couch?

"And you wore the black shirt with the silver Friday. Damn. What about...you could go all retro and wear your Jurassic Park T-shirt?"

He thought about that. "Yeah, maybe. Big belt, cuffs. Boot cut jeans or skinny?" He liked that idea. Super casual. He could pull that off.

"Skinny. Are you going to tell all on Tuesday?"

"Are you buying the Jaeger?" He propped his phone up on his dresser and started moving around the room, gathering clothes and dressing.

"Totally. So, he's caught your attention bad. You were a little floaty yesterday in the shop."

"I thought about him all day. I don't know where it's going, if it can possibly go anywhere, I just know I can't stop thinking about him. I want to..." He tugged on his jeans. God, the things he wanted were huge. They were crazy. "Shoes or boots?"

"Aren't boots sort of a thing with your crowd? You know, lick my boots and all that." He was going to beat her.

Ha.

Beat her.

"You should try it sometime. I'll wear them to work on Tuesday." He rolled his eyes. Boots were good but with these jeans? "How about my Doc Martens?" He had a pair of black eight-eyes that he thought would look great.

"Stompy. I approve. Are you nervous?"

"I shouldn't be, but I am." He grabbed his boots and sat on the bed to pull them on. "I don't... part of me is wondering what the hell I think I'm doing."

"Because he's so much older or what? I can imagine that he's got saggy balls..." Evil woman.

"Funny. He's in great shape, he must run or something." He sighed and flopped back on the bed. "He... he's so established here. He's known the woman who made our coffee last night since her daughter was like, five and now she's married. He's got routines, he's got a whole life, you know? Why would he want someone like me?"

"You said he invited you on another date, though, right?" Em sounded utterly confused. "I mean, seriously. If he's all that stable and solid...is he boring?"

"No. God, no. He's fascinating." Saul wasn't really worried about being wanted. He was far more concerned with being needed. Troy was an experienced sub, and Saul was still learning. He felt like he had something Troy needed, but what if he was wrong?

Then again, why not him? Troy had been without a Dom all these years, if the guy hadn't found anyone else in all that time, why couldn't it be him?

"I don't know why I'm doubting myself now, Friday night I was so sure."

"That's normal, right? I mean, when you're in it, when you're with him, it's cool. Then you start second-guessing. Let me see you."

"Oh. Yeah." He stood and pulled on a studded belt, then

stepped over where Emma could see the outfit. "Cuffs or no?" He showed her his wrists. "I don't want to overdo it."

She was right, he was second-guessing himself and how stupid was that? Why Monday morning quarterback a date? He got an invitation, so Geoff and Carter were cool with him, and Troy wanted him to come.

"Leave the cuffs off. You read Dom, but not scary. Nice and casual."

"Cool. That's perfect. You're awesome, Em. Thank you. I'd still be standing here worrying at this thing." He was such a dork.

"Text if you need me. I'm home." She blew a kiss. "Make some good stories to tell!"

"That's a sure thing. Enjoy your woman." He smiled and waved at her, then hung up and hurried out to catch his bus.

Okay. He had this.

Hopefully.

No, he totally did. And to prove it to himself he used the bus ride to work on his head space. By the time he knocked on Carter's door, he was feeling much more grounded.

Geoff answered the door wearing a pair of jeans, a faded T-shirt, and a lovely, ornamental collar. "Hey there, come on in. I'm glad you could make it."

The house was...totally not something he'd expect from a restaurant owner and a tattoo artist. Open and airy, full of light from huge windows—the bottom story of the house was one big, beautiful space.

"Help yourself to a drink, a snack. Whatever you'd like. Master, Saul is here and..." The doorbell rang. "...and I have to answer the door."

Geoff chuckled and headed back to the foyer, leaving him with Carter and a couple of men he didn't know.

"Hey, man. David, Matt, this is Saul. He's the guy I was telling you about."

"Hey, Carter. Uh-oh." He shook with the men. "What did he tell you? This is the idiot kid that flattened my bike?" He grinned. Might as well own it.

David—who was a mountain of a man with a braided beard—barked out a loud laugh. "No, we were admiring your work when we got there. Matt here is looking for a pair of bikes."

"I still think you need a bicycle built for two, Matt." Carter was obviously comfortable needling these guys.

Matt's eyebrow arched comically. "How are your contacts? I'd have seen blondie here coming."

He laughed. "Whatever you need, Matt, I can hook you up. Come see me, I'll give you the family discount. That should take the sting out of the two-seater."

"Can you see my Krissy on a two-seater? I don't think so. I just want something for him to gain his confidence back on." Matt shook his head. "Have you ever made any modifications for someone with prostheses?"

Oh. Damn. Well, this was what he did, right? "Yeah. There are some great adaptive pedals and we can customize the frame to allow for whatever range of motion he has. But sometimes guys prefer the hand bikes. Is it one leg? Both?"

"One below the knee. He just got home for good. He was a CO in the National Guard." Matt looked toward the great room where a square-jawed man sat in a wheelchair. "The leg bothers him by the evening, so he's in the chair. That's my Krissy."

"Handsome." Saul gave Matt's shoulder a squeeze. That had to suck, and he really wanted to help. "Does he want to ride? Would you like me to talk to him later? I could get a better idea of what he needs and if it's a bigger adaptation than I can handle I know someone."

"We'll come see you sometime this week. Thanks." Matt took a deep breath. "Seriously guys. This hasn't been simple."

Two more men came in, one heading to the great room with Geoff, the other coming in to grab a beer.

"Doc!" Carter clapped him on the back. "How's it going?"

"It's going. Ben and I have been looking forward to this all week." The man held a hand out to him. "Daniel Bush. Call me Doc. You must be Samuel? No. No, that wasn't it..."

"Saul, Master."

"Saul. That was it. Thank you, boy."

He shook hands with Doc. "That's me. Good to meet you, Doc. And your lovely boy is...?" Adorable, and maybe even younger than he was.

"Benjamin. The bane of my existence." The words were warm, the grin that Benjamin gave Doc even warmer. "He's a wicked one, be forewarned." Doc then turned to Matt. "How's it going?"

Matt stared at Doc for a long minute, and then Doc took Matt by the arm. "Keep an eye on the boys, would you?"

"Of course. You're welcome to go upstairs and talk." Carter kept reorganizing food as if nothing was wrong.

He watched the men go, not completely understanding the emotions that followed them. He just saw so much pain.

After a second Saul glanced at Benjamin. "Why don't you see if you can help Master Carter with the food, boy?"

Benjamin looked at him a little confused and then blinked. "Oh. I didn't... Uh. Yes, Sir."

David's deep chuckle sounded like a rumble of thunder. "Don't stress it, boy. Travis and Geoff have Krissy. Where's Troy?"

Carter grinned. "Dozing on the couch, as he does."

"Anyone mind if I wake him up?" Saul didn't really want an answer, he just nodded to them and headed for the couch. Seeing the way the guys were dressed, he silently thanked Emma again, she'd been right on the money.

Troy was on a long, low couch wearing a pair of gauzy white pants and a loose tank. The hints of ink were everywhere, a constant tease. The man really was beautiful, whether he felt that way right now or not. Saul admired the way the tank showed off his muscle and skin, the way his pants sat low on his hips and left little to the imagination below that.

But even with that lovely view, Saul's eyes were drawn back up to the ink and the dozen or so triskelion he could see clearly. They were different sizes, different in character. A patch of three on one shoulder intertwined in a really lovely way, tangled and not, individual but belonging together.

Troy's face was relaxed, passive, and he admired the line of the man's jaw and the set of those cheekbones, but he wanted to see those eyes.

As he stared down, Troy inhaled deeply and stretched, a smile widening his lips. "Someone smells good."

Was that comment meant to give him goosebumps? Must have been the little hint of sleepy gravel in Troy's otherwise smooth voice. "Old Spice. Someone told me not long ago it's what real men wear."

Troy's eyes popped open, the pretty green eyes finding him immediately, the smile not fading a bit. "Well, hello."

He smiled back, couldn't have stopped it if he tried. "Hey. You look great. And bored."

Troy rolled up to sitting, the simple motion fluid and

easy, and so unconsciously sexual it made Saul's mouth dry. "Bored? No, Sir. I was just catnapping."

"Early morning at the diner, huh? Can I sit with you?" *Will you try me out? Sub for me today? How do I ask?*

"Please do." Troy patted the cushion. "I'll share all the good gossip and tell you where Geoff hides the Doritos."

"Clearly I found the right guy." He sat just exactly where Troy had patted the sofa, which put him a little too far away to be assumed a couple but too close to rule the possibility out. "I just met David and Matt, and Doc and Benjamin..."

"Ah. Master Matt is a travel writer, belongs to Kris. Kris just got back from being deployed. He's dealing with some hard-core shit."

"Yeah, I saw that." That was an understatement of vast proportions.

"Master David and Trav are physical therapists—been together for fifteen years, maybe more—and Benji is brand-new to, well, just about everything. He was a figure skater and now he's...not." Troy looked toward Benjamin with a fond expression.

"Yeah? Why did he give it up? Doc?" Doc wasn't young at all. The Dom seemed to easily be the eldest in the group he'd met so far.

"Oh man, he just burnt out. I mean like losing his shit full out on the ice." Troy didn't glance at Benjamin and kept his voice down. "He grew up here, tried to go home and his folks just turned him out. I found him on a bench and recognized him. He stayed with me a few months, met Doc and they connected. It's been great for both of them."

"Whoa, you found him? Wow." *Wow.*

Okay, this was weird. This wasn't a party with a bunch of newbie college grad buttheads sitting around playing beer pong, getting high and fucking around in the bedrooms.

These were, like, *real* men. They had partners and stories. They were interesting. They were friends. He wasn't interesting, he was just guy who worked in a bike shop. He didn't have a story, did he? He had a few things... Deitz and Khloe, a little family shit and college nonsense, but really, he was boring as hell.

The only thing interesting about him was that he and the guy he was sitting next to seemed a lot alike. He usually pulled off mature and authoritative at parties. He wasn't used to feeling young and clueless. It was bizarre.

"Right? I mean, we had a ton in common, honestly, and he's a good guy. He'd just reached the end of what he could handle." Troy smiled, the expression happy, maybe a bit bewildered. "Thank goodness I walk home from work instead of taking my truck."

He wasn't sure what that expression meant. "Were you guys a thing?" That would be a good thing to know, right? If he wasn't the only younger man Troy was into.

"Me and who? Benji? Christ on a purple sparkly pogo stick, no. No, I was just thinking how I wouldn't have noticed him, if I'd driven."

He laughed. "Purple what? Is that the Texas version of you've got to be kidding me?"

"Yessir. It most definitely is."

"I'm impressed. I don't think I could pull that off." He bumped shoulders with Troy, teasing. "What's the matter with Benjamin? He's adorable. Too young for you?"

"Absolutely," Troy teased back. "How did you guess?"

"I don't know. Maybe it was all those telegraphing comments you made about how you're old enough to be my father." He turned to glance at Troy and rested a hand on one thigh, calling on that grounded feeling he'd put such effort into on the bus ride. "I don't want a father. I want a boy."

Troy's lips parted, and he took a breath to answer, when a roar split the room.

"TROY!" Kris, red-faced and near-tears was right there, shaking in his wheelchair. "Take me home. I have to go. Now. Fucking take me home. Now."

"What?" Troy stood, wide-eyed, as Carter and David both came sprinting from the kitchen.

"You fucking take me home or to the bus station, somewhere."

"But Matt—"

"Fuck him. I want out."

Saul stared at Kris. The soldier just radiated panic. He knew two things; first, that as much as he wanted to help right now, this was way out of his league, and second, he still had to do something. "I'll get him."

He took off for the stairs at a run, found the one room with a closed door upstairs and knocked on it, then went right in. "Matt?"

Matt looked up sharply from where he was sitting on the end of the bed with Doc. "What is it?"

"Kris needs you. He's panicking." He got out of the way as Matt ran past him, then followed quickly.

"...dammit, Troy! Just fucking do what I asked. No one here is going to know you're gone. Just get your keys and take me home."

Kris was working himself into a tizzy, and Saul was pleased to see both David and Carter putting themselves between Troy and the wheelchair, even as Geoff and another man he hadn't met were leading Troy out a set of French doors.

"You want to yell at someone, yell at us, boy." David got the words out just in time for Matt to show.

"No." Matt's voice boomed over everyone and the Dom stepped in, standing over Kris. The words that followed were stern but quieter. "No more yelling."

He watched Matt go to one knee next to Kris's chair. There was already a handful of men standing close, and there was nothing Saul could do here, so he squeezed behind them and went after Troy.

The doors led out into a stunning deck with a hot tub and a glorious outdoor kitchen. Geoff was talking hard to Troy, and he heard Troy say, "I'm okay. I'm okay. I just don't want to go back in right now, huh? I'll just... God, that was shitty timing."

Saul walked over slowly, clearing his throat so they knew he could hear them. "Hey."

"Hello there." The man he hadn't been introduced to smiled at him. "You must be Saul? Do you prefer Master Saul? I'm Travis, Master David's boy. Sorry about that. Kris is dealing with some hard-core shit."

"Hey, no worries. Kris is on a hard road. It's nice to meet you, Travis, and just Saul is fine for now. I'm no one's Master at the moment." He smiled at Troy sympathetically. "That was kind of intense, huh? Are you okay?"

"Yes, sir. I'm fine. Poor Kris is just super angry." Troy seemed less than fine, to be honest. He seemed scattered and flustered.

"Hey, Travis. Let's go see what we can do inside." Geoff gave Troy a hard look before they left. "Talk, honey. *Master* Saul came out here for you."

Troy met his eyes, lean cheeks blushing damn near purple. "Would you like to have a seat, Sir?"

"Troy if—" He started to offer the boy an out, but despite

the amazing blush, Troy didn't seem to need that. He wasn't sure yet what the boy did need, but he intended to find out. "I would, thank you."

"Me too. That was unexpected as hell. I don't know if Kris was ready for a get-together."

"No. No, it doesn't seem like it, but I guess you don't know until you try, right? Maybe Matt thought something normal, and people who care about him would help. Maybe Kris did too. He only just got home, huh?"

"Yes, Sir. Master Matt loves him. They'll work it out with time." Troy stared out from the deck. "It's gorgeous out there."

"It really is." Saul glanced out as well, admiring the mountains and the sky, but he was drawn to the view beside him over and over. "Kris really wasn't in control of that timing."

Troy blushed again. Oh, that was a ginger trait he was going to love. "It just was so damn... I was so focused on you I didn't even notice he was there."

"I understand. So was I. Focused on you I mean, like now." And Kris was used to Troy being the single one, just as the boy said, the one no one would miss. He wanted to change that.

"I don't know what to do. I've never actually...I mean, no one's ever asked."

So this was something Troy and Arnie had fallen into. He supposed the whole relationship had to have been that way. "That's okay. I'm asking if you're interested in partnering with me as my sub for this party. This is certainly a safe space to see how it feels, right? So it's just a yes or no question to begin with."

"Right." Troy chuckled, rubbed his scalp with his hand in a motion that Saul would bet was an old self-comforting habit. "That's fair enough. I'm sorry — Kris got my brain all off-kilter. I'm more than happy to partner with you here for the party."

He smiled. "Thank you." So the boy must have thought he was asking for more, which meant Troy was interested. He liked that. Like their first date...he knew you got a second if you left them wanting more. He'd get another chance with Troy for something deeper if this went well.

"I need your safe word or words. And any restrictions or hard limits you think are important for me to know tonight."

"I use yellow and red. I'm not sure that with the tension in the air we'll need any limits, to be honest."

"I don't think so either, Troy, but it's my responsibility to ask anyway. I know your words now, that should be enough... can you tell me—" He hesitated and looked at Troy. "I ask a lot of questions. It's okay not to have... not to know the answers. I just want the truth, you know? And if I overstep just say yellow and I'll go another direction or... just drop it. Okay?"

"Yes, Sir." Troy sat in silence for a long minute, and then a soft chuckle escaped him. "I didn't think I'd be this nervous."

Saul hadn't known he would be either, but his nerves had started long before he'd gotten on the bus out here. He thought that was more about impressing the man than the sub, though. Nerves and uncertainty weren't things a Dom admitted to anyway, right? Not to his sub at least.

It seemed totally understandable for Troy. A sub wanted to please his Master. But a new Master, new friendship, new chemistry... and to just hand over your trust? Damn. He got it. He wanted to hear it in Troy's words though, to make sure he really understood. "Why are you nervous?"

"Because it's been twenty years. I've had a couple of

offers, especially back in the day, but I wasn't interested in biting what they were casting."

He grinned. "Are you saying I'm fresh bait?"

"I would never be so rude. Never." Those green eyes were wicked, promising him no end of trouble.

He returned the look, focused sharply on Troy. He could give as good as he got. "No, of course you wouldn't. Not if you wanted to please me."

Saul swore the electricity that passed between them was real enough he smelled ozone. He watched Troy, curious as to what all those fleeting expressions meant. He'd learn.

If he could keep his hands to himself for a while.

He swallowed hard enough to calm the ache in his balls and laughed softly. "I think we understand each other... a little. Can I ask... what kind of Dom was Arnie?"

"Oh lord... I was a kid, and he was a force of nature. I didn't have any idea what anything meant—" Troy began to smile, the look odd and beautiful all at once. "I tell you, I'm not sure the two of us were ever anything more than consensual. We had troubles with safe and sane. Of course, that was an occupational hazard."

"Oh, man." Saul laughed, trying to imagine the trouble two rodeo guys could get into, and that only made him laugh harder. "Well, if you ask Carter, he might tell you I'm a little challenged there as well, but I'm not, actually. I'm pretty by-the-book with those things."

Saul wished he were a force of nature, but he wasn't really. He was more... like an addict. He had needs, and he'd found the safe and sane way to deal with them. He didn't know who he'd be otherwise, and he didn't want to find out.

"So is subbing more of an adrenaline thing for you, or do you have... is it... necessary?" This was an important question for him, because he wanted more from Troy than his submission.

"I was a two pack a day smoker up until last year. I quit because Master Carter said that was how I earned my ink. I need it. I need my subspace more than the cigarettes. I've been lucky that they're both understanding and willing to help."

"I'd be willing to bet Geoff gets more out of it than you realize." He'd seen the look Geoff had given Troy just a minute ago. Carter had his hands full. "What puts you in your space? Pain? Serving? Sex?"

He was pretty equal opportunity; his needs were narrow, but his methods were broad.

"I've used pain, mostly. Service hasn't been much of an option, not lately, although I help out when a Dom is in between subs." Troy shrugged, and that blush flared again. "I haven't had a regular lover in forever. I go to Denver for a one-off every now and again."

Since Deitz, Saul had been the one-night-stand king. "Do you think it's possible to find everything you need, everything you want in one person? Is that what you want?" He did. But he wasn't sure how it was done. How you actually pulled that off.

"I did it once. Either I can do it again or I can't."

"Right." It was his turn to blush. What a stupid, idiotic question. "Sorry. I... I hope you can. I hope we both can." He let the silence just be for a bit. This wasn't simple for him and it wasn't easy for Troy, of course. When he felt grounded again, he looked at Troy. "Are you ready to go back inside, boy?"

Troy squeezed his hand and met his eyes. "I am, Sir, but before we go, Arnie died a long time ago. I've mourned him.

I'm... I'll never forget him, but I'm not shy about talking about him, about us. No one ever asks."

Saul covered Troy's hand with his free one and nodded. "Thank you. I want to know all about you, and since he was your last Dom, I'd like to know a little about him too."

"Yes, Sir." Troy took a deep breath. "Shall we?"

"Yeah. Can you start by grabbing me a beer, please?" He wasn't sure what they were going to walk into, but he got up and headed inside anyway, letting Troy follow.

"Yes, Sir."

The men were all in the great room, scattered over the couches and on cushions on the floor.

"Hey, Saul. Have a seat. Isn't the view out there amazing?" Matt was sitting in a chair and a half with Kris draped over his lap.

"It's spectacular. Honestly. Troy and I enjoyed it very much." He found a spot on one end of a couch and pulled over a cushion for Troy. "Carter, how did you find this place? It's beautiful."

"When we found it, it was trashed. A starlet had it and had set it on fire; they found a body."

Geoff nodded to Carter, then back at him. "They say it's haunted, you know?"

"Oh, yeah? Well that's a shame about the girl, but a ghost? That is so cool. Have you noticed anything?" He smiled as Troy returned with his beer and gestured to the cushion on the floor. "Thank you, boy. Have a seat."

"Yes, Sir." He noticed all the shocked eyes on them, but he had to give Troy credit. There wasn't so much as a flutter; Troy just curled down onto the cushion and sat.

Carter gave him a nod, which he returned, but that was all. He'd sent Troy for a beer on purpose, and it worked out beautifully. A simple show of their status that didn't need discussion.

"Geoff swears he's heard her, and I've seen shadows in the mirror in the upstairs hall a couple of times, but who knows."

"I know, Sir. I can't make up the things I've heard."

"I know, boy." Carter reached over and squeezed Geoff's shoulder. "You see he's really convinced."

"Regardless, it's a glorious house. I was so pleased when you decided to buy it, and Troy was one hell of a help with the work."

"You're handy, are you boy?" He'd love to fix a place up someday.

"There's not a whole lot of construction stuff I don't have a little experience in. Just enough to get myself in trouble."

"Just enough for Geoff and Travis to get in trouble with you." David rolled his eyes and both Geoff and Travis hid their faces. "There's nothing like hearing from Doc that the EMTs are at your house and Troy's electrocuted himself."

Carter snorted. "Again."

"Again?" Saul laughed and shook his head. He didn't know Troy very well yet, but the guy was obviously fearless. "Did you want to tell me this story, boy? Or is it one of those things better left ambiguous?"

Troy chuckled and turned pink. "They're maligning me, Sir. There was a miscommunication."

Geoff cackled. "A miscommunication. Trav totally flipped the wrong breaker and fried our cook."

"I wasn't trying to kill him...mostly." Travis tossed a throw pillow at Troy, who caught it and winged it back.

"A little decorum, please, boys." Doc's deep voice was soft, but somehow a carried through the room anyway. He caught Doc's grin. "Don't consider those two role models of any sort, Ben."

"No, Master. I won't."

Saul caught the wide-eyed, vaguely horrified look Ben gave Troy. Troy winked at the inexperienced sub, gave him a thumbs up.

His boy was a mischief maker. How charming.

"It's obviously been too long since you had a good spanking, boy. How tempting." He reached over and laid a hand on Troy's shoulder.

It would have been worth it, just for the utter shock on everyone's face, but when he heard the tiny little moan, felt Troy shiver? It was perfect.

He felt a little surge of his own, too. It lifted his shoulders and stroked his ego as he realized he needn't have doubted himself. He was right where he should be. He stroked a hand over Troy's bald head and took a swig of his beer.

"Who is that guy?" He heard Kris ask Matt softly.

"He's the guy I told you ran Carter over on his bike. We're going to see him at his bike shop later in the week." Matt kept touching Kris constantly, as if he were soothing a wounded beast. "I want to get us wheels." Kris opened his mouth, but Matt hushed him with a finger. "Trust me, boy."

All he could think was thank goodness they had this. Without this level of trust where would Kris be right now? Matt was exactly what the boy needed in this moment.

He looked around as the conversation picked up again, watching all the different ways these guys interacted with each other, with their subs. They were so comfortable and casual, familiar. Fascinating.

David caught his eye. "Troy was very tight-lipped about

your date the other night, Saul. But it seems like things went well?"

"We had a very nice evening, thank you." If Troy wasn't sharing, he wasn't going to tell tales either. This was Troy's turf; these weren't his friends... yet.

"Sue said you didn't love her concoction, Troy." Geoff grinned over. "You didn't like the peanut butter and mint?"

"That was your fault?"

Geoff fluttered his eyelashes.

Troy shook his head. "I will get you back, man."

"That was the most disgusting-sounding drink ever, and she handed it to you with a completely straight face? That's awesome. Geoff, you had to see the look when he took a sip. But he didn't complain at all. Not a word. On the way out, all he said was 'too much mint.' That was a pretty good prank."

Troy chuckled softly. "Just remember who cooks your lunch five days a week, hmm? I wield mad amounts of power with my spatula. Mad."

"Mad power? Oh, honey. Let's remember who your boss is, shall we?" Geoff shot back, looking so smug.

"He never forgets." Carter joined in the conversation. "And I swear to God, if you two get into another practical joke war, I will beat you both. I still don't have the superglue off the bedroom ceiling."

"The ceiling!" Geoff's eyes went wide, his expression horrified. "Forget the ceiling, I was peeling it off of my shoes for a week."

Saul just listened to the banter. He had so much to learn about Troy, and how the guy interacted with people was telling.

Doc sighed. "Just cover your ears, boy."

"But, Master, I was there the night that Troy discovered there was Icy Hot in his lube..."

"Boy." Doc tried to sound stern but was having a hard time keeping a straight face now too, and the giggles were peppered around the room.

"You're kidding." Saul glanced down at Geoff and then back at Troy. "How did that feel?"

"Well, at first it was okay—tingling. Then it stopped being okay. I can tell you that the heat made me clench like a nun's fist around a ruler." Troy's voice was dry as dust. "And it took twenty minutes to pant through it and get the plug out."

There was no stopping the gasps and the laughter in the room. "Oh. Shit." Saul tried not to join in, he really did, but he lost it when Geoff spoke up.

"Nobody touches my shoes."

Even Kris was howling with mirth, and, as they all laughed, Saul felt like he could belong here, with these men.

He meant it when he said Troy needed a spanking though, and he was going to keep a very close eye on Geoff.

8

"So, are you having a good time?"

"Shut up, Geoff." Troy tossed over a dishcloth. "Dry dishes and be good."

Geoff caught the cloth and popped him with it. "I am good! Are you going to give him a lift home?"

"I was gonna offer, yeah." He had felt more...present? He thought that was it. He'd laughed, he'd played, and those random little touches had given him goosebumps. "I sort of was thinking that I'd invite him over for a drink. Bad idea?"

Geoff smiled at him. "No, I don't think it's a bad idea at all. But have you thought about why you want to invite him in?"

"I like him." And Saul seemed to like him. And it had been a long time, right? He wasn't going to go all cradle-robbing and seduce Saul, after all.

"Yes, I can see that. He likes you too. Do you want him?" Geoff leaned on the counter and looked at him.

"God yes, but...You know how long it's been since I thought about getting naked with someone?" A long fucking time.

"I'm just saying if you invite him in... he's what, twenty-five? Tops? Saul's different, I know, but he is still a young man. He might just assume..."

Troy wasn't sure what Geoff was warning him off of. "Just speak your mind, honey. Do you think I'm making a mistake?"

"I'm asking you if you plan to fuck him or tell him no. I just think you should know the answer before that drink."

"I don't intend to tell him no, if he asks. If he doesn't want to and if I've had a drink or two, I'll put him in the guest room. Fair enough?" Maybe he'd just take Saul home and go home and jack off in the shower.

"Troy?"

He turned at the sound of his name. "Hey, Kris. You heading home?"

"I am. So, I owe you an apology in a major way."

He waved the words away. "We all have our moments. No worries."

"Thanks. This will get better." Kris gave him a smile. "Your new Master seems like a nice guy. I'm happy for you."

"Thank you." He didn't bother with details. Kris had enough shit to deal with on his own.

"Hey, Kris, let me see you guys out." Geoff stepped around him and followed Kris down the hall. Saul appeared in the kitchen a second later. He didn't think that was a coincidence.

"Hey." Saul smiled at him. "I really appreciate the ride."

"You're more than welcome." *Come over and have a drink?*

"Didn't you say you were off tomorrow? I was thinking maybe we could go for a nightcap. One that doesn't involve mint and peanut butter."

He fought his urge to blush, knowing full well it was a

losing battle. "I did. Would you like to come over to my place? I have beer and coffee, possibly some Cokes."

Saul leaned a shoulder against the doorjamb, fingers tucked into his pockets, the stance and the smile casual and relaxed. "I would love to."

"Good deal." He finished the dishes up real quick and hung his towel on the faucet to dry. "Holler when you're ready."

"I'm ready." Saul was still blocking the doorway though, eyes on him. "Are you?"

"Yessir." He dried off his hands. "Let me grab my shoes."

God, he was flip-flopping it. Seriously, he'd become a Coloradian. Boulderadian? Rocky Mountain man?

"I think our agreement for the evening is over, Troy." Saul hesitated just a second before moving out of his way.

"Pardon me?" He didn't follow. He wasn't expecting Saul to agree to take him on after three hours and a beer.

"You 'Sir'd me. You don't have to do that."

Ah. "Once a Texan, always a Texan." Flip-flops or not. "I'll try and remember."

It was a lost cause, though. He knew that.

"Oh." Saul laughed. "I thought I'd figured out the difference. I'll get better. Get your shoes, Texan." That grin was adorable.

"I'm on it." He went to the little bedroom that he thought of as his, changed from his soft pants and shirt to jeans and his T-shirt and hoodie. He put his clothes away in the dresser and slid his sandals on. It had been nice to be a part of a couple, even for a few hours. Troy thought Saul had been satisfied enough. If nothing else, he had given Saul an opening to another group of like-minded people.

He met Carter in the hallway. "I'm heading out, boss. I'll see you Wednesday if not before."

Carter huffed. "Like you aren't in for breakfast on your days off. We wouldn't know what to do if there was a day you didn't show."

"Yeah, yeah. See you later, man. Have a good one."

He found Saul and Geoff talking by the front door.

"Speak of the devil." Geoff grinned at him. "Hey, before you run. Ink Tuesday? Carter says you've earned it and he'll cover the balance on this one."

"God yes. Please. When?" He ached for it.

"How about ten? Give you the day to relax."

"I'll be there." He leaned in, gave Geoff a quick kiss. "Love you, buddy. Boss is already upstairs. Have fun."

Saul laughed. "Yes, have lots of fun."

Geoff smiled. "We will. Enjoy your evening, you two."

The door closed and he and Saul were alone. "Which is your truck?"

"The red GMC." She was his baby. Fifteen years old, paid off, and in cherry condition.

"Cool. The black one is Carter's, I remember now." Saul jogged around to the passenger's side.

"Yep. And Geoff drives the Mustang convertible." He unlocked the truck and climbed in. He started her up, turning down the radio as it came on blaring. He'd been singing.

Saul laughed. "Aw. You can turn it up, man. I'm game."

"I was having good radio karma." He turned it up a little because it was the Eagles, dammit.

"Right on." Saul jumped right in, singing along. Saul's singing voice had an edge to it he hadn't heard when Saul was speaking. "Who doesn't love the Eagles?"

"You know it. Who are your favorite bands?" He knew that Saul liked French toast and sausage, blond beer, and potatoes, but not much else.

"Pretty much anything with a dirty lead guitar does it for me. Pearl Jam, Foo Fighters, Green Day... uh, and then guys like Aldean, Springsteen, oh and classic rock too. Zeppelin, Pink Floyd." Saul looked at him. "I listen to a lot of music."

"I do too. I love Green Day, although sometimes I wish Billie Joe would enunciate a little more." He headed down into town, the lights shimmering in the night. He loved driving home on Sunday nights, when the whole city was sleepy and getting ready for their Monday.

"So I think it's fair to say that we—or maybe more you— surprised a few people today."

"Yeah, I think we probably did. It was good for them to meet you too." He couldn't wait for the waves of gossip that he'd get over the next week.

"I liked them a lot. That's a really supportive group. I mean, I'd never seen anything like Kris's meltdown. Ever. And by the time we came back in it was all good? That's amazing."

"I haven't seen Kris meltdown before, but I've seen some moments at the gatherings. Matt learned from the best, though. He'd trained under Doc for five years." Carter had wanted him to submit to Matt, but there had been no chemistry, no spark, and thank God, because Kris was made for Matt.

"I've had some training, and I work a lot on instinct too. You made me look good, though. Being new and all, I appreciated that."

"Well, thank you." He hadn't done any formal training, not really, but he'd been watching for years after Arnie had left him. He imagined sometimes how Arnie would have ragged his ass about the monthly meetings.

"I have to tell you, I felt better with Benjamin there. At least I wasn't the youngest in the room." Saul snorted. "I felt a little in over my head for a bit, to be honest. I'm still not sure if I'll really fit in, but I want to."

"Benjamin is a neat guy. I really enjoyed getting to know him. Don't worry— the guys all seemed pleased to get to know you, genuinely." And lord knew, Doc and David could be direct.

"We'll see if I get invited back, right? A lot can happen in a month." Saul reached over and rubbed his shoulder.

"You know it." Oh, that felt good, the random caress.

"Do you bike?" Saul turned the radio down as they pulled into his driveway.

"I do, but I don't have one right now, so I walk a lot." He'd given Ben his bike, and the kid loved it.

"Yeah? Well, I know someone that runs a bike shop, I'll see what he can do for you." Saul chuckled and hopped out of the truck.

"No shit? Lucky for me!" He let them in, turning on the lights, and telling himself not to be nervous. "Please, have a seat. What would you like to drink?"

"A beer works, thanks." Saul moved into the room and took a seat on the sofa.

He grabbed two beers, opened them, and headed back in, trying to decide if it was too forward to sit his happy ass down next to Saul. Hell, he figured he was considering the possibility of intimacy with the man, surely they could sit together.

Troy offered Saul his beer and then sat next to him. Not in his lap or anything, just next to him.

"Thank you. Here's to our first session together." Saul held up his beer. "Cheers."

He clinked their bottles together. "Cheers."

God, he had to wonder if he'd seemed like an asshole,

like some desperate middle-aged dude sitting on the floor at the gathering.

He drank deep, telling himself to relax. Self-doubt wasn't sexy, and it didn't help anything.

As he lowered his bottle, Saul took his other hand and gave it a squeeze. "You have good beer."

"That's the nice part about drinking with a cook, right?" He had to have some taste in his mouth.

"Huh. I didn't know that was a thing. Makes sense I guess." Saul took another sip and set the beer bottle down, then lifted his hand and pressed soft lips to his knuckles. Three long, thoughtful kisses across the back of his hand without a word.

Troy's abs drew in tight, and it was all he could do to swallow back a moan. Goosebumps popped up on his arms and his nipples went rock hard.

Saul reached for him, hooking fingers under his jaw, leaning in and coaxing him closer. He watched Saul swallow and then their eyes finally met. "I've wanted to do this all day."

"That's a long time to wait." He leaned in, letting himself relax toward Saul's hand.

"Yeah." Saul kissed him, slow and sweet, with a surprising patience for a young man, and a less surprising confidence. He sensed the heat simmering just behind Saul's careful restraint, though, and the longer the kiss went on the more of that wild hunger he could taste.

Troy leaned in, one hand settling on Saul's thigh. The strength there made him moan, and this time he didn't hold it in.

Saul answered with a deep sigh, and in one smooth motion, took his beer from his hand, set it down and shifted to face him on the sofa.

He was hard in his jeans, not aching, not yet, but hopeful that it would come to that.

Saul smiled at him, eyes searching his, thumb tracing the line of his cheekbone. "Good?"

One side of his mouth pulled up, the old roper's scar at the corner tugging. "More than, I think."

"All right, then." Saul leaned in, grinning against his lips, tasting him with a curious tongue. It was the easiest thing on earth, to open, to touch the tip of his tongue to Saul's.

Saul circled the tip with his own, then let their tongues slide together and took a deeper kiss, hands stroking over his scalp. The touch on his freshly shaved skin made him dizzy, and he answered the caress by drawing a long line along Saul's spine.

Saul only broke the kiss for a second as a soft T-shirt slipped between them, baring a strong chest sporting fine, light hair.

"Mmm... look at you." Troy dragged his hands along Saul's chest, letting them both feel.

Saul's eyes followed his hands and that chest expanded with a deep breath. "Uh-huh. Your turn." Saul reached over and tugged at the hem of his hoodie.

He struggled out of it before pulling his T-shirt off. He got a gasp as Saul got his first, real look at his chest. He had dozens of triskelions—some were fierce and sharp, others flowed like they were dancing. He had a series of them on his collarbones that were stylized flowers. His nipples were pierced with short barbells, the balls both hugging his nips close.

"Whoa, look at *you*..." Saul's fingers went right to his piercings and tugged on them gently. "Geoff does lovely work."

"H-he does." Oh fuck him, he felt that deep in his balls.

It made him want to beg.

One of Saul's eyebrows lifted. "Like that, huh?" He expected another jolt, but instead, Saul drew wide circles around his hardware, teasing. "I'll remember." Saul's fingers moved on to trace several of the symbols, swirling and twisting with the patterns in ink on his skin. More teasing. "So fascinating. I could do this for hours."

"I have a lot of skin. I lot of ink." A lot of little surprises. He leaned back so Saul could explore.

"We have a lot of time too. Nice." Saul could easily have stepped off the couch to get a better view from behind, but instead the kid climbed over him and the sofa cushions like a monkey, then landed with a plop at his back without once breaking contact. "These are amazing."

"Geoff does wonderful work. Twenty years' worth." He did have a little unmarked skin—his backside, his hands, his groin, the bottoms of his feet.

"I've just never seen anyone do the same symbol over and over and over like this, it's incredible." Warm hands flattened out across his shoulders and Saul pressed a kiss into the base of his neck.

"It is. Geoff says we do good work together." He was an eager canvas. "The blue one on my shoulder was the first."

"This one here?" Saul traced it with his finger, and then with his tongue.

"Mmhmm..." He closed his eyes so he could focus. "I was so fucking nervous."

"Really?" Saul laughed, hot breath brushing his neck. "You'd rodeo but a tattoo made you nervous?" The soft kisses that followed Saul's words traced the line of his neck and across one shoulder.

"I'd quit already. It's a long sordid story." No one wanted to hear that shit. "I was addicted from the start."

"You must be. You're running out of room. Someday you'll tell me all your long sordid stories. When we're in the right frame of mind, which is definitely not right now." Saul chuckled against his back, still landing kisses and tracing ink.

"Mmhmm." Geoff would just cover over the parts he was bored with. Right now that didn't matter. Right now all that mattered were those touches.

Saul moved, this time stepping off the sofa before sitting beside him again, much deeper into the cushions. "Come here." One hand snaked around him and pulled him in for another kiss.

Troy moaned and dared to swing himself over to straddle Saul's lap, the motion as familiar as breathing.

That earned a groan from Saul that he could feel vibrate against his tongue as they kissed. Saul's hands went right to his hips, tugging him even closer. He followed straight away, and when their bellies met, he fed Saul his cry.

Saul's hand slid up his back and the kiss turned hungry, their tongues tangling as Saul's fingers dug into his skin. He met that hunger with his own, refusing to shy away. He wrapped one hand around Saul's head, keeping them together.

Fingers dragged over his abs to his chest and gave one of his piercings a pinch and tug, the other hand kneading his ass through his jeans. Jesus, that was like electricity, lightning sparking between Saul's touches.

Saul rocked under him and he could feel that need pressing against him now, hard and impatient. "Fuck. Troy."

He was willing and able. He reached between them, stroking that hard ridge of need. Oh damn, he wanted some of that.

Saul tightened an arm around him and shifted sideways,

dumping him on his back in the cushions before nimble fingers dove in and started working his jeans open.

He lifted his hips, pushing right up into Saul's hand. He knew he looked like a slut, but he wanted to know what all they had to teach each other.

"Love how you move." Saul wriggled and dragged his jeans down, humming as his cock sprang free of the denim. "No ink here?" Saul dragged his fingers over Troy's bare skin.

"Not yet." He had his piercings, though—one in the head, one where his balls met his cock, and three behind his balls.

"Oh, man. Fucking hot." Saul went after his Prince Albert with curious fingers, alternating slow strokes with fondling his jewelry. "I've never seen one of these for real."

"No?" He wiggled out of his jeans and spread, more than willing to let Saul look his fill.

Saul found the one at the base of his shaft next, and spent a little time exploring. "Seriously hot. I want to..." He got a quick grin before Saul bent and licked the head of his cock, tongue even more curious than Saul's fingers had been.

Jesus fuck. His belly and his toes clenched, as he fought the urge to push into Saul's mouth, just bury himself.

Saul's tongue slipped through his ring and tugged gently, and then he got what he wanted as his cock slipped past Saul's lips.

His mouth popped open, the lights in the ceiling seeming to spin for a minute. He couldn't breathe, but it was worth it, to feel this.

"Mmm." Saul hummed, taking him deeper, tongue working his shaft like a man who knew what felt good. Saul massaged and tugged his balls, making a surprised sound upon discovering the rest of his piercings. He felt that happy noise all the way to his knees.

Saul let him go with a final lick, and looked at him with a wide grin. "That is too fucking cool."

He tried to agree, but his breath caught in his throat. It was goddamn amazing.

Saul plopped down on the couch and bent over to unlace his boots, laughing softly and way too coherent. "These things... they look great, they're comfortable as hell, but they take forever to get off. Such a mood-killer."

"I've become acclimated." He kicked off his flip-flops, fighting the urge to ask if Saul wanted some help. Saul had been crystal clear that sort of thing wasn't welcome outside of a scene.

"Flip-flops are not Dom-like." Saul grinned at him. "And they're no good on my bike either." Once the boots and socks were off, Saul stood and casually stepped out of those black jeans, which had nothing underneath them at all but perfect pale skin and lovely lean muscle.

Troy reached out to touch. So fucking pretty. He wanted to love up on this man everywhere.

But Saul shifted before he got a chance, dragging his jeans the rest of the way off. Saul moved so smoothly, seemed so sure. "Much better. God, you're just gorgeous. You're like a... a living mural or something. A painted sculpture."

He blinked up, shocked as hell. Gorgeous. Huh. "Thank you, Si-Saul. I appreciate it."

"We'll get there, I hope." Saul smiled at him, a flash of promise in those knowing eyes. "Not tonight, though. Tonight's just fun. I just want to know you." Fingers slipped between his legs again to circle and stroke the piercings behind his balls. "Why three down?"

"Three is so many things." God, it was hard to think. "Geoff says he has plans for my shaft."

"Hm. I'm sure he does." Saul leaned over him and kissed him again. More of that slow, hot, easy vibe.

He opened up, rocking gently, finding Saul's internal rhythm and matching it. Saul wrapped fingers around his length, thumb jostling the ring at the tip. "I have plans too."

"Do you?" Oh sweet fuck, yes. He wanted to know all about them.

"I do. Show me your bedroom, Troy." Saul shifted off him and offered him a hand up. "Unless you're into getting fucked on your sofa."

"Come upstairs. I have a great bed." He took Saul's hand, leading him up the stairs to his reason for buying this condo —the loft bedroom took up the whole floor, one wall completely glassed-in with windows.

"Oh my God." Saul gasped and hustled him right to the windows, apparently not caring if he had neighbors. "This is amazing, Troy!" The sun was almost set but it was light enough to take in some of the view, to get an idea of what morning would bring.

"Isn't it perfect? It's why I bought this place." It felt so damn good, knowing that Saul saw it, the beauty of it all.

"I would've too. I love it. This is... oh, I can't wait to see the sunrise." A strong arm tucked him against Saul's chest. So the kid was staying over. Good to know.

"It's gorgeous." He leaned, resting against Saul, soaking up all that heat. They stood there and watched the last of the daylight disappear, taking in their second sunset that weekend. When the sky turned purple, Saul started moving backward toward the bed, pulling him along.

"You're full of surprises. More than I would have expected."

"I'm not a shrinking violet, that's for sure." He was willing to ride.

"No. That I'm less surprised about, with the rodeo and all." Saul spun him so he faced the bed and ran hot hands over his ass. "But I hadn't expected to be invited over so soon. I sure wasn't about to say no, but I hadn't expected to be asked."

"You never know what will happen. Sometimes you have to grab hold and see where you end up."

"Nothing to lose, huh?" Saul gave one cheek a squeeze and then a loud smack that was meant more for effect than to sting. "Let's see where we end up, then."

He pulled the huge comforter back off the bed, leaving it at the bottom. The king-size bed was massive and sturdy with heavy knotted pine posts, one of the few pieces of furniture he'd brought from Texas.

Saul rocked him, that thick cock, which he still hadn't been allowed to touch yet, fitting right into his crack, and naughty fingers crawled over his belly and up to his nipples, rolling his piercings. He propped one leg up on the bed, spreading and stabilizing himself as he rocked between sensations.

"Mmm. Good?" Saul took advantage and leaned into him, dropping one hand to his prick, the rocking pushing him right through that tight fist.

"Oh damn." He blinked down, watching his cock appear and disappear in Saul's grip. It fascinated him, how hard and red he was.

"Yeah, look at you." Saul panted in his ear, voice rough. "Hot. Hard. Wanting, huh? Gorgeous."

His mouth was dry, and he shook as he tried to answer. Yes. Hard. Wanting.

Saul traced a wet line up his neck to just behind his ear

with his tongue, while a thumb swept over the tip of his cock and put pressure on his ring. "I'm gonna fuck you so hard."

"God yes. Bring it on." It had been a while since he'd been fucked, but not long at all since he'd fucked himself.

"Lube and...?" Saul tossed him lightly on the bed and pointed to his nightstand. "In here?"

"Yessir, but—" Troy blinked as Saul opened the drawer, finding his stash of dildos and plugs. "Um..."

"Busy man." Saul chuckled, pulling out a rubber and a bottle of lube. "That's a little intimidating. But I'm more fun than a drawer full of toys."

"I have no doubt." They wouldn't be up here otherwise. "But I'm eager as hell to know for sure."

"Show me that ass and I'll give you what you want." Saul sheathed himself in a second and then popped open the lube. "Let me see you."

He crawled forward on the bed, staying on hands and knees. "This work for you?"

"That's beautiful. You?" Slick fingers put pressure on his hole and Saul moved up behind him.

"Lord yes." He spread his knees and bore back.

"Nice." One finger slipped inside, and Saul quickly added a second, rotating them and putting pressure against the muscle.

Nice seemed like a bit of an understatement, especially when he started moving with Saul.

Saul moaned behind him as he rode those fingers. "Fuck, Troy. You're something else. Tell me I can... want you." The words sounded soft and dark.

"Fuck me. I want to know. Please." That was clear enough, wasn't it?

"Jesus." The fingers disappeared, quickly replaced by

Saul's cock and the guy didn't hesitate a second. The fat head pushed inside, and the rest of Saul's length followed, sinking slowly, persistently, until Saul was balls deep, his ass against hard thighs.

Troy arched and threw his head back, a happy moan tearing out of him. *Fuck*. Fuck, that was good.

Fingers gripped his hips as Saul groaned and started to move, the strokes long and slow at first, then gradually growing intense. "Oh man, you feel so good."

He met every thrust, his entire body full, a coil of need tightening in his belly.

Saul grunted and hauled on his hips, plunging even deeper, driving so hard it was difficult to keep his arms under him.

"Yes." He didn't want Saul to think he was a shrinking violet. He wanted to feel everything.

"Fuck, yeah." Saul changed the angle every so often, obviously searching for just the right spot, but the pace didn't let up.

When Saul found it, Troy surged forward, climbing the bedpost to keep Saul right there.

"Oh, yeah." Saul's forehead landed on his back, hips working hard, hammering him over and over. "Gonna short you right out."

"Yes." He stared at the wall, lights flashing behind his eyes. His prick ached for a touch, and he let that anticipation drive his need higher.

Saul's rhythm faltered for a second, punctuated by a deep grunt and then a hand found him, Saul's fist closing tight around his shaft. "I got you." When those thrusts picked up again, they were stronger but different, first rolling deep and slow, then a few shallow and quick.

The mix-up in the rhythm, added with the reach-around

made him arch impossibly with the burn and buzz. He cried out, so fucking close.

"Jesus. So gorgeous. Fuck, I'm... Troy!" Saul shook, shouting his name, and he could feel the way Saul tensed, every muscle straining through the powerful climax. "Fuck, fuck!"

His breath caught in his chest and his balls throbbed as he shot, pouring himself out into Saul's hand. The whole fucking world spun. Saul moaned through tremors that rocked them both, sucking in air, panting hot breath across his shoulders.

He filled his lungs, then let it out in a long, slow breath. His entire body tingled, and he felt so fucking alive.

"Damn." Saul leaned over his back and rocked into him one more time, then pulled out with a chuckle and headed for the bathroom. "You're incredible."

Troy sat back a bit and tried to remember how to loosen his fingers from the bedpost.

"Hey." Saul returned with a cloth in one hand and helped, playfully maneuvering him onto his back "You okay, old man?"

"I'm fine as frog hair." And getting older every second. He laughed, forcing his post-orgasm mood swing up.

"You sure are." Saul spent a couple of minutes running the damp cloth over him, the gesture warm and caring. "Okay." Saul tossed the cloth on the floor and stretched out beside him with a happy groan. "Jesus. Gingers."

"We're something else, aren't we?"

Saul laughed. "Humble too."

"Totally." He went for arrogant, but the laughter just burst out of him.

Saul rolled over and straddled Troy's thighs, still giggling and grinning. His blond hair was damp, dark with sweat, plastered to his wide forehead in places, and his cheeks were flushed pink. "I'm going to want more of you."

"That works for me." He stroked Saul's hair back. "You gave me one hell of a ride."

"I wanted you. Next time I'll try for a little more... finesse. Or I'll tie you up. You never know with me." Saul bent down and kissed him. He hummed softly and reached up, digging his fingers in to ease those strong muscles. "Mmm. I like that," Saul said against his lips. Saul tugged gently on his bottom lip with cautious teeth. "You like it hard, huh?"

"I do. I'm not real fragile." In fact, he was a stud.

Saul lifted up and looked at him, eyes searching. "We're all fragile."

"You think so?" He made sure to keep the question gentle, not sarcastic at all, but he'd explored what being broken had to teach him. Of course, he'd had a lot more time to be cracked down the center. Rumor was a broken soul got stronger where it healed.

"Well, yeah. Strength and fortitude aren't the same thing, right? Neither is weakness and vulnerability. It's like apples and oranges, you know? All of us need to be handled with care."

"I can see that." Troy wasn't a fan of abuse by any means, but no one was interested in hurting him. Hell, he was way more likely to be completely ignored.

Saul chuckled. "But you're a stud, huh? No fragility in you at all." He got another kiss.

He didn't bother to answer the comment, because he didn't have one. He wasn't sure what Saul meant—he wasn't a mean man, he didn't tolerate meanness in others, and people were rarely mean to him. So he focused on rubbing Saul's shoulders.

Saul sat up again, resting a hand on his chest. "Are you looking for a Dom, Troy? I mean… is that something you want?" The question seemed genuine, honest.

He answered with equal honesty. "I'd stopped looking. I'm long in the tooth, for the most part and I know that. I prayed for someone to work with for a while, then I stopped and just worked on being satisfied with what I had."

"And now?" Saul smiled. "Are you still satisfied with what you had?"

"I said 'worked on'. I was with Arnie for seven years and I've watched the group for another twenty. I miss having that part of my life."

"I would too. I'm not sure how I'd function without it." Saul reached down and smoothed a thumb over his forehead. "What do you want? What do you miss most?"

Not having to pay for what I need. "I miss being a part of something where both people get what they crave."

"Sounds pretty simple. You're not telling me what you crave though." Saul's fingers traveled over his skin, drawing circles and lines, tracing scars. "Do you know?"

"I know that I need to find my headspace. I know that I go to Geoff once every six weeks or so to get it right now."

"Finding your headspace, feeling grounded is important to you. What do you do once you've found it? You're seeing Geoff on Tuesday, right? What happens after he gets you where you need to be?" He understood that Saul wasn't asking questions randomly. They definitely had a purpose.

"That depends on what happens—sometimes I go spend the night in their guest room, sometimes I sleep at the shop, sometimes I come home." It all hinged on Geoff, really. If Geoff was mellow, he went to their place. If Geoff needed, he stayed at the shop or went home, depending on whether he could drive.

Saul looked at him, confused. "That's it? You just go to sleep?"

"What else could there be with Geoff?" Geoff was his friend, helped him out, but Geoff had Carter, and most of the time, Geoff headed home to get what he needed.

"Right, right. Of course." Saul climbed off him and settled in the pillows. "Can I hold you?"

"I'd like that." He moved over, finding the places where they fit together.

"Comfy?"

He nodded and Saul tucked an arm around him, making it that much better.

"I don't have a regular sub anymore. I have a couple of friends that I work with once in a while who don't have Doms, and that's been okay, but it seems like it's better for them than it is for me. I'm not getting a lot of what I need out of that."

He closed his eyes, drawing circles on Saul's chest. "What do you need? What are you into?"

Maybe it was his turn to ask the questions.

"Well I get the power exchange stuff from them. Khloe is really into bondage and spanking and those are big turn-ons, and Brant is more of a deprivation guy. That's all good, I get a workout I guess, skills practice, but I don't often get the high, you know? I need more of that. And I don't get the service."

"Oh, I understand that. The care, the..." Troy searched for what he wanted to say because it was important to him, not to put words in Saul's mouth. "It's hard when you need someone's real submission, I imagine."

"Yeah." He felt Saul's chest rise and fall with a sigh. "They're submitting, but they're not... mine."

"Yes." He nodded, and the action slid his face against

Saul's chest. "I do understand, at least somewhat. I can submit, but it doesn't matter to anyone."

"It would matter to me." The arm around him tightened just slightly. "If you're interested."

"I am." Well, damn. Look at him, reaching for what he wanted. Arnie would be proud.

"That's... I'm—what's the right thing to say?" Saul laughed softly. "Thank you? I'm happy you agreed. And honored. I didn't actually plan to ask so soon, but it felt right."

"Thank you for asking." Geoff was going to rag his ass, no question, but he felt confident in his answer.

Saul kissed his head. "How deep do you want? I guess that's a question we should think about, right? Do you just want to scene together or do you want to—well. I guess don't have to hash it all out in the middle of the night."

"True. We can talk over a lazy breakfast, maybe? I—" He took a deep breath. "I like you. A lot. I'm nervous and excited and there's a huge part of me that's asking thousands of questions."

He felt young and inexperienced again, which he wasn't.

Saul tucked a finger under his chin and lifted his face so their eyes met. "I like you a lot too, Troy. You're fascinating. You're beautiful. I've never been with anyone like you. I want to answer all of your questions, but honestly I'm nervous about whether you'll like the answers." Saul took a light kiss. "Maybe some sleep and some coffee will help us both breathe easier."

"It will." Sleep. Coffee.

Hell, he'd even bought the stuff to make French toast, just in case.

9

Saul shuffled out of the bathroom headed for the warmth of Troy's bed, but those windows and that view distracted him, and he ended up torn between the two. He and Troy had missed most of the sunrise, though they hadn't slept through it. Saul just couldn't keep his hands off his new lover. Despite the second round of fucking at some dark hour, they'd been distracted by lazy blow jobs in the middle of Mother Nature's early morning show.

He wasn't disappointed, and he was fairly sure there'd be plenty more opportunities in his future.

He was pretty sure it was still morning, though he hadn't checked the time, and he hadn't checked his phone for texts, either. He just didn't give a damn about anything right now but the view... the one out the window and the one in that bed.

He was slightly distracted by whether it had been a good idea to ask Troy to sub for him in a haze of lust and hormones, but Troy hadn't said no, and they still had a ton of talking to do about it. He wasn't worried. Maybe just a little bemused.

Troy moaned softly, stretching tall in the bed. "Mmm... Mornin'."

Troy slid out of the sheets and padded to the bathroom to do his business. When he reappeared, Troy unrolled a yoga mat, offering him a lazy smile. "You mind if I get a little stretching in?"

"Not if you mind if I watch. Closely." Because what a sight this was going to be. His balls ached just thinking about it.

"Not at all." Troy stretched up tall before folding himself in half. Saul watched, dry-mouthed, as Troy moved. At one point, Troy went wide-legged and bent forward, resting his head on the floor. Uhn.

Saul thought about joining in but watching was way more fun. Troy's flexibility was something to be remembered, and he was so graceful. Just one more thing to be fascinated by.

"I like that position. I think I'll file it away for later use."

Troy chuckled and slowly stood. "I do love how the morning stretch keeps me loose."

"I'm a fan." He grinned wickedly, hoping to see that ginger blush. "All those toys don't seem to work as well. You felt pretty tight to me."

There it went—a lovely, dark, rosy blush flooding his boy as those green eyes went wide. "Well, thank God for that, right?"

"Yep." Something that sweet deserved a kiss. His fingers were itching to touch anyway. He moved in close and made sure it was a heavy one, something to make Troy's knees weak.

Troy stepped into him, bringing their bodies together with a soft, low sigh. "Damn."

"Mhm. I could watch you stretch all day." He could. "Did you get enough rest?"

"I did. I feel energized today. You?" Troy touched him like he was fascinating, fingers dragging along his body and exploring.

"I feel amazing, thank you." His stomach growled toward the end of that statement and he laughed. "And hungry I guess."

"Good thing I know a short order cook. What's your pleasure?"

He gave Troy a quick peck and headed for the stairs in search of his boxers. All his clothes were still in the living room. "Whatever you've got. I like food. And coffee."

Troy tossed him a terrycloth robe before pulling on a pair of ancient shorts. "I'll make coffee and get breakfast started."

"Hey, thanks." The robe was comfortable and soft, but better than that it smelled like Troy. It was a little bit of a stretch to keep it closed, but it would work. "I'm not useless, I—"

I should let my sub make breakfast.

"Am completely capable of watching you cook." He shook his head at himself. *Dork.*

Troy smiled at him. "You can find some music for us, if you don't mind. Oh, and tell me all about your coffee preferences. I'm the tiniest bit of a coffee whore."

That was easy. He was particular about his morning coffee. "I'm not opposed to a sweet something in the afternoon or evening but my morning coffee needs to be dark, strong enough to take paint off your truck, and with just a splash of milk. Preferably skim. And in the biggest mug you have." He headed for Troy's stereo setup. "Great speakers. I see where your money goes."

"I don't have a ton of vices, and I haven't smoked in a year. Fifteen dollars a day saves up fast." Troy moved around the kitchen easily, the scent of coffee filling the air.

Saul found some Clapton and put it on, the guitar and soulful voice meant to suit the Dominant vibe he was reaching for. They had some talking to do, potentially some negotiating, and he needed to do it in the right frame of mind.

The clothing strewn all over the sofa, the floor, and the coffee table worked against his mood a bit, but he just let himself laugh and started tidying up. It would be hard to have a serious talk over socks and boxers.

"Coffee smells good."

"Thank you, Sir. Here you go. Dark, splash of skim, big mug." Troy didn't sound sarcastic or anything but happy.

He took the mug and cupped a hand around Troy's nape, keeping him there. "Wait." He took a sip, the rich bitter taste giving him that mental slap in the face he liked. He winked. "Pretty good. Thank you, boy."

It was pretty perfect, in fact, but saying so right out of the gate didn't give Troy anything to think about.

"Good deal." Troy gave him a little pressure, leaning into his hand.

After a quick squeeze he let go. "Clapton work for you?" He wandered over to a window and looked out, very much enjoying his coffee.

Troy hummed along with the music, and he could see Troy wandering around the kitchen, almost dancing.

Saul left him to it and didn't bother him with small talk because he seemed so happy. Not that he'd seemed unhappy the past few times they'd been around each other, but he'd been head down and working at the diner, and then Friday night Troy had seemed nervous. But the guy in the kitchen right now was relaxed and in his zone. Saul even caught little hints of a smile now and then.

There were things to be nervous about, but he wasn't going to share most of them with Troy. *What the actual fuck am I doing?* punctuated by the list of what could potentially go south might not go over that well. And it wasn't like the answer to that question was going to stop him from doing it. Hell, no. So he'd just save them and vent with his crew. Maybe Khloe. She got him better than most and would let him get the nerves out without judging.

"Come get it while it's hot." Two plates of French toast with sausage. Surprise surprise.

"Oh, man." He hurried into the kitchen and found himself a chair, stupidly happy over his breakfast. "This is really why I wanted to fuck you, you know."

"Damn, and I haven't pulled out my chili recipe on you yet!" Troy took his mug and went to refill it.

"Oh. Fuck, that's right! You're Texan. I'd totally rim you for chili." He wasn't kidding.

"I will make you chili whenever you want." Troy's voice was rough as a cob.

He couldn't have stopped the laughter if he tried. "Should I—" Words. Words required air, which required breathing. He tried to get a breath in between giggles. "Should I stay for dinner?"

"Hell, that gives me two meals, dessert, and a good-sized snack..." Troy almost cracked a smile but hid it in his coffee cup.

"You are *naughty*." It was maddening, that straight face. "Wicked, evil, and naughty, and now I'm going to give you a solid spanking to go with your rim job. And I'm going to make you wait for next weekend. So there."

Possibly the worst threat of a punishment in history. But it sure sounded like fun.

"So there. Yes, Sir." Troy grinned at him, winked, then waved one hand playfully. "Eat. Eat. Your toast will get cold."

They ate, and he didn't have much to say for a bit because his mouth was full and Troy, sitting there in shorts and sporting all that ink, was enough just to look at. He didn't need words. He did finally slow down after he'd finished two slices. "So so so *so* good. Either I'm going to have to order to you only make this once a week, or I'm going to have to make you part of my workout routine."

Troy beamed at him. "Thank you, Sir. I love hearing that."

"You should have seen all the pushups I was doing to work off waiting you out at the diner every damn day last week. It took you forever to come talk to me." He grinned. It hadn't really, Troy had to get it first, and then get up the nerve. "It was totally worth it, by the way."

"It was. That was a great first date." The smile he got warmed him, all the way down. "Even with all the mint."

"Especially with the mint! One of my best first date stories ever." He leaned back in his chair. "I am stuffed." They needed to refill their coffees and talk. Maybe he could start them off in the shower. Though that might finish them off too.

"Lord, me too. Hand me your plate and I'll toss it in the dishwasher real quick." Troy grabbed his dishes and whisked them away.

"Thank you." God, he wasn't used to this. He was torn between how impolite it was not to offer to help with the dishes and knowing that some part of Troy needed to serve. But the proof of that was in his boy's smile.

He'd talk about it, right? Just tell Troy that he and Deitz were never like this. Right? Maybe.

Yesterday it had worked, just asking Troy straight out, but—

"...like another cup?"

"Another—oh." He peered into his cup. "Just a warmup, please."

"You were a million miles away." Troy's fingers touched his, electricity buzzing through them.

"Yeah, I guess I was. I'm sorry." The touch brought him back to the man he was with.

"You're allowed. No worries." Troy winked at him, then got him more coffee.

"Honestly? I was thinking about service. Wondering about what you need, and whether I should feel like a bad house guest for not helping with the dishes." He watched Troy and smiled as he was handed back his mug.

"That's a little ball of worms, isn't it?" Troy shook his head and grinned at him. "Do you mind coming to the couch?"

He stood up. "Sure." The invitation sounded like Troy had a few things on his mind too. Saul hated talking things to death, but he knew that "consensual" meant they had to talk a little at least.

"Good deal." Troy drew him over and sat with him, grabbing a light blanket to wrap around them both. "I hope you don't mind, but I'm a bit of a cuddler."

"Yeah? Okay." Saul dove for the couch, getting comfy, and held his arms out. That was kind of awesome.

Troy didn't hold back. He cuddled right in with the blanket, connecting them. "This makes talking easier, hmm?"

"I guess so. Feels good to me. My last lover was the anticuddler. He was more of a high-fiver." He snorted. There was nothing cuddly about Deitz.

"Oh. Well, I suppose it's no surprise I'm a romantic."

"I'm not sure what I am, but this it nice." Sure, he knew how to treat a date, but that was just the manners his mother taught him. "You're right though, I'm not surprised about you."

Troy chuckled softly. "Yeah, I wanted to be a rodeo cowboy when I grew up."

"Everybody loves a rodeo cowboy." He kissed Troy on the cheek. "So, tell me what you want me to know about this one."

"I love that you worried about whether you ought to offer to help with the dishes. That makes me feel respected, and it proves you were raised right."

"My mother would be proud. And I did worry. I guess you're saying I shouldn't have?"

"No. We hadn't discussed it, and I hope you would help if I needed it."

"Of course. Whatever you need, whether it's dishes, or a flogging, or a hug. That's a given. Or... Maybe it's not a given with some people, but it is with me. For as long as this is what we want."

He'd been told that his Dom side was way more together and mature than the rest of him. He was oddly aware of that right now, maybe for the first time. He could totally be whatever Troy needed, once they'd agreed on what that was.

"That was how I was used to working before."

"That's how you and Arnie did things? Full-time lifestyle?" That was what he thought he wanted, he just hadn't done it before. "How did Arnie... no, never mind. I don't want to play that game. Sorry."

"It is. Arnie was...I was very young then." Troy chuckled softly. "Very young."

"What's very young? How old was he?"

"He was twenty-three when we hooked up and thirty when he died. I was eighteen, when we got together, I mean."

"Oh, that is young." Eighteen. He didn't even understand himself until two years ago. Which, okay, would have made him the same age Arnie was. But he wasn't attracted to guys that young. Even Deitz was five years older. Troy, if his math was right, was forty-five, give or take? And the hottest man he'd ever been with.

"So I'm up for full-time, but I haven't done it before, so I'll ask for patience in advance. And what does that mean really? Do you want to schedule time off? Do I need to ask to come over? What are your boundaries?"

Troy was quiet for a minute, then he took a deep breath. "That's a lot to think about, too. My biggest request is very few late Friday nights. Saturdays I'm slammed and getting ready for three o'clock Sunday. My hard limit is respect, and that's not a bullshit answer. I need to believe, no matter what I'm doing, that you respect what I'm giving you. You have my word that I will offer you the same."

"Thank you. And you'll let me know if I'm not living up to that requirement. Respect isn't a bullshit answer, it's practically a... what's it called? A... pillar? Yeah. It's a pillar of the practice. And respecting your job is part of that." He stroked a hand over Troy's bald head, tracing the ridges and lines in the bone.

Troy smiled and relaxed deeper into him. "That was a great answer, and I very much appreciate your willingness."

"Everybody has rent to pay, right?" That felt good, that little bit of validation. Knowing he was understood and trusted. And on that note, he figured he better share a couple of things with Troy too. "I need feedback. I need honesty. I need devotion." That was what he was missing. Surrender.

"Of those three, I bet feedback is the hardest. I'm not a complainer. I tend to just suck it up."

"Okay, that's important. I'll remember that. You're the quietest fuck I've ever had too... until you're the loudest. I mean, you barely talked at all." He grinned. "I'm not complaining. The Dom in me will ask for what I want if I need something, but otherwise? You be you."

"Ar—" Troy stopped short. "Are you okay with me talking about him?"

"Oh. Yeah, of course. I'm sure my ex will come up at some point too. I just—" He thought about how to say it so Troy understood. "I'm just not ready for the more personal details of your relationship with him as Dom and sub, you know? Not until we're more... established and have done some scenes of our own. Does that make sense? I can get pretty jealous and I don't want to be drawing comparisons."

"Fair enough." Troy drew lazy circles on his belly, the touch featherlight.

Fair enough. So whatever Troy wanted to share was something he'd just specifically asked not to hear. Shit.

Troy didn't seem upset, though, or tense. Just quiet and there with him.

But quiet wasn't what he wanted. And he didn't want to hash anything else out right now either. He felt like they'd do better creating their normal as they got to know each other better. "Unless there is something pressing on your mind that we didn't cover, I would like a shower, boy."

"Of course." Troy rolled up to standing and grabbed his coffee. "Are you a hot shower type or warm?"

Oh, his boy asked a good question. "Today? I'd like it just a hair too hot for you. And I don't want to have to hunt for condoms if I want one."

"You have my word, Sir. I won't hide them." The words might have sounded glib in another man's voice, but Troy sounded warm, teasing, caring. "I'll get us set up. You'll get to meet my amazing tankless water heater."

"Oh nice. Give me your safe words again, please?" He got up as well and headed for the kitchen with his coffee mug.

"Red and yellow, Sir." Troy finished his coffee on his way up the stairs.

"Red and yellow. Thank you. I'll be right up." He washed his mug, which was more about stalling a minute, doing something mechanical that didn't require him to think, and getting his head right.

By the time he was done and climbing the stairs, he was breathing deep and feeling very ready for a little soapy fun and some personal attention from his sub.

10

"Can we turn on a fan? Please?" Troy's buzz was fading, the burn of Geoff's needle on his skin starting to make him sweat.

"The collarbone is hard, I know. Breathe, baby doll. In and out. I need about ten more minutes to hit a good spot. Tell me more about Saul." Geoff was sweating as much as he was, both of them panting.

"Arnie would like him, I think."

"Yeah? What makes you say that?" He knew that trick. Ask questions. Keep him talking.

"He's hot. He's clever. Opinionated." Oh, fuck. That burned so much.

"He's easy on the eyes that's for sure. Take a breath with me. In deep... good. Out slow. You two looked good together Sunday. How..." Troy felt Geoff shifting his grip. It had been a long session for them both. "How serious is he?"

"I think he's serious? I want him to be. I don't want to be projecting, but it feels good."

"That's amazing. I'm happy for you. Carter likes him, he says Saul is straight up. They're going biking together again soon. I worry for you, but I think Saul's a safe enough bet. Is he good in bed?"

"Glorious. Energetic. He's built like a brick shit house." He groaned as Geoff hit a nerve. "Fuck..."

If Carter was here, there'd be growling about foul language. Geoff had banned his Dom from these sessions years ago.

"I know. Almost done, honey. Hang on." Geoff's voice was a little tight, and even the hum of the needle was starting to irritate him. "Just this last bit. Energetic is good, right?"

"God yes. I feel so goddamn alive. He... he knows how to make a man pay attention."

"That impressive for a wee baby Dom. He makes any mistakes, you send him to Carter, okay?"

"Yeah, that would be a sight... Fuck. Fuck, I'm done, honey." He was pouring sweat, the adrenaline and endorphins worn out.

"Two minutes. You can handle two minutes."

"God, I hate you."

"Liar." Geoff's smile was tight. "You sleeping here tonight?"

"No. I'll walk home and pick the truck up after my shift tomorrow."

"You sure that's a good idea? This has been a long day and you're not always the brightest bulb in your headspace... last little bit here but it's... it's going to right here." Geoff tapped his collar bone with a gloved finger.

"I hate you." Troy turned his head away, forcing himself to breathe, to not panic. It was just chemical. All this shit. It was just hormones flooding his body. "Just do it."

"Deep breath." Geoff touched the needle down. It couldn't have been for more than fifteen seconds, but it felt like forever. It wasn't even the burn; it was the noise. That motherfucking needle was driving into his bones.

"What? Are you drilling to fucking China, man?"

Geoff sighed and pushed away on his stool to turn the machine off. "You're a tough nut today, honey. Pretty. But tough."

"Jesus. Please, Geoff. *Please.*"

"I got you."

Troy grabbed the arms of the chair and braced, telling himself to relax, even though he knew he was too far gone for that—he'd passed that damn near an hour ago—and when the cold soapy water hit his burning skin, he arched, a short scream tearing from his throat.

"Don't honey, leave that be." Hands settled on him, one on his forehead and the other on his wrist. "He's coming around. He was just messing with the compress I have on his forehead. Well, usually yes, but this was maybe a tad longer than I... sure if you... Yes, I can do that. I... sorry. Yes, Sir."

"Geoff?" He blinked, shook his head, trying to shake his brain cells back into their spots.

"Yes, Sir. Gotta go." Geoff's fingers touched his cheek. "Right here, honey."

"Hey." He turned his head and kissed Geoff's palm. "You sent me somewhere else for a second. You okay?"

"That was more than a second, but yes. I'm okay. How do you feel?"

"Sore. Sweaty. Like we've run a marathon." Thirsty. God, he was thirsty.

"We basically did. I'm going to sit you up, let me know if you get dizzy." Geoff helped him upright and locked the table into position. "There. Water?" A bottle with a straw in it was pressed into his hands.

"You know me." He drank deep, and he was so empty he could hear the water splashing in his belly. "I booked you a hand massage at Peter's tomorrow morning at ten, by the by."

"Oh!" Geoff's squeal was totally worth the little extra he had to slip the receptionist to squeeze Geoff in. "Thank you, honey! You're so sweet." He got a happy kiss on the cheek.

"You're more than welcome." *Okay, man. Up. Up and moving. Grab your shirt and go.* The walk wasn't bad, and he could crash in his own bed after a beer and a bagel. It wasn't like this was the first time his truck had slept here.

He glanced at Geoff who was rocking on his heels, watching him anxiously. Someone needed to go home to his man and get what he needed. Carter would be over the moon. Needy Geoff was one of Carter's favorite flavors.

Shirt. Wallet. Phone. He got himself together as quick as he could, then he grabbed the roll of paper towels. "I'm going to get you to tape me up a little so I don't leak on my shirt."

"No problem. And I called Saul. You shouldn't be walking."

"What? But..." Wasn't that cheating somehow? For someone else to call Saul?

"But what? You're his."

"I-I don't know. I don't feel very in control right this second, honey."

Geoff smiled at him and cupped his cheek. "That's why you need him."

He closed his eyes and rested a second, letting his brain be off for a few breaths. Geoff covered his new ink and taped it carefully, the practiced fingers more than capable, and full of care and affection. The little rap at the door startled them both because the shop was so quiet, and Geoff hurried off to answer it.

"He's in here," he heard Geoff say.

When Saul came in, the energy in the room changed completely. "Boy." Saul came right to him and kissed him.

He gasped softly, the touch of their lips electric. Oh. Oh, damn. That was a surprise.

A growl rumbled in Saul's chest, the sound muffled by their kiss, but there was no question what the sound meant, or what his Master's possessive kiss was telling him. Saul didn't let him be until they were both breathless. "Where are your keys?"

"My pocket. I was going to walk." He couldn't risk driving, with his head where it was.

"He usually—"

Saul shot a stern look at Geoff, cutting the words off. After Geoff lowered his eyes, Saul turned back to him and smiled. "I'm going to drive you. Are you ready?"

"Yes, Sir." He was starting to shake—from hunger and pain and adrenaline. "More than ready." He shot Geoff a smile. "I know you are too. Enjoy Carter and don't forget tomorrow. Ten a.m."

"Thank you, sweetie. I'm looking forward to it." Geoff gave him the briefest smile and then his friend's eyes dropped to the floor again.

"Can you get home safely, Geoff?"

"Yes, Sir. Thank you, Sir."

"Very well. Come on, boy. I've got you." Saul put an arm around him and let him lean on the way to his truck.

He didn't know what to say, how to process everything right now, so he didn't try. Sometimes, that was the answer.

"I'm just getting the seatbelt," Saul said, reaching over him. "You just close your eyes. I'm right here."

"Thank you." He focused on slow belly breathing, on finding his center. Saul's scent—soap and sunshine and warmth—kept distracting him, making him smile.

Saul started the truck and then they were moving. "Tell me how you feel."

"I-shaky. Hungry. Sad because coming down sucks. Glad to see you. Sore." That was part of the need, wasn't it? He could feel so much, all at once.

"Oh, Troy. Coming down shouldn't suck. Geoff isn't—" Saul sighed. "I'll make it better. I'm glad to see you too."

He reached out and slid his hand over Saul's arm. Oh, he was feverish; Saul's skin felt chilly to the touch.

"Jesus, Troy." Saul covered his hand for a second. "We're almost there." The truck stopped soon after and Saul came around to help him out. "Easy."

"God, that's hard work. Good work, but it makes a man tired."

Saul waited for him to open the front door. "I want to get you in the shower, boy, and find you something to eat. But first... come sit with me."

"Of course, Sir." Oh fuck. Was he in some sort of trouble? He hadn't asked Geoff to call Saul. At all.

Saul sat deep into his sofa and held out an arm for him to snuggle under. "Come on. As close as you can get."

So not in trouble. Excellent. He cuddled in, taking care to protect his skin on that side. He closed his eyes and sucked in a deep breath, breathing Saul in.

"Coming back from your space—coming down from all those endorphins, and the adrenaline and the pain—" Saul breathed in deep and stroked his shoulders with gentle fingers. "After all that hard work—good work, you called it

—you will feel tired, exhausted sometimes, drained yes. But you shouldn't feel sad. You should feel loved."

Troy wasn't sure how to answer that. "I know that Geoff loves me dearly. He just—" *Has a Master that he needs, that needs him.* "—has to go home to Carter."

"He does. I know he cares about you, but he isn't what you need. He can't be. How did this... ritual start?"

"You mean the ink? I came to Carter to give him Arnie's buckles after he died. I was in a bad way, and they took me in. Geoff started working. An hour or two at first, then four or five. Now it's six, sometimes eight."

"I don't... really mean the ink. I mean using the ink to find what you believe is your subspace. Letting Geoff use your body to... well, I assume to focus on his service. How long has it been that and not just art?"

"A while, I guess. When Carter started coming, so fifteen years? He got banned about ten years ago." Something about Saul's words read like they were doing something wrong, something almost off-putting. He wasn't going to jump to conclusions, though. That got him in trouble, every fucking time.

"Wait. Carter used to be there when Geoff was working? What do you mean got banned?"

"At the beginning, yes, but... Carter has a lot of rules and... he's my boss, not my Dom. It was uncomfortable. So Carter doesn't come in. It means that Geoff hurries home more often, but..." It sounded so complicated. So hard to explain. "He's doing me a favor. I was lonely and not sure how to get help."

Saul sighed. "Well. You have a Dom now." That sounded pretty final.

"Are we all right?" Something was wrong. Troy wasn't sure what, but something was off.

"Yes. Yes, baby. We're fine." Saul hugged him tight and then shifted so he could see those blue eyes. "I'll be very honest. I'm uncomfortable with this thing between you and Geoff, I don't think it's healthy. It has a... it goes against a lot of what I've learned and what I believe. I know there was no malice involved but... I don't like it."

"I don't understand. No one's ever suggested we were being..." He searched for words. "Inappropriate?"

A rush of emotions hit him like a freight train—worry, shame, anger, panic—and he forced them down, finding it hard as all get out to control them.

"Hey. Shh. I didn't say that, Troy. You need food and rest and we will talk about this again, I promise. When you're more yourself, okay? I shouldn't... I'm sorry. I shouldn't have said anything. They're your friends. I respect that."

He squeezed Saul's hand, held it for a long minute while he tried to put his head on straight. Priorities. Right. Feed Saul. Get the shirt and paper towel off. See if Saul would like to spend the night. "Would you like a pizza?"

Saul kissed him. "Sure. I'll order. You get yourself some water and a banana or something and go take a shower."

He grabbed his wallet and handed Saul a twenty and a ten. "That should cover it."

Then he headed upstairs, stripping down.

He needed some cold water. He was burning alive.

11

Saul could hear his mother's voice in the back of his mind. *There are plenty of perfectly good seats to choose from and you're on the damn floor again.*

Well, yeah. He was. He was also on his third slice. Being the youngest, he grew up diving for the food, or he wouldn't get any. He was particularly good at inhaling pizza. He took another bite, caught Troy watching him, and winked.

"You look better with some food in you, boy." He didn't think Troy could look any worse than when he'd shown up at Geoff's shop. Pale, feverish, stressed, and he'd watched as a kind of depression weighed on his boy's shoulders, in Troy's eyes. This was better. Anything was better.

"I hadn't eaten yet. I was getting hungry for sure." Troy was in a tiny pair of shorts, the new ink on his chest a wild, blood red triskelion weaving its way around some others.

"That has to be a long day for Geoff too." He'd been thinking about Geoff, not just today but ever since they'd first talked about Troy's ink. About why Geoff did it.

"It is. He puts so much of himself into the art. By the end he's usually losing his mind with needing Carter."

"Why do you think he does it? Because after so many years, it's not just for you anymore, right? If it ever was. He has to get something personal out of it."

"It's his calling. He's an artist, yeah? And he understands what it's like, to need that rush." Troy leaned back into the cushions. "I let him use my skin, he lets me use his talent."

Okay. The artist thing he could buy. "Humor me, and explain what you use his talent for again?"

"It's all endorphins, right? I manage okay, for a while, but sometimes I need the buzz." Saul couldn't quite see Troy's face with the sinking sun, but his boy didn't sound defensive. "Maybe if I'd never had it, I wouldn't know to miss it, but I did."

"The buzz from the pain. You're not talking about subspace." Troy wasn't equating it to subbing at all.

"It's the closest thing I've had for a long time. Twenty years."

"It's not close at all. It's not anything like subspace. There's no purpose to the pain. What you're talking about is an addiction." An addiction Troy had quit smoking for.

Sometimes I need the buzz.

"A fix."

Troy was quiet for a long minute before he answered. "Well, I suppose so. I wouldn't do it if I wasn't needing something I couldn't give myself."

"Don't, then. I can give you that, I can give you more. Don't do it again." It wasn't a request. He couldn't be a party to it. Not when he knew he could do so much more for the boy than just fill that void.

"I don't understand why you're so angry. I'm trying to, swear to God, but I need your help to do it."

"I'm not... Okay, I'm a little angry, but not at you." He got up and moved next to his boy, close enough to touch and to reassure. "I'll do everything I can for you Troy, and I know I can help. I just didn't understand what you'd been living with for so long."

"No pity, huh? Please? I made my choices. I took a long time to mourn Arnie, and then I admit, I'm picky. I'm picky about my fuckbuddies, and I'm crazy picky about who I open up to."

"That wasn't pity." He grinned. "I was still learning to read and eating my boogers when Arnie died. I should hope you've made your peace. You have a job, hobbies, a fantastic view, and a great support system." If maybe a little misguided. "Wanting to understand what makes you tick isn't pity. It's a Dom loading up his arsenal."

"Good lord and butter, I don't know how much ammunition you need." When Troy chuckled, Saul knew he'd been heard, understood, and it felt pretty damn good.

"There's no such thing as enough." He leaned in closer, pinning Troy with his eyes, and his shoulder. "Never enough." He took a kiss, parting his boy's lips with his tongue. Troy gasped, opening for him. He loved how everything was new—not only for Troy, but for him too.

Saul liked joking about Troy being a ginger, but it wasn't really that. Troy kissed as if it was something holy. He fucked like a starving man. He made Saul feel like it was all so important—like sex could really mean something, and a kiss was almost spiritual.

He took his time and explored the kiss, giving his attention to Troy, his energy, making sure his boy understood he was present and they were okay.

Troy rested one hand over his heart, the touch solid and warm. Sure. Neither one of them pushed the kiss deeper, letting it just stay long and easy.

"I love how you kiss." He covered the hand on his chest with his own.

"Lots of guys don't. I think that's a shame."

"To each his own." Saul liked kissing. "But they really missed out on something if you were involved." He smiled and pulled away enough to see Troy's amazing eyes. He'd never met someone with eyes so intense, so green that they seemed almost like Troy was wearing contacts.

One bright red eyebrow lifted, and Troy grinned at him.

The expression made him laugh. "What?"

"You have a wonderful smile." Troy traced his lips with one finger.

"Thank you." He nipped at Troy's hand. "What is something you've always wanted to try with a Dom? If I'm asking you to give up something as important to you as your sessions with Geoff—and to be clear, I'm not asking, I'm requiring—then I want to replace it with something fun. A fantasy, or a kink you secretly want to explore. Something you think might be exciting. Something new."

"I'll have to think about it. I honestly don't know." Troy frowned, a line forming between his eyebrows. "I'm still working out why you're upset about the ink, to be honest."

"I'm not upset about the ink. I think it's beautiful in fact. But you said yourself that you wouldn't do it if you didn't need something you couldn't get another way. I want to be your addiction." He squeezed the hand he was still holding against his chest.

Troy's lips parted and the expression on his boy's face was pure need, something wild and raw and utterly hungry.

Fuck, he loved the rush of being wanted. A surge of heat spread from the base of his spine, up and out to his fingertips. It gave him goosebumps, made him feel powerful. "What do you want, boy? What do you need?"

"Everything." That single word was heavy, dense. It was what twenty years of waiting sounded like.

The sudden ache in his balls was intense it made him groan. "Knees," he ordered, surprised the rough sound was his own voice. He hauled himself onto the couch and yanked his belt open.

Troy knelt for him, lean and beautiful, erection obvious in the tiny shorts. Saul let his eyes roam over his boy freely and didn't hide his hunger. Fuck, he was well on his way to an addiction himself.

He opened his fly and slipped his jeans low enough that Troy could help him get them off. "Get the shoes too, boy." God, he ached. He gave his balls a tug and then reached back and pulled his T-shirt over his head.

"Flip-flops are easier, you know, Sir." It was sort of fascinating, the way that Troy could tease without seeming disrespectful or rude.

Troy stripped him off, hands sure as they smoothed the fabric from his skin.

"They might be. But it's not my job to make your life easy." He enjoyed the teasing, but if he was serious about this, he needed to set the right tone from the start. He stroked himself slowly, letting the boy watch. "To make my point, you're not allowed to touch yourself for pleasure at all. Understood?"

"Yes, Sir." Troy put his clothes aside, folding them carefully.

In fact, flip-flops were a fine idea for most people, but as someone who didn't own a car, they weren't for him.

Punishments were just fun.

"That looks like it aches." He indicated the healthy outline of Troy's erection with his eyes, and stroked harder, letting his legs fall open more.

"Does it?" Troy glanced down, then that attention turned to him again, so focused. "Remind me to tell you about when I was just beginning to practice yoga. I sprung wood at very inconvenient times."

Really? Now? "If you're asking something of me, I expect you to be respectful. That's two good swats before I'm done with you tonight. Do you own a paddle?"

Troy looked utterly confused for a second, then his expression smoothed out like glass. "No, Sir."

He didn't think it was like Troy to shut down, so he decided that the boy was catching on. It had been a long while since Troy had served anyone, and it was high on his list of things he wanted from a sub. "Good boy. That's more like it. You'll get my bare hand later then. For now, come closer."

Troy slid closer, the motion incredibly graceful and smooth.

"I want your mouth, boy." He slid his fingers around the back of Troy's head and tugged gently, coaxing his boy to kneel.

Troy propped one arm on Saul's knee, resting against it as he curled, lips parting, tongue flicking out to taste. The little shot of heat was followed immediately by a flood as Troy's lips surrounded him.

He hissed and fought the impulse to surge upward as everything in his mind spiraled to his need and his boy's mouth. "That's it." This was going to be epic. And after he watched his boy lick him clean, he had plans for Troy. Thinking about them just made him harder.

Troy bobbed over him, taking him in, inch by inch. Each motion had a rhythm—suction, a slide of that talented tongue, then the pressure eased for a second before the whole pattern started again.

"Fuck, you're good at that." Saul was already having to catch his breath. "Do you practice on your dildos?"

Troy hummed softly around his prick, and he wasn't sure what that answer was. It didn't matter, either way the answer felt amazing. He leaned back in the sofa cushions with a long moan. Troy followed the slightest bit, bald head bobbing faster. He stared, eyes following bare scalp, inked body, then that shockingly pale, unmarked ass.

"Fuck, yes. More." His head fell back, and his fingers dug in where they gripped the boy's scalp. In college he'd had, and given, hundreds of blow jobs. Troy was an artist compared to those rushed, stolen moments. Troy worshipped his prick, the speed slowing as his cock disappeared completely into Troy's mouth. He felt the intense pressure at his tip, Troy swallowing around him.

The sensation made his eyes cross and he curled up reflexively out of the sofa cushions. "Jesus." He sucked in a breath as his vision blurred and his balls did a fucking happy dance. "Again."

Troy obeyed without hesitation or complaint, taking him to the root and swallowing convulsively.

"Oh shit! Fuck!" He flailed for a second, hands closing around Troy's head and hips trying to buck up off the sofa uselessly. He couldn't get any deeper than he already was. Every nerve from his toes to his fucking nipples lit up as a sweet pressure and nearly painful need made his thighs tremble and his ass clench.

Troy reached under Saul's ass with his free hand, supporting his arch, keeping him deep and demanding his release.

Blood roared in his ears, his toes curled and he threw his head back to shout his boy's name, though he had no idea what actually came out. His orgasm rocketed through him, every muscle going tense, hips jerking but everything else about him seemed frozen. Locked in place until he found his breath again. "Shit. Jesus, Troy." He sucked in air and let it out in harsh pants.

Troy eased him down, suction turning to soft licks and careful touches.

He collapsed back on the couch, grinning. "God, I think you sucked my skeleton out, boy."

The sensation of Troy's soft laughter around his prick was almost maddening.

He sighed and relaxed, enjoying his boy's attention until he felt like he could think, and maybe even move. "I'm putting your oral high on my list of favorite things ever." He sat up, pleased to discover he wasn't lightheaded anymore. "How are you feeling?"

Troy eased himself back to kneeling, settling on his heels. "Physically or mentally, Sir?"

"Well done boy. Let's start with mentally." He leaned forward to listen, watching his boy's body language.

"It's been a three re-ride kind of day. You know, up and down and up and down. Right now it's right up there."

That he believed. Troy sucked like a man who was made for it.

"I'm right up there myself." He wanted to keep his boy up there, right where Troy ought to be. "And physically? Are you... up there?" He hid the grin by stroking at his five o'clock shadow.

Troy rolled his eyes and smiled. "Yes, Sir. I'm hard for you. I'm a little tender too, but that's to be expected. Tomorrow is going to be absolutely brutal."

"Let me see it." He could only imagine. Ink over ink, and

this wasn't the first time or the first spot that Geoff had done it. "Is it always like that the next day? Is it really worth it?"

Troy blinked owlishly. "It depends on how long he works and where the ink is."

He noted that his boy didn't answer the second question. That was interesting, but he wasn't surprised.

He looked the new tattoo over, admiring Geoff's work and the clever way the large triskelion obscured some older symbols, but intertwined with others. "And this one is on a lot of bone up here so it's going to hurt to move this shoulder I bet, maybe to turn your head even, right? You can work like that?"

It shocked him, how Troy's entire body flushed. What did that mean?

"You're not answering my questions. And that's interesting because I think you've figured out that I'm not concerned about handing out punishments." He looked at his boy, who couldn't have been more beautiful kneeling and flushed and hard. "Which can only mean you welcome it, hm?" He raised an eyebrow and tried not to grin at the poor boy.

"I keep going back, so I guess I must. Carter has an agreement with us—me and Geoff. I've never done this when I had someone to come home to." Troy blinked. "Unless you mean punishments..."

"I did, but this is more interesting. Tell me about your agreement. In fact, tell me about all of it. It's frustrating to get it bits at a time. Explain it to me." Because when he said he wanted to be Troy's new addiction, he meant it. "I need to understand."

"Right now, I'm not sure I understand, Sir. I didn't think —not once—that we were doing anything wrong." Troy sighed and closed his eyes, hands coming to rest on his thighs. "I go once every six weeks and sit as long as we need. Carter doesn't come because... well, because I'm not his boy. Our agreement with him is that I never miss work after a session, no matter what. So yes. Tomorrow is going to suck. Until the scabs form it'll suck."

"But you like it that way."

Troy frowned. "I like the art. I like the endorphins during. Geoff and Carter are dear to me."

"I'm not asking about Geoff and Carter, boy. I'm asking about you. Do you... like that much pain? Do you like that it lasts so long? Do you enjoy the fact that it's with you all day? Maybe more than a day?" Saul was going to get a handle on his boy's needs no matter how many times he had to drill into this issue.

"I—I like that there's a purpose. I like..." Troy's eyes flew open. "Yellow, Sir. I need to speak with you."

"Of course." He hopped up off the couch and grabbed his boxers. "Are you okay?" When he sat back down again he patted the couch next to him. "Come on up here."

"Yes, Sir." Troy came to sit. "I can't answer your questions fully without bringing up Arnie, and you've asked me not to do that, so I'm stuck against the chute."

He shifted around until he found a way to get his arm around Troy without messing with the boy's tender skin. "Hm. So I should move the stubborn bull, huh? Here's the thing about Arnie. I want to figure out together what works for us as Dom and sub. It's not that I don't want to know about you and Arnie, I just don't want either of us to feel pressured to live up to something. I don't..." Saul snorted and grinned. "You want me to let you into my head a little? I'm just vain and insecure enough to worry that I'm being compared. That's why I asked you not to get into details. But

I want an answer, especially because I need it to understand you better."

Troy smiled at him and gave him a soft yet surprisingly deep kiss. He wasn't sure which part of their discussion had earned that, but he was glad to have the kiss, the connection. "Thank you, Sir. I was serious about needing something. I tried all sorts of things, even hiring a professional Dom. It didn't work. I need it to mean something. Pain for pain's sake just hurts. I need—" Troy sighed. "Am I making sense at all?"

"Yes." He thought about it, looking for the right words to give back to his boy because it wasn't about whether or not he got it. It was about whether or not he got *Troy*. "It's part of what you've been deprived of all this time—the opportunity to serve. You want the pain to be in service of something. It needs to serve a purpose."

"Purpose. Yes. Yes, exactly." Troy waved his hand along his body. "*This*? This is purposeful. Geoff cares about it. I care. It's not the best answer, but it's an answer."

"No, but it's at least a beautiful one." He nodded to Troy. "Okay, I'm with you on all of that. Tell me about Arnie."

"What?" Troy stared at him for a second. "Are you sure? I don't want to cause you worry…"

"Boy. You safeworded because you needed to bring up Arnie. What did you want to tell me?"

"He was very physical, but there were rules—we were in the closet in the deepest way. I never got to explore anything that left marks anywhere because we were in the locker room so much." Troy pulled away a little bit. "I know you don't approve of this, but… Shit, I don't know. Maybe I was trying to be faithful to him, maybe I was paying him back at first, by getting marks. It wasn't about pain at first, and I don't know what it is now. No one's ever asked."

Troy stopped suddenly, like someone turned off a faucet. "And I obviously have diarrhea of the mouth."

"Troy." Saul turned on the sofa to face the boy and took his hands. "You're all grown men. It's not my place to approve or disapprove. And obviously, I didn't have all the details and was drawing my own conclusions. Do I like it? Not really. I'd like you to not... work with Geoff like you have been anymore. If it's important enough to you that you will resent me for making you stop, I'll talk with Carter and we'll figure something out that might satisfy everyone involved. Okay? But I need you to be honest with me. Flat out honest. About all of it."

"Right now I'm hurting and wanting you. I'm not ready to make big decisions. Hell, there's only my cock and my ass left."

Not that that had stopped them today. He knew very well Geoff would continue to overlay if Troy wanted him to. But his boy needed a break right now. "Can we resume, then? You called this time out. I need to you tell me you're ready."

"I am. Thank you for hearing me, Sir. I appreciate it."

"You're welcome, boy. Thank you for trusting me with your safe word. Can I stay the night? I know you have to get up early, so I get it if... but I'd like to."

"I would love that." The response was gratifyingly quick.

"Oh, good." Saul smiled. "Clean up here so you can take me upstairs, boy."

"Yes, Sir." Troy put the pizza box in the trash and rinsed out their glasses. "Did you want water for upstairs?"

"I would, thank you." He stretched as he stood. "I think my skeleton is back."

Troy chuckled softly, shot him a grin, and brought him a bottle of cold water. "Are you ready, Sir?"

He had plans. "A better question might be, are you?" He gestured for the boy to lead the way.

"Yes, Sir."

Oh, he was going to have to remember to make Troy lead the way. The view was... inspirational.

12

L ord have mercy, what a day.

Troy couldn't decide whether he wanted to beg Saul to love on him or to just hide in the bathroom and try to figure out what the hell was going on. He kept telling himself he'd seen this with the guys—the missteps, the nerves, learning what was what.

Right now all the telling in the world didn't make him feel less like a newbie.

Troy headed upstairs, grateful as fuck that he'd changed his sheets this morning.

"Strip off your shorts, please." Saul walked past him into the room and glanced around. "If I want to leave some light on, should you close the shades? Or do people not peep around here?"

"You can't see through the glass, Sir. No one can see." He loved it, because he walked around naked as a jaybird a lot.

"No way, really?" Saul walked right up to it and looked out into the night, seeming even younger than twenty-five, a big smile on that baby face. "Cool. They can't see in at all? For real?"

"When I bought the place, Geoff and I spent a good five minutes making faces at Carter while he watched downstairs. I'm pretty sure..."

Saul laughed, the sound clear and happy, and headed his way. "You two are funny. So, boy, go over and face the window, hands on the glass, legs a little wider than your hips. Be comfortable. Let me know if it bothers your ink."

"Yes, Sir." He headed over, staring out into the night. He positioned his legs first, spreading his toes wide and planting himself into the floor. His arms were a little more of a challenge, but he found a position that didn't pull or wrinkle his skin too much.

Behind him, Saul was puttering around messing with different combinations of lighting. The room went dim, but not dark. "Take some deep breaths. Close your eyes for a minute if you want to. Relax, let yourself just be. I want to try to get your head clear. Don't worry, we're not going to work too hard, I know you're tired."

Troy understood this on a cellular level. He breathed into his belly, letting himself relax and be empty.

Saul stepped up behind him and rested hands on his shoulders at first and then slid them lower, warm fingers finally settling on his hips. "Good boy. I'm going to give you a word, and you're going to give me one back. It doesn't have to be the first thing that comes to mind, it doesn't have to be quick at all. Take your time. Understood?"

"Yes, Sir. I hear you." That he could do. No problem.

Saul's hands were solid on his hips, their bodies close enough his Master barely had to speak above a whisper. "Service."

"Mmm..." That was easy, and he didn't have to hesitate. "Care."

"Lovely, thank you." Saul stepped even closer. "Bondage."

So many words buzzed through him that he smiled. *Release. Leather. Ease. Ropes. Struggle. Peace. Surrender.* Oh, that one was fine. Just fine. "Surrender."

"Good. Submission."

Oh, that was a bit of a challenge. Submission. Christ. It meant so much, but it had been so long. He thought about that rush of emotion, that sinking rush of... "Need."

"Need." Saul's voice was still quiet, but somehow more intense.

Troy nodded, not quite sure if Saul needed another word or not but offering one anyway. "Hunger."

An arm slipped around his waist as Saul closed the space between them. "Pain."

The connection of their skin made him moan, and his toes curled. There were so many levels to that word—from the burn of his ink to the soul-deep tearing when he lost Arnie. He'd known a lot of hurts, from little stings to the kinds a man might not come back from. They'd all taught him a lesson, some more than others. "Lessons."

Saul kissed him on the neck. "Trust."

"Peace." Another easy one.

There was a quiet pause before the next word. "Troy."

Good lord and butter. He was shocked at the lack of words that popped into his head. What was he now? No one's son anymore, not a rodeo man. A friend, he would give himself that. A cook. "Empty."

Saul wrapped the other arm around him, giving him a gentle hug. "Master."

"Home." That was it, wasn't it? A Dom and a sub, at their bests, they were two halves, forming a whole. A home.

"I love that, boy. And I've learned quite a bit." He got

another hug, then Saul tugged on one of the bars in his nipple. "Now it's your turn to choose a few words."

"My—" Oh, that felt so fucking sweet. "Yes, Sir. Um." Okay, he'd start backward. That gave him time to think. "Boy."

Saul answered quickly. "Responsibility."

Hopefully that was a good thing. Like so many things, it could go either way. "Domination."

"Hmm." Saul took a minute to answer. "Essential." With that he got another pinch.

He groaned as he arched, his chest pushing into his Master's hands, ass rubbing against that thick, hard cock.

"S-submission."

"Gift." Saul didn't even breathe before answering that one. "And... care. Truth. Trust. Service." He heard the deep breath his Master took, felt the way Saul's chest expanded.

"Mine."

Goosebumps popped up all over him, and he had to fight a cry. Saul was offering him so much that he desperately wanted.

Saul's hot breath blew past his ear. "Are you mine, boy?"

Saul wouldn't have made the offer lightly, and if he had, best to know now. "Yes, Master, thank you. Yours."

"Thank you, boy." Saul kissed his back, right between the shoulders. "So... what now, if I say 'Troy?'"

This time he knew the right answer, without question.

"Yours, Master."

"Mmm. Good boy. I like the sound of that, don't you?" Saul rocked against him, stiff prick rubbing in his crease.

"Yes, Sir." He braced himself, his entire focus on Saul, on his Master's will.

"Turn around, boy. Take your time." Saul's grip on his hips eased and his Master took a step back, waiting.

He took a deep breath in, bringing his focus back to his body. He straightened up slowly, rolled his hips, and found his center. Then he turned to face Saul.

Saul was smiling gently, and reached for his hands, then led him toward the bed. "I'll have to bring a few things over. I have a little case I can leave here. I'd invite you to my place, but... roommates. Awkward. Do you need a bio break? Some water?"

"You're welcome to bring what you need, Sir. I'll clear you some space of your own, and yes, please. Water sounds perfect."

His Master pulled back the covers for him. "Have mine, I'll run down and grab another. You relax for a minute, but don't lose that beautiful thing." Saul pointed to his cock, where it stretched away from his body. "Be right back."

He drank deep, the water splashing in his belly, his thoughts racing. There was a dresser in the little guest room he could move up here, no problem.

For his Master.

What a truly wild and wonderful thought.

Saul reappeared with an armful of his own clothing and a half-empty bottle of water. "So I can get dressed for my walk of shame in the morning."

"I have a washer up here. Would you like me to throw them in for you?" He could do that, no problem.

"Nah. You have to be at work way earlier than I do. I'll run home and change. Thanks, though." Saul set the clothes down and the water by the bed and grinned at him. "I think you've earned a reward, so let me take care of that for you."

Troy shivered with anticipation. He'd had a full day, and he was more than willing to pack more in. "Yes, Sir. Thank you."

Saul moved over him slowly and kissed him, coaxing

him onto his back. "Good boy." A hand slipped under his balls, teasing the piercings there. Troy moaned softly and spread, giving Saul access. It all felt so new, having someone else's touch.

He got another quick kiss and then Saul slid down his body, kissing and tasting along the way and didn't stop until the head of his cock disappeared past Saul's lips.

Troy's eyes rolled back in his head, as a wash of pleasure shook him. His toes curled, and he sucked in a sharp breath. God, he wanted this to last forever.

It didn't seem like it was going to though, because once Saul started there was no letting up. His Master was hungry, his cock slipping straight into Saul's throat.

"Master. Master. Master." The sound of his own voice seemed like a chant, like a prayer, and he couldn't stop it.

Saul pulled up just long enough to tangle a curious tongue in his Prince Albert and tug gently, and then dove back down again, then repeating the pattern over and over, tongue adding pressure and friction.

There was no way he was going to survive this. None. Nothing had ever felt this good in his life. He flailed, his control shattered as he begged Saul for more.

"Mmm." Saul hummed around him and reached up to twist his nipple hardware. Hard.

Troy barked out a wild scream as the spring inside him, wound so tight he thought his spine would snap, let go in a rush, and he shot, filling his Master's mouth.

Saul bathed his cock, licking and sucking, affectionately staying with him through his climax and beyond, keeping everything sensitive and making him shiver. "Gorgeous, boy. Hot."

Troy blinked, suddenly so exhausted he couldn't breathe, couldn't focus. "Master."

That was all he had.

"My boy." Saul climbed up beside him. "Should I put something on your new ink before you sleep?"

He reached out, slapping around until he found the Aquaphor. He could use a little lubing up.

"Got it." Saul took the tub and carefully smoothed on a layer, coating the sore, angry skin. "Do I need to set an alarm to wake you?"

Troy found the little button on the alarm clock and pressed it. "Little button alarm. Big button snooze."

Saul laughed softly, and curled around him, tangling their fingers. "Got it. Get some sleep, boy. You did great today. I'm totally withdrawing the paddling, in case you think I forgot. Just sleep."

"Sleep." He blinked once, thought about saying thank you, and then he was gone in the next breath.

13

Saul had Deb's mint-green frame up on a rack and he was whistling while he attached the custom chrome fenders. He'd left Troy's condo at the same time as Troy and headed back to his place in an Uber, changed and went to work. But honestly, he barely remembered any of that. He'd been thinking all morning about... *Jesus*. About everything. About Troy.

About his sub.

He couldn't quite get his head around it. It felt like it was too much to process. A guy he liked--a man he wanted--wanted him back. All of him. Not just the company, not just the sex, not just the domination, but everything at the same time.

He was fucking high as a kite.

Sure, it was kind of fast. But it felt right. He'd never felt so complete before.

He'd never had a talk like that with anyone either. Troy was just so... real. Everything Troy did mattered.

That made his responsibility real too. Damn. If he thought too hard about this he might—

"Ow! Shit."

"You okay?" Emma blinked at him from behind the counter, not really looking all that worried.

"Yeah. Pinched myself in the... under the fender." Hard enough the end of his finger went numb for a second.

"Your head is in the clouds, my friend. Completely." She grinned at him. "Good weekend?"

"The best. *The. Best.*" He put his tools down and hurried over. "He's fascinating, and I'm so not enough for him, but I'm going to try to be."

"Yeah? Do tell." Her grin turned wicked. "I'm assuming this means he can get it up?"

He laughed and rolled his eyes. "That is definitely not a problem. He has a ton of stamina. We're totally compatible that way. But he wants that, and he wants a Dom. And... maybe more. Definitely more, I think. Hopefully."

Jesus. *Definitely I think maybe I hope?* What the hell was wrong with him?

"Oh, you are hooked through the balls. Seriously. So, spill. Your party went well, then."

"The party was interesting. Good, but just... so different. There were a bunch of couples there, all couples actually, except Troy. I asked him if he wanted to... well, be mine for the evening, and he agreed. Everyone was shocked. Happy for him I think but, like, seriously shocked. I could totally tell these guys had been hanging out together for a long time, they were really supportive, completely at ease. It was... nice. But man, talk about being out of my comfort zone. I was paying very close attention."

He'd never felt so young and inexperienced, but he hadn't felt judged for it, he'd felt... accepted. Embraced even. Welcome.

"I bet it *was* weird. I mean, they're old enough to be your dad. I like that they were cool, though." Emma went and grabbed them both a Coke. "So, seriously. Was it just like a party or were there guys having formal scenes? Because that might wig me right out."

"It was a social thing. Troy says sometimes they do stuff like that, if it happens it happens, but mostly it's more hanging out, having dinner, casual stuff. And this time, one of the subs had a meltdown and screamed at Troy, and everyone kind of took care of the sub and his Dom, and Troy too. They totally fixed it together. You'll meet them. Matt, the Dom? He wants to get his sub some kind of adaptive bike. The guy lost a lot of one leg overseas. I figured you'd be all over that."

"Oh, you know I love that." Her eyes lit up. Emma was fascinated by the different adaptations that were available, and Saul thought she liked knowing that she was doing something truly useful. The hazards of being the daughter of two doctors, he guessed.

He grinned at her. "You think we can do it for them at no cost? I mean, veteran and all. We can cover it, right?"

"I'll call the big boss, but we have a budget for it, so I vote yes."

The door opened, a guy with a bag in one hand and a cup in the other. "I have an order for Saul?"

"I'm Saul, but I didn't order anything." He looked at Emma. "Did you?"

"No. Are you sure..."

"The note says 'enjoy your lunch, sir'. It's from the Spiked Butterfly?"

"Oh!" The rush was almost inexplicable, but he felt the warmth in his cheeks and the way his heart was beating hard. Damn. "That's uh.... Yeah. That's for me. Thank you." He dug into his pockets for a tip.

"No need. I've been taken care of. Have a good day, dude. Killer shop."

"Thanks. Have a good one." He looked like he'd been taken care of, too. He put the bag on the counter and peered in. "Huh. He sent me lunch."

There was a patty melt, fries, a salad, and a piece of chocolate cake. Wow. Just... wow.

"Huh." Emma imitated him so well. "I guess he maybe kinda sorta definitely likes you."

That just made him blush harder. "Shut up. How sweet is this?"

"Did you guys say twenty-four-seven?"

"I guess?" Had they said that exactly? Is that how this worked? He was good with that. "Or he's just being nice."

"You might want to clarify, but one way or the other, that's cool. I'm jealous. I need to find a girl who cooks."

"It's pretty handy." He grinned. "I guess I'm taking a quick lunch break." That was a joke because really all it meant was that he was going to sit in the chair behind the counter and eat. They couldn't afford to only have one person working at a time, there was always something to do.

He went after the fries first, offering her some. His boy had sent him lunch. He wasn't positive it was meant that way, but he decided that was how he was going to take it. It was kind of awesome having someone care whether he ate today.

"That's so cool, buddy. I mean, seriously. Your new guy sent you lunch."

Yes, and even when he knew Troy had to be tired and sore. He pulled his phone out.

Know ur prob slammed just wanted to say ty for lunch. Yummy. Hang in today. Can I see u tonite?

Troy probably wanted a night off, but Saul wanted to see the boy, make sure he was okay. Let him snuggle.

Not sleep alone.

Emma was right. He *was* hooked through the balls. Shit.

It took about fifteen minutes before his phone buzzed.

I'd love to. Need me to pick you up?

He'd better get a truck; this was starting to get embarrassing. *Do u mind? off at 6.*

I'll be there with bells on :D

Kinky.

Hanging from those nipple bars maybe.

"Oh!" He looked at Emma who was nose-deep in ordering by then. "He is pierced! Nipples, PA, guiche. I think he's considering more. Wow."

"Dude! Okay, that counts as hot, full stop. You going to watch the next one?"

"I hadn't thought about it, but I guess I will. He's—" *Mine.* "I'm his Dom, right?"

"Right. That's one of the bennies, huh?"

He nodded. "It is. One I want to be sure I take advantage of. He's got a complicated relationship with decision-making." Hopefully Troy had gotten the message that he wanted to be in on decisions like piercings and ink. He didn't think he'd say no but wanted the privilege all the same. "He's been alone a long time. A really long time."

"Did he say why? I mean, obviously he's good-looking; he caught your eye." Emma stole another fry.

"Well he lost the love of his life twenty years ago, so... but I don't know if he knows why he stayed single this long. I do know he's had trouble finding a Dom, but he hasn't mentioned why he hasn't found a regular lover." He had thoughts about it, things tied to having been closeted for so long with Arnie, things tied to age, reasons that Troy had given up looking. "I'm pretty sure he didn't expect... I'm pretty direct when I want something."

"I bet you're blowing his mind, which rocks, because he's sure as shit blowing yours." Emma beamed at him, and didn't that feel good?

"I like him a lot. I like how he makes me feel. I love to look at him. All his ink... oh man. I want to know what makes him tick." *I want to see him with my marks. I want to make him scream for me. I want to hold him after.*

"I can't wait to meet him. Seriously. He sounds amazing." She grinned at him. "He sent you salad."

He laughed. "Yeah. You want it? I'm all about calories today. Plus I better get back to Deb's bike."

Not to mention a piece of chocolate cake.

"Sure, if you don't want it. It'll save me going out."

He might share the cake with her later. Maybe.

He handed Emma the salad. "I'm guessing Troy was covering his bases in case I wasn't up for a burger and fries. He'll learn. I'm always up for a burger."

He made his way back over to the fenders, only then remembering his finger, which had a little red mark on it but didn't seem to hurt at all anymore.

"You'll remind me about this moment if I get cold feet, right?" He wanted Troy, he just knew there were going to be those days.

"You have my word. Tell him to send two pieces of cake next time."

He grabbed his wrench and the second fender, and got back to work. "I'll do that."

Maybe he'd ask for personal delivery too.

14

T roy felt like a new man after a nice long shower and a longer nap.

Today had gone by in a daze, which was normal, post-ink. That wasn't strange at all. What was odd was that his whole world, his whole brain was focused on Saul.

His Master.

Carter kept trying to tease, to give him shit, but it didn't matter, he didn't care. He wanted to get through his shift, bathe and rest.

He had someone to pick up from work and to feed.

He hopped in his truck and headed over to the bike shop, singing along with the radio like he was George Strait.

Saul was locking up when he arrived and giving a hug to a woman with wild dreadlocks who had to be the other manager of the store. He got a wave, and Saul led her over to his truck by the hand.

"Hey baby, I wanted you to meet Emma. She runs the store with me."

"Pleased to meet you, ma'am." He held his hand out in greeting. "I hope y'all have had a good day."

Baby. Oh, didn't that feel nice?

"We have. Saul's been in a very good mood today. He even shared his cake."

"Some of it. Mostly I was greedy."

He'd send two next time. "Did y'all like it? I love that one and the chocolate pie best."

"Oh, send the pie next time." Emma winked at him and then smiled at Saul. "I've gotta run. You two have a nice evening. It was very nice to meet you, Troy."

"Night, Em. Be good!"

"Not on your life!" Emma laughed, gave them a wave and headed off in the other direction.

Saul climbed into his truck and gave him a quick kiss before putting on the seatbelt. "I may have mentioned you once or twice today."

"That's good to hear. Did you have a good day? Are you hungry?"

God, Saul was the most beautiful thing he'd seen in forever, and that was saying something because he was a cowboy.

"A little. I had this big lunch. Can we stop by my place real quick?"

"Yes, Sir. Just point me and shoot me. I was pondering tacos."

"Ooh. That sounds good." Saul gave him directions to an apartment complex just a short drive away. "I just wanted to grab my... you don't have to come in. I mean, you can if you want, but I'll just be a minute."

"I'm fine out here. No worries." He offered Saul a smile. The last thing his ego needed was for one of Saul's roommates to think he was Saul's daddy.

"Be right back." Saul hopped out and disappeared into the building. He really was back quick, with a duffle over one shoulder and a big yellow toolbox in the other.

As soon as Saul got settled, he bumped their shoulders together. "I was thinking about having Rincon deliver. I'm addicted to their tacos al carbon."

"Oh yeah. Make it two, please." Saul grinned at him, looking happy as could be, and reached for the radio. "And a beer."

"There's cold fridge in the beer." He stopped, snorted, and rolled his eyes. "Or, beer in the fridge, even."

Saul reached over and gave the back of his neck a squeeze. "Tired, huh? How's the ink?"

"Mmm... It's sore. I lubed it up real good after my shower. I took myself a little nap too, which I needed." *The sheets smelled like you. I liked it.*

"I can imagine. You were so gone last night. I don't think you moved once you fell asleep."

"Yesterday was the wildest day I have had in a long, long time. I slept like a rock." They pulled into his driveway. "Can you hit the garage opener, please Sir?"

Saul glanced at him, then reached up and hit the button. "A truck and a garage. I've got a long way to go."

"Oh, when I moved, I stayed with Geoff and Carter for almost a year, just working as a dishwasher and trying to get through one day at a time. You're already a manager. You're doing good." He'd been a hard-core disaster there for a bit.

"You'd been through a whole lifetime by then. I'm just starting." Saul squeezed his leg and then got out of the truck, hauling the duffel and the toolbox out too.

"Would you like some help?" He got out, locked the truck up. "And, I know it sounds bizarre, but you know what? I feel that way too, in a lot of ways."

"You do?" Saul put the toolbox down. "You can grab that, boy. I'd like it in the bedroom."

"Yes, Sir. There's a spot in the closet this can fit, no problem." He picked up the box. "And yes, I do. I feel like I've been treading water for a very long time."

Saul followed him inside. "I get that. I feel kind of like I've been biking uphill on gravel, you know? I've had a lot of almost."

"I hear you." He'd had a great love affair too, and he didn't regret that for a single second, but the last two decades had been tough.

"Hey." Saul smiled, smoothed a hand over his scalp, and kissed him soundly. "It's good to be here."

"Lord yes." He had to smile—had to. "Let me run this upstairs and I'll grab you a beer and order supper."

"Sounds great. Take my bag too? It's just some stuff in case..." Saul grinned and shrugged.

"Of course." He hauled the stuff upstairs and put the toolbox in the big closet, propping the duffel up against the built-ins there. He called for supper on the way downstairs, stopping in the kitchen to grab a couple of Coronas before he made his way into the front room.

He found Saul sitting on the sofa waiting for him. "For me?"

"Yes, Sir. I ordered supper. They said forty-five minutes to an hour."

"Just enough time to have a cuddle." Saul held an arm out to him.

How could he refuse that? Why would he want to? He sat close, offering Saul his beer. "Cheers."

"Thank you. Cheers." They clinked and sipped, and Saul tucked him a little closer. "You're okay with me just asking to come over?"

"I was tickled. You were on my mind all day."

"Lunch was a nice surprise, thank you. I'm not used to that kind of thing, it was sweet of you." Saul lightly drew little lines and circles on his arm with one finger.

"It was my pleasure. You're more than welcome." He leaned in, soaking up Saul's presence.

"I'm really not used to any of this. Not... like this." Saul chuckled. "That's very specific, huh? What I mean is I've had lovers, I've had subs, but I've never had one person who was both at the same time. And I've never had a round-the-clock arrangement with a sub either."

"It's been a while for me too." And the world was a different place now. "Last time I was someone's sub, it was before smart phones."

"Oh wow. D/s in the age of cell phones is fun. You haven't had the pleasure of receiving a text telling you to do something right away, or asking a personal question, or giving you something to think about until your Dom arrives. Mmm. So much fun."

He blinked. No. No, he hadn't. "I'd never even thought about that."

"Oh, you're going to learn all about it." Saul sounded pretty pleased about that. "FaceTime is fun too. And Snapchat. And the Find Friends feature. Technology is awesome."

"Find Friends?" Troy texted and played a lot of video poker and ordered food.

"Yep. It's an app. I send you an invitation, you accept it, and then I know where you are at all times. Or where your phone is, anyway."

Troy chuckled softly, because he was notorious for being at certain places at certain times. The guys always knew where to find him.

"I guess we can agree to be a little gentle with each other as we work some of this new stuff out. We'll get it, right?" It was hard to tell if Saul was asking a real question or a facetious one.

He went for real. "Yes, Sir. We'll figure our shit out."

"I think so too." Saul sipped his beer. "So, how was work?"

"Work was good. I made a bunch of meatloaf this morning, Carter was riding me some." Geoff had apparently been stressed out.

"Carter? What for? Were you not keeping up?"

Troy shook his head and grinned. "More for fun. Geoff was riled up."

"Oh. I'm sure Carter was really upset with you about that." Saul laughed. "But now I can give him a hard time for giving you a hard time."

"Now that'll be something to see." He fought the urge to crack up, but he thought that Saul could hold his own.

"What would you like to do tonight after our tacos, boy? Movie? Take a walk? Get tied up? As a thank you, a reward for my awesome lunch, I'm at your disposal. Choose wisely." Saul grinned.

Lord, what a list. "I have to say I've never been asked if I wanted to be tied up before."

He'd had it happen, lord yes, but Arnie had never asked.

"Don't get used to me asking. We're new, I'm trying to learn a little about you." Saul leaned close to his ear. "By next week I'll be asking entirely different questions."

The little tease made him blush. "I understand. It feels pushy to ask to be tied up, but I'm curious to learn about you, too."

"I'll do whatever you like. I hit on the bondage because of your answer last night. The way you said 'surrender' was… intriguing to me. But I'd be happy to give you whatever you need; flog you, deprive you, cut you. I'm not great with humiliation but I'm flexible." Saul grinned at him. "Hopefully you are too."

"Yoga. Every single day." He smiled back, and his nerves eased, even if his anticipation didn't. "I'd like to explore that —bondage—with you, Sir."

"Right. Stretching. Got it. Works for me." Saul laughed. "I don't guess your bed is tricky?"

"It's solid as a rock." Not all men had a handmade four-poster bed, but he did.

"Yeah, I had noticed that." Seemed like Saul was having fun with this conversation. "I was thinking rings for tethers, but I think you're saying I don't need them. Cool. I think that's all I need to know." Saul set his beer down, having only had half.

Saul fascinated him, from the way he moved to his little expressions. Troy watched how Saul reached for him, traced his ink.

"Carter tried to tell me that all you do is talk, boy. But you seem to spend more time watching than talking." Saul reached under his shirt and lifted it off over his head. "What would you be doing if I weren't here?"

He peeked at the time. 6:45 p.m. Wednesday. Post-ink. "Jacking off in the shower before I watch TV."

That got him a smile. "Recovering? And… getting off on the last of the soreness from the ink?" Saul sure didn't mind asking direct questions.

"Yes. And letting the pleasure flood me some." He had to prove he could be honest with both of them.

"Mmm. Nice." Saul leaned in, their lips so close. "Thank you." He got a gentle kiss and a tweak to his nipple.

He couldn't hide his little gasp or stop how he arched into Saul's touch.

"You're so sensual, Troy. I'd say you were easily seduced but I'm not sure it's me doing the seducing." Saul followed the lines of his ink like they were a maze, twisting and doubling back, drawing spirals.

"Can I touch you too, Sir?" He was aching to explore.

"Yes, but our dinner is on the way, don't forget." Saul guided his fingers to the buttons of a short-sleeved, striped Oxford.

"I'll remember." He opened the buttons, smoothing the fabric away to caress Saul's chest in return.

His Master's skin was pale with patches of soft blond hair that were very light where it spread out, but dark where it was concentrated at the center of Saul's chest. Saul's nipples were pink, and he dragged his finger around one in a circle.

Saul's fingers hesitated, pausing in their travels across his belly, and his Master took a breath in, chest rising to meet his touch. The air between them was electric.

"Where do you draw the line on marks? That may seem like a ridiculous question because of all your ink, but it's not the same thing. Are they okay? Restraining with rope, for example, even when I'm really careful, can leave marks for a day or so."

"I have an understanding boss, so yes, they're welcome." He hadn't worn anyone's marks but Geoff's ever, and he found himself eager.

"Welcome." Saul smiled at him. "I like how that sounds."

"Thank you, Sir." That smile. Damn. It warmed him up, at the bone.

"Are there rules you really don't care for? Ones you

really like?" Saul took hold of one hand and kissed the back of it. "Ones you need?"

"I'm not good at the no-cursing rule." Watching his mouth wasn't his strong suit. "At all. I'm best at rules for a purpose, but I try hard. I-you'd said not to touch myself for pleasure..."

"I did. There is a purpose to that rule, and you can always ask if you don't know." One light eyebrow climbed toward Saul's hairline. "I can't promise I'll answer. Have you obeyed or broken my rule?"

"I've been good, Master." He wasn't sure he'd bring it up, if he hadn't been. Maybe.

"Thank you, boy." He got a quick kiss and then Saul laughed. "I can't wait to tell you you're not allowed to curse. What fun."

"Yeah, it's really not." He winked before rolling his eyes. "I curse like a sailor."

"Awesome. I love punishments." He got a wink right back, then Saul's abs jumped under his fingers as he dragged them from one side to the other. Oh, someone liked that.

He repeated the caress, keeping his touch light, playful. His focus was on Saul's nipple, on how it would feel between his lips.

"How will you tell me when you need something? For me, I know I can just give orders, but with this D/s all the time thing, I'm worried I'll miss a cue. It's really important to me that this is mutual. Really important."

Troy gave that some thought. He wasn't sure, but he understood that expecting Saul to read his mind was a recipe for disaster. "How about a check-in? Just you and me having a chat?"

"A check-in." Saul nodded. "I could make it a ritual if we

need something more—" Troy's doorbell rang, and that was followed by a loud knocking. "Tacos!"

"Coming!" Troy rolled up off the sofa and padded to the front door. The runner was there with the two taco plates, and he took the bag, handing over a tip in exchange.

God, that smelled good. Meaty goodness.

"I can smell that from here." Saul got up. "I'm ready. Where are we eating?"

"You want to sit in the backyard?" It was fenced, private, little but nice.

"Sure, that sounds great." Saul grabbed their beers. "Can I trade mine for a soda? I don't want to drink if you're going to be bound."

"Of course, Sir. Coke or Dr Pepper?" The care started a little buzz inside him.

"A Coke would be great." Saul set his beer down on the kitchen counter. "What else can I grab?"

"Can you get a dishrag so we can wipe off the table, please Sir?" He worried about birds pooping on it.

"Uh..." Saul looked around the kitchen. He was just about to help when Sir found it. "Got it. I'll get it damp." It was nice, how relaxed and easy Saul was with him, in his house.

"Thanks." He turned the fairy lights on, the whole little yard beginning to sparkle.

"Hey, that looks great." Saul set the drinks on a chair and started wiping down the table.

"You should see them in the snow. They're amazing." He loved the way the ice formed around the lights and made them glow.

"Shhh! Don't say the 'S' word! I only get so much riding time before it's back. Let me enjoy my four days of summer." Saul handed him the dish towel, sat, and opened his Coke, grinning. "Put those bad boys down right here."

He handed Saul his tacos, stealing a quick kiss on the way. Sweet. So sweet.

"Thanks. Oh, this looks so good." Saul spent a minute arranging the food, then rubbed his palms together like a miser. It was adorable.

"I love these tacos. They remind me a little of home." It didn't seem to matter that in a few years he would have been in Colorado more than half his life, Texas was still home.

Saul took a big bite, chewing it some before he tried to speak with his mouth still full. "Well, now they'll remind me of you."

Oh.

Oh, he felt like he was fixin' to light afire with pleasure. Damn.

"Thank you, Sir."

"Enjoy them. You'll need the calories." Saul took another big bite, making yummy noises and bouncing a little in his chair.

He chuckled as he built his taco, making the perfect blend of pico and cheese and crema.

"Do you want to go out again Friday? Do something fun? I know, early... but fun?"

"That sounds good. What are you into?" He was always willing to do something entertaining, especially if he had friends to do it with.

"I don't know. Music? Art? Beer?" Saul laughed. "There's that indoor rock-climbing place, uh... laser tag?"

"Glow in the dark mini golf?"

"Yes! Yes. Let's do that? That sounds ridiculously fun. Where is such a thing?"

"Over off 29th. There's mini golf and a laser maze." He had been a couple of times with the guys.

"It's a date." Saul sucked down his first taco, and shredded his napkin trying to get his fingers clean. "Paper towels. I'll be right back."

His second date. He wondered if he should warn Saul he cheated wildly at mini golf.

Nah...

His entire roll of paper towels landed on the table. "Brought a couple damp ones too. I like your kitchen. You'd think you cooked a lot in it."

"You'd think." He nodded, rolled his eyes at himself. "I cook for the guys, but not a lot for myself."

"I guess when you cook all day the last thing you want to do is cook at night too, huh? How are you so neat with those tacos?" Saul licked at a sticky thumb.

"Years and years of practice." He could do that for Saul. Honest. Sucking was a skill.

Night fell hard while they ate, everything beyond the fairy lights was solid darkness, and the air was getting cool and humid. "Is it supposed to rain tonight?"

"I don't know. Sure feels like it, doesn't it?" He glanced up, hunting for the stars, but not finding many through the clouds.

"Just seems early to be this dark. Em will be happy, she was just complaining about her garden. She grows veggies, brings them in for me all summer long. I don't have a green thumb at all, I always joke with her that I'm better at nurturing people than plants."

"People are a whole different kind of challenge." Troy was good at feeding people.

"They are. Some more than others." Saul pinned him with a blue-eyed stare. "You seem... challenging."

"Me? Nah. I'm an angel." He almost—almost—kept a straight face.

"Yeah, bullshit." Saul laughed, gathering up his dinner mess. "I'm thinking your halo is tarnished and dented."

"Totally caught on my horns." He got the rest picked up. Easy peasy.

They headed inside together, Saul holding the door for him since his hands were full. "Heh. Try to keep those horns from tangling in my rope."

"Thank you, Sir." He dumped the trash and put the paper towels on the counter. "You'll take care of me. I have faith."

"I will. And I appreciate that." Saul carefully washed his hands in the kitchen sink, even cleaning his fingernails. "Anything else you need to do down here?"

"No, Sir. Would you like some water for the scene?"

"Yes, please. Bring a few just in case, you won't be able to get more later." That was followed by a low laugh as Saul headed toward the staircase.

He shook his head and chuckled. Funny funny. Still, he grabbed four water bottles and took them upstairs, didn't he?

"We both need a second to digest, why don't you go wash up? Take your time, boy. Come back ready to work." Saul headed for the duffel he'd brought up earlier.

Troy wandered to the bathroom and took a quick spit bath, then he spent a good few minutes stretching, finding his center, his strength.

He found Saul sitting on the bed when he returned, next to several lengths of neatly coiled rope. Next to those were four instruments: a flogger, a crop, a paddle and a tawse. Saul stood as he got closer.

"Ready? I remember your safe words as yellow and red. Yes?"

"Yes, Sir." Not super imaginative, but easy to remember.

Saul nodded and moved out of his way. "I'm playing things by ear tonight, but I want to know if any of my impact toys are off limits tonight or in the near future. Have a look and let me know, please. Be honest. If you don't know, that's fine."

"I've only ever felt a paddle and a crop." In fact, he remembered a desperate night where Arnie had used the crop on his hole until he'd screamed.

"Oh, good to know. Thank you boy. Kneel right here." Saul pointed to a specific spot on the floor facing the bed and then scooped up all the tools and put them into the toolbox, which sat open next to the dresser. "Ever tied bondage knots?"

"I've tied a lot of knots, Sir, for everything from livestock to Doms when they needed an extra pair of hands."

"Okay." Saul picked up a length of narrow, white nylon rope with a loop in one end. "Can you tie a locking cuff like this?"

"Yes, Sir." Troy took the rope and wound it around his fingers four times before pulling through his cuffs and tightening the center.

"Nice work. I was thinking it would make great homework, but it looks like maybe you could teach me a thing or two as well. So." Saul gestured toward the bed. "Up you go, lie flat on your stomach for now." Saul set the thin rope aside and traded it for a thick black cotton bundle instead. "So you can do some of my prep for me next time, I love that."

"Yes, Sir. You just let me know what all you need." He

did that for Master David quite a bit, when Dave and Trav were working long shifts and needed help.

He crawled up the center of the bed and settled onto his belly, the comforter soft and familiar.

"You've helped out other Doms? Where, at Carter's place? Did you enjoy that?" Saul slipped a loop over his wrist, slid it up to the center of his bicep and tightened the loop until it was just snug against his skin.

"Yes, sometimes, and mostly. Everyone knows I was a roper and that I'm... that I was unattached, so they use me for set up every now and again."

"That you *were* unattached, boy." Saul's voice seemed to drop a full octave and his Master's tone was stern. "Whose sub are you now?"

"Yours, Master." His answer was immediate, and he couldn't have stopped his smile for love or money. It wasn't funny, but God, it was amazing. Wondrous. A blessing.

"Mine." The word was weighty and meaningful. Saul's fingers worked slowly, purposefully, wrapping the rope around his bicep about five or six inches wide and adding another loop to secure it before beginning to do the same on the other side.

"Yes, Sir." He breathed into the ropes like he breathed into his tension, accepting them, letting them hold him.

"How do the ropes feel? Good? Too tight? It should just feel solid not pinching." Saul tied off his right bicep as well, leaving the end of both ropes loose alongside his body.

"They're firm, but not tight-tight." He stretched up taller, rolling his hips.

"Arms down by your sides, boy." Saul climbed up over his back and sat squarely on his ass, then reached out and tugged on his shoulders, making him arch. "Hold that position. When you feel you can't any longer, let me know."

Saul reached for the ends of the ropes on either side and tugged his arms toward his spine, then began weaving.

He closed his eyes and inhaled, the pose familiar enough that he could hold it for a little while. In. Out. In. Out. In. "Master..." he warned.

"Good boy. I want another thirty seconds. Try for me." He could feel Saul's fingers moving faster.

He blew out a long breath, then sucked in another, beginning to count. His abs were trembling, and he fought the need to flop down.

He felt a sharp tug and then Saul shifted quickly around in front of him, hands tucking under him to support his chest. "Good boy, let go. I've got you."

His Master held him in place when his muscles gave out, and lowered him slowly until the knots pulled taut and took his weight. His body wanted to fight, to struggle, but his mind was already fuzzy around the edges, the idea of releasing control amazing.

"Good boy. You'll tell me right away if something hurts, or if something goes numb. Not a little tingly, actually numb." Saul moved again, this time sitting to one side and taking hold of his hips. "Walk your knees up under you."

"Y-yes, Sir." He rocked back and forth between his shoulders, working his legs up where his Master wanted them.

"Oh, that's lovely." The sound of the smack startled him, but the strength and the sting to his upturned ass was what really got his attention.

He stiffened, his surprised gasp loud in his ears. As soon as he processed, he braced himself, in case his Master wanted to give him more.

Saul moved away though, sliding off the bed and returning with more rope and hardware, all of which were laid out where he could see them. Black rope, a pair of thick cuffs with two maybe three rings on each, and a spreader that looked about two feet wide. The cuffs went on first, and quickly.

"What does it mean to be mine, boy?" Saul reached for the spreader and encouraged him to open his knees wide.

The urge to try to figure out the *right* answer was huge, so he forced himself to answer immediately, honestly. "It means my pleasure and pain is yours. It means my focus is yours. My intentions. Submission. Needs."

"Good boy. That's all true." Saul's fingers slid up the inside of his thigh and tugged gently on his sac. "Your body is mine to restrain, to restrict, to make helpless, yes?" The cuffs were tight as Saul put them on his ankles, but they were loosened quickly so they felt more comfortable.

"Yes, Master. Yours." His thighs trembled as they searched for a place to settle.

"Go ahead and move. Get comfortable. I'm going to rope your thighs next and tie you in place. Hopefully you can handle it for a short while." Saul unwrapped the bundle of rope.

He would do his damnedest. He drew his knees up higher, stretching, and bent his head forward to open up his lower back.

"I like it." His Master worked efficiently, wrapping one thigh much like his biceps, running the rope through the rings on his cuffs and then wrapping the other thigh. "Boy. You're beautiful, exposed for me like this. At my mercy. Would you like to see?" Saul pulled a square mirror with a long handle from the toolbox and held it for him, angling it this way and that. The ropes bisected him, the black stripes shocking against his skin. He'd never seen himself like this—bound and held.

"Do you like it? How do you feel?" Saul took the mirror away, leaving him blinking, trying to remember the image. Warm fingers landed on his ass, massaging, working deep into the muscle.

He cried out, the muscles there surprising him with how tight they were. When they let loose, he had a moment of panic, suddenly off-balance.

"That's it. I'm right here, boy." Saul shifted to steady him. "I've got you, just breathe. Relax."

"Relax." He nodded and leaned into those sure, strong hands, trusting them to hold him up.

"All right?" His Master let go. "There, see? You were fighting the bonds. You have to give in, it's the only way this works. You want to fight, we can try that another day." That was followed by a low laugh.

"That's a whole 'nother scene." He didn't want to fight the ropes, but his body had a different idea.

"Oh, I like those scenes too. We'll chat about the fantasy stuff, hm? This is the flogger." The leather tails fell firmly but not painfully on his backside, Saul alternating one side, and then the other. "It's iconic. It's not ideal for ass play, but you said you'd never felt one so I thought I'd give you a taste."

"'S different. Good thud." He felt at once dazed and intensely focused.

"Breathe, boy. I'll let you feel it a little. Relax. Less thud and more sting, I don't have a lot of room to work." The flogger made a swooping sound and the tips of the falls bit into his skin as they landed.

Troy hummed softly, stretching where he could as he processed the sensations.

His Master chuckled. "Oh, you're going to be fun." The

next set of blows landed harder and came quickly; seven, eight, nine...

He rocked forward, driving his chest deeper into the mattress. He'd forgotten what this was like, having a master work him.

Saul went on, more than doubling that count before the blows stopped abruptly. "Tell me how you feel, boy."

"Lit up, Sir." Between his chest and his ass, he was all lit up.

"Good, good." Saul put the flogger down and drew a hot, wet tongue across one sensitive ass cheek.

Troy's eyes flew open, making him realize they'd been closed. He felt everything. Everything.

His Master licked and nibbled, soft, subtle torture up to his lower back and down again to the top of his thigh. "Mmm."

Every exhale made him shiver, made him want to moan and beg. His skin was awake, every inch of it.

"Oh, good boy. It's all right, let me hear you." Saul's fingers found his piercings, gently nudging and tugging on them, then slipped around to fondle his balls.

"Master..." He let a deep, needy groan slide out of him, and he leaned hard into the ropes, letting them hold him.

"Being mine means other things too. It means that I have a responsibility *to* you, and that I am responsible *for* you. That I make sure your needs are met. All of your needs." Saul reached farther and made a fist around his cock, stroking it once from the root outward until there was sweet pressure against his ring. "Not just this one."

A sudden inexplicable emotion flooded him, tears prickling at his eyes. He nodded for Saul, praying that the man didn't see because he knew his Master would ask what was wrong and he didn't know.

Saul released him, and both hands glided over his restraints, checking them, tugging here and there, squeezing his fingers and his toes. Safety checks were part of the process, but this felt more like a caress than anything else. "Everything... feel okay? Fingers?"

He wiggled them, one at a time, and cleared his throat. "Yes, Sir."

There was a second of hesitation and then his Master sighed softly. "All right." He felt Saul move away, dig around in the toolbox, and without another word his Master clamped a heavy ring around the top of his sac, weighing his balls down.

"Did I do something wrong, Sir?" He was wearing down —beginning to itch a little, the knowledge that those tears were going to come sooner or later weighing on him.

"No, my boy. I'm just not sure you heard me when I said *all* your needs." Saul cleared his throat. "You've felt the crop before. I'm giving you four. Two for me, lighter to check my arm, and then two for you. Breathe."

He didn't know if he could breathe. He didn't know if he remembered how. "Yes, Master."

Saul didn't keep him waiting. As promised, the first two were solid but not painful. His Master paced into view and he could see the concentration on Saul's face. It was only a moment after his Master moved out of his sight that the second set of blows fell flat across his ass, one just slightly higher than the other, hard enough they seemed to burn into his skin.

The first tear fell without his permission, and he went to slap it away, tugging needlessly at the ropes. He let his head fall forward, hiding his face as he did his damnedest to breathe.

Saul moved to the top of the bed, sitting close to him

and smoothing a hand over his scalp. "Your intentions are mine. You said it yourself. Your needs are *mine*. Let go, boy. You need to let go. You've surrendered everything but this."

He groaned, his entire body shuddering. Why hadn't anyone cared for him before this? In twenty years, why hadn't anyone wanted him?

"Not yet? All right, boy." Saul stood again and moved away. He knew the crop was coming again, he could hear it swoop through the air as Saul practiced behind him. "Two more."

That was all the warning he got.

He bit out a scream, and he twisted to one side, fighting the tears and the ropes, needing Saul to help him. "Please!"

Saul sat with him again and stroked his head, his shoulders. "If you need out of the ropes I need a safeword, boy. Otherwise, I'll assume you're asking something else. 'Please' can mean so many things. You need something, and I need to help you. You may be bound right now but I'm the one whose hands are tied. You have to give me something. *Something.*"

He pushed into that touch, soaking up the connection. *Calm down, man. Seriously. You're scaring him. You have to control yourself.* "That-that was... bigger than anything in recent memory. Can I rest here a second with you, please Sir?"

He thought he felt Saul hesitate, disconnect for just a second maybe, but then again maybe he was reading into something that wasn't there. "Of course. I'm... I'm right here. You've worked very hard."

"We both did." Troy rested his head on the solid warmth of Saul's thigh, letting his cheeks dry, cool off.

"You're beautiful, you know. You really are." Saul kept touching him. Soothing him with strong, warm hands.

"I don't know how to process that yet, but I want to believe it." His panic faded, thank God, Saul smoothing it away.

"I get it. But you'll only ever get the truth from me." Saul shifted, kissing the places where his fingers had been, starting with the top of his head. As the slow progression reached his ropes, Saul started to undo them.

"Thank you. I freaked a little bit on you." And he felt a little like a fool for worrying Saul. He'd done it to Geoff too. Maybe he was getting older than he thought.

"A little." Saul worked quietly, undoing the hogtie first and then freeing his thighs. "Not enough."

"I have to admit it felt remarkably 'enough', Master."

"It was good. I'm proud of you. That was your first real scene in how long? You did great." Saul took the spreader off his ankles and helped him stretch out flat again. "I like to do this part slowly, so be patient with me and rest."

"Yes, Sir, and thank you. I was worried." He melted and let Saul move him where he would.

"Me too. I was honestly disappointed in myself for a bit, but we need to remember we're just starting. It's not a race, we'll go deeper soon. It'll happen."

His wrists were freed of the cuffs first, and then he felt the rope loosen, wrap by wrap and knot by knot.

"Twenty years ago." He knew that question had been a few back, but it was important.

"Yeah." Saul laughed softly. "Sorry I kept you waiting so long. I had to grow up."

"You did. I still want to pinch myself that you took an interest."

"You have the most beautiful eyes I've ever seen, and you make the best French toast in town. I've never met anyone that gave off such stubborn I'm-not-interested vibes, though.

I mean, how much can a guy eat?" Saul removed the heavy ball stretcher last.

"I don't know, Master. You went through most of my French toast designs..." Troy began to chuckle, the amusement bubbling up inside of him.

"I did. And I got your point loud and clear. But I'm not, in fact, a child, in case you hadn't noticed. And how will you ever get what you want if you don't go after it?"

"What?" He sat up in a rush, his entire body screaming with the unexpected motion. "Is that what you thought I was saying?"

The first time it had been a tease, but after had been... obviously clumsy wooing.

"Whoa. What are you doing? Lie down." Saul coaxed him back down into the pillows. "At first. After the train and the dinosaur yeah, I did. But the third one, the CU logo? That was genius and then I figured it out. And I loved the flower."

"Oh good. I wanted you to feel special." Troy wanted Saul to know that he cared, that the urge to take care was near impossible to deny.

"I did. I do." Saul grabbed a tube out of the toolbox and sat on the bed next to his sore backside.

"I'm glad. It's important." It was his part of giving back, of sharing himself.

"I only broke the skin in one spot, but the welts are pretty. Like a big, red equal sign across your butt." Saul chuckled and tended to the welt with some ointment and gentle fingers.

"Good thing I work standing up." He shivered at the touch, goosebumps popping up all over his legs and back.

"Good thing." Saul practically sang to him, sounding gleeful and hopping off the bed. "That should do it for now."

Saul's jeans hit the floor and his Master climbed into bed with him. "Now I want to hold you."

"Yes, Master. That sounds... like heaven." Troy moved right in, soaking up Saul's strength, his heat.

"Yeah, this is what we need." They settled together, and Saul let the silence take over.

Troy sighed, settled, stress eased back. "Thank you, Sir. For everything."

"It was my pleasure boy. Thank you for your trust." Saul tilted his chin up and kissed him.

Oh, goodnight kisses were one of the things he'd missed the most. He was going to rest, he thought, deep and quiet.

15

"Is the boy toy picking you up again?"

"Yes, Emma. Troy is picking me up. Again. And he's not a toy, he's more like..." He snorted. "Okay, fine. He is my favorite thing to play with."

Emma laughed, pleased with herself and pointed out the door. "That's his truck."

"It is. Thanks for covering so I could leave early."

"Is this going to be a regular Friday thing now?"

"Well, it's just that he has to be at work so early on Saturday and—"

"Oh shut up, Saul. Go play. You're opening on Saturdays from now on."

He grinned at her and kissed her cheek. "It's a deal. Night." Troy had him up before dawn on Saturdays anyway.

She made a shooing gesture and he ran out the door to the truck.

Troy waved at him, his boy all smiles. "Happy Friday. How did you enjoy your lunch?"

Every day lunch appeared in the shop, and today's lunch

had been chicken and dumplings and double blackberry cobbler.

"Your dumplings are better than my mom's." Saul climbed into the truck, then leaned over the armrest to kiss him. "Hey, baby." He'd stayed the night Wednesday, but they hadn't seen each other yesterday and it felt like it had been forever.

"Mmm... I missed you." Troy cupped his jaw, the caress gentle as hell.

"I missed you too." Okay, so this was serious. It was still all tangled up with the D/s stuff, which he was only just starting to get a handle on, but this was real. *Thank you, Universe. I get it.*

"Golf first or food, Sir?" God, Troy seemed so happy, those green eyes smiling.

"Golf. I had this huge lunch." Wait. Did he want to be 'Sir' right now? Wasn't this a date? Did it matter? What if he just wanted a boyfriend tonight? Was that weird? Dammit. Why wasn't there a manual for this shit?

"Sounds good to me. There's a laser maze at this place too." Troy headed out. "How was your day?"

"It was... oh! Oh, it was a good day. Matt brought Kris in. It was amazing. Kris was better than last weekend, like he'd gotten some sleep." Emma had been so in her element, she was brilliant.

"Good deal." Troy nodded. "They deserve a little good. I introduced them to my yoga teacher, Nate. He's going to give them some moves."

"That's fantastic. Emma's arranging to give them the bike for free. Don't tell; adaptive stuff is kind of her hobby and she's really excited."

"I won't spoil the surprise." No, there was something

inherently trustworthy about Troy, something solid as a rock.

"Did you say laser maze?" It was a lovely afternoon, so he rolled his window down, turned up the radio and rested a hand on Troy's knee. "Do you have an advantage because you're a yogi? I think that might be cheating."

"Yeah, but I'm an old man, so it evens it up."

"You're the youngest old man I've ever met. The ass I beat the other night is in amazing shape." That had been sweet. Marking that ass in one of the few spots his boy wasn't otherwise marked? It was like claiming territory. Troy had serious depth, and sometimes he had serious needs. They were going to be so good together.

Troy's blush proved that his boy not only heard him but was pleased.

They pulled into the parking lot, settled, and Troy grinned at him. "You ready to play?"

"Born ready." He stole another kiss before they jumped out of the truck. This was going to be fun. "I have never played neon before. Actually I can't remember the last time I played at all."

"Really? That's a shame. Do you like rafting?"

"I love rafting. I'm not very experienced, I've only been a few times, but I have always come off the water intending to do it again. I do a lot of camping though." Saul recalled that Troy had said he didn't enjoy camping alone, but maybe they could go together now.

"I'd like to go. I've done it quite a few times in Idaho Springs. Maybe... I'm owed a day or two off..."

"We'd have to go midweek. Emma needs me on the weekends. Maybe head up on a Sunday afternoon and stay through Wednesday or even Thursday. Think about it, I'm game. I have camping gear." They went into the building and he had to blink to get his eyes to adjust to the light. "Whoa."

One hand rested on his shoulder. "You got it?"

He leaned into it, even though he didn't need to, and smiled. "I'm good."

"Good deal. You want to try the maze and golf both?" Troy's voice was soft, breath tickling his ear.

"Why not?" Oh, he liked that. The touch, the care, Troy's subtle seduction.

"Excellent. Let me grab our tickets, hmm? You'll need to pick out a club."

"Thank you. I'll go do that." He fought the urge to offer to pitch in. He'd treated the last time and he knew about that pride thing, he felt it himself. He headed over to the rack of clubs, grinning as he picked out one with a neon green head, a zebra-striped pole and a matching green handle.

A couple of guys came over to pick out clubs, jostling and teasing, making fun of each other.

"Hey." He nodded to them and got out of their way to wait for Troy.

"Hey, man. You want to join us?"

"A foursome? Sure. Sounds like fun." He offered a hand. "I'm Saul."

The blond shook with him. "I'm Kenny, this butthead here is Devon. Who's four?"

"Oh. My boyfriend, Troy." He looked toward the ticket counter. "Bald guy."

"He's your boyfriend?" Devon glanced at Kenny. "Wow."

He grinned. Wow was right.

"Lucky, man. You guys local?"

"Oh yeah. I run the Cycle Rack in town and Troy cooks at the Spiked Butterfly. You guys too?"

"Yeah. We're up at CU, man."

"I graduated three years ago. I never came here in college. I can't believe it. The guys I hung out with would have loved this shit."

"Rock on. You doing the maze after?" Kenny winked at Devon. "It's pretty cool. There are some places in there you can slip off course."

"We are. With my luck I'll won't make it far enough to take advantage of that. Troy does yoga though. I bet he makes it." He waved at Troy. "Over here!"

Troy caught sight of them, heading over with a smile. "Hey y'all."

The guys exchanged a knowing glance before Kenny grinned. "Hey, Tex."

"These two jokers want to have a foursome." He blinked. "Uh. Play as a foursome. Golf. Just golf."

Devon laughed good and loud. "Golf. Is that what they're calling it now?"

Kenny snorted. "Going for a hole in one?"

Troy chuckled softly and grabbed a club. "You kids can't keep up with me."

He laughed. "Oh, but I can." He herded Troy toward the first hole, pinching his lover's ass once they were more out of sight of the ticket desk.

Troy leaned into the touch, then waved them all ahead. "Go ahead, y'all."

Devon shook his head. "Age before beauty, man."

"Well now what do we do? Troy is older *and* prettier than all of us." He put an arm around Troy's waist and grinned. "Go on, Devon."

"You better go, Dev. In case he's smarter too."

"Shut up, asshole." Dev stuck his tongue out at Kenny and lined up a shot.

"Don't stick that out unless you intend to use it, Dev." Kenny poked Dev in the ass with the club as he swung.

"Hey!" Dev's ball went wild, bouncing off a neon dinosaur egg and rolling almost all the way back to where it started.

"Oops." Kenny laughed. "I guess it's my turn?" Dev stuck his club out in front of Kenny's ball, sending it right off the course.

"This might be a long game." He looked at Troy. "You next, or me?"

"Go for it." Troy grinned, watching him like a man with a secret.

"Okay." He stepped up and placed his ball, glancing at Troy before lining up his shot. "Okay. Here goes nothing." He pulled his club back gently and swung at the ball.

"Oh, nice one, dude!"

The ball went up and over the hill, bouncing off a dinosaur tail, almost getting him a hole-in-one.

"Huh. Right on. Your turn, baby." He went and stood at the far end where his ball was and watched. "Impress me."

Troy grinned, and Saul watched as he swung, knocking his ball clear out of the way. "Oops."

"Ah! You didn't tell me you were good at this game." He laughed, staying out of Devon and Kenny's way as they joked around their next shots. Neither of them touched Troy's ball, but Devon managed to knock his even farther, and Kenny rolled past the hole. Eventually the two of them sank their balls and moved onto the next hole.

He eyeballed Troy and lined up his shot, his ball rolling pretty much right on target.

"You almost got it in the hole..." Troy was asking for it.

He leaned on his club. "I can pretty much guarantee you won't."

"You think?" That soft laughter bubbled out of Troy, the sound warm and so happy.

It just got happier as Troy banked a shot and sank both their balls.

"Why, thank you. Show off." He hugged his arms around Troy. "Nice shot."

"I figure we both needed in the hole." Troy kissed his cheek.

"We better catch up with the boys." He winked at Troy. The boys, who weren't more than a few years younger than he was. Was it weird that he felt like he'd grown up some since meeting Troy?

"They were hoping I was your father and you were available."

"What?" He blinked over at Kenny and Devon. "They were?"

"They most definitely were." Troy waggled his eyebrow. "And you're not."

"I told them you were my boyfriend, so I'm pretty sure they got the message. Devon said I was lucky." He kissed Troy behind the ear. "And I am. Go show them how a real man plays mini golf."

Troy's laugh filled the air, drawing stares from the other players.

What a wonderful sound that was. He grinned and headed to the next green. "Ooh. Spaceships."

"If you stay on the green, I'll give you a blow job." Troy was in a lovely mood.

He laughed. "Oh. Incentive. Or is that more self-serving than it sounds?"

"Totally incentive. If I was being self-serving, I'd say the winner got the blow job."

His first shot went a little off course but stayed on the

green. "I like how you think you make the rules." He gave his boy a look, and then a grin. "It's cute."

"I'm adorable, remember?" And feeling his oats.

"Are you, *pup*?" He made sure to put emphasis on the diminutive. "Oh, that might stick. I like it."

"Woof. Should I wag?" Troy rolled his eyes, that grin wicked as he took his shot. Christ, how many times had he played this?

He stepped up to take his turn, grabbing Troy's ass on the way by. "I can appreciate a nice tail." He lined up his shot and sank his ball. "Ha. One blow job. And I don't even have to order you."

Troy applauded, bumping against him as he passed. He almost missed the whispered, "You can have it when you want it."

But he didn't.

He crossed his arms and watched Troy's shot. Maybe on the way home. He'd just make Troy pull over somewhere. "Nice one."

Troy bowed dramatically. "Thank you, Sir."

"Hey, are you two going to flirt or play golf?" Kenny shouted as the two of them moved onto the next hole.

"We're going to flirt, whippersnapper," Troy shot back.

"Yeah! And you kids get off my lawn!" He cracked up and totally missed his next shot, but it was worth it watching Kenny and Devon lose it, especially when Troy just flew past them like they were standing still.

"Dude, you can play some golf," Kenny said, and Troy just bowed.

"You should watch me play tiddlywinks."

Saul pretty much laughed himself sick during the next three holes, and Troy had to rescue him more than once. Mini golf was not his game. But it was fun.

"Shark! Okay. I've got this one."

"Sure you do. Once Troy bails you out again." Kenny slapped him on the back.

"Shut up." He lined up his ball. "I was just getting warmed up."

Troy watched him, the gaze heated enough he swore he could feel it like a physical touch.

Jesus, who knew golf could be foreplay? No wonder he was missing every damn shot. He swung and the ball rolled up the shark's tail, down onto the green, and right into its mouth.

"Boom! Hole in one. Told you."

"That took Dev four shots."

"Shut up, Kenny."

Troy hummed with approval. "What do you want for a reward for that shot?"

"Well, since I can't throw you over the glowing, green dinosaur, I guess I'll have to think about that." He laughed.

"They might frown on that, yeah. I could be wrong, but I don't think so."

"You know what I want?" He caught Troy's arm at the end of the green. "Toasted marshmallows."

"Toasted marshmallows? Like on a stick?" God, that was the cutest expression.

"Yes, exactly. On a stick." He took Troy's arm on the way to the next hole. "Over a fire."

"All right. I will make that happen. Sunday night?"

Saul loved that—how Troy worked to make things happen for him.

"Thank you. Perfect." He gave Troy a quick peck on the cheek. "Your turn."

"We'll see if I can manage the hammerhead shark this

time. This one is tough-ish." Troy lined up, and Devon goosed him, making Troy jump. "Hey!"

Saul was at Troy's side in a heartbeat and used his slight height advantage to get in Dev's face a second later. "Not cool." *Never, ever, touch my sub.* "Keep your hands to yourself."

Dev put his hands up. "Hey, no harm, no foul, man."

Troy, though, watched him like a hawk, and he could see a quiet approval in his eyes.

"Maybe." He wasn't ready to back down just yet. "That's for him to say, not you. Apologize."

"Seriously?"

He just raised an eyebrow.

"Uh." Devon looked at Troy. "Sorry, man. I was just goofing around."

"No worries. Thanks." Troy hummed for him, the sound deep and so sweet.

Devon backed away and whispered something to Kenny. Saul rested a hand low on Troy's back and leaned in close. "Take your shot at the hammerhead, baby."

"Yes, Sir. Thank you." Troy beamed as his took his shot. Simply beamed.

He'd had a brief moment wondering whether Troy would be weird about him stepping in, but that smile said it all. He knew he had a bit of a possessive streak and sometimes it was more trouble than it was worth, but this time it worked out great.

Troy's ball banked around and across the head and then dumped out on the green before slowly rolling right into the hole. "Look at that. Nice shot."

Troy bowed for him, graceful as anything. "Thank you, thank you."

The next hole was a little awkward with Devon and

Kenny, but a couple more down the line they were back to having a good time. He'd apparently had his one good shot, though, and he was getting pity putts and gimmes and a lot of teasing. Troy was having a ball with him, though, his boy relaxed and playful, flirting with him wildly.

"Do not play croquet with me on this last hole, or I will dream up something very uncomfortable." He grinned at Troy as he lined up his shot.

Kenny and Devon whistled. "You heard the man."

"I did." Troy chuckled for him. "I'll let you use your imagination for something fun, thanks."

"Hey, Kenny, is that supposed to be a squid or an octopus?"

He took his shot and the ball rolled neatly past the tentacles of the huge octopus... and got stuck. "Damn." He snorted, about to give up when one tentacle swung down, scooped his ball up and deposited it in the hole.

"What?" Devon gasped and Kenny hooted.

"No. Way." He laughed. "Holy shit."

"I think you win the whole fucking night." Troy nodded to him. "Seriously. You win."

"That was crazy!" He looked at Kenny and Dev and then bumped shoulders with Troy. "Crazy. Did you know it did that?"

Troy's answer was a warm chuckle, a wink, and then Troy scooped up his ball and didn't take his shot.

"You did." He followed Troy, poking and tickling, playing with him. "Dork. That was so much fun!"

Troy cracked up for him and tossed his ball in the net. "You want a drink before we have our maze?"

"Sure, sounds great." He let Troy lead the way. "You didn't tell me you were so good at this. Do you play a lot?"

"Yeah, it's quiet in the winter when I get off and I've got no plans."

"Do you ski?" He tucked an arm into Troy's. "I'll have whatever you're having."

"They have cherry Coke. I love that. And I do! I ski, snowmobile, even tried snowshoeing a few times."

"Awesome. We are never going to run out of things to do." Saul loved that they had things in common, but also a lot of things to teach each other.

"You guys taking a break?" Kenny called over.

"Yeah, quick drink before the maze."

Devon waved. "If we don't run into you again, have a great night!"

He waved back and watched them disappear through the dark doors at the maze entrance. "They were fun. Mostly."

"They were." Troy shot him a heated glance. "Thank you for standing up for me. That was hot as hell."

"You're mine." He couldn't have kept the little growl of pride out of his voice if he'd wanted to.

"I am."

It turned him on so much, watching the way Troy seemed to get taller, spine straighter.

The other night hadn't been perfect; he knew Troy had been holding something back, and he hadn't managed to get at it. It wasn't because of him, though, Troy trusted him that was obvious. So whatever it was, he'd just keep working until his boy could let it go. They'd gotten close; they'd both felt good after. Watching Troy, he was convinced that they were on the right path.

Troy got their drinks before sitting next to him again. "So I was thinking we could head out this weekend. See if there are campsites at West Chicago Creek or whathaveyou."

"With marshmallows?" He laughed. "I'd love to. You're actually ready to try staying overnight?"

"If it's uncomfortable, we can stay in Idaho Springs."

"I love camping. I will make sure you are very comfortable. Or very comfortably uncomfortable, depending on how much privacy we have." He got an image of Troy tied naked to a tree and part of him wanted to laugh, but part of him...? A little rope, maybe a blindfold, a roaring fire? There was something there worth exploring.

"I have a camp stove, a hammock, sleeping bag. You have a tent?"

"I have a tent, lanterns, a bear bag and bug spray." Saul winked. "And a bunch of other random crap. And you have a truck, which makes this so much easier."

"I do. I'll grab the air mattress out of the garage, even."

"Glamping. I like it. A couple of steaks, lawn chairs, beer, enough rubbers for a small army." Hell yeah. "Lock the phones in the glove compartment."

"Sounds like heaven. With bears." Little shit.

Saul leaned closer to Troy. "I know a couple I can invite if you're into that."

"I'm into you, Sir. All the way."

God, that immediate answer suited him just fine. He nodded, finding those green eyes and holding them. "Thank you. How do you feel about heading out? We could take a walk or... something." He was thinking he'd rather get lost in Troy than a maze. He'd been promised a blow job after all.

"Sounds perfect. Let's go. I owe you a reward." Oh, good boy. Great minds thinking alike and all that.

"Golf was fun. You're a wonderful date, you know that?"

Troy seemed to have the transition stuff or integration thing, or whatever it was down already. He was keeping up, but it was far from comfortable yet.

"Thank you. I'm having a ball, playing with you."

"I like that we can just hang out. It's... different. I mean, I love all of it obviously, but sometimes I just want to be a regular guy on a regular date. I'm just used to that being separate."

Troy glanced at him, stood, and then held out a hand. "You ready to hit the road?"

He jumped up and took Troy's hand. If he'd smiled any broader he'd have hurt himself. "I am." Saying something was his second good call of the day.

"Good deal. Holler when you're ready for supper." Troy led him out in the air and got them moving toward the truck.

He hooked an arm around Troy's back. "Nice evening, huh? Okay, I know what I'm getting for my hole in one... what do you want for yours?"

"It's a gorgeous night, and if you're rewarding me for mine you'll get damn tired. I rocked that course." Troy shot him a grin.

He laughed and slid his hand lower, tucking it into Troy's back pocket. "Such a show off."

"That's me, short order cook and gooney golf player extraordinaire."

He tugged on Troy, leaning his lover's back against the driver's side door. "Extraordinaire?" He planted a kiss with intentions that had nothing to do with dinner.

Troy's eyes flew open wide. Saul did love how easy it was to surprise his boy.

"Know a place to park?" He nuzzled Troy's ear.

"I might know a place out of town a ways." Troy patted

his hip, the touch intimate. "Come on and we can see what we can see."

"Sounds good." He wondered how Troy knew a place but didn't really want to know either. He liked the naughty feeling of not knowing more than he wanted details. He pushed away with a grin and headed around to the passenger side.

Troy waited until he got settled before he got the country station going, grabbed a gimme cap off the dash, and directed them both out of town. They headed west, the sun right in their eyes, the city disappearing.

He found himself watching Troy, kind of sidelong at first and then watching frankly. Casual, easy, comfortable in that tattooed skin. "You look great." He gave Troy's shoulder a squeeze.

Troy glanced over, blinked, and then offered him a smile. "Well, thank you."

"Really. Your vibe is hot as hell." He drew a hand along Troy's side and slid it along one thigh.

"I have a vibe?" Troy stretched up tall under his hand.

"Yeah. This casually masculine thing. It's hard to describe but it's a total turn-on." He teased, tugging at the button on Troy's jeans.

"Well, thank God for that. It would suck if I didn't crank your tractor."

"Ha!" Saul barked out a laugh, pulled his hand away and socked Troy in the shoulder. "Buzzkill."

"Never say so." Troy hooted, cheeks bright pink. "Seriously. I appreciate it. It's been a long time."

"Yeah, yeah. Twenty years, blah, blah." He snorted, teasing, hand going right back where it had been. "I've been fucking you for more than a week. I think you should believe me now."

"Fair enough. More than a whole week, huh? That's pretty damned impressive."

"It is for me." He shrugged. "Subs I stick with. Lovers are more of an issue."

"Hey, I wasn't mocking. I'm more the seven-years-on, twenty-years-off type, and don't ask me to do that math. I don't got that kind of focus with you right here."

"No math. You just find us that spot." He toyed with Troy's belt but gave up, he'd never get it undone with one hand, and instead pushed his fingers lower to cup Troy through the denim.

Troy gasped, hips rolling up as his fingers tightened around the steering wheel. "Damn."

"Now who is cranking whose tractor, cowboy?" He gave a squeeze but backed off pretty quickly. Driving off into a ditch wasn't sexy.

"You do. Crank all sorts of things, I mean."

"Uh-huh." His own cock was starting to complain about tight quarters, and he adjusted himself, grunting just loud enough to be heard over the radio, and lowered his fly, letting it out to play.

"That is totally cheating, you know. Completely." Troy reached over, fingers sliding up over his shaft.

"What fun is playing by the rules?" Whoa. His voice was pretty tight. Damn. He ground the heel of his hand along the ridge in Troy's jeans.

"I don't know. I think you don't mind when I follow them." Troy pulled off onto a dirt road and pulled over on a wide spot, throwing the truck in park.

"I like you to do as you're told." He reached over and hauled on Troy, forcing their mouths together in an awkward but needy kiss. Troy held his prick, stroking him steadily as they devoured each other.

He loved this. They could have gone back to Troy's place, but he was craving something wild. Something naughty. He wrestled out of his seatbelt and shifted to get a better grip on his lover's shoulders, letting himself get lost in Troy.

Troy leaned and fiddled, and suddenly the seat shifted back with a click, and they had more room.

He laughed against Troy's lips. "Nice."

"Thank you, thank you." Troy winked at him, playing hard.

He went after Troy's buckle again. He wanted to touch. To rub. To get off. "This fucking thing is like... birth control. It's like a chastity belt, or one of those bar puzzles, or... ah! Got it! So there, Fort Knox."

"Lord have mercy. Am I fixin' to have to make you practice belt buckles?" Troy grabbed him and kissed him good and hard.

Fuck yeah. Who needed air anyway? He tore Troy's fly open and got his hand around his prize, giving the solid cock a squeeze.

Troy gasped into their kiss, the sound rough and raw, and more than a little happy.

"Hottest... man on the planet." He stroked, making sure to pay attention to the piercing, giving it a nudge, putting pressure on it with every stroke.

"Oh Jesus..." Troy's whimper felt so good. "You make it feel so fucking good."

"Your hardware is amazing." Troy's touch was just right, his prick ached just enough to distract him, but he was focused on winding Troy up. "I love to watch you."

"Love how you touch me like you mean it."

He chuckled softly. "I mean it. I want you to feel good. Too much talking." He kissed Troy lightly. "Shut up and suck me."

"Bossy." Troy eased him back and away. "Give me some room to work."

"I thought you liked bossy?" He shifted and wiggled his jeans down farther. "I can't help wanting you."

Troy hummed and leaned, mouth dropping over his cock like a lead balloon.

He gasped and fell back against the passenger side door, fingers playing over Troy's pale scalp curiously. So odd not to have a fistful of that ginger hair to pull on. He had to wonder, if he asked, would Troy grow it out, let him see?

Troy took him in deep, making his eyes cross, and he realized he wasn't going to be doing much seeing anyway. "Jesus." He braced one foot on the steering column and reached for the oh-shit handle.

Troy's hands slid under his ass and pulled, drawing him in deep before backing off and teasing the tip.

He moaned, eyes locked on his lover, breath catching in his chest. Troy had the sweetest mouth. He had an urge to bind his boy's hands with the seatbelt but ignored it and let Troy steer, keeping contact with his free hand, touching everywhere he could reach. Troy slapped his shaft, the sting from his tongue perfect.

There was no way it had been twenty years since Troy had given head.

"Fuck, baby." He was pretty sure he'd said that out loud, though he could barely hear it. God, his breath was thin, and that heat in his belly was building fast. His toes curled and he dropped his head back against the window.

Troy sucked and moaned and worked him like a popsicle, suction loose on the way down and dragging on the way up.

"Troy. 'S good." He said that, and a bunch of other stuff, but it was all needy babbling. His balls ached and his thigh muscles started to tremble and stiffen. "Fuck!" He sat up, grabbing Troy's head and curling over it. "So close... Troy!"

Troy rolled his sac, pushing at him and rolling him as the suction became almost unbearable.

He sucked in a breath, every nerve on fire. For a long, horrific moment he felt like he might hang on the edge forever, but finally the dam broke, forcing a strained cry from him. His orgasm seemed to go on and on, leaving him shaking and breathless.

Every time Troy made a noise—a deep hum, a soft moan, anything—Saul wanted to scream. Scream, jerk away, beg Troy to stop, beg him for more... something. So many conflicted sensations Saul kind of froze. "Fuck, fuck. Troy."

Troy let him slide free, long slow licks cleaning him off. "I got you, honey."

He nodded. "Jesus." He took as deep a breath as he could manage and grinned. "Damn. You're... that... wow."

"Mmm...You're more than welcome."

He relaxed, leaning back against the door. "You earned yourself pretty much anything you want, baby." As soon as his brain remembered how to make his body move.

"Spend the night?"

He blinked, surprised by the sincere request and by the little rush of emotion he felt in his chest. "I'd like that."

"I would too." Troy kissed his belly, the touch featherlight, a little maddening.

"Come kiss me." He pulled on Troy. He knew his lover had to work early, and that the Saturday into Sunday shift was a really long haul, so he'd make sure they got to sleep when they got home. But he got what Troy was asking. Since they'd met, the nights had seemed really long when he was alone.

Troy climbed right up his body, taking a half dozen kisses along the way before bringing their lips together.

"Mmm." He could do this all day. Troy's kisses made him dizzy. He worked a hand between them and teased Troy's ring, gently wrapping his fingers around that heavy prick. "I feel you."

Troy moaned for him, lips parting as his pinkie finger nudged that little barbell at the base. It was an embarrassment of riches.

He traced Troy's upper lip with his tongue and stroked gently, keeping his lover's buzz on. "You want this now, baby, or do you want to wait until we get to your place?"

"I'll wait. I like a pre-bedtime orgasm when I can get it."

He smiled. "Right, you can't get it unless I'm around. If I didn't know better, I'd think that was why you asked me to stay the night." He kissed Troy's nose. "But I know better."

"Yeah, you do." Troy grinned back. "I'm starving. Let's get some supper."

He let Troy go reluctantly, playing at disappointment. "Oh, all right. If we have to." He wiggled his jeans back up, stretching and twisting, and laughing softly. "Truck sex always seems like such a great idea until you have to get dressed again."

"No shit. Of course, I've gotten dressed and undressed in a lot of trucks." Troy kissed him again, then pulled back.

"Was that your MO with Arnie? Or is that your MO in Denver?" He gave Troy a wink and a grin. He'd had his fair share of car sex too.

"Sleeping in your truck is a young cowboy standard, but Arnie and me had a few moments, sure." Troy chuckled, but didn't quite meet his eyes. "Now Denver? No. I went into the city a couple times a year for a one-off. Something not my own hand."

"I've picked up some guys in Denver. I mean, that's where the bars are right? I used to go with some friends from school once in a while when..." He shook his head feeling a little embarrassed, but Troy was honest so he could be. "When we were bored with each other."

"Yeah. Have you been to the big club there?"

"If you mean Tracks, yeah. When I can afford the cover. It's the go-to when I want to dance." And when he wanted to pick someone up.

"I bet you're a good dancer."

"Oh, I am definitely better after a beer or two." He gave Troy's knee a squeeze as they pulled back out onto the road. "You?"

"Me? You mean dancing? I'm not the world's best dancer, but I've done it before."

He gave Troy a sidelong look. "I'd like to see that sometime." The way his lover moved, that could be something to see.

Troy shot him a smile. "It's been a while, but I can probably manage."

"What do you like to dance to?" He leaned back in his seat and stretched one leg out, his brain was still foggy after Troy's incredible blow job and he was feeling lazy.

"I've mostly two-stepped, waltzed. I've done some line dancing too, but not much."

"I've mostly danced in clubs, but I know how to two-step. Deitz—my last regular sub—taught me. I'm not good at it, but I could get better with practice." Deitz had been very good at it. His friend and former sub had been good at a lot of things.

"We could practice at the house, if you want. How do you feel about Thai?"

"Love Thai." He hummed happily. "This is my second-best date ever." His best date ever had been last Friday.

"Good deal. There's a great little hole in the wall place—does a stunning tom kha ga. The tom yum is good too."

"And here I thought nothing could make tonight any better. That sounds perfect." He slid a hand down Troy's arm.

Troy's smile suited him to the bone. "Golf. Making out. Thai food. Coffee. I'm having a ball."

"Yep." Saul turned the radio up loud and started singing along.

16

Troy packed up his truck and tried to lose his shitty mood.

He was tired, and he knew it. The new backup cook had crapped out and he'd cooked his ass off for two days before trying to plan all the shit for camping.

Now he was ready to take a long, hot shower and die.

Maybe it was too much, heading out right after his weekend shift. Maybe he should call Saul and put it off until tomorrow. He didn't know if he was going to be great company tonight.

Hell, he was hoping Saul might be convinced to drive even if they left tomorrow. He was just... tired. Tired and a little emotional, which he hated.

A familiar truck pulled up, the horn honked, and Saul got out, giving him a wave. Emma helped Saul unload some gear and left it next to Troy's rear tire. So much for waiting until tomorrow.

"You guys have fun."

"Thanks for the ride, Em."

"Nice to see you again." Emma smiled at Troy and

climbed back into her truck, and Saul came right to him, smiling.

"Hey, baby."

"Hey, honey. How goes it?" Troy still wasn't quite sure how to know whether he should be 'sir'-ing or not, but he thought not now.

"I'm excited." Saul slipped an arm around him and pulled him in close. "You okay?"

"Yeah. Long couple of days. You?"

"I'm great." Saul definitely had more energy than he did. "The store was busy, we had some great people in, the weather is perfect... I'm ready for some time alone with you —with my boy."

He took a deep breath and released it, relaxing into Saul's strength, almost hysterically grateful for the clue as to what Saul expected.

Whoa. *You gotta watch that shit, man. You remember how you lost your mind after you lost Arnie. You have to keep your feet under you.*

Sometimes Troy hated that little voice of reason.

"Wow. Okay, I'm here." Saul held him, stroking a hand over his back. "Should I have waited for you to call me? Emma offered me the ride and I just jumped on it. What do you need?"

He found a laugh and let Saul have it as he straightened up. "Just a long few shifts. I'll be glad when it's fall and I can take some of my vacation days. I put some frozen hamburger meat in the cooler with the beer and bacon."

He'd grabbed a loaf of bread and a bag of chips too, along with the makings for s'mores.

Saul kissed his forehead. "I'll see if I can't make these couple of days feel like a vacation for you. Ooh. Chocolate. I want to grab something from upstairs. Be right back."

Saul took off at a jog with the bounce of a twenty-five-year-old.

God, he was old.

Still, it felt good to be wanted, didn't it?

He did a forward fold, wrapping his arms around his legs as he relaxed.

"Look at you, pretzel." Saul came back quickly and gave his ass a slap, and he was pretty sure he caught sight of some cuffs disappearing into Saul's bag. "I should really do some yoga with you. I could use a good stretch."

"Yeah? It helps me more than I thought it could." He practiced every day, had before Arnie had left, and it brought him back to himself.

He nodded. "Yeah, I get tight biking and running. I bet we could find a great spot up in the mountains when we get up in the morning. It might be fun doing it together."

"I'll grab a couple mats." He wasn't sure he wasn't going to beg to spend Monday night in one of the hot springs hotels, to be honest.

"Cool."

When he got back, Saul had loaded the gear he and Emma brought into the back of his truck, and his lover was sitting on the tailgate looking at a cell phone.

"Everything okay?" The shop was closed, so it shouldn't be that...

"Oh yeah. I was just checking the weather and looking for any alerts. Looks clear, and I didn't see any critter warnings."

"Good deal. I... I don't suppose you'd like to drive." He'd never let someone drive this truck, but he'd be a way better person without having to pay attention.

Saul glanced up at him sharply and hopped of the tailgate. "Sure. I'll drive, no problem." Saul slid a hand over his scalp and kissed him, gentle and slow, leaving him swaying as they parted. "Are you sure you still want to go?"

"I am. I'm just tired. We had a cook quit, so I worked a double yesterday and a hellacious shift today." Was that whining?

"Thank you for telling me, boy. That sounds exhausting. I get to take care of you, though, and I'm very okay with that. I really am. Hop in when you're ready; you can nap while I drive if you want to."

He blinked, pleased as hell. Like down to the bone. "Thank you, Sir. I appreciate it."

Saul smiled at him. "You're welcome. Keys?"

He handed them over without hesitation. "We're going to have a ball. Relax. I intend to turn my phone off."

"No phones. Sound perfect." Saul opened the passenger door for him. "Ready?"

"I am." He laughed at himself. Seriously, his humor had flipped from bleak to cheery in a heartbeat.

Saul ran around and climbed in behind the wheel, started the truck and then played with the seat, sliding it back. "This is awesome." He watched Saul run eager fingers over the steering wheel. "Okay. Where are we going anyway?" Saul grinned at him, on the verge of giggles.

"To hell, if we don't change our ways?" He wasn't going to be able to hold it together. Not at all.

"I don't plan on changing my ways so I guess you might as well get the lighter fluid."

Troy cracked up, managing to plug in the phone and get the GPS started. "Ta-da!"

"Ooh." Saul was laughing hard enough even those strong shoulders were shaking. "Good to have, particularly if you're asleep!"

"I'd just have to drive with my toes." Wait. Did that even make sense?

"Hey." Saul leaned close. "Close your eyes. What's the worst that can happen? We sleep in the truck bed? I got this." He got a quick kiss. "I do."

"I trust you." He did close his eyes, focusing on listening, relaxing. Focusing on Saul.

He felt the truck start to move. Saul turned the radio down low and just kept talking to him. "I want you to relax, boy. I want you to leave your job and your tough day behind. All you have to do for the next two days is breathe. Serve and breathe. You're with me now."

"Yes, Sir." He focused on his breath, deep, full-belly inhalations, slow, steady exhalations.

"That's it. Get some sleep."

He reached out, hand finding Saul's thigh, trailing as he sank deeper. He was aware of Saul fingers in his, tangling them together, as the song on the radio faded into the monotonous hum of the engine.

HE WOKE UP TO THE FRONT OF THE TRUCK DIPPING AND bouncing, and blinked to clear his eyes in the dim light. Saul's hand pressed into his chest. "All good. Almost there."

"Mmm. Smells good out here. How you doing?" Troy stretched up tall, his back snapping and popping.

"Great. It was a gorgeous drive. Lots of time to let my mind wander. Did you have a good nap?"

"I did, thank you. I was wore." And he felt refreshed, awake, and he actually was looking forward to their 'weekend'.

Saul drove his truck carefully up the narrow, bumpy road and past a stand of trees. "I think this is it."

The camp site was simple, isolated, and lovely—with a cleared space for a tent, a firepit, and battered picnic table.

"Looks like! It's going to be chilly. We'll have to snuggle tonight."

"If we must." The truck came to a stop, Saul shut the engine off and handed him back his keys. "I like how your truck drives."

"Thank you." He leaned close. "I appreciate the hell out of you driving. I was in a state."

"You looked it. We'll make it an early night." He got a hug, but then Saul hopped out of the cab. "I'll get started on the tent. You want to figure out a fire?"

"I'm on it." He'd packed in a bunch of firewood, unloading about half of it so that he could get the fire going. Once he'd done that, he set up their chairs and pulled the cooler out.

The tent went up quick and Saul anchored it down like a pro, stretching the guy-lines out and marking them so they wouldn't trip. "That looks totally comfy." Saul hooked an arm around him. "Let me just get the sleeping gear, and then I'll be ready to sit for a minute."

"Sounds great. Would you like a drink? We have Cokes, beer, water."

"Coke sounds good for now." Saul pulled their sleeping bags from the truck and headed for the tent. "Man, I'm glad you reminded me to bring a jacket. I almost didn't. I forget how much cooler it gets once the sun goes down."

It was getting dark, but they'd gotten the complicated stuff set up. Dinner would be easy enough by lantern and firelight.

"We're a hell of a lot higher, hmm?" He had blankets in the cab, so they were good.

"Yeah, I feel that a little too. You?" Saul zipped the tent

closed and joined him at the fire, looping arms around him and nuzzling his neck. "Okay. We're set up."

"We are." He leaned back, sighing with pleasure. "Happy Sunday, Sir."

"Mmm." Saul hummed in his ear. "Thank you, boy. It is now. I missed you last night."

"Mmhmm. I dreamed about you." All night long. He'd woken up hard as a rock.

"Not too tired to dream? I hope they were good." A hand slid over his abs. "Do you need help with dinner?"

"I have stuff for burgers. Does that work for you?" Carter had let him grab the fixins for a couple days; he was damn lucky.

"Anything works. I'm more interested in you than dinner anyway." Saul was just holding him, nothing more, and that somehow made those words seem more sincere.

"We should just have sandwiches. I brought some already made up."

"Yeah. Simple dinner, beautiful night, campfire, and my arms around my boy. Sounds great to me."

Troy leaned into him, humming deep in his chest and thanking God that he hadn't canceled. This felt like balm for the soul.

Saul kissed his neck and then his temple. "I love a fire. I like watching the flames, I like how the wood hisses. It's nice to just watch it, or poke at it, and soak in the heat. Fire is fascinating."

"That's why there's a fireplace in the bedroom too. In the winters I can lay in bed and watch it forever." Right now, though, his focus was on his Master, on the solid heat behind him.

"Now I'm looking forward to winter." Saul gave him a

squeeze and let him go. "Okay. Let's eat before it gets even darker. I've got a lantern in my bag, I'll grab it."

"Sounds good to me." He grabbed the turkey and provolone from the cooler, along with a bag of chips. It wasn't glamping, but it totally didn't suck.

Saul met him at the picnic table with the lantern. "You've been to this site before? Did you have to reserve it? Or is it just something you found?"

"I reserved it. I used to drive out here and go to the hot springs after. Beau Jo's pizza, soaking, and mountains." It had been magic. Maybe it still was.

"Oh wow. Let's try that sometime." Saul opened up one of the sandwiches and popped the top on his Coke. "When I come up, I usually figure out some way to get up to the mountains, bring a pack, and hike in. It's handy having a truck."

"I've hiked a bunch of these trails. I could spend a lifetime up here, I love Rocky Mountain National Park, but house payments and all..." Still, if he was rich, he'd go find himself a fourteener and build a cabin.

"If you spent a lifetime up here you wouldn't have a house payment." Saul winked at him and bit into the sandwich.

"Logic is totally overrated." The sandwich was good, even a few hours later. Man, he made a fine bite of food.

"True. I wouldn't want you thinking for yourself." Saul gave him a wide grin. "I mean, thinking too hard."

"Yeah, yeah, yeah. Good for you that I'm not the sharpest tack in the box then." He was good at consistency—ride the bull for eight, cook the perfect pancake—but he wasn't brilliant. That was okay. Steady was a good thing.

"I didn't mean that, boy. I value who a person is way more than what they know. I was teasing my sub, was all.

You're more than sharp enough for me. Please. I have a degree, but I am clearly not smart enough to figure out how to use it." Saul laughed.

Troy snorted and leaned harder. "You're happy, right? You like it?"

"The shop? I love it. It's my favorite hobby made into a job. Someday I'll open my own shop. Or buy this one out. Emma and I talk about it all the time."

"That would be something, wouldn't it?" He could totally see that—Saul owning his own shop. He liked it.

Saul nodded. "It's a plan. What about you? Do you have plans?"

He didn't know how to answer that without sounding like he'd given up. He didn't have plans. He stopped making them years ago. He would work until he couldn't anymore.

Jesus. Come on. Think of something.

"I'm going to retire and get my teacher hours in yoga. Have my own studio."

Wait. What? Where the everloving fuck did that come from?

"Oh, wow. That's fantastic." Saul's smile lit up that baby face, eyes reflecting the firelight. "What a great idea. You'll be a great instructor, you're good with people, you're super patient, and you definitely love it."

"Thank you. I do love it. It saved my life."

"Thank goodness." Saul kissed his jaw. "Clean up dinner, boy, and then we'll sit and enjoy the fire."

"Yes, Sir." It was easy to clean up, pack the trash and the food and haul it up high in Saul's bear bag where the bears wouldn't get at it. The last thing they needed was random critters looking for a snack.

It didn't take long, but it was long enough for Saul to fold up his chair and put a yoga mat in its place. His Master pointed to the mat as he got close. "I want you to kneel for a bit. I think we both could use to find our center."

"Yes, Master." Hell yes. He was eager to settle, to sink in and focus on Saul, Saul's will.

Saul helped him get there. They pulled a couple of rocks and sticks out from under his mat and shifted it until he was comfortable. "Good boy." Saul smoothed a hand over his head, behind his ear, and under his jaw. "Cross your ankles please, and grasp one wrist with the opposite hand behind your back. Whichever one is more comfortable and helps you keep your balance."

He murmured his agreement, inhaled, and as he exhaled, he moved into position. Thank goodness he'd worn his flip-flops in the truck and not his hiking boots.

His Master moved around him, checked his grip and put his flip-flops to one side. "Lower your chin a little, eyes down or closed, if you prefer. If you get cold, or you feel like something is falling asleep, make sure you tell me."

Sir sat close enough to touch, close enough to rest a hand on his shoulder.

Troy closed his eyes, the way the fire light danced against his eyelids simply fascinating, hypnotic.

Saul let him sit there quietly for a while, and listen to the logs pop and crackle, but eventually broke the silence. "Tell me what's on your mind right now."

"I was enjoying the rest, knowing you were with me."

"It's good, isn't it? The energy between us when we're together. It feels easy to me."

"Yes, Sir. You have a vibe that calls to me." That wasn't another good way to explain it.

"I think that might be the need. That calling. But I know what you mean." Saul slid a hand over his shoulders. "To find your space though you need to focus on something specific. Is there anything you want to talk about? Think about? We did that word thing to try to stir up something. We talked a little about service already. What else comes to mind for you?"

"I have no idea. I'm so glad I didn't cancel today. It was so good, to see you."

"I'm glad too. You needed me. I could see that. You were worn pretty thin. Canceling would have been exactly the wrong thing to do. When you feel that way, I can help you settle."

"I appreciate it. Seriously." He inhaled deeply, stretching with the breath and settling with his exhale.

"I know you do. But you don't need to tell me, you can show me with your service. With your submission. That's how this works, right? That what I need from you." Saul leaned forward in the chair, watching the fire. "I need to understand what this feels like twenty-four-seven. I need you to help me with that, okay? It seems like the ideal to me, you know? But I don't have a feel for how it works. How we each get what we need out of it. Everything we need."

"I'll do my best." Troy wasn't sure how to help. He'd never known anything else, and he'd never had to worry with Arnie. He'd been too fucking young and too fucking wet behind the ears to stress. He'd just been so in the moment every single second. Now he worried about seeming like some old needy queen who was pushing Saul into a situation he was uncomfortable with.

Maybe he needed to talk with Geoff and Carter.

Or just Geoff.

"I definitely can't ask for more than that, boy. Except maybe for some patience. Thank you." Saul relaxed back in the chair, and he could feel his Master breathing easier. "Are you warm enough?"

"Yes, Sir. The fire's doing its job." He spread his knees a bit, giving himself a little hip stretch.

"It's nice. I'd love to see you naked in this firelight, but I'm not going to do that to you tonight. I'll save that for the sleeping bags." Saul laughed softly. "Maybe tomorrow night, if you've been a good boy, I'll figure out a way to keep you warm out here with my crop or my flogger. I think we're both a little tired for that right now."

It had been a long few days, no question.

He knelt, breathing into all the little hurts, the nagging pain from the burn on his wrist, the ache in one shoulder, letting them go.

"I was thinking last night about how much I'm looking forward to the next get-together at Carter and Geoff's house. I guess it's a couple of weeks away still, but I liked those guys. I liked how I felt like I belonged there."

Troy wasn't sure whether he was supposed to answer or just listen, so he smiled and nodded. He got that. He'd been drifting, and Geoff and Carter and the others had become the family he'd lost, and God knew he'd lost a ton of that. The guys were his safe space.

Saul's fingers were warm on his shoulder despite the chilly night. "You're a good boy," his Master said in a soft voice, after another long silence. "You've been good for me. Everything matters when I'm with you. You... make me want to get it right. I like that."

He leaned and lifted one shoulder, kissing Saul's fingers gently. He tried to be a decent man, a faithful friend, a solid lover, so maybe he was doing something right.

"Why don't you bank the fire and do whatever stretching you want to do and then come to bed. I'll go get the tent in shape for us to sleep in. Sound good?"

"Yes, Sir. I'm on it." He slowly moved out of the position

Saul had asked for, aching in the cold parts. He put his shoes on and covered the fire up. Then he grabbed a pair of sweats and a sweatshirt, heavy socks, and changed out of his jeans there by the truck.

Jeans weren't stretch friendly, and he hadn't worn loose work jeans in a long time.

He saw another lantern go on inside the tent and Saul's shadow moving around inside like a fly in a lampshade, distorted and shadowy. His Master was humming something catchy, happy, but he didn't recognize what it was.

Troy put the chairs away, then focused on stretching out, bending himself in half, eyes closed. He loved the song of Saul's happiness, and he let it pour over him and make him smile. That wasn't someone who was stressed or worried. He figured he couldn't be pushing Saul all that hard, or his lover wouldn't sound that way.

The tent went quiet and still after a bit. He could tell by the shadow that Saul was sitting up, but couldn't quite make out what his Master was doing.

He draped his mat over the chair and went to slip into the tent. "Master."

Saul looked up from the book in his hands and smiled. "My boy. All done?"

"Yes, Sir." He settled down and zipped the door closed, enclosing them in a little cocoon.

"I made us a little, like, nest in here. So we don't have to squeeze into each other's sleeping bags. I just unzipped them and spread them out." Saul grinned and tossed his book into a corner of the tent. "Body heat."

"Sounds perfect." He crawled right into Saul's space, wanting to touch.

"That's the stuff." Saul hunkered right down with him,

burying them both in a heavy sleeping bag. "What should we do tomorrow? Hike? Fish? Swim and freeze our nuts off?"

"There's a couple of great trails, a couple of hippie pools. What's your pleasure?" He was happy just knowing he could sleep tomorrow, that the alarm wasn't going to ring and he would be in Saul's arms.

"Mmm. Bacon and coffee. And then... we'll see." Saul laughed and nipped at his ear. "Maybe a nap."

"Bacon is best eaten outside." He might even indulge himself.

"See? I'm not as dumb as I look. So, bacon outside, a hike, and... oh. Maybe we'll do some training and let you earn a handful of stripes. Then we can go sun ourselves on a rock somewhere like a couple of lizards and ponder a scene for after dinner."

He shivered, a tiny hum escaping him. "You have some good ideas, Sir."

All of the sudden, Troy wanted a kiss, so badly.

"I think so too, boy. You have any good ideas?" Saul teased him, lips close enough to share breath.

"I'm looking forward to focusing on us, on you, on being together." He was easy. He wanted to remember how to breathe.

"I am too. I really am. That's exactly what I want for us this weekend. Focus. Maybe there will be some clarity, maybe a few more questions, it's all good as long as we're communicating." Saul brought their lips together in a kiss that was pretty patient, considering the twenty-five-year-old's libido.

Troy opened for Saul, encouraging him to take more, to take what he needed.

Saul took his invitation with a moan and leaned into him, muscling him onto his back. Saul took other things too, his mouth, his breath, and kept pushing his hands away every time he tried to touch.

He panted, his nipples hard as rocks, his cock filling as Saul made him forget everything but his Master, his lover.

He shivered as Saul pulled the zipper down on his sweatshirt and growled at the T-shirt he was wearing, then shoved them both up high and pulled one of his nipples, barbell and all into his mouth, sucking hard.

Troy dragged his shirts off, as if that would help him grab control, process that amazing suction. Oh sweet fuck, he'd played with the rings, but this... this was heaven.

He threaded fingers into Saul's hair, but Saul pushed his hand away again with a grunt. God, that was getting frustrating. Saul pressed a hip into his groin and teeth closed around his nipple, pinching hard.

"Fuck!" White-hot sensation shot through him, and he arched, not entirely sure whether he was angling close or away.

His Master let go quickly and hummed to him, licking and soothing his nipple where those savage teeth had been, and praised him in a dark tone. "Good boy."

That praise made him whimper, made his cock jerk. Fuck him, he'd do damn near anything to hear that. Saul made the words seem like a promise of the best possible kind.

Saul pulled his own T-shirt off with one hand. "That one was a surprise. This time, you know what's coming. Eventually." His Master ducked again, short blond curls falling this way and that, tickling his chest, and a hot tongue circled his other nipple.

He moaned, the world seeming to swim for a second. The anticipation was maddening and wonderful, and he let himself stop waiting, and just felt.

The slow, deliberate attention went on, Saul teased at his hardware and sucked it in hard. Everything was sensitive by the time those teeth closed down, pinching him again.

He pushed up on his elbows, and his hips jerked up in a few uncontrollable thrusts. That was wrong in the most right way.

Saul gripped his hip, pinning it to the ground, and held on this time until the whole area around his nipple went numb before letting go. The burn of the blood coming back was almost as painful as the bite had been. His Master laughed softly, and kissed over his shoulder and up one side of his neck.

He leaned his chin and let Saul have him. His world was that mouth, his nipple, and the way he was grinding them together.

"I think about you, about this, every day. Every damn day, I mean it." Saul sat back and tugged his sweats down, helping him get them off.

"I ache for you," he admitted. Like he'd never ached for anyone.

"Oh. God, Troy." His Master undressed quickly and pulled the sleeping bag back over them both. They kissed again, hips rocking.

He held on, dragging them closer as they tried to eat each other up. Troy liked to set his happy ass on fire.

"You—" Whatever Saul was going to say he swallowed up with his tongue. Eventually Saul broke the kiss off, pressed their foreheads together and tried again. "You on top?"

"You want me to ride you?" He was easy.

"Yeah. Wanna watch you move." Saul shifted and retrieved a bottle of lube from somewhere above his head. "In a minute."

He knew how to ride and ride hard. Some things a man never forgot.

They were nice and warm under the covers, but that lube felt cold as ice as Saul's fingers touched him, teasing his hole. Saul chuckled at his gasp, obviously enjoying his reaction.

"Trying to freeze me in places ice don't go." He winked up at Saul, loving that smile.

"Oh, my boy. Ice goes everywhere. I'll show you sometime." Saul winked back, the pressure easing as two slick fingers pushed inside him.

His lips parted, and he bore down, taking Saul's fingers all the way to the hand.

"Jesus. The way you *want*..." Saul moved inside him, stroking and stretching, and finally added a third.

It was bigger than that. Vast. What Troy felt was need.

Saul kept at him, fucking him with those fingers, well beyond what he would have needed to be ready. "Talk, boy. I want to hear you. Is it enough? Do you want more? Do you need me?"

"I do. I need you like breathing." He wasn't ashamed. Saul was on his mind, all the fucking time. "You make me burn, swear to God."

"Mmm. Good boy. That was lovely. You should talk more often." Saul rolled off him, leaving him empty and letting in some of the chilly night air. "Come on, boy. I need you too. Now."

"Hell yes." Troy moved to straddle Saul, rocking his ass back to tease them both.

That earned him a heated grin. Saul arched under him and pulled him down into a hungry kiss. Troy stretched out tall against Saul, rubbing them together. It made him think maybe he could dance with his Sir.

Saul grabbed a rubber from wherever the lube had come from and reached down between them, parting them just enough to roll it on. "So ready for you, boy."

"Going to give you a good ride, Sir. Best one of your life."

"Fuck, I believe that." His Master took hold of his hips and guided him back until the head of Saul's hungry prick pressed tight against him.

"Yes." Troy hissed as he sank down, filling himself up. Damn, this was... His eyes flew open as Saul took him in.

Saul groaned as their bodies came together again. He knew that long, low, heated sound was for all him. "God. You feel so good."

"Yes." He rocked, not bouncing yet, just moving in a slow, torturous roll.

Saul watched him, blue eyes intense and honest. His Master didn't try to rush him at all, just held on and let him move. He groaned, loving the way Saul stretched him and made him dizzy.

Sir gripped him hard and held him steady where they had some room to move and started gently thrusting, pulling out until Troy felt the head start to stretch him and then pressing back in again. The burn was so sweet and the long, slow strokes were driving them both a little mad.

He didn't fight the thrusts. No. He gave himself over to the steady, building pleasure.

"I can't get enough of you." Saul let him go and took another kiss. The contact was more than need this time, it was something more urgent and full of questions.

All of the sudden Troy couldn't breathe, couldn't focus on anything but Saul. "Master."

He wasn't sure if he spoke out loud or just thought the honorific.

"Mine." He could feel his Master's growl and the groan that followed rumble in his own chest.

"Yours." God yes. Please. With all the faults and scars.

Saul caught his eyes again. "Move, boy. I need you."

His head bobbed with his agreement. Move. Yes. Troy sat up tall and began to ride, counting on his thighs to keep him going and his core to keep him balanced.

"Yeah." Saul slid a hand over his abs, fingers tracing the line up the center of his chest to his collarbone. "Fuck, yeah."

It was the most natural thing in the world, to reach up and put his hands behind his head, interlocking his fingers, offering his Master everything as he rode.

"So beautiful." Sir slid fingers up his neck and pushed one into his mouth. "Such a good boy."

His eyelids drooped as he began to suck, and he swore Saul's cock swelled inside him as he tightened.

"Best... of my life." Saul kept watching him, twisting the finger in his mouth for a while. When it did slip away, that hand dropped right down to his cock, tucking under his sac to tug on his piercings. "Fascinating."

"Oh fuck. Make me feel so good." He flew—that touch was perfect, hard and sure and perfect.

"So good." Saul's free hand groped along his thigh, hot fingers sliding over his skin, and his Master's hips rolled slightly to meet him on each downward stroke.

He began to bounce, riding good and hard, Saul dragging inside him in the best possible way. Saul grunted and moved a hand to his cock, closing it tight around his shaft and working him like his Master knew just how good it felt. Handy, because he was just about as far gone as he wanted to be.

He glanced down at Saul, admiring the way his Master's

pale skin reflected the angular light from their small lantern. It was damp despite the chilly air, and the shadows made the ridges in Saul's chest and abs seem even deeper and more pronounced.

Troy whimpered, reaching out to stroke the toned muscles. "Jesus. Beautiful." He bore down, gripping at that fine cock, milking it.

Saul gasped and arched, hands flying to his hips and holding on tight. "Fuck, boy. See what you do to me? Gonna come so fucking hard for you. You, boy. You make me feel this way." His Master's voice was rough and tight, the words meant for him alone.

Fuck, he'd never felt so alive, so powerful, so necessary. "Yours."

Saul planted one foot flat, lifting him, and thrust frantically a handful of times. "Mine. Fuck. Yes!"

He felt that hungry cock jerk and pulse inside him and watched the expression on Saul's face go from desperate need to blissful relief, so fucking far gone.

Troy let himself soak in Saul's orgasm, let the joy of it fill him up before his own need reminded him that he was in serious danger of blue balls.

Saul looked at him wordlessly, fingers tightening as they started to stroke again. Troy swallowed hard and began to rock, his balls aching and heavy with the need to shoot.

Saul moaned and moved inside him, still breathless. "That's it boy. Take what you need. All of it. My gorgeous boy. Let this be enough." His Master worked him skillfully, stroking and nudging his ring. "Let me be all you need."

He blinked hard, trying to focus, but he couldn't. All he could do was hear his Master and obey the way he needed to. He shot so hard that he went boneless, leaning against Saul's chest.

Saul kissed his scalp and held him, arms strong and warm as his skin started to remember the night air. His Master must have gotten a little chilly too, because it wasn't long before they were back under the sleeping bag.

Troy snuggled in, his body melting, his exhaustion catching up to him, taking him over. "Master."

The word meant a lot of things—thank you, tired, good night, so happy.

Even, I love you.

"My boy." His Master hummed for him, the low, smooth sound as soothing as it was affirming. "Sleep well."

17

Holy shit.

Holy fucking shit. What an amazing night. Beyond amazing.

It was fucking epic.

Troy was right, it really was the best ride he'd ever had. But that...

That was more than sex. What he and Troy shared, what they created together was something he'd never experienced with anyone. Troy's complete submission made him better. It made him strong and confident, it forced him to focus, to stay in the moment. To be what Troy needed him to be.

Troy's submission made him a better Dom.

And yeah, the sex was pretty fucking mind-blowing.

Troy slept in Saul's arms all night. His lover was still sleeping hard as the sun came up. It had taken Saul a while to fall asleep, but his mind woke him just before dawn anyway, and this morning, for some reason he just felt different. He couldn't figure out exactly how but all he'd been doing since he woke up was thinking about Troy.

About everything he'd seen, everything he'd figured out about his boy last night.

He shifted so he could watch Troy sleep, so beautiful and trusting, and he knew he wanted to find a way to make the full-time arrangement work. He felt like he had to, he was convinced that Troy needed it, and he knew deep down that he did too. He didn't have reasons, just intuition, but he knew.

Troy stretched against him, this slow, undulating arch that rubbed them together. There was a peaceful smile on his boy's face, eyes moving under the lids. Oh. Dreaming.

He hoped it was a good dream. He didn't know all the details of Troy's story, just enough to guess that his lover's dreams might not always be easy. He didn't know for sure, but it seemed like Troy had given up on a lot of things. He wanted more for his boy.

He used Troy's stretch as an opportunity to move a little and then settled again, making sure to keep close. He wanted to be close when his boy woke.

He blinked slowly, hoping to doze a while, or even fall back asleep. But he wasn't tired, he felt like he could run a marathon.

Bright green eyes blinked up at him, all of the sudden, wide for a second, then going heavy. "Mmm... morning."

He was so struck by that beautiful green that it took him a second to respond. "Hi. Good morning, sleepyhead."

One hand slid along his arm, his side, his hip. "You did good with the bed. It's so soft."

"Thank you. I've had a little practice." He winked at Troy and gave him a gentle kiss. "We don't want to be all sore from sleeping on the ground."

"No, Sir. You sleep good?" Troy seemed happy to stay curled up with him, twined with him.

"I did." He gave his boy a smile. This morning, answering to "Sir" seemed as natural as breathing. "I watched you sleep some also. You were dreaming."

"Was I? I dream a lot, always have." Troy reached up, tracing his lips. "I used to have terrible nightmares, but not in a while."

"I hope not. You deserve good dreams." Yeah, something was different. He felt protective, possessive. He didn't want to let Troy go. "No more nightmares."

"Wouldn't that be stunning? No more nightmares?"

"I think it's possible." He did. What they had was good. It was solid. New for sure, but real. "I've got you."

"Mmm..." Troy kissed his jaw, his throat, his collarbone. It felt like a blessing.

"Last night was... incredible." He just didn't have a better word. It probably went without saying at all, but he felt like if they didn't acknowledge it, the memory might disappear.

"Yes, Sir. I felt... I felt like I was... yours."

He nodded. "I felt... I *feel* like I'm starting to understand what you need from me. I feel like I can give that to you. I want to be that man, that Dom, for you. I wish I could explain it better than that... I've been thinking about it a lot, but I don't seem to have the words yet."

All of that slow burn, the need, the heat... Saul got what he needed, and he knew Troy did too, but there were no ropes or cuffs, no crops or spankings, no pain at all. No marks. No need for safewords.

They were Dom and sub for sure, but they were lovers, just Saul and Troy at the same time, and he felt... he felt— Oh.

Oh shit. Maybe he did have the words after all.

Holy shit, was this what love felt like? Was he really falling for Troy?

Holy shit.

Troy lifted his head. "You okay? You stopped breathing there for a second."

"Yeah." He took an exaggerated breath and smiled at Troy. "That's what you do to me."

"I hear you." Troy's grin was simple, real. So happy.

"I guess we're both a little high this morning. I like that. Coming up here was a great idea." He took another little kiss, and Troy held him, hands running over his body, learning him all over.

He let Troy touch. Last night he'd been controlling things just to give his boy something to focus on. He leaned in harder, giving his boy his tongue.

Troy took him, yielding beautifully to his need. When the kiss broke, they were both panting, and he was warm as hell.

"My beautiful boy," Saul whispered. "I still want that bacon." What they needed was a little space between them or they'd be in bed all day.

"Busman's holiday." Troy's laugh was soft and happy. "Bacon, coffee, eggs, yes? I brought some challah too."

"You're sweet to me. Save it for tomorrow." He leaned back and stretched long, groaning with it. His fingers itched to touch Troy again, to make the boy his again, and he decided they should both ride that wave for a while.

"I want you wanting today, boy. That prick doesn't have to cut glass, but it needs to stay interested, got me? You have permission to touch, just for today. Wear whatever you want, I don't need to see. I know you'll obey."

Troy blinked from where he was retrieving clothes, the surprise patent, absolutely perfect.

He hid his smile and opted to not acknowledge the look at all. "Do you need help?"

"I— Pardon?"

He glanced down at Troy's cock, which had gone from vaguely interested to rock hard.

Fuck, that was a sight.

"Pardon, *Sir*. That's one stroke for you tonight." He got the feeling that this was going to be a very good day. He reached for his backpack and pulled out his crop, then answered Troy evenly. "With breakfast, boy. Do you need my help?"

Troy shook his head, more like he was clearing it. "Do you mind getting the fire going while I start breakfast, Sir? It's chilly out there."

"No problem." He hung the crop on a loop along the roof of the tent making sure that Troy saw him do it, then went after jeans, a clean T-shirt and his CU Buffs sweatshirt.

Troy got the camp stove set up with the coffee first, before he started to work on the breakfast. The soft random whisper was just quiet enough that he couldn't recognize the song.

Troy had banked their coals like a pro, and he was able to find a log still smoldering at the bottom of the pile. He swept the ash out of the way, added some kindling and a couple of fresh logs from the back of Troy's truck, and then he just had to wait.

"Should have fire in a few. Is that coffee I smell already?" He moved behind Troy and slid a hand down to cup his boy's ass.

"Mmm... Yes, Sir. Coffee is important, hmm?" Troy leaned into his touch. "Do you want three pieces of bacon?"

"I want bacon more than the eggs. So yes, please." He kissed Troy's neck and then went to fish out mugs for the coffee. "Coffee is like comfort food. And it tastes better outdoors."

"This is when I miss cigarettes the most, with my first cup of coffee."

"If it's distracting, we should talk about adding a morning ritual to give you something else to focus on." He set their mugs down.

"Thank you, Sir. I'm usually at work for my first cup. It hasn't been long since Carter had me quit."

"I'm glad he did. Do you feel better?" He poured them each a cup.

"I still miss it, smoking, but it's easier now." Troy put the bacon in the pan, the smell hitting Saul's nose almost immediately.

"Oh... smell that." He sipped his coffee. "Subbing when you're jonesing for a light sucks. I've seen it. Carter did you a bigger favor than you know."

"I started after Arnie died, so that wasn't an issue for me." Troy drank deep, a near sexual sound leaving him.

"You do what you need to, right?" He wasn't judging, but he was glad Troy had quit. "Oh. Fire." He picked up a stick and went over the make sure it was burning evenly.

"How do you want your eggs, Sir?"

"Scrambled hard, please. Are you feeling a little of this warm?" He made his way back over and cupped the front of his boy's jeans without warning, pleased by the hard length under his hand. "Good boy."

The way Troy jerked, abs tightening at his touch, was gratifying. "Yes, Sir."

"What else do you need me to do?" He gave the poor boy a little space to recover and perched on the rickety picnic table.

"Eat." A paper plate was handed over with bacon, eggs, and a slice of grilled bread. Impressive.

"Look at this." He smiled at Troy and took a seat. "Thank

you, boy." He sat at the table and waited for Troy to join him before eating, admiring again how his boy moved with a purpose, no effort wasted and graceful as a cat. Troy was sensual without trying, beautiful but didn't know it. And that body, that mind still had stories to tell and he wanted to hear them.

Troy sat with his fingers wrapped around his coffee cup, breathing in the steam. "Do you mind if I do my morning practice, Sir?"

"I'm sorry, of course not. Your routine is important. Thank you for reminding me." He ought to have remembered. He promised himself he wouldn't forget again. "Actually, would you be distracted if I tried it with you?"

"Of course not." Troy smiled at him, the look warm, the agreement immediate. "You'll just need to remember to take it easy, hmm? It's cold and you just ate."

"I will do that. Thank you, boy." Thankfully, he was in decent shape. He was pretty sure he could almost touch his toes too, although he hadn't tried in a while. This could turn out to be a hilarious disaster, but what the hell? It could turn into a really cool shared routine too. He loved the idea; he'd just have to see how he and yoga got along.

He munched on his bacon and sipped his coffee, about as happy as he'd ever been. "Have you ever done any training to heel?"

"I'm sorry?" Troy tilted his head. "I don't know what you mean, Sir."

"Walking to heel? That's a no? Cool." He finished off that slice and started another. "Something we can work on for the next Sunday gathering. I know they're informal and everything, but I kind of want to make an entrance." Him, in a carefully chosen outfit, and his boy in something like last time, comfy and loose, eyes low and tucked in right behind his shoulder. Mmm. Yes, please.

Truthfully, though? He wanted to impress them. He didn't want to be the cute baby Dom on the block. He wanted to be the young guy who had his shit together. They all knew Troy, but he wanted them to know *his boy*.

"Yes, Sir." Troy smiled for him, and Saul wanted to know what was behind those gorgeous eyes.

"What are you thinking?" He smiled back. "That you're already a good show sub? You are. You made me look damn good that night. This is another level. Traditional stuff."

"What?" The smile was replaced by pure, wide-eyed shock. "Lord no. No, that was the absolute opposite of what I was thinking."

His eyebrow lifted, surprised himself. "No? Tell me what you were thinking, then."

"That—that my life has changed so much. The last time I was someone's, the whole point was that no one would guess about me, ever." Troy chuckled, shook his head. "I feel like I'm trying to catch up."

"Oh, I hear you." He took Troy's hand and gave it a squeeze. "You're not catching up, though. I don't want you to feel that way. There is a lot of this that's new to me too, and I want to make sure we're taking steps together. I don't want to get ahead of you, you know?"

Yeah, you know. Like, falling for a guy that maybe isn't ready for that? No, he wasn't getting ahead of Troy at all. He didn't roll his eyes, but he wanted to. What the hell was he going to do? It was what it was, and it felt great, so... he'd just have to see where it led him.

"Thank you. It wasn't bad thoughts, you know. More... with wonder, you know?"

"Wonder." He chuckled softly and nodded. "Yeah. I do

know. I know exactly. It's not just you." He took his last bite of eggs and swallowed it down with his last sip of coffee. "I can't do yoga in jeans. I better go change while I digest."

"Good deal, Sir. I brought two mats, just in case you might like to practice." Troy stood and began clearing the dishes, that happy whistle sounding again. His little bird.

He knew exactly nothing about yoga, but Emma had suggested he try to find a hobby they had in common, and he didn't see Troy getting on a mountain bike, so he was really hoping he enjoyed this. He had this feeling it would be good for him.

When he came back out in sweats, he went and poked at the fire. It was warming up a little so he wasn't going to waste another log right now, he just got it going on a nice simmer and let it be.

Troy had stripped his shirt and shoes off and was standing and breathing, slow and steady. His boy could focus, Saul had to admit.

He followed suit and tugged off his sweatshirt, ditched his sneakers, then stepped up to the open mat quietly. Troy stayed still so he tried closing his eyes and listening to the pop and hiss of the fire.

"Spread your feet just a bit. It will help you ground. This pose is tadasana, mountain pose." Troy's voice seemed to wrap around him, hold him.

"Mountain pose. Appropriate." He wasn't sure what grounding meant exactly, but he followed Troy's instructions, widening his stance and focusing on his boy's voice.

"Yes. This is like being the mountain, connected to the earth through the soles of your feet." Troy stepped over to him, easing his shoulders down from his ears. "Breathe, Master. Nice and deep."

"Oh, I didn't even realize I was... right. Breathe." *Connected to the earth...* He took a breath and tried to make everything relax as he let it out, imagining that tension going right through his feet into the ground.

"There. Just like that." Troy sounded so pleased. "Perfect."

"Yeah? Cool." Go him. He stayed focused on Troy, and on letting the tension go.

After a dozen breaths or so, Troy spoke again. "Now, next time you inhale, lift your hands and stretch out your spine, relaxing them down on the exhale."

He didn't think too hard about it, he just did what Troy told him to, raising his hands as he inhaled and stretching. This time he noticed his shoulders creeping up as he brought his arms down and tried to relax.

Slowly, gently, Troy moved him through poses, hands adjusting his position every so often, once in a while praising him. Always making him refocus on his breath.

Saul did his best, and it felt great, but it didn't take him long to learn two things. One, he wasn't very flexible, and two, yoga was fucking hard.

They ended up lying on their mats, eyes closed.

"Focus on your breathing."

"Breathing." He tried, but his mind kept focusing on fishing instead. He was about focused out. In fact, he was aching to break Troy's focus and make the man lean on him for control.

He stayed still a little longer, not wanting to disrespect Troy's ritual, but his patience finally frayed and he sat up. "Oh." Damn. The world was sort of soft...vaguely sparkly. He blinked to clear his vision and shook his head.

Troy bowed to him, folding in half, forehead on the ground. "*Namaste.*"

"Oh, I like that. Good boy." He should've returned the gesture, but as Troy's Dom he chose not to. "Thank you for teaching me."

"Thank you for sharing a practice with me." Troy smiled as he sat up and stretched tall. "That was a lovely thing."

"It was. It felt good, I'm just stiff. That was real work, but I'd like to do it again." He hooked a finger under Troy's chin. "Put the mats away please, and then join me by the fire." He needed to dig a couple of things out of his bag and then see if he could breathe more life into the fire without adding more fuel. They'd need the wood, and the warmth, more at night.

Troy pushed himself up and shook out the mats, before gathering up socks and sweatshirts. Troy handed Saul his half with a peaceful, easy smile,

"Thanks. Shoes are fine for you, no shirt yet though. I'll hold onto your sweatshirt." He held his hand out for it.

"Yes, Sir." Troy handed him the sweatshirt and worked on his shoes.

He smiled, leaving Troy to puzzle things out. He folded Troy's sweatshirt and set it on the picnic table, took his time dressing and getting what he needed, and went back to the fire. "Hm. This might be about done." There was still heat, but the ashes needed to be cleared before they built the nighttime fire.

The sun was well up now and it was a gorgeous morning. He didn't have a watch on and his phone was off and in the glove compartment, so he didn't know for sure what time it was, but he didn't care. They weren't on any kind of clock.

It was the finest Monday he'd had in a long time.

Troy settled beside him, silent as a mouse, arms just brushing together.

"Last night was so powerful, I want to keep you in that space today. Be honest, were you able to stay hard through morning practice?"

"I don't know, Sir. I was focused on our practice." Troy glanced at him. "I didn't have anything but our breath in my mind."

"That's fine, boy. I didn't expect it, I'll be clearer next time. I was just curious. I'll assume you are now, however." If Troy wasn't he would be in about fifteen seconds.

Saul pulled the soft leather collar out of his pocket and held it out where his boy could see it. "Training collar. Have you worn one before?"

"No, Sir." Troy's cheeks flamed as he shook his head. "I-No. I haven't."

Oh, he'd been hoping that was the answer. He felt as if his shoulders were suddenly four feet wide. He turned the collar over in his fingers, letting his boy look at it, so Troy could see the pattern stamped into the sides, the lock at the back, and the circular ring in front. "Now, this is not my collar, it's a training collar. Do you know the difference?"

"Yes, Sir. This isn't a show of commitment, but a tool." His boy was having no trouble staying erect now, was he?

"Exactly. This one is a tool, well said. It's important you understand that." When they got to that point, Troy would be the first boy to wear his collar. After last night, he pretty much knew they'd get there, which was crazy when he really thought about it. He wasn't anxious about any of that, he was just awed. It was all new to him. "Face me and I'll put it on you."

"Yes Sir." Troy turned toward him, fingers opening and closing a couple of times.

He thought about that and slowed down a little. "Your

words are yellow and red, and I'm listening for them. Are you cool, or do I need to know something?"

"I'm excited, Sir."

What was that in Troy's voice? Curiosity? Shame? Eagerness?

Whatever it was, he'd find out soon enough. He reached up and circled Troy's neck with the leather, then moved around behind Troy to check the fit and set the lock in place. He kept his hands on his boy, the contact meant to be reassuring and grounding.

"Good boy. Oh, it looks great." He smiled, tracing the line where the collar crossed his boy's throat.

The sight of his boy swallowing, testing the way the collar moved against the tanned throat, was inspiring. "Thank you, Sir."

"If it starts to feel tight, if you feel anxious or panicky, if you just need it off, I want to know right away. No matter what we're doing. Is that clear?"

"Do people feel panicked?" Troy sounded honestly confused.

That made him laugh gently. "No one you know, clearly. Good." He reached into his pocket and pulled out two tiny keys. One was on a keychain and one a ribbon. The one with the ribbon he hung around his neck and tucked into his sweatshirt. The other one he handed to Troy. "Put this one in your glove compartment with our phones, please."

Troy nodded in approval. "Yes, Sir. Smart call."

"Your safety is important. Run along." He'd learned well, sometimes with training, occasionally the hard way. But locks weren't something you wanted to learn about the hard way.

While Troy was gone, he watched the embers smolder

and thought about how the afternoon would go. He wanted to work, but he wanted to have some fun too.

Saul heard Troy lock the doors, and he sat up as his boy came back and handed him the truck keys.

"Oh." Surprised, he took them, then closed his fingers around the ring carefully. He hadn't asked, he hadn't even had plans to. "This is unexpected. Thank you." He smiled at Troy and rewarded his boy with a kiss.

Troy hummed on his exhale, the pretty eyelines going deep.

He put the keys in his pocket as he pulled away. "I'll keep them safe. Close your eyes." He ran his hand over his boy's barely stubbled head and down to where the collar sat, perfect against Troy's skin. "You can keep them closed as long as you like but when you open them again, you're to keep them low and not look me in the eye again. At all, for any reason, until I say it's all right."

"Yes, Sir." Troy inhaled deeply and released it in a slow breath.

"Good boy." Saul wandered back to the picnic table to get Troy's sweatshirt, wondering how many times his boy would forget between now and nightfall. He was looking forward to adding stripes to the single one Troy had earned this morning.

Troy stood where he was, solid, strong, steady as a rock. No, it was a mountain, right?

He watched quietly from a short distance. Troy's level of concentration was a little intimidating. It was going to take him a while to piece his sub together. The boy hadn't ever worn a collar, didn't seem to have training at all really, but had no trouble finding the headspace to serve. Troy had been around Doms and their subs for twenty years or more but had mostly been observing rather than participating.

He realized he didn't know what his boy's goals were yet. He didn't know why Troy wanted or needed to serve. He wasn't sure Troy even knew. And he didn't completely understand his boy's relationship with pain yet either. He did know his boy was athletic, generous, and remarkably willing to try, in bed and out. What Saul had to decide was whether he was going to be excited about all they had to learn together or nervous about all he didn't know.

Or maybe just go with it and be both. He was totally ready for the ride.

Saul brought the sweatshirt back over, still waiting for Troy's eyes to open. This was standard training, but he was going to miss those eyes looking into his today. "How long a hike is it to the water, do you know?"

Troy's lips twisted, brows drawing down. "Maybe six hundred feet to the southeast, give or take? Not bad."

"That's it? I don't guess you brought a fishing pole or two?"

Troy chuckled, eyes rolling. "You are joking, aren't you, Sir? I never go anywhere without a rod and reel. I just happen to have a spare too."

"Excellent. And that's a second stripe. Eyes down, please." Troy hadn't had them open a minute yet. This was going to be fun. He held out Troy's sweatshirt. "You can put this back on, and then grab the fishing gear."

"I promise I didn't look at you, Sir." Troy tugged the sweatshirt on. "Toss me the keys, please?"

Saul chuckled and handed Troy the keys, closing his hands around his boy's for a second. It was meant to be an annoyingly unforgiving rule. Troy would figure it out. "Maybe not. But I saw your eyes, boy." Was he going to be a stickler about respectfully asking questions too? Maybe not today. Maybe he'd add that tomorrow.

Troy dipped his chin in a nod and unlocked the truck, digging around in the back for a minute before pulling out a tackle box and a couple of rods and reels. "You want a hat, Sir?"

"I have mine in the tent. Thank you, boy. You need any help?" That was a good reminder. He ducked into the tent to get his ball cap and fished out sunglasses while he was at it.

"Nah, I got it, thank you." Troy plopped an old straw cowboy hat on his head and snatched his sunglasses off the dash.

"A little-known fact about your Dom," he offered, making his way toward the truck. "I can gut and clean a fish." He thought maybe they'd just found a hobby they had in common. Yoga was good, but fishing was fun. And usually involved beer.

"Yeah? Good deal. I have been known to cook a little bit, so the rumor goes."

"I do seem to recall fish-shaped French toast." He laughed and snagged a pole from his boy, and the truck keys. "You ready to go?" They didn't need to bring much. The water was so close by they could come back when they got hungry.

"Yes, Sir." Troy waved to a trail. "Damn near any of these trails lead to the creek, so far as I know."

"Yeah?" Saul looked around and chose one. "We're off, then." He started walking and let his boy follow. "Did you tell me you reserved this spot, or just hope that it's available when you want to use it?" It was a Monday, maybe Troy just didn't run into that much competition during the week.

"I reserved this one. I've been up here... oh, Christ, maybe a hundred times?" Troy chuckled softly. "When I first moved up, I spent every waking moment working and out in the mountains."

"It's a great spot." They wandered through the woods, just trees everywhere, then suddenly he heard water and boom. There was the creek. "Oh, hey. Nice spot."

Troy cast his eyes out over the water and heaved a big sigh. "Hopefully the trout are biting. It's a gorgeous day."

"It is." Saul paid attention to that sigh, not sure whether it was relief or something else that the boy was letting off his shoulders. "If they're not biting, we'll still have the view and some good conversation."

"Absolutely." Troy reached out and squeezed his fingers quickly before opening up the tackle box and offering him a fly.

He took it and sat down to get it hooked up. "Do you wade out usually? Or just hang here on the rocks?"

"I tend to hang here. I get cold in my bones and I don't have the waders in my truck."

He and his stupid college buddies used to wade in wearing their sneakers. He'd tried that last summer and didn't last all that long—he didn't get the kind of cold Troy was talking about, but it wasn't as fun without being drunk and surrounded by fellow moronic college idiots.

"That's cool. If I get hot, I'll dip my toes in." He headed for an outcropping of rocks that stuck out into the water a few feet. It was fairly flat with room for them both. It was as if someone had put it there just for them.

Troy stood on the far side of the rocks close to him and started throwing his line in and reeling it in, face a study in concentration.

He smiled, watching Troy fish just as gracefully as his boy did everything else. They had slightly different casting styles, but he wasn't going to make it a competition. He tossed his line out and let the current take it downstream a bit.

"Do you ever think about goals you have as a sub? Things you want to learn or do more of? Things you want to accomplish?"

It took Troy a second to answer. "No, Sir. I—I haven't."

He wasn't shocked, considering this relationship was surprising and new for both of them. He pulled on his line and reeled it in slowly, then cast it out again.

"I'd like you to. I can do all the formal training with you, and I can see that you get the things you need, but you should really grow in your submission, you know? You should always be working toward something. It can be small, but it should be specific."

"Yes, Sir." Troy cast again, backlit by the sun.

Yes, sir. No, sir. He struck a chord there didn't he? Or, for all he knew, Troy just took fishing that seriously. Saul cast his line again and let it be, leaving the boy to his own thoughts for now.

"Can I ask you a quick question, Sir?"

"Of course. It doesn't have to be quick. You can speak freely, boy."

"Can I?" The question wasn't the slightest bit sarcastic, possibly a bit wistful. "I was thinking you didn't want me jabbering."

"Hm." He reeled his line in and set his pole aside. "I don't think I said that, did I?" He moved behind Troy and hugged his arms around his boy. "How did I confuse you?"

Troy blinked, stiff for half a breath before he just melted. "You just seemed pretty clear early on that you didn't like me chattering. I get it. I try real hard to keep my mouth shut unless I'm with Geoff."

What in the world had he said? "You must have misunderstood me. I love to hear you talk. There's no need to try to keep your mouth shut, ever. Just the opposite.

Chatter away. I'll chatter right back, you can count on that."

"Oh. That's...that's good to know."

How long had Troy been stressing this, for God's sake?

Keep his mouth shut unless he was with Geoff? Geoff? Okay, so Saul might have confused Troy, but this went back further than that. Was it Carter? Arnie?

He gave Troy a squeeze and dropped the formality for a minute, hoping to help his boy relax. "I'm sorry, baby. I don't know what I said, but that's not what I meant at all. I want to hear everything you want to tell me."

"No need to apologize. We're learning each other still. Thank you, though. I'm glad I came out and asked. I get tired listening to myself talk."

"I don't." He kissed Troy's neck and then let his lover go. "Come out and ask anything. Don't let things like that stew, it doesn't do either of us any good." He backed away a couple of steps, smiling. "Feel better?"

"Yes, Sir. Thank you." Troy chuckled softly, casting again. "You remember your first time fishing?"

"A boy doesn't forget that, does he? My Uncle and my oldest brother, Abner, took me out on the Schuykill River in a boat. Abner was getting ready to graduate high school so I was about ten I guess? I was a fifth wheel for sure, but they set me up with a pole and I had a blast. You?"

"Lord have mercy, I doubt I do remember. The first time I recollect though, I was out with my pappy on his old bass boat, and he was singing."

It was the first time he remembered Troy saying a single word about his family.

"Were you little? Do you remember what he was singing? Was he the ginger or your mom?" He laughed. "I'll hold off on the other questions for a minute."

"My momma was about as redheaded as they come. She was pretty as all get out. And I must have been just little. He was singing *I'll Fly Away*."

"That sounds like a good memory. Doesn't everyone think their mom is the prettiest ever? I do." *Why did you shave off all that red hair?*

"I reckon."

Listen to that. Suddenly Troy was so Texan it hurt. Was that memory? Pain? Nerves?

"Do you miss them?" There were a bunch of ways he could have asked what he wanted to know, but that one seemed to cover them all.

"Every day."

He nodded, feeling a little braver about digging deeper. "Are they still alive? Do they know where you are?"

Troy sighed, shoulders hunching as he cast again. "My mother killed herself when my sister passed away. When I left home, my daddy told me to never come back. I did once, and it was a mistake."

He never quite knew what to do when he opened up a can of worms. Should he watch them wiggle around a while? Slam the lid back on the can? Or pull one out, put it on a hook and go fishing.

"What happened to your sister?"

Oh, good, Saul. Not I'm sorry about your mom, or fuck that guy anyway... no, just go for the gut idiot.

"Leukemia. She was four, I was eight. It was hard and fast." Troy cast, rhythmically, steadily, totally focused. "I know that it's a cliché to say it was a blessing, but in this case it was."

He hadn't picked up his rod again yet and he just didn't, moving back to Troy and resting a hand on his boy's shoulder. "I hear you. But it doesn't sound like your mom thought so. I'm really sorry."

"Thank you. It was a long, long time ago."

Still, he couldn't imagine a little boy losing half his family just like that. And then to lose his dad, and his home, and Arnie... damn.

"So what happened with your dad?" He had Troy talking and his lover hadn't told him to back off yet.

Troy snorted. "What didn't happen? He got stuck with queer rodeo trash for a son, and then, when I went home after..."

"After Arnie died?" Saul circled an arm around Troy again. "What happened?"

"He handed me a gun and told me to put it in my mouth and pull the trigger."

He tightened his grip on his boy protectively. "Jesus, Troy." Who needed that fucking asshole anyway? He'd ask why his boy even bothered to go home in the first place, but that would be like pouring salt in a wound at this point. "I'm not sure I wouldn't have shot him instead."

"I didn't. I took the gun, though, and I came up here to give Carter Arnie's buckles."

"And you just stayed. I remember that part. You're lucky to have them." Whatever went on between Carter and Geoff and Troy wasn't his business and he wasn't going to ask. Whatever it was probably saved Troy's life and that was enough for him.

"I am. They're my family."

He rested his head against Troy's and sighed. "Why did you shave your head?"

"There are a lot of answers to that question, but the short answer is I was dared."

"Geoff?"

"Exceptional guess."

He laughed. "Well. It really wasn't that hard. Okay, so he dared you, but why did you keep it?"

"Maybe I looked younger? I don't know. I don't have to take care of it, and no one cared that it was gone. It wasn't like I had someone to mourn it."

He let his next question rumble in his chest a second before whispering in Troy's ear. "Would you grow it for me?"

A shudder rocked his boy, that focus going from the past to him so quickly he swore he heard it. "Y-yes. Yes, Sir."

Fuck if that didn't make him feel like he'd been filled with rocket fuel. He felt that powerful. Never mind that his cock had turned to granite in his jeans. "Good boy."

"Can I kiss you, Master? Please?" Troy was doing a good job of needing him.

"Yeah. Yes." He didn't wait for Troy, though. He circled around and took the kiss, careful not to get caught up in the fishing rod. Troy stepped close, all the distance between them dissolving.

He couldn't stop his moan and caught Troy's face in his hands, sliding their tongues together. The stubble on the lean cheeks tickled his palms, the tiny hairs rasping at his skin.

Every time they kissed, it felt new. He'd just learned something, or they were trying something out together. Sometimes his boy was asking for something, and sometimes he was. Saul hadn't gotten that familiar feeling yet, that I-know-you feeling. Kissing Troy was always good, but it was still about exploring, about being curious. It was still about offering his boy whatever he had in the moment and seeing what he got back.

Troy held him by his waistband, thumb stroking his erection through his jeans.

Yeah. He wanted that too. He could demand the boy's mouth if he wanted to, and leave Troy wanting. Sure he could. Or, he could hold out, ride the buzz, and just let his boy salivate.

He chuckled into their kiss and withdrew, then scooped up Troy's naughty fingers and kissed them. "I'm not biting."

Troy's laugh made the camp robber birds fly, the sound winging out into the blue sky.

He smiled and stole one more quick kiss before stepping away. "We've got a bright future you and I, let's see if it includes dinner."

"Yes, Sir. I'm on it."

18

"What's your position on weed, Sir?" Troy had the trout ready to go; all he needed was for the potatoes to cook in their foil.

He found green to be vastly superior to beer. No puking. No hangover. No calories. He tried not to smoke it too much, because it made him crave a Marlboro Light, but sure knew how.

"Favorable. If you have it, you better share it."

Was Sir grinning at him or levelling an order? This not looking Saul in the eye thing made things tough.

"Good to know." He could share a couple shotguns. In fact, that thought made him about hard; the idea of passing the smoke between them hot as all get out.

"I'm not hitting you with anything if either of us is high though, boy. Or tying you up." Saul sauntered over from the tent and kissed his shoulder. "Sex is totally okay though."

He made a sound that was vaguely like a startled duck. "Shit, sex is totally better than okay, Master."

"Kinda thought you'd feel that way." Saul sniffed at the fish. "Dinner smells good."

"Thank you. Hopefully it tastes good." He wasn't worried. He knew it would taste just fine.

Saul just laughed. "Get serious, boy. You want a Coke?"

"I do, thank you. A Dr Pepper, please Sir." Troy grinned. A guy had to fish for compliments sometimes. Oh. Fish. *Ha!*

Saul dug around in the truck and came back with his Dr Pepper and a ginger ale. "I like you in a collar. I could get used to that look."

Troy's cheeks liked to burn. "Thank you, Sir."

He was buzzing already, just a little off-center.

"I like that look too. The blush I mean." Saul was sitting close, but just out of reach. "So think for a minute, and then tell me how you feel about my order to not meet my eyes today."

This was a challenge, wasn't it? Was he totally honest, good and bad? Did he fudge the bit where he'd been grateful for his hat and sunglasses? He was pretty used to not meeting Doms' eyes, but 'I don't want to see your eyes'? That was headache-inducing.

"Yes, Sir."

He checked the potatoes, checked the green beans bubbling in the can. One more turn for the trout and it was time to eat.

Saul sat quietly, sipping ginger ale and being patient. When Sir said take your time, or think for a minute, he really meant it and never rushed Troy into an answer. That was good and bad, because a man could think himself in circles on a question like this one.

"So how much do you want to hear, Master?"

"Anything that comes to mind. You're still welcome to speak freely."

"It wasn't terrible. We were busy and both had sunglasses on. I'm careful at the gatherings." He plated their plates and handed Saul his supper. "The sunglasses saved me from the seeing my eyes rule. That's hard on the head, looking down."

"Thank you." Saul grabbed a fork and took it over to the table, looking thoughtful, and dug right into his fish. "Okay. Well, first of all I'm lifting that rule for the rest of the day. Oh. So good. Mm."

"Thank you. It's special, cooking outside." Today had been special too. It had felt like they'd made some breakthroughs that he hadn't even known they'd needed to make.

"And catching dinner. It's been an awesome day so far. I had a reason for giving that order, and for wanting you hard all day—which I assume you had no trouble with. It's hard to make sure you're constantly mindful out here, there are so many really worthy distractions. It was meant to be inconvenient, even annoying. But I think it served my purpose."

"I did my best for you, Sir." And he'd never thought Saul didn't have a reason. He'd watched that with the other couples for years. He assumed that his Master had his best interests at heart.

Otherwise he would never have shared about his past, about how he'd come here to die and had learned to live.

"I don't have any doubt about that. You really honored me the way you trusted me with your past. Maybe it's not Dom-like, but I was kind of humbled by your honesty. It was more than I expected. I thought for sure you'd want to stop answering my questions at some point."

"It feels good to tell some of my stories." No one else cared to hear them. Geoff and Carter had heard the first half and lived the second with him.

"It feels good to hear them, honestly. Sometimes you're

such a mystery to me." The affection in Saul's eyes was obvious, and he was glad that he was allowed to see it. "I don't mean that's a bad thing. I just..." Sir smiled and shrugged, and took a bite of potatoes.

"I've spent years in my own head. I forget sometimes." And Arnie had hated noise. He'd spent days not allowed to talk, so he'd learned how to stay quiet.

"I don't want you to be in your head. I don't know if that's some holdover, or something I said, but I need a partner I can talk to. There will be times you'll wish you could shut me up. Like now, maybe." Saul popped a bite into his mouth and gave him a goofy look.

"I love listening to you." A partner. He liked that. He liked that a lot. "The potatoes came out good. I haven't done them like that in a while."

"So good. Not that I'm surprised. So, I think I got a little sun on my neck waiting for that second trout to bite." Saul snorted. "I thought maybe I was going to lose you into the river on the first one."

"I have aloe in the truck, and if you hadn't kissed me into stupidity, I'd have been fine." He winked, playing with his Sir.

"I regret it completely. I'll never do it again." Damn, Sir actually pulled off a straight face on that one.

"That would be a shame. Your kisses are..." He didn't have words for the way Saul made him feel.

Saul winked. "A lot like yours, apparently."

"I hope so." This felt a lot like flirting, like getting to know each other.

"I enjoyed the yoga this morning. I thought I'd feel all clumsy and clueless, but I didn't feel that way at all. You're a good teacher."

"Thank you. A lot of people think yoga is competitive,

but it's about listening to your body and your breath. When I started, I was just worried about tight hamstrings."

"I'm not very good at listening to my body usually. I've always got bruises. I've broken practically everything, including other people's bikes, as you probably know."

"Yes." Carter had been livid, so the rumor went, but when he'd found out Saul was a bike store manager, things got way calmer. "He loves his bike. I should get one again; I used to love riding."

Saul's eyes lit up and he turned into a kid right before his eyes. "Yeah? Let me build it for you? I can make whatever you want. I put a lot of mea culpa into that bike of Carter's. I felt like a first-class asshole. Did you ride street or mountain?"

"Street when I was a kid, of course, but I had a mountain bike here. I don't even know why I stopped, really." Sure he did. He'd met a kid that needed transportation to school, one of the dishwashers. "I would be honored if you would, Master. Honestly."

"Next week... uh, next Tuesday when you're off and I'm working, you come in and we'll talk shop. It'll be fun." Saul took one more bite and leaned back from the table. "Oh. That was yummy. Thank you."

"You're more than welcome. This has been a great day. Thank you." He reached over and squeezed Saul's hand.

"So far. It's not even over yet." Saul squeezed back and leaned over to kiss him across the table. "We still have to clean up the dishes."

"I have the bucket filled up with water." He stood and started gathering dishes, the routine of washing and cleaning, putting the world to right almost as good as his practice.

Sir moved around him easily, drying dishes and stowing

things away with lots of little touches and smiles as they worked. They may still have been learning each other, but the contact came naturally to both of them.

"French toast tomorrow?" Saul hung the dish towel to dry on the clothesline he'd strung from the truck to a nearby tree trunk.

His French toast addict. "Yes, Sir. I'd be happy to."

"Awesome. So listen, we have to talk about your yoga practice." Saul raised a hand and laughed. "That didn't... it's not ominous. Pull up a chair by the fire with me?"

His yoga practice? Huh.

"Yes, Sir. Would you like a blanket?" He was going to need one, for sure.

"Sure. Thanks." Saul started moving their chairs closer to the fire.

He grabbed a couple of old blankets from the truck, along with the sticks he'd whittled to points earlier and the bag of marshmallows for later.

He settled in the chair, wrapped himself up, and forced himself to relax. Sir had said nothing ominous, right?

"Breathe boy, it's good stuff, I swear. It's just, like, timing and diligence and things." Saul had set their chairs close and Sir reached for his hand.

Troy took it, rubbing slow circles on Saul's knuckles with his thumb. "Diligence is something I happen to excel at."

Practice, practice, practice.

"Well, good. Because I don't always. Maybe you can help me then." Saul smiled. "Okay. So here's the thing. As a Dom, I think discipline for a sub is important. I think atonement is also important. Obviously, the traditional way these things are done is with rituals—some kind of devotion in the morning and stripes for missteps at night, something like that. Do you have experience with this? Did you have something in place with Arnie?"

"Not so much experience, Sir, but I've seen it; I understand it. My relationship with Arnie was... different." He didn't elaborate because Saul didn't want to know, but his time with Arnie involved a lot of time on his knees and making sure no one suspected. "I did have a bag of stones with him. It was the same basic idea."

God, he remembered that, so clear. Arnie had been a small man, birdlike, and he'd felt gangly and awkward kneeling naked on a shitty comforter. He'd been hard as nails, willing to accept anything if Arn would just love him.

Arn had held out a little leather bag to him and told him to take it.

"There are ten polished stones in there, boy. I take one for every fuck up. Give one back when you please me. You understand?"

"Yes, Sir."

"Good. Remember, though, you ever make me empty this bag, we're done. That's it. You're out."

"Yes, Sir." He hadn't wanted to take the bag, but he had, and he'd never lost more than a half dozen stones.

He'd buried the stones with Arnie; the leather bag was in his dresser drawer, emptied.

He blinked and caught Saul's eyes on him.

"Where'd you go? Tell me about the bag of stones."

"I was a million miles away. I used to have a bag with stones in it. I lost one for every mistake and worked to get them back, so I get it."

"For every mistake? Like, every day?" Saul was watching him closely.

"Yeah. I guess. I mean, I don't know." He'd never known exactly what the rules were with Arnie. They were... flexible.

Saul took his hand. "And how did you... earn them back?"

"Mostly blowjobs. Lots of blowjobs. Keeping my mouth shut when Arnie was driving. Uh... I just made sure to not piss him off, please him." He grinned at Saul, holding on. "Don't worry. I never ran out."

"I—okay..." That didn't seem to make Saul feel any better. "But what would have happened if you'd run out?"

"Everything was over."

"You mean the scene?"

"I mean the... affair. I didn't, though. I never once did. Not even close." He was good. Genuinely.

Saul was silent long enough that it became uncomfortable, but finally gave his hand a squeeze. "This isn't an affair. There's nothing you could do that would just end this outright. You don't have to earn anything to stay with me. I want you to know that."

"I—" Fuck. Fuck, what could he say that wasn't disrespectful to Arnie? He couldn't handle that again. He'd seen how it could be with the other guys; he couldn't go back. "You're not Arnie."

He got a serious nod, but then Saul smiled. "I'm not at all." Saul took a deep breath and squeezed his hand. "All good?"

"Yes, Sir. I'm solid as a rock." He stifled the laugh, because he was afraid if it got loose it would sound closer to hysteria than humor.

"I hope so. There's no reason not to be." Sir's hand was strong and steady holding his. "Okay, so here's where I need your help. This morning I had the idea that I would let you earn stripes today and then we'd talk about them and you'd take them for me tonight. That's one pretty common way

Doms deal with atonement. A lot of them call it punishment. But..."

Saul watched the fire for a breath or two. "It doesn't feel good to me now that the day's gone by. Nothing about you as a sub makes me think you'd respond positively to punishment. Also, you already have a morning and evening ritual, and I want to be respectful of that. So I'm trying to think how you can keep your ritual whole, and we can still incorporate affirmation and atonement into our day. You see what I'm getting at?"

"I think so?" He liked the words 'our day'. He liked them a lot. "I'm not sure I'm any help, but I think I understand what you're saying. We are trying to start each day whole, new, without yesterday's problems following us."

"Yes, that's exactly it. I don't want a bad day to make us worry the next won't be a good one. And I want you to be able to atone and get tools to do better if I'm not satisfied. I don't want that pain you need to be a negative thing, ever. It's sacred. It's not a punishment." Saul snorted. "I'm rambling. Sorry. It just feels so important to me right now."

"Don't be sorry. Please." He was forty-five years old and he'd been lonely for most of his life. He liked listening to Saul work things out. It made him feel like he was a part of something. "I appreciate it—both the not using pain as a punishment and that..." He swallowed hard, because it shouldn't be weird that he needed, not after so long, but the cowboy in him insisted it might be fucked up. One way or the other, though, fucked or not, he wasn't going to be a shrinking violet. *Own it.* That was what he told the younger subs. *Own your shit.* "...that you appreciate how much I need this—from the service to the pain to the sex to surrendering control."

"I do And, well. I'm really grateful for it I guess because I don't really want to know what I'd be if I hadn't found an outlet for..." Saul glanced at his free hand, flipped it over, made a fist. "This. The rules and the rituals are important, so it stays purposeful and doesn't become something wild."

"I've spent twenty years learning that." He hadn't had someone to work with, but he wasn't a stupid man.

"It's kind of *the* big lesson, right?" Saul glanced at him and smiled. "Okay. I don't think the morning will be an issue, I have an idea there, but what about at night? There's all that breathing and focusing in your yoga practice right? Is there a way we could weave something in? I guess you're not really supposed to talk though. Hm."

"Master? Yoga doesn't have supposed to. Practice changes every day, depending on what I—what we—need. Some nights can be vigorous, exhausting if we need. Practice can be sensual, relaxing, energizing." Troy stroked Saul's hand. "Some days I have to spend an hour just trying to open my chest, when I realize I'm hunching and I haven't been able to talk to anyone. I spent two years learning a headstand for my practice, every night." Was he even making sense?

"Really? That makes me feel a little less like a bull in a china shop. I thought it was supposed to be all Zen and quiet. Maybe we could figure something out then." The fire popped and the logs collapsed, and Saul let his hand go to pick up a stick and poke at the pile of logs. "Whatever we do I just want it to be us. I'm not just your Dom and you're not just my sub. We're more than that, too."

"We are. We're lovers. I haven't been in love for a while. I thought maybe I'd forgotten how." In all the things he'd done in his life, and he'd done a lot, this might be the hardest, to bare his heart, his soul.

"I've never been. I just realized this morning how hard

I'm falling." Saul looked away from the fire and smiled at him. "I thought I was supposed to be all nervous about it but I'm not. I'm loving this ride."

"Good. I thought I was supposed to be quiet, you know? I feel a little like my world is lighter." Like his universe was opened to something new.

"That's the point." Saul tossed his stick into the fire and knelt in front of his chair. "It's how this is supposed to work. And about the best compliment you could give me right now."

He reached out, cupping Saul's face. "My heart is racing, Master."

"Mine too. I think it's a good thing." Saul kissed his palm, then his wrist, then his lips just gently. "You're good for me. I can't explain it but I *know* it, I feel it every morning when I wake up."

Troy couldn't stop smiling. There wasn't a bit of sorrow inside him right now.

"I love it when you smile. Show me how we celebrate a good day."

"Marshmallows?" he teased, rubbing their noses together.

Saul laughed. "Wait. Is it still yoga if we sit on our mats and chat and eat marshmallows?"

"So long as we remember to breathe..."

"Never happen." Sir was still giggling. "Can we make worship part of our nighttime practice? You know, of each other?" Saul slipped a hand under his shirt.

"Yes, Sir. I could spend hours worshipping you." His Master's hand was cold, and his entire body woke up.

The chilly fingers found his piercing and gave it a tug. "You bank the fire and I'll make the bed. And if you want some time on the mats before bed, with or without me, just speak up. Always speak up."

"Yes, Sir." He licked his lips, his eyes crossing as that tug happened again, hard, sure.

"Good boy." Saul's hand traveled from his chest to the bulge in his jeans that had been with him all day, and then Saul stood and headed for the tent. "Very good boy."

19

S aul locked up the bike shop over an hour late, after one of the busiest days they'd had all summer. Emma had a date, so she'd left at about six, but it was coming up on seven thirty now. Late summer was damn good for business.

He leaned on his bike and pulled out his phone to text Troy a little love. *Thinking about you, so is my dick.*

It took longer than he'd expected to get an answer, Troy sending him a heart.

Hearts were good, though. *What's for dinner?* He knew Troy liked to bring something from the grill home. He also knew it was usually a patty melt and a hundred French fries but he liked to ask anyway.

I'll order you something.

Wait. No. Troy only ate one meal a day; Saul knew that. He wasn't going to let his boy not eat. And he never saw Troy on Saturdays, that was their agreement. So was that an invitation? Sometimes he wished this was easier.

You want me to come over? I'll bring food.

Another pause, then his phone rang.

"Master?" His boy's voice sounded... weak. Rough.

"I'm here."

"I'm having a shit day. You got a minute?"

A shit day wasn't going to get better being alone and without food. And a big piece of him was surprised and relieved that Troy had even told him. "I have all the time you need. Can I come over?" He could leave his bike inside the shop and take the bus.

"Do you want me to come pick you up?" That was a definite yes.

Jesus this was some bad day. Made his long one look easy. "It's faster than the bus. I just locked up the shop. Are you okay to drive?"

"Yes, Sir. I was considering smoking a joint, but I'd be at the convenience store buying a pack of smokes, so I'm sober."

"Good choice, boy. I'll wait right here. Please breathe and drive carefully." Maybe his boy could have a supervised smoke later. "Okay? Breathe."

That actually got him a soft laugh. "Yes, Sir. In and out. I'll be right there."

Okay. He needed to breathe himself. His lover, his boy needed him. He walked his bike back to the shop and put it inside, grabbed a couple of bottles of water, and locked up again. It was a nice evening and he didn't mind waiting out in it at all.

Troy pulled up and offered him a wan smile through the open window. "Hey, stranger."

His boy seemed so tired, unhappy, drawn, hat pulled down low to shadow his face.

"Hey, you. Slide over. I'll drive." He handed Troy one of the waters through the window and opened the driver's side door.

"Thank you, Sir." Troy scooted over, moving stiffly.

It would take some maneuvering to lean over and kiss Troy, not to mention he'd have to mess with that hat, so for now he just put a hand on his boy's thigh. "You're okay. Drink some water."

"I am. It's just been a shit day, all day long."

He pulled away from the curb and headed toward Troy's place. "I'm sorry. That sucks. Was work crazy?"

"Yes. God, yes. The shipment didn't come in until late. I burned the fuck out of my hand, and—" Troy stopped, sighed. "Sorry."

"For what? I asked, I want to know. Go ahead and vent. Is your hand okay?" He tried to glance at it, but it was in shadow and he was driving so he couldn't get a good look. He pushed the speed limit a little just to get Troy home, he wanted to be where he could get his arms around his boy, see what was in those green eyes.

"There's a blister, but it wasn't serious. Nothing's been serious, but I'm so fucking aggravated!"

Jesus. There was a lot of emotion in that one sentence. Troy was pretty worked up, and he decided to help his boy get it out for now. Just get it all said. "I hear that. What happened with the shipment?"

"Someone fucked up the order, and I won't name names, but my fucking signature wasn't on the invoice. It was a mistake, and I get that, but God fucking forbid anyone take notice, or you're on the boss' radar all damn day."

So Carter was in a mood. Great. "Can't say I haven't been there. It sucks. You think you were actually on his radar, or did you just kind of feel that way, you know? Like you didn't want to add to his mistake?"

"If he got on my ass about my hair, one more time, I was fixin' to pop him in the mouth. He made the mistake, own it.

I hate that, you know? If I fuck up, I'm expected to be a man about it, take responsibility. How hard is that?"

"Not hard, man. Not hard at all." The gray area here was that Troy was an employee but also a sub, and Carter was Dom but also Troy's boss, and they were like family too... wow. It was so tangled up he decided he'd just lighten things a bit. He grinned at Troy. "Working for family is a complicated business."

"No shit on that, honey." Troy nodded and took a deep, deep breath. "And it builds, don't it? One tiny thing after another."

"Sure. And then something stupid you said over a beer becomes something you pay for in the kitchen at work the next morning. And then a month later it comes up in an argument. I totally get that." He turned into Troy's neighborhood and headed up the quiet street. "You think there's been something building?"

"I—" Troy pursed his lips and shook his head. "I don't know."

"That's not a no." He pulled into Troy's driveway and hit the remote to open the garage door.

"I don't have a better answer for you. I'm sorry."

He shut the truck off, handed the keys back to Troy, and closed the garage door. "Okay. Let's go sit on the couch. Want to?"

"Yes, Sir. Please."

He wondered what not having a better answer meant but there wasn't any point in pushing right now. He waited for Troy to open the door, crowding his boy a little as they went inside. "I'm gonna kick my sneaks off okay?" He toed them off by the stairs. "So we can get comfy."

"Kick away. You want a drink?" Troy hung his hat up near the door and offered him a smile.

Did he? He had no idea what Troy was going to need tonight. This was one of those places that the full time thing kicked his ass every time. Were they going to work? Did he need to be sober? Or could he have a beer?

It kind of felt like a normal day could turn into anything at any time.

He wanted a piece of that smile more than he wanted a beer anyway. He tugged Troy closer and kissed him. "Just a Coke, thanks."

"Yes, Sir." Troy rested their foreheads together. "Hey. I'm glad to see you."

He nodded against Troy's forehead and cupped the nape of his boy's neck. "I'm glad you called me. It feels good that you... I want to be what you need." It felt strange to say he needed to be needed, but it was true, and it wouldn't serve either of them not to be honest.

"You are. I'm surprised your ears weren't burning all day."

"I was slammed busy. We closed over an hour late and I handled the last hour by myself. Probably if I hadn't been so distracted I'd have felt something." He winked.

"Wow. Late summer rush?" Troy straightened up and headed for the kitchen.

"Every year. We run a sale, so it's part mountain bikes for fall runs and part back-to-school."

"Yeah, we're having a little rush of tourists." Troy led him to the sofa and sat close. It felt good, the way Troy was showing his need.

"Hey." He put an arm around Troy's back. "So, the hand, work... I'm sure you've handled worse days. What tipped it over for you? You look kind of fried."

"I am. I couldn't center this morning for love or money. All I wanted in all the world was to crawl back into the bed."

"You think maybe going away for those two days was too much?"

"No. I've..." Troy sighed and rested against him. "It's Arnie's birthday. I always head out to the cemetery, but... I didn't want to. He's not there."

"You usually do, but you decided not to this year?" That was interesting.

"Yeah." Troy sat up and pulled away like he'd been stung. "I didn't want to."

"Why not?" He felt like if he moved too quickly or followed Troy too closely the boy would spook, so he let Troy have the space, but watched carefully.

"Because I did for twenty years. Isn't that long enough? He's not there." Troy sighed and dropped his head into his hands. "What do you want for supper?"

Troy liked routines and rituals; he knew that. They were comforting, he assumed. There was only one reason Troy would change up a twenty-year long routine now. This year. The timing wasn't a coincidence, it had something to do with him.

"I don't know what's long enough, I've never lost anyone so close to me."

Was it grief? Guilt?

"What do you think you can stomach?"

"I want something... shit, I don't know. Do you think I'm an asshole? I mean, I loved the son of a bitch. He was a good guy, but..."

He wanted to answer that question but he wanted to know what came after that 'but' too. "You're not an asshole. But what? If you look at it from my perspective, it was literally a lifetime ago."

"I mourned him a long time. I was your age when he died. Everyone deserves to move on." Troy stood, his boy stiff, angry. "I didn't want to be in a graveyard talking to a ghost. I want you."

Shit. What was the right thing to do? Go to him? Give him space? Saul didn't understand the anger. Was this a normal grief thing?

How would he know? "I want you too."

"Good." The single word held so much emotion. So much need.

That got him moving. He stood and put his arms around his boy, pulling Troy in whether it was what the boy wanted or not. "Why are you so angry? Isn't it okay to have both? Why can't you miss him and love me too?"

"It is. I do. Someone made a smartassed comment and pissed me off."

Someone.

Troy had said Carter was on his case about his hair. "You mean Carter?" Troy had only just started growing it, and Saul assumed Troy's friends would rib him a little about it. It would probably be obvious that Saul had asked; why else grow it after all that time?

"Yeah. It shouldn't have been a big deal, but goddamn it, it felt like a big fucking deal."

He wouldn't say it where Troy could hear him, but he wondered if that wasn't more about him giving the orders now than about Troy's hair. Old habits die hard, his mom always said.

"Will you tell me what he said?"

"When I said I wasn't going to go to the cemetery he said that he guessed you could teach old dogs new tricks."

Saul sighed and held Troy at arm's length. "Hey. All of you need to stop talking like you have one foot in the grave. You're not old, baby. You have no trouble keeping up with me. And you're the hottest man I've ever seen. I mean that. You're beautiful."

"I loved him, but he's gone. I didn't know you were out there, but you are, and you make me so fucking happy."

He smiled and pulled his boy in for a kiss. One of those kisses that Troy made feel so important, like nothing meant more in the world. Those words made him feel like his heart might burst right out of his chest. He'd never had a man keep his whole focus before, he hadn't known one person could be enough—could be everything—until Troy.

His boy melted into him, holding him tight, the kiss going deeper as Troy opened.

Maybe he could be enough for Troy, too. He didn't have as much experience, and he'd never even want to try to catch up to what Troy and Arnie had obviously had together, but he paid attention, and he loved Troy. Maybe that would make up for being young and dumb.

Their kiss was almost enough to make him believe it.

Troy kissed his jaw, his cheek, his temple. "Thank you for coming. I needed you."

"Thank you for trusting me. I'll do my best to live up to it, I promise." Everything about this felt good. Not that his boy was hurting, but that Troy seemed better, that he felt like he had this. He could see he was helping.

"I believe you." Troy let Saul hold him, support him, and it felt amazing.

He didn't let go for a long while and it didn't feel awkward at all. He realized after a couple of minutes that they'd started breathing together, kind of like they did in yoga practice, just breathing each other in and letting out the tension and the worry.

"How do you feel about pizza?" He asked finally, loosening his grip on his boy a little.

"Sounds perfect. What kind?" Troy straightened up, relaxing for him.

"Veggies, whatever. I'm easy." He gave Troy a pat on the backside.

"Me too." Troy wiggled for him, flirting just the barest bit.

He snorted. "Jesus Christ. No kidding." Flirting, teasing, that was good stuff. He watched Troy call in the pizza, polite as anything and even managing a smile.

Having him there didn't change certain facts, though. Carter had still been an ass, it was still Arnie's birthday, and Troy still looked exhausted. Pizza wasn't going to make those dark circles go away.

As soon as Troy hung up, he held out one hand and Troy came right to him. "All ordered. They're busy. It'll be an hour."

An hour. Okay. Troy needed out of his head. "I'd like to sit out back, boy. It's nice night. Bring something to kneel on." He kissed Troy's temple and went after his Coke.

Troy followed him, grabbing one of the yoga mats that was rolled by the door. The fairy lights were just flickering on, the sun beginning to set.

He settled outside with Troy at his feet. "I want you to settle and see if you can find a good space. If your day starts creeping in, don't fight it, just breathe through it. You can be silent, you can talk if you like—as freely as you like—whatever. I'm here."

"Yes, Sir." Troy spread out the mat, moving carefully, as if he was trying to focus on every single motion.

"That's it boy. I like how mindful you are. In fact, if you'd prefer to stretch and try to center I would be fine with that." Why not, right? What he wanted for Troy was to settle, however it happened was fine.

"Thank you, Sir. I feel like the world has shifted under my feet." Troy took a deep breath, arms lifting, lowering with his exhale.

"Maybe it has. Maybe the new road will be better." Saul reached down and rubbed the top of his boy's fuzzy head, the new hair growing in slowly. He wouldn't make Troy keep it if the boy didn't like it, but how would they know until it grew?

"It's curly." Troy pushed into the touch like a cat having a scritch.

"Is it? I can't wait to see it. I hope it's not a real pain, growing it in. It's cool if you don't like it, just so you know."

"I grew it for ten years. I loved it. I'll show you a picture later." Troy blinked up at him. "Can I rest my head in your lap, Sir? Just for a minute?"

That made him smile. "Go ahead. As long as you like."

"Thank you." Troy moved closer, resting against him, and God, it felt good. He could feel Troy soaking up his presence, his care.

"I like this. Are you tired? You look pretty exhausted." He hadn't realized how much the contact was what they needed.

"Yeah. Yes, Sir. I feel like I've run the gauntlet today."

"You haven't eaten anything, that doesn't help. We'll get you fed and showered and then I'm putting you to bed." He should stay again, which meant another 5:00 a.m. Uber home when Troy left for work. The early trek home was starting to wear on him a bit, but Troy could be a restless sleeper, and if he didn't stay, the boy might not sleep at all.

"Can you stay? You can take the truck, if you want. I walk to work anyway."

"Happy to stay." He didn't have anywhere to park the truck, but he wasn't going to get into all of that now. He wanted to anyway, he wanted to keep his arms around his boy.

"Thank you." Troy dropped a kiss on his thigh. "It's so easy, getting used to sleeping with you."

"I'd much rather sleep beside you than alone anyway. But tonight especially, I know you need me, and I want to stay with you." He told himself the early morning would be worth it.

"I want you to stay too." One of Troy's hands wrapped around his ankle, holding on tight.

Saul wondered how Troy was going to be able to work tomorrow. Another full day with Carter on him about everything? "Do you get sick time? What happens if you can't make it into work?"

"I don't know."

Wait. What? How long had Troy worked there? "Haven't you ever missed a day?"

"No, Sir. Not once."

That didn't even make sense. "Why not? I mean, are you never sick? Are you worried about your job?" How do you not miss a single day of work in twenty years?

"I don't get sick often, no, and I didn't have a lot of reasons to skip work, I guess."

"You might have a reason tomorrow." If ever a sanity day was called for, tomorrow was the day. "Think about it."

He'd never do it, but he really wished he could order the boy to stay home.

"Yes, Sir."

Every time he stroked Troy's soft stubble, his boy relaxed deeper against him.

"I really do like it back here. The lights and everything. Do you sit out here a lot?"

"I do. I love it. It's my magical space. Stupid, I know."

"Why do you say that?"

Troy snorted, cheek heating against his thigh. "I guess because having a magical hidey-hole doesn't sound real macho?"

"Macho?" He wondered if that a Texas thing, a cowboy thing or both. "Macho isn't high on my priority list. Magic is interesting though."

"Yeah. You know this is my first place that I lived alone? I was fucking terrified the first few nights, and I slept out here, telling myself I was just camping."

He tucked his hand around Troy's shoulder and gave it a squeeze. That sounded so horribly lonely. "How long did it take you to buy the place after you moved here?"

"Lord... I stayed with Geoff and Carter for nine months, give or take." Troy looked up at him, grinned. "I swear to God, I needed to move out, but a part of me just wanted to stay."

He got that. Geoff and Carter were pretty much Troy's whole world. That was changing, part of him was actively trying to change it. Hopefully Troy was good with that. "I've never lived alone."

"No? You got a ton of roommates, huh?"

"Three buddies from college, though we're all doing different things now. Open-minded guys, if you know what I mean. But a lot of bodies in one place."

"Yeah. I been there a few times—living with a bunch of folks. It's tough, sometimes." Troy took a deep breath. "You know, I never thought about asking someone to come stay with me. Never."

Saul blinked and froze for a second. Was Troy asking or just supposing? Did "stay" mean move in or crash? Should he worry that he was totally ready to say yes? "No?"

"No, Sir. I'm asking you, though. If you'd like to come and share with me, I'd love to have you here."

Troy was brave as hell, wasn't he? Because it had to mean something, to make the offer, not knowing the answer.

"I... Yes, I want to. I'd love that, but are you sure? It's only been a few weeks, you know? Can we do that? Is it weird? Like, too soon, weird?"

"I'm not an authority in what's not weird, but I figure we're both over twenty-one—some of us more than others—and we can do what we want."

He nodded, letting Troy's confidence convince him. "I'm in. And I'm glad you asked. I was trying hard not to dread another early morning Uber ride."

Troy lifted his face to smile at him. "I'm glad you said yes. It'll be good, having you beside me every night."

"It will. I—" Troy's doorbell rang, and he gave his boy a pat on the shoulder. "Pizza?"

"Yes, Sir." Troy pushed himself up into a downward dog, before hopping up to where his feet met his hands. "I just got to find my wallet."

"Mine's in my backpack on the stairs if you want." Hm. Rent. Utilities. Groceries. Beer. They had some things to talk about. And then there was the longer commute to work. The actual move wasn't going to be an issue; everything he owned would fit in Troy's truck no problem.

It didn't take long for Troy to come back with the box. "Do you need another Coke, Sir?"

"I'm good. Thank you." His stomach growled loudly. Apparently, food would be good for both of them. "I'm ready for dinner though." He sat up and helped Troy with the plates.

"I bet. You worked your ass off today, you said."

"I did." And he hadn't gotten lunch, which, now that he

thought about it, ought to have been a clue about Troy's day. Damn. He needed to pay better attention. "It was a good day though. Just busy." He served up a slice for Troy. "Sit and eat. Maybe we'll turn in early."

"Yes, Sir. I could just go rest with you and watch stupid TV." Troy was easy to please.

He laughed. "That sounds great. It really does." He loved just holding Troy, the way he could feel his boy relax in his arms. He didn't need to ask if Troy if he was helping, he knew. He could feel it.

Saul waited to make sure Troy was eating before he took a bite of his pizza. It tasted like heaven, honestly. "Mm. Yummy."

"You have to have the right oven to make pizza, I think." Troy took another bite, humming softly. "It's a skill set all on its own."

"Yeah? I just know what I like. I'll leave the complicated cook stuff to the pros." He winked at Troy. "You needed to eat."

"I think so. I don't know. I sure wasn't hungry." Troy winked at him. "Stupid sandpaper day."

He was annoyed with Carter, but he still didn't know where he fit into that relationship. He wasn't going to step in between a boss and his employee, but he wasn't sure Carter recognized a line anymore. He knew Geoff didn't. All three of them were just used to what they had, operating by habit. But he was Troy's Dom now and some of those habits were his business.

"You look like you might survive it." He grinned at his boy. "Maybe."

"Possibly. If I'm lucky." Troy teased right back.

"You're lucky." He wasn't blowing his own horn, though maybe it sounded that way. At the moment he felt lucky that he managed to be what Troy needed after a day from hell. He didn't give a damn about the age difference, but just like how Troy had made a single kiss feel like it mattered, his boy made him feel like everything mattered. Troy was deeper. Troy was... mature. Things with Troy had more meaning. And the opportunity to fuck up seemed more real. So far it seemed like he was doing okay. "We both are."

"Yes, Sir. We really are." Troy reached out and squeezed his leg.

Well, he was just going to have to eat his pizza one-handed because he liked that hand there, and he covered it with his own to make sure it stayed put. "You're a good boy." And a good friend, and a great lover, and a lot of things he'd never had all in one person before.

"Thank you." Troy smiled, relaxed and easy in his skin.

There. That's what he wanted to see. *Take that, bad day*.

They sucked down most of the pizza and goofed around while they cleaned up. He had Troy grab a couple of waters before they went upstairs to the bedroom for their snuggle and bad TV night, and he gave that sweet ass a pinch as he chased it up the stairs. "Feeling better, cowboy?"

"Yes, Sir. I truly am. Thank you ever so."

"You're welcome. I'm happy you called, that you felt like you needed me, wanted me to come over. It was good, you know?" He plucked the water bottles out of Troy's hands as they went into the bedroom and set them next to the bed.

"I do. You were the only one that could make it better."

He smiled and slipped an arm around Troy's waist to pull his boy in. "I'm not making any hard moves here, but I've been waiting since before dinner just to kiss you."

Troy offered over his lips, the expression sweet as hell. "I'm all yours."

Saul nodded, believing every word. He took his kiss, not

needing or even wanting more than Troy had energy for, just craving a little taste. Wanting their connection. They breathed together, sharing their air, their focus, and Saul could feel their energies connecting.

That was another new thing Troy had given him. That energy, that awareness. He kind of basked in it a while, soaking in what his boy was giving him, letting it fill him up and make him smile until it bubbled over and he started giggling.

Troy's smile seemed to hold secrets. He loved it.

He gave Troy one more peck and leaned back to peer into those green eyes, still chuckling. "All right, troublemaker. What are we watching? Boomerang? The Cowboy Channel? Wait, I know. Food Network, right?"

"It's Saturday. Ghost hunting night."

"Oh, right on." He stepped back and tugged his shirt off over his head, then tossed it into a corner before stripping out of his jeans. "I'm a sucker for those shows. I fall for everything. We can be creeped out together."

"I knew I was attracted to you for a reason." Troy pulled the sheets back before stripping down, baring himself.

"Which, that I fall for everything? Or that I'm a *sucker*?" He laughed at his really bad pun as he climbed into Troy's bed. He was reminded for a minute of the Saturday nights in college that he'd spent three or four or more in a hotel room fooling around and watching porn. Good times. He didn't really miss them, though. This way better.

Even the view was better. Troy was solid and lean, and sexy as hell.

"That you'll watch ghost hunting shows with me and snuggle. I've been waiting for you."

"Aw. Come here." He held his arms out. "I wonder, you

know? If all the rest of it was so we could have this. This is kind of the best part."

"I love that idea." Troy came right to him, burrowing into his arms.

He stuck the remote in Troy's fingers and hugged his lover close. "Right? Me too." He watched as the TV came on and Troy messed with the channels feeling pretty ready to shut his brain off for a while and just enjoy Troy's company.

Troy's cheek rested on his chest, and they both settled, the spooky music and melodrama filling the air.

20

Troy woke up with vicious heartburn and a throbbing head. All he wanted in all the world was to stay in bed and sleep.

He sat up, the room spinning, and dropped his head in his hands. "Goddamn."

"Whassup?" Saul asked sleepily, sitting up beside him. "Oh. Headache?" A warm hand landed on his neck and started massaging.

"Uh-huh." Oh God. That felt so good. "Please."

Please don't stop.

"That bad?" Saul shifted around behind him and started working his neck with both hands.

"Yeah. Just throbbing and like to split."

Saul stopped just long enough to hand him some water and then went back to rubbing, Sir's fingers finding spots that made fireworks go off behind his eyelids. "Did we stay up too late maybe? Do you have Advil or Tylenol or something? Tell me where, I'll get it for you."

"Excedrin Migraine in the medicine cabinet, please."

Saul climbed around him carefully and got up,

returning with the bottle. He could hear it rattling in Saul's fingers and then the top pop off. "How many?"

"Four." He was hurting. Bad. Bad enough that he could see his heart beating behind his eyelids.

"Jesus, that sounds bad. You're pale too. Do you get migraines usually?" Saul put four pills in his hand.

"I don't think so." He just got headaches. He popped the pills into his mouth and swallowed them dry, swearing that he heard them clicking all the way down.

"You've got water, baby. Right in your hands." Saul tapped the bottle and then took the cap off for him. "Drink it down." Saul moved around him again and went back to rubbing.

He drank deep, the cold water splashing in his belly. Oh fuck.

"You should lie down again. What time do you have to be at work?" He felt his lover trying to coax him back down into the pillows. "Come on. Lie down."

"Today is Sunday? Six." He stretched out, not even caring what time it was.

"Baby, it's already five-twenty. You need to call out. Or at least say you'll be late and give the meds time to work." Saul shifted and stretched out beside him. "You... you want me to call?"

Did he want Saul to? Fuck yes, but that was cowardly, and he wasn't a titty baby. "I'll do it."

He sighed and forced himself to sit back up. *Come on. Focus. Phone. Carter.*

He hit 2 on his phone and waited for Carter to answer. "If the place has burned down, just call me later."

"I'm sick, boss." There was no way Carter was going to be okay with this.

"Too bad. You're my only cook. You're coming in."

"I'm—"

"Look. I know you have a new, hot lover. That's great. But if he wears your ass out, you deal. You don't call in sick on Sundays. Period."

"Back off, man." He stood, grabbing a pair of jeans. He couldn't stop shaking — whether from fury or pain, he wasn't sure. "Don't you snarl at me."

"Troy? Whoa. Whoa! Hey." Saul followed him, hands gently fighting with him, trying to get him to let go of the jeans. "You need to get back in bed."

"He's there. I knew it. Tell your baby Dom you're an adult and adults don't play hooky to stay in bed like college students do."

He felt like Carter just poured ice water over him, and for a second he couldn't quite breathe. He turned off the phone without another word and turned to Saul. "I have to go in. There's no one else."

"Baby, you can't even... are you kidding? What did he say to you? He can't find anyone else?"

"Yeah. He's still hiring people." No way on earth would he hurt Saul's feelings. Not a chance. Baby Dom his ass.

Something flashed in Saul's eyes but then his lover let his jeans go and sighed. "What can I do? You want coffee?"

"Please." He wanted to go back to bed, to have Saul hold him, but Carter was part right. He was a grownup; this was his job.

"Okay. I'll... go make some. Put that Excedrin in your pocket." Saul kissed him and left the room.

He sat down to put his jeans on, a cold sweat shaking him. Dammit. He was hurting, and he felt a little like he was fixin' to hurl.

"All you have to do is get dressed. Once you get moving, you'll feel better." All he had to do was convince himself.

It took him damn near five minutes to get dressed and another five to make it down the stairs. Thank God Saul was in the kitchen.

"Jesus, Troy. You look awful. Are you sure you can do this?" Saul handed him a mug of coffee. "I'm kind of worried about you."

"Thank you, honey. I'm kind of worried about me too." He found a smile, though, even though he didn't mean it. "Nine hours and I have two days off, right?"

"Nine hours. If you can't handle it, you have to tell Carter, okay? I'll come over when I get off work and we'll get you feeling better." Saul glanced around the room. "Shit, I better get dressed. Why don't you let me drive you? That's something anyway, right? You don't need to walk."

"I'll make it. Thank you, though. Please, take the truck, huh? You'll need it more than me."

"I guess it will get me back here faster tonight. I have to figure out where to park it. Let me just run up and get clothes on." Saul bounded up the stairs, taking two at a time. He hadn't had three sips off his coffee before his lover reappeared, dressed.

He handed Saul the spare truck keys, before heading for the little hidden drawer in his desk and digging out a house key. "Here you go. Truck keys. House keys."

Saul stared at him for a second and took the key to his house. "Wow. Thanks. I mean, yeah. Thank you." Saul pressed a hand against his jaw and kissed him. There was a whole lot of Dom about it and not a bit of baby. "You take care of yourself today."

"I will. All I have to do is get through today, right?" He rubbed their noses together. "See you later."

He headed out into the early dawn without waiting for Saul. He knew his Master needed to get to his apartment, change, and get to work. Troy marched across the park, shivering as he forced himself to hurry.

About halfway there, he frowned, a crushing pain slamming through his left arm. He reached for his phone, but somehow he couldn't reach it from where he was on the grass.

Oh.

"Please. I need..." Help. He needed help.

21

S aul stood in the middle of Troy's living room for a long while just looking around and running his fingers over the house key.

When that didn't seem to lend him one ounce of clarity he got in the shower. He had a key now, he could lock up any time.

This situation was seriously screwed up. Carter still only had one weekend cook? And after twenty years of coming in every single day without ever calling out, Carter didn't understand Troy wouldn't do it if it wasn't the real deal.

Giving the guy the benefit of the doubt, maybe Carter was panicking and when he got a good look at Troy he'd realize his *friend* really needed to be in bed. Right? There was still that chance.

It wasn't his place to interfere with Troy's livelihood. He understood that. But this was something else. Carter had strong-armed his boy, something he felt was way beyond an employer's right to do.

Kind of more like what a Dom might do.

And where exactly did that leave him? Did he need to set Carter straight?

His shower was long, and when he got out, he pulled on some clean shorts and a T-shirt he'd stuffed into one of the drawers Troy had cleaned out for him, then headed downstairs to have another cup of coffee before he left.

He was about halfway through it when the door to the condo started shaking violently, someone banging on it hard.

What the fuck?

"Who's there?" he shouted through the door, hand hovering over the deadbolt. "Troy?"

"It's Troy's fucking boss! Where is he? Open the damn door!"

Wait. What?

He flipped the lock and yanked the door open. "What the hell is your problem, Carter?"

"He hangs up on me and doesn't open the restaurant? He could have at least told me to fuck off."

"Oh, bullshit Carter. He left like forty minutes ago. He's there." He held his ground and didn't let Carter over the threshold.

"What? I just left the place. He's not there." Carter frowned at him. "Are you sure he's not here?"

"He has to be." Had to be. Where else would Troy go? "He hurried out of here, left me his key. He was headed straight there, I swear. If he's not there, where is he?" The expression on his face must have convinced Carter because the man's expression changed. Saul's heart started pounding. "He... he was really sick, Carter. Really sick."

"Call the hospitals. I'll trace his path. Maybe he passed out."

"I'm calling." He pulled his cell phone from his pocket so

fast he dropped it, reached and missed it, and finally just sat on the floor as he picked it up.

He called several hospitals and had only just found Troy when Carter came back through the door. "He's... it's Anderson Medical. They said he's there." His hands were shaking. "They wouldn't tell me anything else."

"Let's go. Geoff will meet us there." Carter reached down for him. "Come on. Geoff has his power of attorney. We'll get you in."

He let Carter help him up and took a deep breath once he got to his feet. Lock the door, right? He needed to lock the door. He dug out the key. "He had a migraine. A really bad one. He could hardly sit up."

"He's never had a migraine. Never in twenty years." Carter sighed. "I didn't believe him. I thought he had been up too late, playing."

"No, Carter." He locked the door and turned to glare at his boy's boss. "We don't usually see each other on Saturday nights because he knows how tired he gets, and I respect that. But Troy had a shit-ass day at work yesterday and needed me, so we had a very quiet evening watching TV. I guess that's shocking to you, huh?" He pulled the truck keys out of his pocket.

"You can chew my ass after we go see Troy. I fucked up. Let's go." Carter was pale as milk, eyes wide and bloodshot.

"Sure, if that's more convenient," he muttered as Carter looped around the truck to get into the passenger seat. He was worried sick, and he was pissed off. He really didn't know which one was winning at the moment.

And he was mad that the lady on the phone refused to tell him anything. Next of kin? Troy didn't fucking have kin. Troy had him.

He opened the garage, started the truck, and tore out of the driveway. "Arapahoe, right?"

"Yeah." Carter put his phone to his ear. "Babe, bring Troy's paperwork to the heart hospital. I don't know. Saul says a bad headache."

"He took a bunch of Excedrin. Like four." He hadn't even given that a thought. He took four Advil all the time. Maybe he shouldn't have let Troy take so many?

Shit, maybe he should have ordered Troy to stay home. Or insisted on giving his boy a ride. If he'd given Troy a ride to work maybe—

"Right, Saul! It's a right here."

"Shit." He hauled the wheel over and the tires sang at them as they took the corner.

"Jesus!"

"Sorry. I—" He puffed out a breath. "Sorry."

"No worries. Breathe. I'm sure he's fine."

Right, because people who were fine got taken to the hospital all the time.

"It was a bad headache, maybe he just passed out." That was plausible. Sure. He took another hard turn into the hospital entrance and through to the emergency room parking.

"Geoff is right behind us. He'll bring the paperwork. They might talk to you, but..."

He screeched into a parking lot and threw the truck into park. He needed to see Troy.

"We'll see what they say. Come on." He jumped out of the truck, ready to stand up for himself this time, like he should have done when Carter was ordering his boy in to work. He didn't wait, he stormed in through the ER doors and stopped at the desk. "Where did they take Troy Finch?"

The girl behind the desk blinked at him. "I'll have to check. Do you want to have a seat?"

"No. I don't."

She shook her head, and he leaned over the counter. "Please. Please, I'm scared. He left for work and he never showed up."

"Oh. Oh!" Her eyes went wide. "He's in emergency surgery. He had a heart attack."

He had a heart attack.

He stared at the nurse, frozen. "Surgery?"

Carter rested a hand on his shoulder. "Where do we wait? We have power of attorney."

"MedSurg, second floor. I'll tell them you're coming, just stop at the desk."

"Thank you." Carter steered him away from the desk, stopping near the elevators. "We'll go on up. I'll text Geoff."

A heart attack? He was pretty sure people died from heart attacks all the time. "He can't have had a heart attack. He does yoga and walks everywhere. He's healthy." Jesus, he felt young and dumb all of a sudden. Broken bones and concussions he understood, but he didn't know anything about hearts or scary things like that.

"He is. Ridiculously healthy. The man is thin, for fuck's sake." Carter sounded as shocked as he did.

The ride up in the elevator was totally silent, and he assumed Carter was feeling a lot like he was. Just... stunned. Worried.

Kind of helpless.

Geoff appeared on the next elevator, and he and Carter both jumped up out of their chairs.

"Hey." Geoff went right to Carter and into his arms. "What do you know so far? Just the heart attack?"

He nodded. "That's it, yeah. And he's in surgery."

"Okay. Let's go talk to the nurses at the desk, see what we can see." Geoff offered him a weak, watery smile. "Has he shown any signs of being sick?"

"He was exhausted and wound up after work last night, and I went over just to give him some company. This morning he woke up with a headache. Like a migraine or something. He could hardly sit up. It was bad. He was pale and just looked really awful. Can you find out how long they think he'll be in surgery?"

"Of course. Come on. Let's do this." Geoff went up to the desk. "Good morning. We're Troy Finch's family. We just arrived."

There was the nonsense with the paperwork, with registering his boy, and a metric ton of signatures for Geoff.

It felt good that Geoff hadn't hesitated at all in calling him family. He honestly wasn't sure where he stood with these two, but that was a solid start at least.

They didn't really find out anything new after all of that, just that Troy had been found by a jogger, and that someone would be out with a status soon. He slumped into a chair with his arms crossed, just staying quiet. He didn't have words for any of this. Not for how the worry felt, not for how he felt about Carter right now, or himself either. Everything about this just felt wrong. Wrong, and unfair.

"I don't understand. Troy's the healthiest man I've ever met." Geoff shook his head. "He was a smoker, sure, but he stopped."

"I ordered pizza last night. Maybe I should have ordered salads." That was stupid and he knew it. They were all just grasping at straws right now.

"And I should have told him to stay home," Carter sighed. "I was an asshole."

Geoff snorted. "And what would have happened if Troy

had collapsed at home? Saul would have found him this evening?"

Oh, God. That would have been... he didn't want to think about that. He shrugged, feeling stupid. "I probably should have insisted he let me drive him to work, though."

"Stop it. You two stop. He's going to need us when he's out of surgery. We all have to focus." Geoff could snap when he wanted to.

Saul glanced over at Carter and then gave the man's knee a squeeze. It wasn't an apology exactly; he was still mad. But he was mad because Carter had been an ass of a boss, not because he thought this was Carter's fault or anything. Geoff was right, it could just as easily have happened in the kitchen.

"He's right."

Carter sighed dramatically. "I hate when he's right."

He fought a grin because it just didn't seem appropriate in the moment, but he couldn't hold out long. He snickered, and that made Geoff huff out a laugh, and then he was giggling. "I bet you do."

"You have no idea, man. He's going to milk this for months." Carter reached out and squeezed his hand. "He's going to be fine."

He nodded and squeezed back. He really didn't know what to say.

"Mr. Lee?" A tall man came through a door to the left, pulling on a doctor's white coat.

They all stood in a rush, and Saul thought for a second he might just pass out.

"We're his family. How is he?" Geoff sounded so confident.

"I'm Dr. Marks. Troy is resting. He's very strong and he

made it through surgery just fine." The doc smiled. "Now, everybody breathe."

Saul took a huge breath on cue, not realizing he'd been holding it. He thought he heard Carter do the same.

Geoff nodded. "Good news. Thank you."

"It is. He was pretty weak when he came in. His myocardial infarction—the heart attack—was caused by a congenital valve defect he probably didn't even know he had. It's more common than you might think. He didn't arrest, which was good because we don't know how long it was before he was found."

Saul sighed. "Might have been twenty minutes."

The doctor glanced at him. "Then he was very lucky. We'll keep him under for a day or so to make sure the valve repair is doing its job and then once he's released he'll need meds and therapy..." The doctor waved a hand. "We can talk about all of that later. Come on, I'll take you back. I'm sure you're all anxious to see him. You'll have to scrub up and visit one at a time. He'll be going to ICU for a bit, then the cardiac unit from there."

Scrub up? ICU? Wasn't that for really sick people? Didn't the doc just say Troy was okay? He had a lot to learn about hospitals.

His phone buzzed as they were walking, and he pulled it out to find a text from Emma.

Where ru?

Oh shit. He was supposed to work today. He texted back, quickly. *Troy is in the hospital. He'll be ok but can I have the day?*

Oh no! Of course. I got this. Call me later.

Thanks Em. Will do. He sighed. She was going to have a hell of a day. Hopefully she could call someone in to cover for him. Craig was always looking for more hours.

He followed the others. He wanted Geoff and Carter to go first, and then he was hoping they'd go home. He had Troy's truck, and he just wanted to be alone with Troy for a while.

"Did you want to go in first, Saul?" Geoff asked. The question was gentle, careful, almost tentative.

"No. No... thank you, Geoff. Really. You go ahead. I'll go last if that's okay with you guys."

Geoff nodded and went to scrub and he and Carter sat, waiting their turn.

"This shit never gets easier, does it?"

How the hell did he know?

"You've done this before?" He sure hadn't. He had no idea what to expect when he went into that room.

"Yeah, with my dad." Carter sighed softly. "And then with my younger brother."

Oh, man. Had Carter lost them both? He'd lost his dad when he was really young, but he had a bunch of siblings and his mom too. He couldn't imagine what he'd do. He leaned back in his chair and glanced at Carter. "That really sucks. I'm sorry."

"Dad lost a short, awful battle with cancer. Thomas had issues with heroin and his body couldn't handle it."

Heroin. That shit was ugly. Or so he'd heard. "That must have been hard." That was okay to say right? The last thing he needed to do was put his foot in his mouth today.

"I don't know. I think it was less hurtful than the constant backsliding, to be honest."

He reached over and rested a hand on Carter's shoulder. He'd heard stories. Addiction was a disease with no cure. But that was literally all he knew about it. "I've been lucky I guess."

"That's good. I'm glad." He searched for sarcasm, but there wasn't any.

"Puts me at a loss with Troy sometimes. But I'm managing." Troy had lost a lot. A lot.

"I can't imagine making the age difference work, but there's no doubt that you and Troy are."

"The age really isn't a thing at all. I don't even notice that. It's more just the things he's been through and how long he's... been alone." He didn't feel like they were making it work. They just worked. It wasn't hard.

"Yes. He waited a long time, and..." Carter broke off and stood as Geoff stumbled out crying.

"Master. He looks so gray."

Gray? Saul stood slowly and glanced toward where Geoff had come from, then back at Geoff, who was a little gray himself.

"Boy, he just had open heart surgery. Of course he's pale."

Open heart surgery. God, could they make this thing with Troy sound any worse? He was going to be okay. The doc said so. "Go on in, Carter. I'll hang here with Geoff for you." Carter was sounding pretty stressed. *Of course he's pale* probably wasn't all that helpful. It sure wasn't to him.

"I'm going to take Geoff down to the cafeteria for coffee. Troy needs you, and he needs me. Remember, he can hear you talk."

"Oh. Oh, sure. Thanks." He suddenly felt nervous about going in, but he followed what Geoff had done and started scrubbing. His boy was in there, he told himself. And Carter was right, Troy needed him. After yesterday he was absolutely sure of that.

A nurse handed him a mask and he was allowed into the room, and for a second he wasn't sure Troy was even in bed.

There were monitors and machines, lights and crazy technology everywhere, and Troy was small lying there in the middle of all of it. Small and pale, and not really like Troy at all.

"Can I touch him?" He asked the nurse before she left the room. "Can I hold his hand?"

"Carefully, yes." The nurse acted as if maybe he didn't know what "carefully" meant.

He sighed, went to Troy, and curled his fingers around his boy's hand. "Hey, it's Saul. It's me, Troy. I think you can hear me, right? I was told you could. So... I'm here." He watched Troy's pale, still face. He didn't know what he was looking for exactly. "You're going to be okay, did Geoff tell you? They're just keeping you out for a day or so to rest. Really. They said you'd—"

His vision went blurry with tears all of a sudden and he was so stunned he let go of Troy's hand to rub them away. It didn't do much good. "I'm going to sit, okay?" He plopped down hard into a chair by the bed and took Troy's hand again. "I was worried."

Was. Am. Probably not going to get over it real soon.

Troy's heartbeat sped up, fingers trembling in his hand.

Oh.

Oh, damn.

He squeezed them a little tighter. God. He needed to keep it together, at least while he was here. He took a breath and pushed the emotion down. "I'm here, boy. You're okay. They're going to move you a room in the cardiac unit soon and I'm hoping they'll let me stay with you. Okay? I want to stay, and I will if they let me. Your job is to rest. That's all. Breathe, relax, and rest. I'm here." If he were in Troy's place, he'd have questions. Lots of questions. He started thinking about what he should and maybe shouldn't say.

As he spoke, he watched Troy's heartbeat slow again, easing.

"That's perfect," the nurse whispered. "Just keep doing what you're doing."

He blinked up, startled. He didn't know she was still there. He gave her a nod and focused back on his boy. "That's good, Troy. You can feel my hand, right? I've got you." He stroked the back of Troy's hand and let the room go quiet a minute.

Troy looked like hell, but somehow he seemed better than he had this morning—less panicked and pained.

"I think if I were you, I'd want to know, so I'll tell you what happened. What I understand anyway. But only if you promise not to get worked up." He laughed softly, knowing Troy was tuned into him, and trying to take the tension out of the air.

"So, a jogger found you and called an ambulance, and in the meantime, Carter came over to ream you a new asshole for not showing up. We both kind of stared at each other for a minute like maybe you given up on both of us and moved to Bora Bora or something, but no, you went way more dramatic than that. You had a heart attack."

Since Troy wasn't able to interrupt him, he rambled on, explaining about the birth defect and the surgery, and made the tension between him and Carter sound like they almost entered a boxing ring just to be entertaining. Geoff of course, saved the day and put them both in their place.

That part wasn't really exaggerated.

He swore he could see Troy relaxing as he talked, and it felt amazing that he could do this—give Troy so much ease.

"So that's the whole saga, and now you're here. All you have to do now is rest up and get better." Get better. He wasn't sure if it was a simple as it sounded but he wasn't going to go into that. He didn't really have any details about what that meant anyway. "Dr. Marks is kind of hot too. If you had to have open heart surgery, you came in on a good day."

He looked up at the nurse and winked. He thought maybe she might be blushing.

She just rolled her eyes at him, though, and shook her head. "If you'd like, you can go to the cardiac unit waiting area. They'll let you in once he's settled down there."

"Yeah? Okay, I'll do that. You hear that, baby? I have to let them move you, so I'll meet you down in your new room. I'll be there, I promise. You stay relaxed. You have one job— rest. Got me?" He leaned over and kissed Troy's fingers through his mask. "Be good."

He gave Troy's hand another squeeze, left the room slowly, thanking the nurse on the way out, then bolted blindly for the men's room as the tears came flooding back.

He was pretty sure he was going to hurl.

22

The first thing Troy knew when he woke up was pain, and the second was utter panic. He fought to sit up, to find out where he was, who was hurting him, but he couldn't. He couldn't sit up.

Fuck. Fuck, it hurt.

He tried to scream, but all that came out was a long, low moan.

"I'm here." He knew the voice, but it was so far away, and the warm, steady grip on his fingers didn't seem to fit at all with what he was feeling.

Help me. Help me, please. I'm in trouble. He kept trying to force the words out through a throat that wasn't working.

"Hey. Shh. I can see your heart rate you know, you're not fooling me. You're okay. You have one job, remember? Rest. Wow. That's kind of high. Maybe I should call the nurse."

Nurse. Nurse. Okay. Hospital. He knew that.

He fought to get his eyes open, but he couldn't figure it out.

He felt the grip around his fingers tighten but it seemed so far away, just like the voice. "You need to breathe, boy.

Listen to me. You're in the hospital, you had a heart attack but you're going to be fine. I've told you this already but maybe it's hard to remember with the drugs. They have you sedated and on pain meds... you're supposed to be resting. They said you shouldn't really wake up at all but... I'm calling the nurse right now, okay?"

Saul. The recognition came right along with the name. Saul. His Master. His lover.

Resting. It hurt too much to rest.

"Mr. Finch, you're fighting hard to come back to us, aren't you? Your partner is here with you, but you need to try and sleep. You can't heal if you don't rest."

"I think he's in pain. He's all tense, you see that? And he was moaning."

"Let me see when he's due for more meds."

"He's hurting now."

"Well, as it happens, I can give him some now. I'll be back."

Saul sighed. "She's right though, boy. You have to rest. They'll let you wake up tomorrow if you're stable enough."

Love you. Stay. I'm so tired. I want to go home. Stay. Please.

"Okay Mr. Finch. This should help."

"I'm here, baby. I'm not going anywhere I promise."

Oh, thank God. Yes, please.

"Oh, he liked hearing that, didn't he?"

"Yeah. He wants me to stay, you know? He needs me."

"You definitely relax him. He trusts you."

"He does. I love him. He asked me to move in just yesterday." Saul sounded happy.

"Oh, that's wonderful. And good for him too, he'll need help when he gets home."

"Yeah. I guess he will."

That isn't why I asked, though. I would never do that to you. Never.

"So that stuff will help the pain?"

"Should work pretty quickly. It'll put him out for a while too."

"Oh. Good." Saul's fingers shifted and tangled with his. "You should feel better in a minute, baby. Rest up. I'll be right here like I promised, okay?"

He tried to open his eyes again, but it was a lost cause. He didn't have the energy. "Love."

Hopefully that was real.

23

Saul startled awake when one of his feet slid off the bed rail where apparently, he'd had it perched when he fell asleep. He didn't remember doing that, or falling asleep, but the sound his sneaker made when it hit the floor was real enough. He pulled his other leg down with a groan and sat up, rubbing his hands across his face.

Ooh, stubble. He wondered if it was long enough people could actually see it. It took him weeks to grow enough scruff to call a beard.

It had been a long couple of days. They'd let Troy wake for a bit but that didn't work out so well pain-wise so they put him under again. The second time they let the sedation wear off went better, but Troy was taking his orders well and spent a lot of time sleeping hard.

He hadn't left the hospital yet, but he was going to later tonight. Geoff was going to come spell him overnight so he could get a shower and sleep in a bed.

Hopefully. He needed to stop promising he wasn't going to leave the hospital.

"I want to go home. Tell them." Troy's green eyes were

bloodshot, and the command wasn't making him leap to his feet.

"Sure, I'll tell them. And then they'll laugh at us both. Or, we could just stick around and share some more green Jell-O. That was fun."

"No more Jell-O." Oh, his boy was *grumpy*.

"You only had two bites. I ate most of it." He pushed up out of his chair and perched next to Troy in bed, smiling. "Look, no more mask. Want a kiss?" He leaned in, made a kissy face and crossed his eyes.

"Making fun of me." Troy leaned up, wincing as he brought their lips together.

Saul kissed him, leaning down and pushing Troy's shoulders back into the mattress. He hadn't intended it to be longer than a peck but they both wanted more. "Cheering you up," he said when they parted.

He hadn't realized how much he'd missed that kiss. It was a little low energy, but it was definitely Troy. Thank God.

"I want my own bed. I have to get back to work. I—"

Saul quieted his boy with another soft kiss. That was enough for now.

"You have one job." He brushed his hand across the short fuzz on Troy's head. It was soft and a coppery red, tickling his palm.

"Only one?"

"Yes. Rest. That's it. I'm conspiring with your boss, so there's no point in arguing with me." He had to assume Carter had found someone to fill in for Troy by now. He knew Carter was paying Troy and that the man had insurance, so all his boy had to do was breathe.

"Think of it as taking twenty years of sick days all at

once." He winked. "With the handsomest nurse on the planet."

"I'll give you that, for sure." Troy rubbed his cheek as the IV line tugged. "I hate this thing." Then his boy sighed and shook his head. "And I'm whining. I'm sorry."

"A little." He shrugged. "I like that thing. And I like this hospital bed. And I even like those bloodshot eyes. Because all of those things mean you're still here."

"I can't believe this happened to me."

He couldn't believe it either, but he couldn't say that. He had to say something positive. That was his job, right? "You're going to be fine. Do what you're told, and you'll be out of here before too long."

He yawned through that last bit. God, he was tired.

"Honey, go home." The words were warm, gentle. "I can handle this for a day. I swear. You look exhausted."

"I'm fine. Geoff is coming soon, and then I'll go. I don't want you to be alone." He half expected Troy to try to get up out of bed or something.

"With all these nurses with their psycho refusal to let me sleep and another night of infomercials? I'm never alone."

He laughed and gave Troy's knees a pat.

"Well look at the lovebirds. Are you through with this pathetic cry for attention, honey, or what?" Geoff breezed in looking... like Geoff. Khakis and perfect hair. "Hello, junior."

He rolled his eyes. "Geoff."

"I am. Take me home, and you can go home to Carter."

"Good luck." He smiled at Geoff and slid off the bed.

"Nice try, honey. You've got a week minimum sentence."

"Traitor." Troy winked at Geoff. "Did you bring me my coffee?"

"I did. Special brew for the heart patient." Geoff set a

cup down on the table by the bed. "Don't ask me what that means. Sue made it."

"I guess we'll find out." Troy caught his gaze, like he was a touchstone.

He leaned over the bed rail and kissed Troy again. "Are you going to be okay if I go?"

"I will. I swear. You deserve a night in a real bed." Troy squeezed his arm. "Good night."

He just needed a shower and one good night's sleep. "I'll be back in the morning."

Geoff snorted. "It's one night, Saul. Troy's a big boy."

He ignored Geoff and gave Troy's hand a squeeze. "I'll be at your place and I have my phone. I love you."

"Our place." Troy held on for a second. "I love you."

Oh. Wow. "Our place." He nodded. "See you in the morning."

Geoff was saying something snarky as he left but he didn't hear it. He loved Troy, but he needed out of the damn hospital. Just for a while. Some real food, a real bed.

He got into Troy's truck, started it up, and headed... home.

24

"Don' be ugly, butthead." Troy was tired and feeling weirdly vulnerable and scared. "How's you?"

"I'm just playing. I'm fine. I'm not the one in a hospital bed. Carter and I are worried about you. How are you feeling?" Geoff sat just where Saul had been perched on his bed.

"Like I been rode hard and put away wet. They keep making me blow in all these tubes." He was exhausted and hurting, but he'd say he was fine to get out of there.

A fucking heart attack. Jesus.

Geoff touched his shoulder. "You're going to have to be patient with it, Troy. It's frustrating, I'm sure, but you had no control over this. It was a congenital failure, and you just have to do the rehab and be grateful you didn't die."

"Right. I am. I'm just... I'm ready to get back to normal."

"Honey." Geoff sighed and took his hand. "I don't think it works like that. You have to find a new normal. Have the docs talked to you about... everything?"

"Yeah." Two months his ass. He'd already talked to Solomon. He'd be back at yoga in a few days.

Geoff gave him the eye. "You better follow orders. We want you around for a while."

"I'm not going anywhere." He wasn't that old. Middle-aged, sure, but not *old*. "I'm making a miraculous recovery."

Geoff smiled at him. "Yeah? I'm into miracles. Personally, I think it's a miracle you're awake. You look pretty tired. Get real, honey. How do you feel?"

"It hurts. I've never hurt so deep." And he'd never felt so weak.

"Oh, Troy." Geoff reached out and gave him a gentle hug. "I can only imagine. But you've got a few days here whether you like it or not, so take advantage of them. Get the pain meds and rest. I'm here because I wanted to see you, I don't need you to entertain me. Plus, I think Saul would be upset with me if I didn't make sure you rested. He's been very... clear with Carter and me."

"Oh fuck. He's really stressed out, isn't he?" He didn't know what to say, for chrissake.

"He needs some sleep and a little perspective, I think. He's okay. He's young, you know? He's never seen any of this before, none of his buddies have ever seen this before. But his heart is in the right place."

"Yeah." He was old, wasn't he? Like too old for Saul. God. His eyes filled with tears. What the fuck was wrong with him?

"He's been really good, Troy. The nurses all said he's been good to have here." Geoff rubbed his shoulder. "Hey. It's okay. You're tired, honey. Close your eyes for a while."

"I'm not okay. I can't keep my shit together somehow." He wanted Saul there. He wouldn't ask, but the heart wanted what it wanted.

"So don't. Who am I going to tell? Jesus, Troy. What

haven't we been through together?" Geoff took his hand and squeezed it hard.

"Right?" Troy held on to his best friend, tears sliding down his face without his permission.

"This is fucked up. It's scary. It changes things. Why should that be easy? It's not. I was so scared for you." He could hear the emotion in Geoff's voice too.

"I don't remember it—not the whole day."

"Just as well, it was scary as fuck. Your surgery took forever. Hours."

"I just remember hearing Saul talking to me, telling the nurse I hurt." It had been the thing he held onto, that kept him sane.

"I'm not surprised, you know. He pays attention. He may be young, but he knows you. He loves you, that's obvious to me and Carter, both."

"He does. I've asked him to move in, did you know?" He thought, maybe, he'd mentioned it.

"I didn't know until just a minute ago when you and Saul were talking. I was surprised, you've been alone there so long. Congratulations."

"Do you think we'll... that he'll forgive me?" His eyelids were so heavy.

"There's nothing to forgive. Saul loves you." Geoff touched his cheek. "That's how this works. In for a penny, in for a pound."

"Ask them to let me sleep? Please?"

"I will. I'll keep everybody out tonight, okay? You tell me if you need pain meds. I'm here all night, honey."

"I'm sorry." He wasn't sure what for, not at all, but he was.

Geoff kissed his cheek. "Stop. You're my best friend. No apologies."

"I am." He sighed, the world sort of falling away from him.

Good night, Saul. Sir. Love you.

25

Saul rolled over with a sigh and stared at the ceiling. He'd been awake for a bit thinking, worrying, wondering what the hell he should do next. He knew he needed to get back to the hospital, Troy would be missing him.

God, he hated that hospital. He was starting to understand what Carter had been talking about the other day. And keeping up a strong front for Troy was hard. Maybe the hardest thing he'd ever done.

It was weird sleeping in this house alone. Wrong.

He dragged his phone off the nightstand and looked at it, a little shocked to realize it was already Friday. He also had a string of texts from Emma. Jesus, what was he going to do about work? He didn't read them all, he just called her. He needed a reality check or a kick in the pants or something.

"Dude. You have to come back to work. Please." Emma chuckled softly, but he could hear the stress. "Also, how is Troy?"

Fuck. Work. "He's... I don't know. In pain? Weak. Not

himself. He'll be in the hospital at least a few more days." He was going to have to figure it out. Troy was going to have to manage. Maybe Geoff and Carter could pitch in more? Maybe.

"That sucks. Seriously. A few more days sounds... better than I thought. Is there a chance you can come today and tomorrow? Please? I'll buy pizza."

"Yeah. Yeah, of course. I just need to go by the hospital first and see Troy. Let him know what's up." Okay, so Emma wasn't going to be the one to vent to. And honestly, it wasn't fair to her to have to run things on her own. How did people do this? "I might be a little late, but I'll be there."

"Sure. How are you? I've missed the hell out of you, man. Seriously." Emma sighed. "I want to hug you and tell you it's all okay."

"I'm... good. I got a good night's sleep." He couldn't dump on her now, she'd feel guilty for asking him to come in. And that hug sounded like a terrible idea. He might lose it. "Listen, I'm going to run, okay? I need to get dressed and get to the hospital so I can get to the shop."

"No running. Now that I've heard your voice, I feel better."

"I'm sorry I didn't call sooner. I was... I lost track of time. I can't believe it's Friday already."

"Of course you did. Your guy's in the hospital. Dork."

"They said he's gonna be okay. I'll see you in a bit." He hung up the phone before he had to get into any more details.

He just needed to breathe and figure it out, that was all. He got dressed, cleaned the room, made the bed, tossed his towel into the hamper. He didn't want to leave a mess for when he brought his boy home.

Then he made himself a cup of coffee, which he drank

in the truck on the way to the hospital. He could do this. He could work and look after his boy too. He'd talk to Emma, cut his schedule back as much as they could, and then Troy was just going to have to manage with other people when he had to work. He had an idea, he didn't think Troy would like it much, but Geoff and Carter might. Truthfully, he didn't think Troy was going to like anything much.

The way Troy was talking yesterday, he was going to walk out of the hospital and go back to work. Fat chance. Saul knew damn well that wasn't going to happen, and deep down? Troy probably knew it too.

He parked the truck and eyed the building as he headed inside. He was fine before last weekend but now he really didn't like hospitals.

His phone buzzed, Troy's name popping up.

Morning. Did you sleep?

He smiled. He wasn't expecting Troy to be up for texting yet. Or for worrying about him.

Like a log. I'm here. B there in a sec.

He got a smile in response, a thumbs up.

He'd wanted to stop for coffee, and bring Troy some real food too, but since Emma needed him at work he didn't have time. When he got to the room he poked his head in the door and grinned. "Hey, baby."

"Hey, it's sleeping beauty!" Geoff laughed and stood.

"Shut up, I wasn't talking to you." He went right over to Troy. He'd been hoping his boy would look better today, but no. Troy still seemed so damn tired. "Did you sleep?"

"I did. I just got up and let them change the bedding. The physical therapist is coming around again this afternoon." Troy leaned back into the pillows. "I did a good job."

He bent over and kissed his boy, gave him a smile. "Good for you. You better rest up for that therapy, he means business."

"I kept the evil vampires at bay all night so he got about six hours in a row. Not too bad." Geoff was texting and heading for the door.

"Thank you for your help, man." Troy waved goodbye even as he turned his attention to Saul. "Good morning."

"You're welcome. I'll be back in a bit. Carter's coming to say hi to you and then take me to breakfast."

"Thanks Geoff. Really." He was glad they were coming back so Troy wouldn't be alone all day. He sat on the edge of his boy's bed and tangled their fingers. "How are you feeling this morning?"

"Tired, right now, but I walked around. You're a sight for sore eyes."

"I slept hard, but it was weird as hell waking up in your house alone." He grinned and ducked his head. "Our house. Alone."

"Yeah. I bet. We didn't even get your stuff over yet. Soon. They're saying Monday at the latest, maybe even Sunday."

"Let's hope for Monday. I have to work all weekend." He caught Troy's eyes and held them. "And today. I'm sorry. Emma is drowning."

"I'm a big boy. I'll be fine. I swear." Troy held his hand, thumb drawing circles on his palm.

Maybe that was true, but it didn't make him feel less guilty. "I'll be here after work, and I'm going to talk to Carter, see what we can work out so you're not alone all day. Okay?"

"Hey. Hey, I have my phone and my charger. I'll be okay. It'll be when I have to walk up the stairs at home that I'll need help."

He nodded and looked away, swallowing hard against the rush of emotion. A good night's sleep was supposed to make things easier, not harder wasn't it? He took a deep breath.

Pull it together, man. Doms don't cry.

Lovers might though. Maybe? God, this was so confusing.

"Thank you for being here. I fell asleep dreaming about you." Troy cupped his jaw. "I love you."

He looked back at Troy, just letting his lover see whatever there was to see. "I love you too. You scared the fuck out of me is all. We'll figure it out." He didn't want to talk about his dreams, they were scary too.

"I bet. I don't remember much. I remember your voice making it better."

"Yeah? It seemed like you could hear me. Carter said you would." That made him happy. "I knew you needed me and I'm glad it helped."

"I do. I'm sorry about this. I swear, I've been trying to stay healthy." Troy sighed and rubbed his chest. "Jesus."

"The surgeon said you're really strong. You *are* healthy. This is some weird thing you were born with. He said there wasn't any reason you'd have known about it." He put his hand over Troy's. "Still hurts, huh?"

"Yeah. It's freaking me out that they wired my breastbone together, you know?"

"That is kind of freaky. I had a really hard time with the words 'open heart surgery'. It still makes me a little queasy to think about it."

"Yeah. I don't know... they... I can't..." Troy shook his head. "My ink's all messed up too. I hope we can fix it."

"You know Geoff is going to love trying." He smiled and squeezed Troy's fingers. "It's going to be okay, Troy. I haven't figured it all out yet, but I will. I'm going to make it okay."

"You already have."

A knock came to the door, a lean man with a shock of white-blond hair and a pair of gauzy pants that barely hung off his hips appeared. "Good morning, my friend. Are you up to breathing this morning?"

Saul saw the bare shake of Troy's head. "Solomon, come in and meet my partner, Saul. Saul, this is my yoga teacher."

"Oh. Hey." He shifted off the bed, smiling at Solomon. "It's good to meet you."

"It's excellent to meet you too." Solomon grabbed him and hugged him like they were friends. "Finally."

He blinked for a second but damn, the man gave good hugs and he needed one. He gave Solomon a quick squeeze in return. "Troy talks about you a lot. He's even taught me some things."

"You're welcome at class, any time. I figured since Troy can't make practice, I'd come to him."

He looked at Troy and winked. "Doesn't sound like he's giving you a choice, baby."

"He never does. Butthead." Troy sighed, but there was a grin on his boy's face.

Solomon would help Troy relax, maybe his boy would sleep some. "I have to get to work, so this seems like a good time to leave you to your breathing." He leaned in and kissed Troy again, longer this time, making sure his boy felt the connection.

"Don't work too hard." Troy cupped his jaw, stroking him. "I'll text you later."

"I'll bring dinner." He grinned. "Be good. Great to meet you, Solomon. I think you're exactly what he needs today."

"I'll make sure he relaxes. No worries."

God, could Solomon sound more Colorado?

"Thanks, man." He patted Troy's leg. "Love you." He turned and left the room feeling better that Solomon was there.

Now he just had to face Emma. And work.

26

Troy woke up at four a.m. convinced that Saul was hurt, was bleeding, was needing him.

The monitors started going off, alarms warning everyone that his heart rate spiked, even as he flailed to find his phone.

Someone got in his way, fought with his hand, pushed him back down into the mattress.

"Stop, Troy. Hey! You're okay, baby."

"Saul! Be careful! I'll get you help!" He loved Saul; he wouldn't let him bleed out in the arena.

"Troy. It's me. I'm fine, baby. You're dreaming. Look. Look at me."

He tried to look but the lights got bright all of a sudden making him squint.

"Mr. Finch?"

"He's dreaming. I think if I just—"

"Mr. Finch, I need you to take a deep breath for me. Can you do that? A deep breath."

"Saul." He sucked in a breath, the lights sparkling in his eyes.

Saul took his hand. "I'm right here, boy. I'm fine. It was just a dream."

"He needs a sedative—"

"No. Pain meds yes, but all he does is fight the sedation. He doesn't need it. Shut the lights off, please."

"Sir—"

"Shut the lights off, I've got this." The grip on his hand grew tighter. "Boy. Relax and breathe. You're fine. I'm fine. It was a bad dream."

"Oh. Oh, you were hurt, Sir. You were hurt." He focused on Saul, on that sure gaze.

Saul spoke slowly, reassuring him over and over. "I'm not hurt. I'm totally fine. We're in the hospital, remember? You have to calm down, or these ladies are going to sedate you again. Deep breath. We're okay."

"I love you. I thought... Terrible dream. It was so real."

Saul glanced over at the nurses. "Better, right?"

"Better. He's got another hour before he can have anything more for pain."

"We'll call you. Thank you so much for coming running."

Saul waited as they left the room and then turned back to him. "Do you want to talk about it? Tell me what it was about?"

"You were bleeding out on the arena floor, and I couldn't save you." He held on to Saul's hand, feeling himself tremble uncontrollably.

"Oh God. How scary." Saul leaned closer and looped an arm around his shoulders, hugging him carefully. "I'm so sorry, baby. You're not gonna lose me. I'm not going anywhere."

He leaned over, breathing in the now-familiar scent of his lover.

Saul held him quietly, patiently until he wasn't trembling anymore and then released him. "It must have worried you, being alone today."

"I just... I'm ready to go home, to sleep with you in our bed." Surely he wasn't that bad, that he couldn't be left alone for a minute...

"Soon. I want that too. I really do. You have to meet their criteria though. I don't want you home too soon. You don't want to end up right back here again."

"I never want to be here again. I've been in the hospital enough." He leaned harder, stroking Saul's arm, belly. "My granddaddy called it the horse pistol."

"Horse pistol—oh!" Saul laughed. "That's great. I like it." Saul looked at him. "Suppose you slide over and make some room for me. You think we could fit?"

"I know you could." He scooted over, the tape over his chest pulling and irritating his skin, but it didn't matter. He needed Saul with him.

"Awesome. I'm coming in." Saul smiled at him and climbed up, settling on one side, sharing his pillow and resting a hand on his belly. "Hey, this is pretty good."

"It is." He could hear Saul's heartbeat, the sound steady and strong, like music. "Do I get to go home, soon?"

"Didn't you tell me Monday? It's Saturday, so yeah. Soon. Then you'll just need to build your stamina back up. I'm looking forward to working on that with you." The suggestive tone in Saul's voice was a little dirty.

He laughed. He actually laughed, and it felt so good. Like he might not be permanently broken.

Saul laughed with him. "You like that idea? Me too. Who says physical therapy can't be fun? I'll be your favorite therapist. Dedicated, creative, attentive. You're gonna love it."

"I already do." He twined his fingers with Saul's, taking another deep breath. "I bet you're way more fun than Sylvia the Torturer."

"I bet I'm better looking too." Saul sat up on one elbow, smiling. "I'll give you a sample." Saul kissed Troy, tongue sliding along his lips until he opened.

Oh.

A part of him—a huge part, really—had been afraid that this part of his life was fucked up, was gone. Stupid, but he'd had a ton of stupid shit in his brain in the last week.

Geoff swore it was just the drugs.

Saul's kiss was deep but not demanding, offering and not asking for anything in return but his focus. When they parted, his Master smiled at him. "I'm not going anywhere. Okay? If I'm not here, it's always just a matter of time before we're together again. I promise."

"I'm sorry, Sir. You have to be so tired of me." Such a needy titty baby.

"No. I'm not. And I won't get tired of reassuring you either if that's what you need." Sir drew a finger across his cheek, voice patient, kind. "We've made some promises to each other haven't we?"

"Yes, Sir. More than some. I'm yours, full stop." He turned his face, kissed Saul's fingertip.

"Mine." It was Saul who took the deep breath this time. It might be four in the morning, but that smile lit up his room. "Thank you, boy. I... needed to hear that."

"I needed to say it." He traced Saul's lips, feeling decadent and lazy, the horror from the dream all fading away.

"Time to sleep. I told them not to sedate you again, so you better prove you don't need it." Saul chuckled. "And I have the dreaded Saturday shift at the bike shop in a few hours."

"Sleep. Day after tomorrow we'll be in our own bed. I'll make you French toast."

"You're on. Goodnight, baby." Saul settled next to him, relaxing easily, and was off to sleep in minutes.

He sighed softly, kissing Saul's forehead. "Goodnight, Master. Sleep well."

Soon he'd be doing this in his own bed.

27

Saul's eyes popped open wide and he sat up in bed. It was Monday morning, a bright sunny day, and he was bringing his boy home.

He took a quick shower, made some coffee, then sat out back for a second to soak up a few minutes of sun, catch up on email and text Carter.

Hey man, if you have a second can you call me today? Everything is fine just want to chat.

He sipped his coffee. He'd come home last night after Troy had fallen asleep just to make sure the house was in order and to get just a breath or two of air before the real work started. Troy was much better, but he was going to need a lot of help, and if he knew his boy at all, a lot of reassurance. It was going to be a full-time job—on top of his full-time job.

He dreaded it a little, but he liked the idea a hell of a lot better than not having Troy at all.

Sure, bud. Now? Carter was on it—partially because he was training new cooks, partially because Saul thought Carter and Geoff were ready to be away from the hospital.

Works for me. He waited for the phone to ring. "Hey. Thanks for calling me so fast."

"No worries. Everything good with the plan to get him home today?"

"As far as I know. I'm at the condo right now, I'm going to head back to the hospital in a few." He took another sip of his coffee. "That's kind of what I'm calling about."

"I think Geoff can come help."

He nodded. "That's great if he can, but I'm thinking more about what happens on Wednesday when I go back to work. He really shouldn't be alone for a while. I had an idea."

"Of course. What do you need? I'm on it." God, that felt good, that immediate willingness to help, to be on it.

"Well, I was thinking maybe some of the subs in your Sunday group might be willing to work out a schedule? I mean, anyone really, but I think he'd be less... I think he'd accept help from the subs more readily, you know?"

"Sure. Sure, man. Troy has a lot of friends. Do you need meals too?"

"Some. Yeah, some would be great. I think he wants to cook some too, so I'm hoping he can do that." He wasn't hoping, he was going to make it happen. That, and his boy's yoga. He and Troy needed some normal.

"Well, I do know a decent diner..." Carter laughed for him. "Are you sure you don't want me to get him a hospital bed?"

"We'll be sure to come eat at it." There was no telling when Troy might be ready to pull even a partial shift again. All that time on his feet... it would be a while yet.

And to hell with staying out of Troy's work life. Carter wasn't going to be the one who decided when *his* boy came into work anymore.

"I think Troy would set a hospital bed on fire and possibly me with it if he walked in and saw that. But thank you." Saul laughed. "One thing I know, he wants his own bed. I don't think he cares if it takes him half the day to get out of it and the other half to get back in."

Carter chuckled softly. "Well, then, his own bed he'll have. Do you need help with the first day home things, or do you prefer privacy?"

"Today I think we'll be just us. Can I call you tomorrow? I'll have a better idea of what Troy really needs then. I really appreciate your help, and your experience. I hadn't even thought about food yet." There were probably a lot of things he should have thought about by now and hadn't. He had a feeling he was going to learn some things the hard way.

"Don't worry about dinner. I'll have a runner bring by soup and rolls tonight. That will be easy and gentle."

This was one of those moments when he didn't know if he was young and dumb or just overwhelmed and normal. Maybe it didn't matter, he needed the help either way.

"Thanks, Carter. I really appreciate it. I'll call you tomorrow and give you guys an update."

"Can you text Geoff tonight? He's having troubles sleeping from stress."

"Yeah, of course. Is it about Troy? Tell him I'll text him tonight, and he can come by tomorrow. I just think Troy will want quiet tonight, you know?" However he felt about the whole tattoo thing, Geoff had been really helpful and he was Troy's best friend.

"I think Geoff will need me tonight, but I'll set him to making a plan, okay?"

"Sounds good. I'm gonna go over to the hospital. Have a good one." He hung up and sighed, taking the last sip if his coffee before heading out the door.

This time he did stop first for good coffee, and for a couple of egg sandwiches for him and Troy, and he ducked through the door into Troy's hospital room smiling, and carrying gifts like it was Christmas. "Good morning, handsome. Happy release day!"

Troy was sitting up in bed, fiddling with the heart monitor he had to wear for the next thirty days. "Hey, stranger. I'm more than ready. Let's go."

"I brought breakfast. We have to get you checked out. Did they bring paperwork already? I don't even know how this works." He went to Troy, gave him a kiss and sat a sandwich in his lap. "Eat. Also, coffee." He set Troy's cup on the table by the bed.

"Coffee. Thank you. They want to send me a nurse twice a week for a month, and they say I can't drive or go back to work for six weeks."

He'd spoken to the doctors. It was six weeks at least just to pick up ten pounds. It was going to be a while before Troy got back to cooking full-time.

"That's a lot of puzzles." He winked at his boy. "And porn."

"I'm thinking about painting the guest room."

"Yeah? Like a mural?" He was teasing, trying to get Troy's spirits up. Six weeks at minimum sucked. Especially for someone that had never even called in sick.

"Like a nice deep blue." Troy rolled his shoulders, wincing. "Maybe not today."

Okay, so cheering up might be a stretch. Maybe he should shoot for no breakdowns and getting home in one piece. "We can do it together if you want. Eat."

"Yeah. Eat." Troy unwrapped the sandwich, and those pretty eyes lit up. "Oh. Avocado. My favorite. Thank you!"

"You're welcome." The way to a man's heart... his mom

said that all the time. You'd think he'd have been a better cook. He sat on the end of the bed and took a bite of his sandwich. "Beats hospital food, huh? Have to start a big day off right."

"It does. I'll cook for you tomorrow morning." Troy slipped out a piece of avocado and ate it, moaning as he did.

"French toast. I haven't forgotten." He grinned. Watching Troy enjoy the breakfast kind of made his day. He wouldn't push Troy on cooking at all tomorrow, he had a feeling a lot of normally easy things were going to be hard for the next week or two at least. But he wasn't going discourage anything Troy said he wanted to do.

He bit into his sandwich again and hummed as the salty bacon made his mouth water. "I was hungry, man."

"You can have half of mine, if you want."

"No, thank you. You want to get your strength back, you need to eat, boy." He raised an eyebrow at Troy, though he wasn't all that surprised his boy didn't feel like eating. "Have the egg at least if you can't manage the biscuit."

Troy blinked at him, and that little buzz of electricity felt good in the pit of his belly. "I—"

He let Troy see the smile slightly tugging at one corner of his lips, then took a slow sip of his coffee before answering. "Something to say?"

Troy shook his head. "No, Sir."

His boy ate a bite, watching him, and Saul could feel the way Troy stopped thinking about all this garbage at the hospital and started focusing on him.

He finished his last bite and took another sip of his coffee, enjoying the moment more than he'd enjoyed anything in a week. Troy's change in focus, in body language, even in heart rate was totally gratifying. His usually familiar confidence wasn't actually gone after all, it was just being tested. It made his spine tingle when Troy stared at him that way. "Good boy. I want to find out about the paperwork and—"

"Mr. Finch!" A short, happy nurse came shuffling into the room pushing a wheelchair. "All I need is two more signatures and you're outta here."

"Seriously?"

"Yep. We have your nurse scheduled, your cardiologist, physical therapist, nutritionist. All that." She handed Troy a bag of pill bottles. "And these are yours."

"God." Troy looked a little panicked.

Saul tried not to look it, but he knew how Troy was feeling. "So... do all those people come to the house? Or do I need to get him to appointments? Is it all written down somewhere?"

"The nurse will come to the house, starting day after tomorrow. He isn't cleared to drive for six weeks, but you can get medical transport, and yes, everything is written down in the discharge papers."

"Okay. I'm on it." He'd sit with a calendar while Troy was napping later, and then he'd talk to Carter. Medical transport would suck. "Thanks."

"So sign here and on the next page, Mr. Finch."

Troy scribbled his name on both pages, then grabbed his shirt.

"If you want to get the car, we'll get him downstairs."

"I'll walk myself."

Saul shot Troy a look, then smiled at the nurse. "Can I take him? He can just hang in the lobby while I get the car, right?"

"Well."

"Please? I'd really appreciate it."

"You've got a good one here, Mr. Finch. Feel better soon." She smiled at him and left the room.

"Sit, boy."

"The temptation to bark is huge. I won't, because I respect you to death, but God, Sir, I want to." Troy gave him a wry grin.

He snorted. "Wow. It's a shame I can't levy stripes as punishment right now. Maybe I should order you to bark all the way to the car."

"If I could feel up to it, I'd welcome them." Troy sighed and sat. "I guess I'll be grateful that I feel good enough to tease and drink good coffee."

"I know you would. But remember, there is more to submission than that. You and I need to work, and we will. But teasing and drinking coffee is good too." He smiled and shouldered Troy's bag, then wheeled him out of the room.

Troy leaned his head back, smiled up at Saul. "Going home. Thank God."

"Oh, look at you smiling at me. I like that. I like that a lot." He leaned over and kissed Troy upside down. "We can snuggle and watch more creepy ghost shows. Carter is sending soup for dinner." He rolled Troy onto the elevator and sighed as the door closed.

"That sounds like heaven. You want to know something weird?"

He grinned. His boy could come out with just about anything. "Shoot."

"I think I feel better today with my sternum wired shut than I did last Saturday." Troy smiled at him, the expression open, easy.

That was kind of weird, Troy was right. "Good. That was a bad day. This is a good one." The elevator doors opened, and they rolled out into the lobby. "Want to wait outside while I get the truck? Soak up a little sun?"

"Yes, Sir. It'll be cold before we know it." Troy smiled at the people in the lobby, in the parking area. His boy was perking up, second by second.

"Right on. Out we go." Troy hadn't been outside in a week, so he parked the chair directly in the sun. His boy wouldn't be there long enough for it to be an issue. "Soak up that vitamin D. I'll be right back." He hitched Troy's bag higher on his shoulder and went to find the truck.

28

Troy stood in his front room feeling a couple three things. First? He was grateful as all get out to be here in the quiet, in his house. Second? He wanted a Dr Pepper. Third? There'd never been a longer set of stairs.

"You better sit, baby." Saul scooped an arm around him, and suddenly he was halfway to the couch. Had he lost that much weight? "What can I get you? Would you like a snack? Something to drink? Remote is on the arm there."

"Can I have a Coke, please?" The whole world seemed just a little different, a little fuzzy.

"Yeah. Dr Pepper?" Saul helped him sit and then headed for the kitchen.

"Yes, Sir. Please." He sat there for a second, blinking. God, he was fixin' to burst into tears like an idiot. *Come on, cowboy, suck it up.*

He'd damn near died, lying in the fucking park like a homeless man. If that guy hadn't found him, or had walked by thinking he was a drunk...

A weird panic rushed him, and the damn heart monitor started alarming, just making it worse.

Saul sprinted back from the kitchen looking panicked, tossed the can of Dr Pepper on the couch, and knelt in front of him, hands on his knees. "What's wrong? Troy?"

"I almost died there in that park." He hadn't believed it, not really. Not until he got home.

Saul took a deep breath and nodded. "Right after your surgery I went in to see you—well, I let Geoff go in first because honestly I wasn't ready—I'd never been in a recovery room. All the machines... and you looked so small in that bed and gray... I felt sick. Like deep in my soul sick. I think I know some of what you're feeling. I almost lost you." Saul's voice held steady until that last bit, he could hear the emotion but Saul stayed steady. "But I didn't. And you're home now."

The beeping slowed and the alarm stopped as he breathed with his lover. "I am. I'm home. With you. Thank God."

Saul shifted to the couch, put the Coke in his hands and an arm around his shoulders. "So. Scary shit over. I mean, in a way you're healthier than before, you know? They fixed the problem."

"That's what they said, that I'm going to recover and be better off." He already felt himself healing. He reckoned that's why he'd freaked. A man had to believe there was a god to be scared of the devil.

Saul kissed his temple. "I have big plans today. I'm going to sit here with you and hold you until you can't stand me anymore."

"Yeah? It's a hell of a job, but somebody needs you to do it." He opened his Coke, took a deep drink, then leaned in hard.

"I'm totally prepared." He felt Saul settle with him. "Breathing?"

"In and out, Master. Steady as it goes." Troy wondered if they were ever going to just be able to have a scene one day, just be two normal men.

"Good boy. How would you feel about my buddies bringing my stuff over tomorrow? Too soon? Too many people? I really don't have much."

"Bring it on. This is your home, you should have your things."

Saul glanced over and smiled at him. "Thank you. We need to talk about rent and utilities, food and stuff. Beer." Saul laughed. "Soon. Not this minute but think about it."

"Yeah. We'll do okay, though. I got some savings, and I will get back to work as soon as I can." Maybe even next week. Maybe.

"Six weeks minimum, and don't even think earlier is a possibility. Carter and I have discussed that. Sorry, boy. You get one shot at this recovery thing and you're going to get it right."

There were downsides to working for another Dom. Downsides, but shit, there was a huge comfort knowing that Saul and Carter had his back, that someone was caring for him. "Y'all are talking behind my back."

"Yes. We are." Saul sighed. "I was in over my head for a bit."

"You were there for me. I'll never forget it." Saul had been with him, every time Troy had needed him.

"Of course. I didn't want to be—I *don't* want to be anywhere else. I love you. Turn on the TV. We're talking ourselves in circles." Saul chuckled and pointed to the remote next to him.

"Yes, Sir." Ghost hunting. Laughing. Snoozing together on the sofa.

Just like last week.

Except he didn't think he'd seen five minutes of anything before he'd fallen asleep. He woke up feeling a little stiff, lying against Saul, his Master's chest rising and falling rhythmically under him. The light had shifted, and he knew by the shadows it was afternoon, maybe two or three already. They'd been asleep for a couple of hours.

He needed to sit up, to pee, and to take half a pain pill. He clenched his teeth and forced himself to push up and not moan. Oh fuck him sideways, he was sore, and he needed to think about supper.

Had Saul mentioned supper? Maybe? Hell, he didn't know.

"Hold on. I'll help," Saul said sleepily. Troy watched him drag himself awake and stretch long and tall like a cat. "Got this."

"Didn't mean to wake you up, love." God. Okay. Sitting. Maybe he'd just wait to piss until, well, maybe next week.

"I was just dozing." Dozing for two hours. Sure.

Saul sat up, took a breath and then stood. "Okay. Where were you headed? Kitchen? Bathroom?"

"Bathroom. I gotta go." He sighed and held one hand up to his Dom. He needed help. "Please."

Saul nodded and helped him up, giving him a moment to get his balance. They started moving together, Saul's arm around his back, supporting him. "We should get you upstairs after this while you still have some strength."

"Maybe I'll just sleep on the sofa. That looks like a long way." Maybe tomorrow he could crawl up.

"Carter offered to get you a hospital bed." Saul grinned at him and stopped outside the bathroom.

"I'd beat his toppy ass," he growled, before heading in to relieve himself. He'd waited so long it hurt, and he was panting and sweating by the time he came back out.

"Oh, baby. Come sit in the kitchen. There's food." Saul got an arm under him and he felt like he'd floated across the kitchen to his seat. "Chicken soup."

"I don't know if I'm hungry." He didn't know if he could pick up a spoon right now, but he didn't want to let on.

"Well, then you don't know you're not. Might as well try." Saul let him sit and started moving around, finding a pot, warming the oven. "Carter will be disappointed if we don't."

"It's time for a pill after, yeah?" *Please?* He hurt.

"Uh." Saul checked the time on his phone. "You have a little less than an hour." The soup went on the stove and Saul put a few soft rolls in the oven to warm up. "How bad is it?"

"Worse than a mosquito bite for sure." He hurt like his chest had been cracked open.

"I'll sneak it to you a little early. In the meantime, maybe you can pretend it's a tattoo." Saul winked at him. "I mean... it's not the same, but, pain, right?"

"You're right, it's not the same." He smiled though, letting the tease be what it needed to be, a way to distract him, relax him.

Saul chuckled and set a glass of water down in front of him. "Shame, right? Uh... soup bowls are where?"

"Left side of the sink. Do I need to make room for your dishes?"

Saul shook his head. "I don't have any."

"Well, now you do." He had Fiestaware. Tons of it. Carter had teased him at the beginning, but the guys always found him some fabulous piece for Christmas, birthdays.

"I'm not kidding, I have like, almost no stuff. Most of what I'm bringing should probably live in the garage. My bikes, and my freestanding punch bag. My skateboard, skis, crap like that. Otherwise, I guess I have a suitcase and some books and stuff."

Saul sat a bowl of soup in front of him. "You need help with that, just ask."

"I'd like to go riding with you, and I love to ski." He grabbed the spoon, hand trembling like an old man's. He could do this. He could.

"You're on. I'm going to build you a bike when you're ready to ride." Saul set rolls out and then came back with a bowl of soup for himself. To his credit, he didn't say a thing or offer to help again. He just let Troy be.

"Good deal. I need to paint the spare room, replace that vanity in the guest bath..." Learn how to hold a spoon steady.

"I'm no designer but I'm pretty handy if you want help. Could be fun, doing it together." Saul took a bite of the soup and snagged a roll off the plate between them. "Good. Not as good as yours, and I'm not blowing smoke."

"I'd love help. I like the whole idea of together." He needed his pain pill, so he ate his soup. He didn't need to be tossing cookies.

"It's early, but I'm getting your pills. You look like a ghost." Saul hopped up and came back with the bag of meds from the hospital, unpacking it on the kitchen counter. "Damn, this is a lot of shit."

"Yeah, it makes my head hurt to look at it." He pushed the soup away. "I'm going to bed."

"Sit one more second, boy." Saul pushed a roll at him. "Eat that, take your pill, and then we'll get you upstairs. I promise."

"I'm so angry." He wasn't sure if he'd said the words out loud, but he meant them.

"Eat so you can take this thing, will you?" Saul rubbed his back gently. "You're exhausted is all. And hurting."

"Yes. I think I might be going crazy."

"The doctors said this was normal, boy. That your brain chemistry and hormones would be horked. We just have to be patient with it. Easy for me to say, I guess." Saul kissed the top of his head. "This grew in a lot this week. It's more like hair and less like fuzz."

"Do you like it?" Given length it would become heavy ringlets, all over his head.

"So far. The color is great. I like having something to play with up here. But the more important thing is, do you?"

"I don't think about it much." He reached up, smiling as the soft mini curls tickled his fingers.

"My adventurous ginger." Saul leaned close to his ear. "Finish that roll and I'll take you to bed. Our bed. And I'll climb in with you."

"Our bed." God, he ached for that. "I'll eat it."

"Good boy." Saul waited patiently while he forced it down, and then slid the pain pill over to him. "Lots of water."

He nodded. He wished he didn't need it, but he did. Bad. He took it and drank deep, the water cold and necessary.

Then he forced himself up to standing and took the bowls to the sink to rinse them.

Saul hovered but didn't stop him, staying close while putting away the leftovers. They moved around in the kitchen so easily together anyone would've thought they'd done it forever.

By the time he was done, the pill was starting to make the world fuzzy around the edges.

"I think, I, uh..." He blinked, staring down at his hands. What had he been doing?

"We were... going upstairs." Saul handed him a towel. "Dry your hands, baby. We better get moving before your knees go to Jell-O."

Saul let him dry his hands, then hooked an arm around his back to support him. "Ready?"

"Uh-huh. Longest damn staircase on earth. Should've bought a ranch style. Swear to God." Words kept falling out of his mouth.

"One foot in front of the other. This is easy shit. You can do this." They made it up one step, and then another, and then he lost count. "That's it. Just keep moving. I've got you."

"I want to do a scene with you one day. Have you ever given anyone your collar? Arnie would have laughed at me for even going there, daring to ask. Seriously. I have to wonder how he and Carter ever became friends. He's so formal, and Arnie just expected me to toe the line because... I guess because the first time he pushed down I sucked him off... weird, huh?"

"Two more steps, okay? That's it. One... and two. Good job." Saul wasn't answering his questions. He had asked them out loud, right? "I'm going to help you get undressed. Do you need the bathroom?"

"I'd better I guess. I want a shower. Not now. Tomorrow. God, I'm glad we're home. I finally get to be naked with you." He sucked in his gut, blinking as his sweats fell off. "Oops."

Saul laughed. "Saves me a step, skinny. God, you need to eat more." Saul got him untangled from the sweats and helped him to the bathroom. "You're getting woozy, I'm coming in. Falling in here would be bad."

"Uh-huh. I've fallen a lot in my time." The doctors had asked a ton of questions, all answered with 'rodeo'. He did his business, chatting away like his common sense had been derailed. "It's fixin' to get chilly, I think. Not cold, not yet, but too bad to camp. I'd freeze my balls off."

"We still have a couple of weeks before it's just not fun anymore. I'd like to go, I think it might be good for you." Saul followed him to the sink. "Hands. Then teeth."

"Teeth. No marks." How many times had he heard that? Watch your teeth, boy. No marks. None. Hundreds.

He brushed his teeth, the world swinging dangerously from present to past, hiccupping around. Arnie. Saul. Geoff. Saul. Carter. Saul. Saul.

Saul placed a cup of water in his fingers so he could rinse and then he was moving again, this time toward the bed. It seemed so big after a week in that narrow torture chamber.

"Climb in, I'm coming." Saul undressed quickly, adding his clothing to the pile in the center of the floor. "What do we do with this monitor? It just... stays like that?"

"Uh-huh. Just leave it on my chest." The thing was a little like an alien pod, stuck on his pec. "Turning into a robot. Beep boop beep." God, he was funny.

"Yea, okay. Come here, Data." Saul chuckled and dragged him in, the sudden touch of hot skin against him sobering him just enough to see the way Saul was staring at him. So much worry.

"Home." He reached for Saul, stroked his cheek, trying his dead level best to comfort his lover. "God, we're home."

"We are. Sounds good right? Home? Love you, baby. Close your eyes, you need to rest. I'm right here." Saul was everywhere, heart beating against his temple, arms around him, legs tangled up with his.

"I love you, Master. You make it better. Make the weirdness tolerable."

"You make everything better, Troy. Confusing sometimes

but better. We've got this." Saul kissed his forehead. "Sleep, boy."

"Yes, Sir."

Sleep. In his own bed.

Yes.

29

Saul spent an hour trying to fall asleep and another just allowing himself to hold Troy and be happy with that before getting restless. He wasn't tired, not enough to sleep, and his mind was going a million miles an hour.

Troy had thrown him talking about Arnie and Carter, asking about his collar, and getting a good look at that heart monitor hadn't helped anything. Neither had the really scary way those sweatpants just slipped off his boy's hips. He had work to do.

God, so much work.

He managed to sit up and then slowly extract himself from Troy who barely even moved. His lover was out hard. He needed his phone so he could text Geoff like he'd promised, and he wanted a cup of coffee. He pulled on his jeans and dragged his phone out of the pocket.

We're home, Troy's sleeping. Chicken soup was good. I'm sure he'd love to see you tomorrow. When he didn't get an immediate response he added, *he's okay. Heart monitor looks a little scary to me, but I'm a newbie with this shit.*

Okay, coffee.

He tucked Troy in and jogged down the stairs. Maybe he didn't need coffee. Maybe he needed some green. He felt wound up, thoughts spinning like a top.

Have you covered for work. Have suppers covered for 3 weeks. What else can I do? Geoff texted. So kind.

What else could Geoff do? Saul wanted to know about Arnie. He wanted to know everything.

And he wanted a joint.

He didn't text any of that, though.

I'm good. You okay? Carter said you weren't sleeping. Can I help?

Could he help? He couldn't fucking help himself.

You want company? Carter's sleeping and I'm going a little crazy.

Oh good. Yes. Company is what he needed. *Come on over. Troy's out cold. We have beer. You have any green?*

Are you kidding? I'll be there in 15. I'll let C know.

Was it mean to hope that his boy stayed asleep long enough for him to enjoy this?

He ran back upstairs for a hoodie, it was getting cooler, and as much as he'd have liked to hang outside just in his jeans, he'd freeze his ass off. Troy hadn't even moved. Didn't look like his boy had so much as twitched since he'd left the room.

He and Geoff hadn't spent a lot of time together really, but they had Troy in common, in a big way, and he figured they were better off as friends.

Geoff pulled up in fourteen minutes as promised, coming right up to him on the little front steps. "Hey there, man. I'm glad to see you home."

He smiled. He liked that Geoff called it home. "It's good to be here. It's good to have him here finally too. Come on in. You want a beer?"

"God yes. I brought a spliff for us to share. You'll let me crash on the sofa if I can't drive, yeah?" Geoff's smile was warm, and he imagined Geoff had crashed here more than once.

"I've taken many a nap there. It's comfy as hell, right?" He led Geoff into the kitchen and opened two beers. "Let's take it outside. Thanks for coming. I needed company. I can't get out of my own head."

"I can't imagine, man. Seriously."

Oh, he thought maybe Geoff could. Geoff loved Troy dearly, had been stressing this too.

"Be honest. You can. You said you were going crazy." He pulled a chair out from the outdoor table for Geoff and then one for himself. "Carter said you couldn't sleep. Talk." That was a little more Dom-like than he'd intended, but fuck it, he was a Dom. Geoff knew it.

"He's my best friend. Closer than anyone but my Master." Geoff met his eyes, those big brown eyes wide, shimmering. "I can't imagine him being gone. It scares me to death. He's... I've taken care of him for a long time."

He smiled and shook his head, knowing what Geoff was saying. "And now he has me, that's true. But he needs you too, for other things."

"Yeah, I know. I'm not trying to take your place or anything, I just... I love him too. You two are our family."

"Troy says that all the time about you and Carter. He loves you guys, you're all the family he's had for years. And as much as I hate it, I need you guys like family right now for sure."

He knew he'd complicated things for everyone when he showed up. Carter was learning to pull back, Geoff was learning to let go a little... he sometimes felt as if he'd broken up a triad. At least an emotional one.

"I mean—that didn't come out right. I don't hate that it's you guys, sorry. I just hate that I have to ask for so much help. I hate that this is so *hard*. Like, really fucking hard." He reached over and picked up the big lighter Troy had out here for the fire pit. "Let's light that puppy up."

"Fuck yeah." Geoff pulled a hand-rolled joint out and offered it over. "And you don't have to be so careful with me. I'm on your side, me and Carter."

"No?" He lit up, took a nice drag and held it in, then handed the joint back to Geoff. He leaned back in his chair and exhaled slowly. "I never know if you'll think I'm overstepping. Troy is... he needs me."

"Yeah. It's hard, huh?" Geoff took a drag, holding it easily before letting it go. "I've almost been acting as a switch with him."

"Not almost. You totally have. You're the one who gave him what he needed. You made the choices about the art. That's a lot of ink. Hundreds of hours' worth. What did you get out of it? What need was that filling for you? It can't have all been about him."

"Do you know how heady it is, as an artist to have a whole body to do what I want to with? It's... fucking awesome. It's like a drug a little bit."

"No, not as an artist, but as a Dom I do." Heady was a good word. And it was definitely a high. Speaking of... he reached for the joint and took another hit. Geoff knew the good stuff.

"And before you there was Arnie." He sighed. "I don't mean to... I mean, I didn't know him obviously since he died when I was five and all. But the few things Troy has said about him make me... uncomfortable."

"You mean the bag deal? That pissed me right off. It

felt... creepy." Geoff blinked at him. "This is between us, huh? I wouldn't hurt Troy for the world."

"Yeah, the bag. And today he said that Arnie just expected him to toe the line. Toe the line? It will stay between us, but I think I should know what the deal is." He handed the spliff back to Geoff and took a swig of his beer.

Geoff sighed and took time for another deep hit before he answered. "So, it was a different world, right? No one in rodeo was out. No one. It was a death sentence. Arnie was..." Geoff sighed. "Arnie was a Top, no question, and he didn't take no for an answer. There was Arnie's way, or you left. Arnie adored Troy, but it wasn't a formal arrangement. It wasn't always sane."

A different time. Okay, that he understood. Things weren't great for a lot of people even now, in rodeo or otherwise. But the rest was... "He was a Top. He wasn't a Dom." He sighed. He wanted to rant and get angry but that wasn't going to make it better. It was twenty years ago. His job was to look after Troy now, treat his boy right.

"I hope Troy understands the difference. I hope he knows there's no line, no bag of rocks. That it's our way, not mine." Oh, the green was kicking in nicely, he was relaxing for the first time in days.

"He's been with all of us—our little group—for twenty years. He knows how to say no, how to ask questions. I've tried to help, to release the pressure valve. I've done okay, huh? I helped?"

"Oh, Geoff. Man, he wouldn't be here without you. Both of you. He told me he'd intended to disappear after he brought Carter Arnie's buckles." And given the state Arnie had left Troy in, he was pretty sure Troy would have succeeded in doing just that. "You saved him I think." He glanced at Geoff, it seemed important that Geoff heard him. "I really believe that. You saved him."

"He's my best friend, so that means a lot. Thank you. You should have seen him then, this scared, skinny kid who fully intended to walk up into the mountains and die." Geoff shook his head. "It was Carter who found out he could cook."

"He's working hard. He wants my collar." Troy would get it eventually; he already knew that. It was about timing now, finding the right boundary, working through something.

"Oh..." Geoff fluttered a little bit, and it was utterly adorable. "That's so fucking cool!"

He grinned and nodded. "Yeah." He'd noticed that Geoff wasn't collared. Not in any traditional way that he could see. "It'll be a while, especially now. But he'll earn it." He sipped his beer again and dug at the label with his thumb. "It's going to be a long few weeks."

"It's a black light tattoo."

"What?"

"My collar. I saw you looking. It's only visible under black light."

"No way." Damn. He got a sudden image of Carter and Geoff's bedroom, their teeth and Geoff's collar glowing under an overhead black light. Oh. That he could never unsee. "Tattoo artist, of course. That's... crazy. How cool."

"Thank you. It was perfect. Just like what you two do will be. Assuming you survive the next six weeks. Drag?" Geoff was just giving him shit now.

"Troy's going to wake up and be the sober one." But he took that joint, didn't he? And he inhaled one more nice drag, keeping it in as long as he could manage before exhaling. "We'll survive. I don't know about Carter, though. I can't promise Troy will be back."

"Not ever? Seriously?" Geoff looked totally stunned, wide eyes, lips parted. "No way."

He shrugged. "He wants to open a yoga studio. I'm going to encourage him to do it." Plus six weeks from now Troy could go back to work, but he couldn't be on his feet all day. He couldn't carry anything heavy. He wouldn't be able to do his job anyway.

"He what? He's never said that to me..."

Oh, interesting.

He smiled. "He'd given up on it. I think he thought he knew how the next twenty years were going to go, and then..." And then Saul had crashed into Carter on the mountain. "Also, you're married to the man who told Troy he couldn't call in sick. What do you think Carter would have said if Troy said he was thinking about a studio?"

He liked Carter, but the man wasn't stupid. Carter knew what he had in Troy.

"Carter was jealous." Geoff blinked, his hand slapping over his lips.

"Oh, no. Out with it. Of who? Of me and Troy? You and Troy?" He grinned, giving Geoff shit now, and the joint back. "Drag?"

"God yes. Please." Geoff took the joint and inhaled deep, holding it. Eventually he was going to have to breathe and answer Saul's questions.

"Troy told me he used to come to your tattoo sessions and then he just couldn't anymore. He's the jealous type, huh?" He never understood that. A Dom shouldn't ever need to be jealous. But he wondered if he would get it now. He'd never had the lover and sub in one person thing like he had with Troy before. "It's okay, I'm patient. I can wait you out."

Geoff groaned, smoke blowing out his nose. "Dude...

Doms, man. Carter was ejected because he has a no-cursing rule, and Troy, man, he cusses like a sailor. He was just hurt that Troy has allegiance to someone not him. He's used to having the final say, and he needs to hire more people. Troy gets a life."

He nodded. He'd gotten that exact vibe from Carter. And he didn't know exactly what Carter had said to Troy on the phone, but whatever it was made Troy... mad? Upset? Whatever it was, he was pretty sure it had been about him.

He was totally going to swear around Carter.

"So... is he over that shit yet?"

"Yeah. Yeah, he is." Geoff grinned at him, blinking a little owlishly. "You took care of Troy. You were there in the trenches, and you can see the love, man. You're his Master." Geoff turned a bright pink. "He's been... I mean, he's been real focused the last week."

Oh, he believed that. Carter probably needed to remind himself what was his. But he wasn't going to give Dom secrets away. Nope. "You totally needed that. You... man, you were as gray as Troy when you came out of his room after the surgery. Your Master has been worried about you."

He put his hand up when Geoff offered him the spliff again. "I'm good. Really good. Troy will need me when he wakes up. He's going to sleep for a while though, those pain pills are serious shit. Are you hungry?"

"I'm always hungry. Always. I can't cook worth a damn, though." Geoff worked the cherry off the joint. "There's enough for another puff later."

He needed to get up. "I wonder if Troy can have it?" He wiggled his toes, leaned forward and stood up. "Oh. Look at me. Peanut butter and jelly or queso? Does your Master know you're here, man?"

"Peanut butter and queso sounds scary, and of course,

my Master knows. I told him there would be green, and he said he trusted you to take care of me."

"No, idiot. Peanut butter and jelly. God." He offered Geoff a hand up. He wanted queso though. "If you're crashing, you can have another beer. I live here now, so I can offer."

"I'd love one. Thank you. What can I do to help? DoorDash?"

"Oh, that would be fantastic. I want queso. And tacos. Maybe order a couple for Troy? He won't eat them but it's nice to be thought of, you know?" Maybe Troy would eat them, who knew? Maybe he'd make his boy eat one. "Guess what? I ordered him to eat his breakfast this morning."

"No shit?" Geoff stared for a second. "He doesn't eat breakfast, man."

"Yeah, I know. But that, like, one meal a day thing? That's not gonna support his medication or his physical therapy. And wow, he needs to gain, like, ten or fifteen pounds. His sweats fell off him. Like, fell. To the floor. Just *whoop!*" He laughed. It wasn't funny really, except that it was. A little. "*Whoop!*"

They started giggling, just leaning together like kids, holding on as they howled. God, he needed to remember this, that he wasn't alone, that he and Troy as a couple had a community.

"Beer. You need a beer." He was still catching his breath and giggling between words as he headed for the fridge. "I'm so glad you came over. God, I was... whoa. You know?"

"I do. I shut the studio down for a few weeks. I just... Whoa." Geoff pushed his hair behind his ears. "It's crazy, but it just shocked me, bad."

He nodded. That made him feel better, that it wasn't all because he was just young and stupid. That Geoff had been shocked and off-balance too. Worried. All of that was okay he guessed.

"I should have told you to order extra guac. Troy loves avocado."

He knew about Arnie now and so much of what Troy had said made more sense. Troy hadn't had this before really either. Troy had watched for twenty years, had learned, but he hadn't experienced it a bit.

Damn.

"I know. I did."

"Right. Of course." He laughed again. "Have you and Troy ever... you know?"

"No." Geoff's cheeks lit up and he groaned. Oh, Saul knew there was a story there, so he just waited for Geoff to confess. "Well, you see, once I walked in on him when he was jacking off. It was... it was weird and embarrassing. He was crying. I may have freaked."

Crying. That he hadn't seen yet. "Shit. That sounds kind of fucked up."

"It was a long time ago. He was so lonely, you know?" Geoff swigged his beer. "I wanted to tell him he didn't have to torture himself at the get-togethers, but... I needed him to know he was welcome."

"I'm glad it got better. I liked that gathering. I can't wait for the next one." It might not be the grand entrance he was hoping for anymore, but it would be enough. Comfortable. Troy would feel safe and cared for. It would be good.

"There will be this one, then Halloween! I love the holiday gatherings. Love them."

Oh man. Holidays. It hadn't even occurred to him what he was going to do. That'd be a hell of a conversation with Troy, wouldn't it? "I usually spend the big holidays with my mom..."

"Well, I don't know the situation, but you know Troy always has a place with us. Always. He can always help Carter cook."

"No, no. If I go, he's coming. If he doesn't want to, then we'll... do whatever we do together. With you or whatever. I've brought guys home before. I brought Deitz home, and he was wearing a collar even." Maybe TMI. Oops. Well, his mom was okay.

"Oh! Oh, that rocks! I thought you couldn't take him. We're careful to plan our celebrations so that we can all make them."

"Oh. No. I can take him, I just don't know how he'd feel about it. There'll be some family there—siblings, nieces and nephews. Might be a crowd. I don't know how all of that will sit with him." Christmas could be chaotic. Fun as hell, but crazy.

"He misses being in a family, I think." Geoff shot him a grin. "I bet he'll say yes."

"Yeah? Awesome. I think my mom would love him, I really do. She's rolled her eyes a some of the guys I've brought home, but none of them have been like Troy. You and Carter don't have family?"

"Both of Carter's parents are gone, and mine. My family is here with him, Troy, you, Doc, Trav, David, all of you."

That wasn't the first time he'd heard that story. He counted himself lucky to still have family to spend time with. "You could do a lot worse, man. I was fascinated by Doc—is that weird to say? He kind of looked at me like I was from outer space or something."

"Right? He goes through subs madly too. He's kept little Ben, though, for a good long while." Geoff shook his head but kept his smile. "The first time I met him I wanted to cry."

"Cry? How come?" Doc was older, and a big guy, but there wasn't anything about him that made him feel that way.

"I don't know—he's super-imposing, and I was still working out where I belonged with Carter. I was... just overwhelmed."

"He's big. And yeah, I mean the way he was watching me was like he knew something about me that I didn't. I guess I see what you mean. How did you and Carter hook up?"

"I was a tattoo model at a convention in Denver—collared, bound, shown off. My boss had pretty much forgotten I was there. Carter hadn't. He unchained me, helped me take the collar off, and asked me to supper." Geoff curled up on the sofa, feet under him. "It's like the best romance novel, isn't it?"

"I love it. I hope you quit your job after. Oh." He handed Geoff the beer he'd been holding all this time. "Man, I forgot that was still in my hand. I think my fingers are kinda numb." He snorted. "Wow."

"Lightweight," Geoff teased. "And yes. I... well... to be honest, Carter just kept me and brought me to Boulder. I had been living in LA."

"He kept you." Saul laughed. "I don't know, I like how that sounds for some reason." He started to sit down on the couch with Geoff but hesitated. "I'm going to run up and just check on Troy, okay? Make sure he's..." *Not trying to get out of bed.* "Comfortable. I'll be right back."

He just suddenly felt like he needed to touch Troy. Make sure his boy was whole.

"I'll keep an ear out for the food." Geoff waved him off with a smile. "Tell him hi if he's awake."

Oh.

326 | JODI PAYNE & BA TORTUGA

"You want to come up and see him? Even if he's asleep, it's okay. I get it."

"Nope. You're his Master. If he needs anything, it's you."

He squeezed Geoff's hand and smiled. "I'll be right back."

He usually took the stairs two at a time, but he was moving slowly; the green doing just what it was supposed to do, relaxing him. At the top of the steps he peeked around the doorframe and then moved quietly into the room.

Troy was curled up with his pillows, holding them, rocking with them, muttering in his sleep.

Hm. He climbed up behind his boy in bed and tucked an arm over Troy's side. "Shh."

Troy immediately eased, sinking into his arms. He sucked in a breath, letting in that relaxation, the peace suiting him to the bone.

He could stay, maybe even should stay, but honestly, he wanted a little more time with Geoff. And tacos. He knew these times when Troy was sleeping hard were the only time he was going to get a break, and he needed breaks, right? It was okay. When Troy was awake, his attention belonged to his boy one hundred percent.

He was struck suddenly by the strangest flash of a memory from a very long time ago. Mom and Aunt Ellie talking about Dad. He was about... well, he had to have been six—that was the year his dad died. They were standing in the hall in his old house in Philly and Aunt Ellie was telling Mom she had to take care of herself.

Whoa. He thought he'd forgotten everything about that time. He tried to get more out of the memory but couldn't, it faded as fast as it had come on.

Aunt Ellie, who was Dad's sister, had joined Dad about

five years ago. Maybe she was looking out for him. Huh. He laughed softly.

Or, maybe I'm just high.

Either way, there was queso on the way, guacamole, salsa, and he was starving. Surely his snarling belly would disturb Troy.

Surely.

"Love you," he whispered, kissed Troy on his not-so-bald head and slipped carefully out of bed again.

30

T roy wasn't sure if he was tired to death or if he was so ramped up that he couldn't sleep. He couldn't settle, not even for a second, so he headed back to the kitchen.

He needed to make Saul's lunch for tomorrow and do some goddamn laundry. Make room for Saul's things in the drawers. Mow the grass.

Troy rubbed his chest, shook his head. Focus, man. Lunch.

Saul came trotting down from upstairs and hurried to his side, catching him under one elbow. "Whoa, you're up? Why didn't you call me? You okay?"

"I need to make your lunch." Of course he wasn't okay, but he wasn't going to get better sitting on his ass.

"You sit, baby. I can do it." Saul stopped him. "Really. You go rest. Why don't you put on some football?"

"It's Tuesday. We have two more days." Wasn't it Tuesday? God, he felt like the world was moving on without him.

"Right. I'm losing days, sorry. Want to find a movie? I was just going to start some laundry for you."

"You don't want me to do it?" A huge part of him was fucking relieved.

"Nope. I got it. It's too heavy for you right now, you're not allowed to lift it, remember? Six weeks." Saul kissed his cheek.

"Hasn't it been six weeks?" he teased. God, there was no way. None. He would lose his mind.

Saul grinned at him. "Yeah, but it's like Groundhog Day. You have to live them all over again. Will you sit, please? You're making me nervous standing here. Are you hungry?"

"I don't think I'll ever be hungry again, some days. Do you think I can do yoga soon?" He wasn't sure. If he asked the nurse, she'd say no. She said no to everything. He didn't want to hurt his sternum, but he wanted to move.

"Six weeks, and ten pounds. You're going to have to find a way to be Zen about this, Troy. Do the time, gain the weight, and then we can talk about adding things back." Saul shook his head. "I'll get lunch. Carter sent you some a cream of something soup and some sourdough."

God, he wanted to just throw a temper tantrum, which would not help anything. Nothing. Well, maybe he'd feel good after. "I'm not hungry."

His little monitor started beeping, warning him to calm the fuck down.

Saul sighed. "You have to take it easy and you have to eat. This isn't going to last forever."

"I know. I know. I'm sorry. I just... I'm sorry." Fuck.

Saul moved in closer, cupped his jaw with one hand. "Don't be sorry. Just breathe. Maybe we can call Solomon and see what he'd suggest? But even he is going to want me to fatten you up."

"He'd say, focus on your breathing, on your restorative

practice." And Solomon would be right. He just didn't seem to have a calm center anymore.

"Is that something I can help with?" They were moving, Saul pulling him gently into the kitchen. "I will if I can."

How the hell was he supposed to answer that? "I honestly don't know. I've lost my center. There's no balance right now."

"Hm. You have to accept. You know who said that to me? Kris. The day he and his Master, came in to design him a bike with Emma."

Accept. At least Kris was a hero. He was a cook with a heart defect and six weeks before he could get back to work.

"I can feel you mentally grumbling at me, you know." Saul sat him in a chair at the kitchen table. "Man, this is going to be a long six weeks if you can't breathe a little."

"I'm sorry. It'll be better tomorrow. You'll be able to get back to work, back on your schedule." He just needed to shut up and fucking deal. He'd been dealing for twenty fucking years just fine. Saul had a whole life ahead of him. If Troy wanted to be a part of it, he needed to suck it up and not run him off.

Saul glanced at him, brow furrowed, and then at the floor. After a thoughtful couple of second Saul pulled out a chair and sat with him. "This isn't about me. It's not about my schedule, or my work. It's about you, Troy. It's about your health. I don't want you to find some peace with these first few weeks so I can get on with my life. I want you to recover, to be whole again so that *we* can get on with *ours*. Together. I swear to you it's not about me. It's about us."

He didn't know how to deal with this. No. No, that wasn't true. He knew how. He just couldn't *do* it. "It's like someone else took up residence in my brain."

"Is that someone else still my sub?" Saul looked at him

meaningfully. "If the rest of it is too hard right now, you can serve me and not have to think about any of it."

"I'm yours, Sir, good and bad." Hopefully, Saul could take him. "And it is hard. Fucking exhausting."

"You hurt, boy. The pain meds do a number on you. You're sleeping but maybe not getting good rest. You're not eating enough. I'm a nag, the nurses are nags..." Saul grinned at him. "You're up against some big hurdles. And tomorrow Geoff is coming to hang out with you. You think I can be an asshole?"

"I'll just send him home if he's not nice." He did grin back at his Master, taking Saul's hand.

"Can we please agree that you have to eat three times a day so you can gain some weight? Hungry or not? You've got meds to support and you need your energy."

"I haven't done that since I started rodeoing. You'll say if I get too puffy?"

Saul shook his head. "You can watch the scale. Ten pounds and you can back down to two. Fifteen and I'll stop nagging altogether. Deal?"

"Fifteen pounds... that much?" He'd lost that much? Really? That was almost scary.

"You lost ten and the docs want you up five. You were underweight." Saul leaned over and kissed him, then stood up. "Skinny. I'm feeding you this soup."

"What kind of soup?" He told himself he could do this— breathe, focus, let Saul care for him.

Saul opened the container. "Cream of potato? I think?" And some yummy-looking crunchy things. Maybe croutons? I'll tell you what. You eat a good bit of this, and we'll snuggle on the couch for a while and find something stupid on TV."

"I do like snuggling on the sofa with you." He could get

used to it. Hell, he was already used to it. "Make sure you make yourself some."

He nodded, smiling. "I will. I'm hungry and this smells really good. I think Geoff said tomorrow he's bringing something you can chew. How is your pain right now?"

"I don't want another pill. They make me stupid." Although, maybe half a pill would take the edge off...

"You don't have to have one unless you need one. You're allowed Tylenol too, if you think that's enough. They do make you pretty loopy. You said some weird shit yesterday."

"Oh God. Like what?" Weird as in 'I like mustard on my Saltines' or weird like 'I called you Arnie'?

Saul shook his head and shrugged. "It's not important, it was just nonsense. You were high. What do you think about having a glass of milk instead of just water? Add some calories?"

"Sure. Thank you, Sir." He could drink a glass of milk, no problem.

"Great. My evil plot to fatten you up is underway." Saul laughed and brought him a bowl of soup, a spoon and some crackers. "One thing I'll say for soup, it heats up quick."

"It does. That's one of the best things." He loved making soups—chicken and rice, potato, beef stew. Oh. Chili.

Saul set a glass of milk down and sat at the table to eat with him. They were quiet as they each took their first few bites, but he knew Saul was watching him. Not watching what he was eating—watching *him*.

He kept stealing glances in return, curious at first, and then admiring. His Saul was lovely, and Troy thought he could admire him for hours.

"Hey, Troy?"

Uh oh. Something was on his lover's mind. "Something wrong?"

"No, no. I just... I'm trying very hard not to judge, okay? But... I just wanted you to know that I won't ever have a bag with some arbitrary number of chances in it. There is no line with me, okay? I love you. I'm not keeping score or... and I won't try to trip you up. Okay? I just wanted to say that."

"Oh." What was he supposed to say to that? That he knew, because he did? That he'd let Arnie do that to him? That he'd been a stupid, desperate kid? "Thank you. I love you too."

That was honest and true.

"I know everything is different now. You're different now. I just... needed you to know. So, now you do." Saul gave him a shrug and a smile. "How's the soup?"

"Carter's not half the cook I am. It needs garlic."

"Carter's hired someone." Saul winked at him. "Finally."

"Huh." Okay, that was both good and bad. Good because he'd need help when he got back, but bad because, damn, he wanted Carter to need him to be back.

Saul touched his hand. "Don't worry. Carter will have a job for you—if you decide you want to go back."

"It's not like I have another job waiting for me..." He turned his hand over, twining their fingers together.

"Well, you kind of do though. You were talking about retiring, remember? To get your instructor hours in so you could open a yoga studio. I remember it clearly because I thought it was such a great idea."

"When I retire, yeah." Maybe in another ten years—the condo would be paid off; he could save a ton of money and teach some classes.

Saul raised an eyebrow. "You could retire any time... right? What's stopping you?"

"I'm forty-five." You didn't retire at forty-five.

"Sounds like the perfect time to start a new career to me. You have twenty years in the diner. Aren't you bored yet?"

"God yes." He didn't mind it, but it was just another job. It sure as shit wasn't rodeoing. Still, Carter and Geoff were his friends, his boss and his tattoo artist.

"So move on. Get your teaching hours in. I bet your mortgage can't be much more than what I was paying in rent. I can help support you through it some, right?" Saul grinned at him and picked up a cracker.

"I... I think I should be careful. Think about this." Nothing good ever just happened, right?

"Well, you have time. Six weeks, at minimum." Saul winked. "And look at you, you just about finished your soup." He got a quick kiss on his forehead and then Saul took his bowl. "Good boy. How do you feel? Nap? Meds?"

"I think I'll take a half of a pill before we settle on the sofa." That had been the plan, and he intended to enjoy it.

"I wasn't sure you'd really be up for it. Awesome. Why don't you head out there? I'll do the dishes and start the laundry and then I'll be out." Saul started up the water and dropped all the dishes in the kitchen sink.

"You sure you don't want me to do laundry?"

"Boy."

That single word, that tone, made him shiver.

"Go sit. No, wait. Go... kneel." Saul went back to the dishes. "Now."

Oh God. God. What if he got down and couldn't get up? What if...

Stop it.

If he got down and couldn't get up, his Master would help him. He knew that like he knew his own name.

"Yes, Sir." He wasn't sure if he was supposed to take his pill or not, so he erred on the side of caution. He eased himself down onto the sofa, then laboriously worked on getting to his knees.

He'd managed it by the time Saul finally joined him. His Master held out a bottle of water and half a pain pill. "Good boy." Saul sat on the couch behind him and rested hands on his shoulders, kneading gently.

He felt like his skin was resting directly on his bones. He sighed, took his pill, and let himself relax, feel that touch.

"Ready to come sit with me, boy? Let me know if you need a hand." Saul gave his shoulders a squeeze.

"Yes, Sir. Please." He was at that place where the world was held back with a thin piece of tissue.

Saul helped him up enough that he could slide back onto the couch. "Are you feeling more weak or more in pain? Your meds tend to kick in pretty quick." They settled together and Saul helped him get close, get comfortable. "There. Just lean right on me. Good?"

"Good. Thank you, Sir." He felt fragile, but not weak. It felt like an important distinction.

"So. Food Network? B movie? Weather Channel?" Saul kissed his head. "Did I tell you Geoff is coming to hang with you tomorrow? And he has a whole schedule of people to keep you company while I'm working. Subs from the Sunday gathering."

"You're good to me, Sir." He didn't really need the company, but the idea that Saul and all his buddies cared? That was the best medicine. Geoff would be a butt, but he knew he and Kris could get into trouble together.

Saul turned on the TV and found the Food Network. "Oh, that was all Geoff and Carter. All I did was call and panic at them." Saul laughed. "I'm new at this."

"I think we all are. Usually I do it—make the calls and food, all that."

"Yeah? Did you do it for Kris and Matt?" His Master was playing with his hair, combing fingers through the short curls.

"I did. I helped with all the details—accessibility, getting Matt to Germany, getting them both back."

"Wow. That's pretty amazing, actually. And kind. No wonder they are all over being helpful. That, and maybe the whole bike thing. I got a call from Matt asking how I was yesterday. It was pretty cool of him."

"They're all good guys. My family." God, he loved this fine son of a bitch.

Saul nodded. "They are. You couldn't pick a better one. Feeling that pain med yet?"

"Little bit, yeah." The whole world was a little blue around the edges.

"*Chopped*." Saul pointed to the TV. "I love this show. It's like the *MacGyver* of cooking."

"Oh man. There is some gross shit on this show, especially the Halloween episodes. I love it."

"The grosser the better. Have you seen the one with the cocktail onions and the fruit punch? Ugh." Saul laughed. "Sometimes I wonder what it's like to be a judge."

"Sort of like training a new kid at the diner, right?" Troy chuckled softly at himself. Sometimes he wondered about his sense of humor; mostly he just went with it.

Saul was stroking a solid hand over his shoulder and down his side, the touch warm, soothing. "God, I hope not. I hate to think what you would end up putting into my French toast."

"I take great care with your French toast, I'll have you know." He turned to face Saul, leaning for a kiss. "Great care."

"Mmm. Best I ever had." Saul kissed him, slow and deep,

tongue gliding along his. He leaned in and breathed, letting Saul control this.

Saul moaned softly and pulled him closer, though their kiss simmered rather than flared, his Master keeping them both in check. Just the act of breathing together made him feel like a million bucks. Made him feel healthier.

"Mmm. That was a good idea, boy." Saul smiled at him, a little buzzed. His lover stole another kiss, then tasted his jaw, his ear, breathed hot air on his neck.

"Oh God. That tingles so good, Master. All over."

"How long do you have to wear that monitor? I'm ready to make it squeal so loud it shorts out." Saul drew a thumb over one pierced nipple.

"Three more weeks. Damn thing." He hated it, but he had to be honest, he wasn't cleared for sex yet and his lover didn't seem to be interested in breaking the doctor's rules.

"Mother of God." Saul laughed, and caught his eye. "We're not getting out of bed on day twenty-two."

"Promise? I need you in the worst way."

Saul smiled and sighed. "I'm sorry, boy. I know. We have to wait, though. We have to do this right the first time so we don't have to ever do it again. Right? Your heart isn't something to fuck around with." His Master chuckled. "Like, literally."

"Right? I'm pretty sure I can't get it up yet. Soon, but not yet."

"It's only six weeks. That's all. I can wait six weeks, I think. I'm pretty sure. I'm trying to think of the last time I waited that long. I'm sure I have..." Saul seemed completely serious. "Maybe?"

"Shut up, you turkey. I was on a once, maybe twice a year diet for twenty years."

Saul laughed. "Well, let's see. For many of those same

years I was completely celibate. Although, I was under fifteen..."

"Yeah, yeah, yeah. I'm an old fuck. At least I have good ink."

"Your ink is the hottest. Seriously, I mean that. I love tracing it with my fingers, following the lines, trying to figure out Geoff's patterns. Not everyone can pull off that much ink, but it suits you. It's complicated and interesting." Saul did just what he said, and started tracing the pattern on his forearm. "Major turn on."

"Your illustrated man." He could feel each touch, every centimeter of that caress.

"Mhm. This is cool. The arm of this triskelion is all tangled up with this one over here, and then that one is twisted into this purple one. So cool." Saul did seem to into it, sharp eyes following curious fingers.

"Balance in all things, yes?" Troy leaned back, humming deep in his chest.

"Balance, moderation, patience... not things I have much of a grasp on, but I'm learning." Saul laughed softly, fingers pushing his shirt up, tracing ink over his ribs. "I think."

"Do you think he'll be able to fix it? My ink?" He hated how the incision looked. It was still raw and puffy with stitches.

"Oh, yeah. I bet it heals up way smaller than you think it's going to. Artists mask scars and stuff all the time, don't they? Geoff totally has this." Saul gingerly patted the skin around the incision. "Although this placement's is going to hurt like hell. We'll have to put all your piercings back in soon too."

"Yeah. I know, but it will be worth it." It was the most handsome thing about him.

"If you say so. You could also just be proud of your scar.

It's like a war wound, you know? It's the thing that could have killed you but didn't." Saul kissed his chest, just to one side of the stitches, and then the other side too. "You beat it."

"I hope so. I hope I come back stronger." He would settle for coming back all the way, but stronger would be better.

"You will. I know you will. How could you not? You're better now than you were. Get your teaching hours and everything, you'll dump all that stress too. Win-win." Saul was really into the yoga teacher idea.

"I don't know. It's a huge chance." What if he fucked up? Lost the house? Hurt someone in class?

"It's a lot, I know. You think about it. Maybe you could start out partnering with Solomon? Invest in his studio. Or teach for him. Anyway, sleep on it for a couple of weeks. You have time." Saul was still exploring his ink, fingers moving lazily over his skin. "Remember I'm here now, I can pitch in, right? It's not all on you anymore."

He wasn't sure how to think about that. He didn't want to be that guy who took advantage, but he didn't want to be the one that held his thoughts away from Saul, either.

Shit, did that even make sense?

"How are you feeling, boy?" The switch from lover to Dom was deliberate, he knew. "Do you hurt or was half enough? Do you want to lie down for a while? Or maybe just crash here?"

"Stoned, Master. I want to sit with you for a while. Please." He didn't want to sleep anymore. He was tired of sleeping.

Saul's laugh was low and seemed knowing in a way that someone Saul's age probably shouldn't. Saul was part reckless twenty-something and part steady confidence. Or wisdom. Or maybe Saul just got him.

He didn't care, one way or the other. He just wanted to be with his Dom. That suited him to the bone.

His Master let the room go quiet except for the TV, but warm fingers kept touching him, kept soothing, reminding him Saul was right there and paying attention. "So is it a good stoned? Like mellow? Or is it like whoa, pink rhinos, dude?"

"It's more like being slowed down, backed off away from you. Everything is blue. Like literally. Blue."

"That's wild. Well, you're not away from me. You're right here where I can get my blue arms around you." Saul grinned.

"You're keeping me, are you?" God, he sure hoped so.

"Hell yeah. I'm going to take you home to Mom."

"I would love that." The words were out without a single hesitation, mainly because they were true.

"Yeah? Me too. I think she'll like you. I think everybody will like you. I was thinking you'd like to do the holidays. Thanksgiving, Christmas? Geoff said they plan parties for the group around people's travel schedules, so we won't miss out."

"Either way works for me. Are y'all slammed at Christmas at the bike shop?" Carter would give him time off, no matter what. He knew it.

"Nope. We're sort of busy with snow bikes and stuff after Thanksgiving until the week before Christmas but then we close for a month, right through January. It's winter. February is totally dead. We have short hours and a four-day week, and we spend a lot of time cleaning and restocking for the spring."

"Let's go for Christmas, then. Do y'all have a big to-do?" Troy had loved Christmas when he was a little boy, then he'd learned to love it again here.

"Huge. Family, extended family, family friends. Anyone who needs a home. We don't get all my siblings at once, but there are always three or four of us and kids and dogs. Enough food for an army. It's a nuthouse." Saul sounded excited about it, those had to be good memories.

"I'll be happy to help with anything. Honest. You just let me know." He'd have to just see where he fit in.

"I will do that." Saul kissed his temple. "Geoff said you'd want to go. I wasn't sure. People are funny about family sometimes."

"I miss having a bunch of family around. I haven't had it for a long, long time."

"Well, you get me, you get those jokers too. At least at Christmas. Otherwise, we just text mostly. Mom's in Syracuse now, with Abner and his family, so we'll go there. Hope you like snow. Like, a lot."

"I live in the Rockies, man. I like snow." He grinned, his nose wrinkling with how big it was. "Otherwise I'd be a masochist."

Saul blinked at him. "Heaven forbid!" Saul lost it, giggling so hard he shook them both.

He cackled, just tickled as all get-out. Damn, he was funny.

"I'll remember that the next time you're tied up. Which isn't aerobic and is still in my toolbox of things we can do until I can fuck you again." Saul's laugh grew softer and darker. "Just for the record."

"I like your records, Sir. I like them a lot." He reached up to touch Saul's laugh, trace his lips.

Saul smiled for him. Touched his finger with the tip of a naughty tongue. "Good. And? I'm taking you out on a date Friday night, so decide where you'd like to eat for dinner."

"You are?" How dear. Honestly. "I'd like that. I'll even let you drive."

Saul laughed. "You're not allowed to drive, you nut. I was thinking dinner, and then depending on your energy level, a movie out, or here. We can have popcorn either way."

A date, holidays with family, talk about teaching yoga... Saul seemed pretty serious about planning a future together despite... everything. Maybe Saul was right. Maybe six weeks wasn't forever.

Maybe it was just a pause, a really long shavasana.

Troy could maybe live with that.

31

S aul was grateful for all the help Geoff and everybody was giving them.

Really.

Okay, so he did have to laugh at everyone's interpretation of making sure Troy ate and rested. It was like when his mom used to leave him with Nanna and she'd give him cookies and turn on cartoons, and then he'd go home where he had to eat broccoli and there was no TV allowed on a school night.

Nanna was fun. Mom was mean.

It was a pretty decent analogy, actually.

He was looking forward to their date for a lot of reasons; they needed to get out of the house, he wouldn't have to watch Troy every second to make sure his lover wasn't trying to do things alone, like climb stairs or bend over. But mostly he was just hoping to lift Troy's spirits, help Troy feel human. Have a little fun. Spoil the boy.

He knew Troy's energy faded as the day went on, so he wasn't going to be too ambitious. He'd seen it all week. Troy

344 | JODI PAYNE & BA TORTUGA

would have a decent day and by the time Saul got home from work, his boy was exhausted, impatient, hurting.

So, a short evening meal somewhere with different walls. That was as ambitious as he was going to get.

He parked his bike in the garage and keyed into the house, thinking maybe he'd grab a quick shower first.

He found his boy on his worn blue yoga mat, cross-legged, sound asleep, the expression on Troy's face pure bliss.

Ben was sitting on the couch, reading. When he saw Saul, he whispered, "I didn't want to wake him up."

He nodded, moving close to Ben and whispering back. "Thank you. Was the day okay?"

"He's been quiet, but not down really. Just quiet. He hasn't eaten much, though. Says he's saving up for your dinner."

Oh. He glanced back at Troy, smiling. He'd started to feel disappointed, but now he understood. Troy was saving his energy, and his appetite, for their date. How sweet was that? "I've got him from here. Thank you so much for coming over. Will we see you next week?"

"Yes, Sir. I'll be here Sunday, Wednesday, and Friday." Ben was the most gentle person he'd ever met. It was the slightest bit unnerving.

Especially given that he was paired up with Doc at the moment. Dude.

"See you Sunday then." He held the door for Ben, whose tiny car was parked in the driveway. "Thanks again."

"Of course, Sir. It was my pleasure."

He closed the door and then turned to watch Troy, wondering what the least jarring way to wake his boy up would be. Finally he went over and knelt in front of Troy, then reached out and touched his boy's shoulder gently. "Hey, you. I'm home."

"Mmm... You smell good." Oh, that was a lovely smile, warm and relaxed. "How was work?"

"Easy. Quiet, compared to the last few days. More like normal. How was your day? Ben said you were pretty quiet." He wanted to kiss those smiling lips so bad, but he was going to give Troy another minute or two to shake the sleep off.

"Solomon came and we did a restorative practice. I watched a movie with Ben, but my mat was calling me."

Saul quietly approved. He didn't want to push the yoga thing too hard and turn Troy off. But he was determined to help Troy start on a new path.

One that belonged to Troy, not Carter.

He didn't mean any disrespect by that, just that it was time for that relationship to change somewhat. Let Carter just be Troy's best friend's Dom and not his employer.

"You look very relaxed. Are you still up for going out? I understand if you're not." He did understand. And he wanted to go out. Was that bad?

"Oh, I want out of this house. I want to go sit in a different chair. Maybe have a beer."

He smiled, relieved. "I checked it out. You can totally have a little beer." He stood up. "What do you want to wear? I can run up and grab it for you."

"I saved a shirt and pair of jeans out of the laundry." Before he could growl about doing laundry, Troy winked. "Don't worry. Ben helped."

"He better have. No lifting for you. Is it me or does Ben have a... thing? Something." He had no idea how to explain why Ben wigged him out just a little.

He offered Troy both hands. "Ready? Up?"

"Ready."

He almost had to lift all of Troy's weight off the floor. His boy had stiffened up, and they rested together, breathing.

"You good? Do you need a hot shower or a stretch before we go?" Saul let Troy lean all he needed and just stayed patient. It wouldn't do their evening any good to rush this.

"Mmm... No. This is perfect. I was soaking you in while I remembered how to stand up."

He laughed softly. "Okay. Let's get you changed, and then I'm going to run up and find something clean too."

Dressing took a little while between getting Troy settled and then picking out what he wanted to wear. It sure was nice to have all his clothes here now, though. Most of his stuff was still in the garage, but he thought maybe he'd figure that all out on his day off.

He came downstairs in a plaid button-down, gray jeans, and his black Converse. He knew he was coming off hipster, but he really loved the shirt.

"Getting hungry? Did you decide where we're going?"

Troy looked good, if skinny, in his jeans and green shirt. His hair was beginning to move from auburn stubble to soft, tiny curls. Best of all was the smile, warm and relaxed and ready to go. "I was thinking about Argentinian food. That place on Arapahoe has great empanadas."

"Oh, I'm all over that. Great idea." He moved into Troy's space and kissed him. "You look good, baby."

"Thank you. I'm feeling pretty solid today." Troy wrapped around him, humming softly. "Almost healed."

He wouldn't go that far, but he was glad Troy felt good. He wanted them to have a nice dinner. Enjoy each other. "Truck, ho?"

"Who you calling a ho?" The joke was old and goofy, and it suited the mood he wanted to create.

"Heh. I set you up good, huh?" They made it out the door and into the truck, and he helped Troy put on the seatbelt. "Oh look, the stupid little pillow from the hospital is still in here." He tucked it in between the seatbelt and Troy's sternum. "Good?"

"Th-thank you, Sir."

Okay, still very tender. Good to know. They were going to have the stitches removed Monday. He needed to make sure the pillow was in here still.

"I'll take it slow." The last thing he needed to do was slam on his brakes. "I went easy at lunch so I could eat tonight." And he could definitely eat. He felt practically hollow.

"I want a criolla empanada. I'm craving caramelized onions. I might get a steak one too. Maybe chicken." Troy chuckled, shook his head. "I think I might be hungry."

That was excellent news. Even if Troy's eyes were bigger than his stomach. This was the first time Troy had actually wanted food. "I'm having a steak one. Or the spicy chorizo. Both maybe. Oh, my mouth is watering now." He wanted a margarita. Maybe he could just sip half of one.

There was very little in the way of traffic and he managed to find a parking spot in easy walking distance. "You think you can make the walk if we take it slow?"

"Yes, Sir. We'll just go easy. I knew it was time to get out of the house when I started stressing leaving, you know?"

"Yeah, I do. I was stressing taking you out. But you can't get back to normal, even slowly, without doing things. It's just dinner. With people around." He grinned and helped Troy out of the truck. "Easy. There you go. Nice job."

"Do I get a gold star if I'm good?" The warm tease didn't hold an ounce of sarcasm.

"No. You get a beer." Saul put an arm around him,

natural as anything, but helping to steady him discreetly at the same time.

"That's an encouragement, isn't it?" Troy shot him a quick—and fairly shaky—smile.

"Yes." He leaned over and kissed Troy's temple. "Almost there. You've got this."

"I'm fine. I totally do. The nurse wants me to gain another ten pounds. That's good, huh? I'm almost back to rights."

"That is good. You're doing great. You still have those pesky five weeks, though." He was teasing, but serious at the same time. But he was encouraged by this Troy, who was closer to the man he knew than anything he'd seen since they left the hospital.

"It'll go fast. This week did."

Yeah, he was fairly sure he was going to have to start binding Troy about week four.

Gee, what a shame. A hardship. How would he possibly cope?

Jesus. He cracked himself up.

Seriously though, they needed that. He needed to create some of those moments, just short scenes to keep Troy from getting restless and to keep him feeling like he had this under control. He had ideas. If Troy wasn't exhausted, he thought he might try one later.

He pulled open the door to the restaurant. "Empanadas!"

"Oh smell that." Troy groaned, a huge grin on his face. "I may eat forty of them."

"Listen to you." Yeah, that was his Troy in there. God, what a relief.

"Two?" The host grabbed a couple of menus. The place

was busy but not packed, the din of conversation nice but not overwhelming.

"Yes, please." They followed at Troy's pace, and were seated at a nice table near a window with a view of a garden out back.

Troy settled carefully, still managing to offer the host a smile. "It smells delicious. I can't wait."

"We'll take care of you, promise. Can I get you both some water?"

"Yes, please. And I'll have a margarita on the rocks, please. You want a beer, baby?"

"I do, with my meal, please." Troy shrugged as the host headed off. "I don't like a warm beer, and there's no way I can drink a beer on an empty stomach."

"Good call." Saul opened his menu. "Oh, man. I thought I knew what I wanted but... look at this menu!" There was whole page of just empanadas. And then four more pages of other amazing looking things.

Troy nodded. "It all looks like heaven. We'll just get one of each and share."

"You may be overestimating what your tummy can handle, just a wee bit." He laughed though, because Troy was having fun and it showed. "I think I better go with Plan A or I'll never be able to order." He put the menu down.

"We'll start slow then. Beer and yumminess. God, it's good to get out and about."

"It is. With other people, right? New scenery. I wanted you to get a little normal, even if it's just a taste. Remind you that this... this is your life. Your *real* life." Saul leaned back in his chair, watching Troy. "This is our town."

"Yes. I came here and knew I belonged here." Troy stroked his chest, right at the top of where Saul knew the incision was.

He felt the worry lines forming on his forehead and he pointed to the spot. "Hurts?"

"Itches. I keep telling myself that it's going to be worse before it gets better, but it doesn't work."

He grinned and waggled his eyebrows. "I'll make a big thing out of putting stuff on it for you later."

Troy's smile burned him to the ground. "I'm looking forward to Monday. It's got to be better, having the stitches out, right?"

"Yeah, stitches itch like crazy. I've had dozens." He laughed. He wasn't sure he remembered them all. "I got like, six or seven in my hand once, three in my eyebrow, a couple of fingers, some on my elbow—oh, both elbows actually. I'm a mess."

"Your eyebrow? Is that your roper scar?" Troy stroked his own eyebrow, tracing where Saul had his scar.

Saul snorted. That was cute. "You know I've never roped anything but subs, cowboy. I fell off my bike. Most of them are from wipeouts."

"When did you know that bikes were your thing?"

"Oh, man. I don't know." He thought about it, remembering when Abner had taught him how to ride, his first street bike, and when he'd gotten his first mountain bike. "High school? I spent a lot of time on my bike, I loved it. I'd bike to school and take crazy long routes home. And then I moved out here and got completely addicted to the mountains. I was out riding every weekend in college."

Troy nodded, a wry smile quirking his lips. "I hear you. For me, cooking is a job. I mean, I'm not a chef. I'm a cook. So not addicted."

"No, you're addicted to yoga." He gave Troy a sly smile. "Which could be so much more than a job."

"It already is more than a job. I just have to see if I can

make a living doing it." Troy shook his head, and Saul wasn't sure what the emotions that crossed Troy's face meant.

"You know I'll listen, Troy. What's holding you back?" Their server brought his margarita and took their dinner order, interrupting the conversation. He sipped his drink and sighed. "Oh, that's good. Want a taste?"

"Yes, please. Thank you."

He offered the glass and Troy took a sip, humming softly. "That is delicious. I should have chosen that instead of my beer."

"Never too late. You were waiting for your meal anyway." He looked at Troy and decided to let his other question go. This wasn't supposed to be a stressful evening. They had lots of time to hash that out. "Geoff says their Thanksgiving gathering is fun. Is that our plan?"

"I would like to, if you'd like. It's fun, joyful, informal. There's cooking and laughing and drinking. I'd love to go now that I'm yours."

Now that you're mine. "It's good, don't you think? Thanksgiving with your family and Christmas with mine?"

Troy nodded and touched his knee under the table, the caress light as feathers.

He could blame his warm cheeks on the first few sips of his margarita, but he wouldn't be kidding anyone. That feeling belonged to Troy. Of course, if Troy said anything, he might deny it. He was stupid happy, though. And stupidly in love, which was both amazing and sobering at the same time. So serious, and so much fun all at once.

"I've got some ideas for your bike. Emma thinks the titanium frames are going to come down in price in the spring, but I think you'd do just fine with the standard aluminum-alloy. I'm going to bring home a catalog for you to look at. You want to hit the mountain, right? Or did you want to stay on the road?"

"I'd like to try the mountain again. I'm strong enough. Hell, Carter does it. I ought to be in better shape, huh?" The touch never stopped, teasing him, the tablecloth not so much as twitching.

"Carter is pretty good, he's solid and smart. I think he thinks I'm reckless, which maybe I am, a little. He likes the game, I like the rush. We ride together well, though. The last time he actually started pointing out routes he thought I'd like." He slid his hand over Troy's, tangled their fingers and winked. "Naughty. I think you're right, you're stronger. And you're... I don't know what the word is. More free? Looser? Carter is really left-brain about it. I think you'd be more in tune."

"Yeah. I got on a two-thousand-pound bull every weekend on purpose. You wouldn't believe it about me now, but I understand liking the rush." Troy squeezed his fingers.

"Are you kidding? I totally believe it. You maybe think a little safer, but you still like the rush. You can fly, baby I've seen it."

Something in what he said made Troy light up, and that attention snapped right to him. God, that was heady, knowing how much Troy cared.

He returned the look, unable to keep the heat in. "We're going to tear up that mountain."

"We are. We'll tear all sorts of things up together. Soon, huh?"

"Soon. It'll go by quickly, you'll see. We'll make it work." The server walked by and he flagged her down, canceled Troy's beer and ordered his boy a margarita instead. "There. We can start by tearing up some tequila."

"Thank you, Sir." Troy pinked, and the smile he gave Saul was so pleased, warm and happy.

Going out was such a good idea. They'd both enjoyed their Friday night dates before he'd moved in, and given how well this evening was going, he'd make sure they kept up the tradition.

Their food arrived and he dug in like he hadn't eaten in days, but he kept an eye on Troy.

Troy ate hearty for about half of his first empanada, then he began to slow down, focusing more on that margarita.

"Good, right? This was a great choice. I haven't been in here before." Half an empanada was more than Troy had eaten in one sitting since they'd gotten him home. He wasn't going to nag his boy about it.

"I love it here. I spent a year or so coming every Monday for lunch, trying all the different things on the menu."

"Oh, that's cool. That's something a chef would do, you know." He sipped his margarita. He'd eaten enough that he wasn't getting much of a buzz, but man, it tasted good. "You're a good cook, Troy. I hope you don't think I'm putting that down. I love that diner. It's simple food, maybe, but you do it well. I've been going for years, and I've never left unhappy."

"I am a good cook. It's about keeping all your balls up in the air and paying attention, you know? Try to make sure your people are happy and taken care of."

"You've got that down." He wasn't talking about cooking, and he could tell Troy got it.

"Thank you." Troy leaned back, and Saul thought he could see the little bulge in his boy's belly. "So good."

"Stuffed, huh? We can take home a doggie bag and have it for dinner tomorrow night too." He wanted a kiss for dessert. Truthfully, he wanted more than that, but he was on the same six-week wait as his sub.

"Works for me. My eyes were bigger than my stomach. It was damn good food, though, Sir. Thanks for the invite."

"I had a feeling. It's much richer than what you've been eating lately too. And thank you for saving your energy so we could enjoy the time." He waved for the check and a couple of to-go containers. He wasn't rushing them, but he wanted to get Troy home and upstairs before his boy got too tired, so they could end the night on a high note.

"I wanted us to have a good evening. You deserve it."

"Thank you. We both do. It's been a stressful week, right?" He paid the tab, packed up their food, then stood up and offered Troy a hand. "How about we snuggle and watch a movie in bed?"

"That sounds perfect." Troy stood, moving slower now, his boy sweating the barest bit.

"I thought so." He offered his arm, like had on previous dates, just to be something familiar, romantic even. Polite, like mom taught him. And if it happened to give his boy some extra stability, that could stay between them. He leaned in, smiling. "You've got this."

"I totally do. I'm okay." Troy held on, though, didn't he? Held on and came with him. By the time they reached the car, Troy was leaning hard.

He waited a second for Troy get his breath. He helped his boy in, then ran around to the driver's side. He was watching Troy carefully, but kept things light. "You're a total stud." He tucked the pillow over Troy's chest and fastened the seatbelt.

"Thank you, Sir." Troy stroked his wrist. "Thank you for being here."

"I'm where I belong, boy." Yeah, that sounded like his

boy needed pain meds. He didn't waste time, and made sure to take the shortest route home, pushing the speed limit the whole way.

Troy didn't say much. He rested back into the seat, breathing a little shallow, but the heart monitor never went off.

He kind of felt like the trip inside from the truck was enough of an effort. "Do you want to just crash on the couch for a while? The stairs might be too much."

"I think I'll try to go up. The idea of snuggling is too good to pass up." Troy kissed his cheek. "I'm okay. I want to be with you."

He started to ask if Troy was sure, but that was a stupid question. He heard what Troy wanted. His boy was just going to have to dig deep. "I'll reward you with some meds when we get up there. And maybe a kiss." He winked, teasing. "Let's go."

"Maybe, huh?" Troy took the stairs slowly, one at a time, and that damn heart monitor was beginning to beep by the top.

He got them clear of the top step and let Troy lean on him for a second, but he didn't want to stay there long. He steered Troy toward the bed, sat his boy down and knelt where he could peer into Troy's eyes. "You're good. Look at me and breathe."

"Breathe. In and out." Troy nodded, focused on his gaze, watching him close. "I hear you."

"Good boy." He stayed put, breathing with Troy until the monitor went quiet. "There you go. Better, right? I'll get you a pain pill. A whole one so you can sleep. Okay?" He got to his feet. "Sit tight. Undress if you can, I'll be back to help."

He jogged back down the stairs into the kitchen, grabbed a pill and a couple bottles of water, took a second to put their doggie bag in the fridge, and then headed back up to his boy.

Troy was undressed and was pulling back the sheets and comforter. Stubborn boy. Beautiful stubborn boy.

He leaned in the bedroom doorway, eyes on Troy, watching his sub, his lover, move. Even tired and in pain Troy was graceful; no wasted effort, no hesitation.

Saul was looking forward to getting his arms around that tired boy.

"Naughty," he chastised softly, but he didn't really mean it. As much as he wished Troy would take it easy, his knew his boy wanted... needed to serve, and there was precious little Troy could physically do to take care of him right now. This small gesture was good for his boy too. "Thank you, boy. Climb on in. I've got your happy pill."

Troy beamed at him and crawled in the bed, holding the covers up. "Come snuggle, Master. We'll watch silly TV together. This feels so decadent."

"Might as well take advantage of doctor's orders while we can, right? No guilt." He tugged his clothes off, dropping them in a heap on the floor at the foot of the bed, and handed over a bottle of water before climbing in with Troy.

"Meds." He held one hand out flat, a white pill sitting on his palm.

"Maybe this is the last one, huh?"

Yeah, he didn't think so. Monday was going to hurt like hell. He had to believe Troy knew that, but he wasn't going to spit in the man's drink. "Maybe."

He watched Troy take it and then leaned back in the pillows with the remote so his boy could settle in.

Troy snuggled right up, cheek on his chest, one arm draped over his belly. "I love you."

He knew it was true, but that didn't stop his heart from

beating hard for a minute every time he heard it. "I love you too. You're mine. Thanks for letting me take you out. Pretty soon I'll be showing you off again. Dancing maybe."

"Oh, isn't that a pretty thought. I'd like that a lot, Sir. A whole lot."

"Then it's a promise. And speaking of promises..." He angled his head enough to catch his boy's lips in a kiss.

Troy hummed, licking his lips, the kiss slow and sweet, the love undeniable. His boy.

He could tell, just with a kiss, that Troy was feeling better. Maybe even getting better. He knew the pain meds would kick in shortly, but this was the real thing.

This was love.

32

The next person who asked him how he was doing was going to die. Troy growled at Saul and Geoff and stormed upstairs, as best as he could—fucking heart monitor. He wanted a shower, a beer, a blowjob, and... and...

Shit.

He didn't have an 'and'.

He didn't fucking need an 'and'.

Damn near a month after surgery, and he wasn't right yet.

His chest hurt, and it was ugly—the scar fat and thick and raw, his ink destroyed.

God.

He was going to take down every mirror in this entire fucking house.

"Troy?" He heard Saul call up the stairs after him and ignored it, starting the shower so he had an excuse not to listen. He half expected Saul to come find him in the bathroom and give him hell, or try to baby him, but he made it all the way through without being harassed.

By the end, his temper was cooler, and he felt almost—almost—human again.

He left the bathroom with a towel around his waist, and found Saul waiting for him, sitting on the end of the bed, back straight and arms crossed. Those blue eyes pegging him with a stern look. "Boy."

Goddamn it.

"Yes, Sir?"

Saul stood and stepped close to him, hooked a finger into the towel and it fell to the floor. "I sent Geoff home. You'll apologize to him tomorrow."

"Yes, Sir." That was no skin off his nose. Geoff would understand. Geoff got him.

"Go lie down on your back, hands up over your head if it's not too uncomfortable for you."

He wanted to ask questions. Hell, to be honest, he really wanted to struggle and fight and just be an asshole because he was ugly and tired and frustrated.

He was also Saul's, and Saul deserved his respect, so he did as he was told. He stretched out on the bed and lifted his arms.

Hell, he didn't even sigh.

"Good boy." Saul lifted a pair of cuffs he hadn't noticed sitting on the dresser and sat on the bed beside him. "You're frustrated? Angry? Speak freely."

"I am. I'm pissed. Frustrated. I hate this."

"What do you hate?" His Master gently buckled the cuffs on his wrists, taking time, moving slow.

"Being tired. Being weak. Being ugly. Not being real. I need to start working, to start feeling better. I want my life back!" The anger in the words couldn't be hidden.

Saul stayed silent and clipped the cuffs together, then

tethered the cuffs to the headboard with a thin length of rope.

And then a heavy hand landed on his sternum, covering his entire scar.

"I hate it," he whispered. "It's huge. Ugly."

"I don't." Saul's chest was bare, and he could see the way those ribs expanded with his Master's deep breath. Saul climbed over him, straddling his thighs and bent to kiss his collarbone while that hand stayed put, warming the scarred skin beneath it. "Under this scar is your heart. And this is how they saved it. How they saved you."

Saul's mouth traveled over his throat and down to one nipple to taste it, tongue rolling it between his lover's soft words. "Your scar is proof that you're strong and healthy, that you fought to stay here with me."

Troy blinked slowly, seduced and surprised by the words and that touch. He'd forgotten that his body could feel good, that Saul could do this for him.

"I'd rather have you frustrated than not have you at all. Frustrated I can fix. I might even be able to fix angry." Saul traveled lower, finding that scar and covering it with gentle kisses. "I'm as proud of this scar as I am of you."

Troy moved to stroke Saul's head, brought up short by the cuffs. "Master."

How could he comprehend this? No one had ever loved him, cared for him like this, even when he was failing.

"Mmm. A different kind of frustrating. Relax. You're just going to have to accept that this is all about you." Saul moved lower still, licking across his belly. "Do you think blowing you counts as sex? I mean, what do doctors know?"

"You make it hard to maintain a temper tantrum. Thank you, Sir." Troy licked his lips, the thought of Saul's cock in his mouth even more of a turn on than a blow job of his own.

"You're welcome, but I've been watching you, boy. You make me hungry. And you're hot when you're pissed off. Damn." Finger slid over the piercings just behind his sac.

He whimpered deep in his chest, one leg drawing up, bending to expose himself more. He would give Saul anything the fine son of a bitch would take.

"Oh, man. I've missed that sound." Saul teased him, circling his hardware, jostling it, tugging on it gently.

He rocked down into Saul's hands, a soft moan splitting the air. "That... Please, Sir."

"And that, too." A hungry tongue circled the head of his cock, tasted his ring, burrowed through his slit. Lightning buzzed along his spine, making his eyes cross. His balls drew up, and he panted, forcing himself not to jerk, drive him into that heat.

"Don't forget to breathe," his Master reminded him with a dark chuckle.

He tried, until his cock slid past Saul's lips. Saul's throat closed around him, swallowing, the pressure and suction making his eyes cross.

Then he did stop breathing, because the whole world screeched to a halt, trapped in Saul's heat. He shook, going from damn-that's-good to Jesus-fuck-I'm-fixin'-to-shoot in a heartbeat.

"Mm." Saul seemed to know and hummed around him, then swallowed him deep. That was all she wrote. He shot so hard his bones rattled, and he poured himself out in a rush.

His Master kept up the gentle attention until he relaxed, before climbing up and stretching out long beside him. Saul touched his chest again, fingers tracing the scar. "Good boy. Beautiful."

"Master." Tears prickled his eyes, hot and stinging, and he tried to blink them back.

Saul kissed his cheek. "You're mine, boy. My gorgeous boy. My crazy-hot lover. Mine."

"Yours. As long as you'll keep me." Troy turned his head, stole a kiss.

"Hmm." Saul grinned and kissed him back, sliding a finger along his jaw. "As long as you want me."

"Then we're golden." Troy inhaled, let the breath out, and allowed himself to melt. "Thank you, Master."

"My pleasure." His Master reached up and loosened the knot holding his cuffs to the headboard. "Move a little, I don't want you getting stiff."

"Yes, Sir." He wiggled, flexed, rolled his shoulders. Oh, he needed a few sessions with a massage table, but he felt so damn good.

"I'm going to take these off. You keep your hands to yourself." Saul grinned at him and started removing the cuffs.

No fair... "Are you sure, Sir? I could make you a happy man."

"I know you can. But I want you to rest, and," Saul laughed. "Your meds are going to fuck you up any minute."

"I want to suck you, have you fuck my mouth. I dream about it at night now." He smiled, remembering last night's dream, the hard-on he'd woken up with.

"You—" Saul swallowed and shifted beside him. "Really shouldn't... you're naughty."

"You can beat me later, Master. Please. I need to taste you. I need you." He was willing to risk this.

Troy watched Saul try to hold back a moan and fail,

miserably. "You're trouble, boy." Apparently, the kind of trouble worth getting into, because Saul's hands were shaking as he opened his jeans.

"Yes, Master." He wasn't playing a game. He wanted to be taken, he wanted to bring Saul off, and he needed his Master to want him.

"Fuck." Saul kicked the jeans away and settled on one elbow, holding out the other hand to draw him in. "Come on."

"Thank you, Sir." Troy took a kiss before he eased himself down, breathing deep with his nose against Saul's skin.

"Mm. So fucking hard. Your fault." Saul gripped the back of his head, managing to tug on his short curls.

"Yes, Sir." He opened up, dragging his tongue along Saul's slit before taking his lover in. He moaned, the sound muffled by that sweet prick.

"Oh, fuck." His Master bent a knee, planting a foot flat on the bed, and that voice was rough. "Need you."

He nodded, the action slipping Saul in deep. *Yours. Yours, Master. Take me. Remind me I'm yours.*

Saul gasped and froze, and for a moment he thought his Master was going to hold back, but that was followed by a long groan. "Boy." The hand around his head held him tight as Saul's hips rocked up off the bed, pulled back and shoved in deep again.

Troy opened, taking every inch, accepting his lover's will with a happy groan.

Saul was trembling, and using the foot braced in the sheets to take what he needed, everything in that moment was about that heavy cock for both of them. Sir wasn't going to last long. Troy grabbed Saul's ass and dragged him in deeper, swallowing hard and demanding his Master's spunk.

"Troy!" Saul curled up with a gasp and then fell heavily back to the mattress as he shot, ass going tight in his hands and hot liquid going down his throat.

Troy took it—every drop—then cleaned his Master's cock with gentle, careful laps. Oh. Better.

He closed his eyes, relaxing against Saul's belly.

"Love you, boy," Saul said between deep breaths. "Needed you bad. Damn."

"Love you, Sir. Thank you." He stroked Saul's thigh, breathing his Master in.

Saul pulled on him, guiding him up to take a kiss, smiling against his lips. "Docs don't know everything."

"No. Sometimes touch is more important than anything." They had needed this, them, together.

"Yeah." Saul nodded. "I get it, but I don't like to see you like that. Angry. Maybe this week will be easier."

"I hope so. I'm ready for a little inner peace."

Sir's fingers scritched through the short curls on his once-bald head. "How do you feel right now?"

"Loved. Taken. A little stoned." Maybe a lot.

"Sounds pretty peaceful. Close your eyes and take advantage of it, boy."

"Yes, Master." He sighed and snuggled in, cocooning them in the comforter. He was ready to rest.

33

Troy still had some time before he was released from restrictions, and although they'd now shared numerous mutual blow jobs, it didn't look to Saul like a little switch was going to flip at that six week mark that would suddenly allow the boy to go back to work.

Stamina was a thing, standing all day was a thing, and moving quickly? Yeah, that was still a thing.

Saul wasn't sure what was in Troy's mind. He'd carefully avoiding asking his boy about it because Troy's mood seemed better recently—mostly—and he really didn't want to rock the boat. But they were in Troy's truck on the way to Geoff and Carter's for their first Sunday gathering since Troy's surgery, and he had a bad feeling it was going to come up.

He probably should have thought of that before now, huh? What was he going to say when there were five minutes out that wouldn't ruin Troy's reasonably decent mood?

Not a damn thing.

Shit.

"Turn here, right?"

"Turn here, left." Troy winked at him, teasing gently.

"Smartass." He turned left. "Okay, boy. Quick ground rules. I'd like to treat tonight kind of like a scene. I'd like to make an impression, if you're agreeable." He wanted to do more than make an impression. He wanted to claim his place with the Doms, prove he wasn't just young, that he wasn't green. He knew people liked him, that wasn't an issue, he wanted to earn their respect.

Maybe that was petty, but Troy was smart and loyal, and he knew his boy could make him look damn good. And a little formality might help Troy stay in a comfortable headspace.

"Yes, Sir. What do you expect, or will you let me know as it comes up?" Troy stopped short, and that grin bloomed like the sun through the clouds. "Pun totally not intentional."

He started giggling as they pulled into the driveway and he glanced at Troy, his own grin nearly as wide as he put the truck in park. "Really?"

"Swear to God and my next hard-on."

"Whenever it comes up?" He giggled hard enough that he snorted, and that just made him laugh harder.

They leaned together, howling with it, both of them ridiculously tickled. He caught Troy's face in his hands and kissed his boy. "It feels good to laugh. That smile looks good on you." Maybe not the best timing, but he'd take it when he could get it.

"Thank you. It does. I'm looking forward to seeing everyone and saying thank you. Everyone helped so much."

"Yeah, I need to make sure to do the same. It's been pretty amazing." He let Troy go, took a deep breath and leaned back in his seat. "Okay. Expectations. I expect you to do what already comes naturally to you. Use your best judgment as to where you should be and what you should be doing. Or just ask. I have total faith in you." He winked at his boy. "I just want the Doms to know I'm doing my job, and make sure the subs know how proud of you I am. Easy."

"I love you too, Master." Troy's smile felt like an expression of pure trust.

Saul nodded, then took Troy's hand and squeezed it. "Ready to show off?"

"I am ready to make you proud, Sir."

"Prouder... more proud?" He shook his head. "Come on." He climbed out of the truck and waited for Troy to join him before knocking on the front door.

Geoff answered the door with a warm, happy smile. "You guys made it! Oh, come in!" Geoff pounced on Troy, hugging him tight.

He stepped inside, smiling at Geoff and his boy. "I don't think I could have kept Troy home if I wanted to. Which, I didn't."

"Saul." Carter appeared in the foyer, offering him a hand to shake. "Welcome. It's good to see you both."

"Thank you. You too. We've been looking forward to this all week."

"We have too. We were ready for all our family to be home." Carter's smile was warm, genuine. "Ben and Travis are making nachos and margaritas, and we heated up the hot tub and the fire pit."

"Oh, right on. Sounds great. Do they need help with the nachos? I know a Texan who's a good cook." He grinned and winked at Troy.

"I'm sure they could use a supervisor. Geoff and Kris are just driving them mad."

He laughed. "Go on, boy. See if you can help... if your

friend will let go of you." He raised an eyebrow at Geoff, teasing.

Carter just cleared his throat.

He heard Geoff whisper to Troy, "Never. Never, honey," but the man did back off.

Saul stepped back as Troy headed for the kitchen.

"He looks good," Carter said as soon as Troy was out of earshot.

"He is good. Not as good as he wishes he were, I don't think, but better than the docs expected." Good enough that Saul didn't worry much anymore.

"That's exceptional. We miss him at the diner, here, all over."

"He misses everything. He's ready to get his life back. He feels so much better that I spend a lot of time reminding him to take it easy." His boy growled at him a lot, but it wasn't angry at least.

"I can imagine. He's one hell of a hard worker." Carter pointed toward the back deck. "Come join us?"

"Sounds great." He liked Carter's deck; it had such a great view. He'd sent Troy to the kitchen on purpose, to let him feel useful, normal. Hopefully all the how-is-he questions would be out of the way before the boy joined him again.

Doc was out there, along with Matt and David, the three men all in the hot tub, bubbling away. Doc raised a beer to him, nodded. "You made it! Welcome!"

Oh, he wanted in on that party. "Thank you. We're really glad we could come. Look at all of you!" He grinned, tugged his T-shirt off and tossed it over a chair before shaking hands all around. "Mind if I join?" This month's invitation included a mention of time in the hot tub so he had worn his suit. His boy was going to have to stay dry, but Geoff had sworn that Troy wouldn't be the odd man out.

"Of course not. Come on in." David's booming laughter filled the air, the sound warm and happy.

He loved a good soak. He'd love it more with Troy, and he'd promised his boy when the restrictions were lifted he'd ask Carter for another evening. "Awesome."

He climbed in, ending up next to Matt and across from Doc, who had the longest legs of anyone he'd ever shared a hot tub with. He pulled his feet back after accidentally playing footsie. "Oh. Sorry."

Doc laughed. "Not to worry. My feet are a hazard in tight spaces."

"They're canoes." Matt winked at him. "You need a beer, Saul."

"I guess I do."

"Krissy, Master Saul needs a beer, please."

"Yes, Sir. We have Fat Tire, Coors Light, and Shiners." Kris pulled over in his chair, more confident every time Saul saw him.

"Fat Tire is perfect. Thank you." He had to smile. Shit happened, people got better. Kris and Troy were lucky to have people that got it. People that supported them.

Hell, he and Matt were pretty damned lucky, when you got right down to it.

"One Fat Tire, Sir." Kris handed it over with a smile.

He nodded to Kris, and took a big swig. "Ah. This is fantastic." He glanced at the others, trying to make eye contact with each of them. "I really have to thank all of you for your help, your boys' help. I don't know what I would have done without it and it meant a lot to both of us."

"We're family." Doc nodded at him, so sure, so steady.

This was a man who was used to being in control, to being obeyed, it rang in his voice.

"Yeah. We are." He smiled at Doc and raised his beer before taking a sip. "So what else is going on? What have we missed?"

"David, Doc and I took Little Ben to the Sanctuary for his first visit."

"He hadn't been? I love it there. I'm a big fan of the tigers."

David grinned nice and slow. "I think Little Ben likes the bears best."

"Yeah? I haven't been in forever. Do they still have the polar bears?" Maybe he should take Troy. That would be some low-key fun for their next date.

Mike shared a laugh with Doc. "Why do I feel like we need a field trip?"

"You two hooligans be good." Carter rolled his eyes. "The Sanctuaty is a private membership club in Denver, man. They have a shit ton of parties, scenes, even a TNG group. Hell, you, Ben, and Kris could go to that together."

"Oh. So... not the zoo." Saul snorted and shook his head at himself. "Bears. I get it now. Funny."

David laughed. "I couldn't resist."

How did he not know about this club? "You guys are members?" He couldn't imagine going without Troy, who had apparently aged out of the TNG—The Next Generation--group.

"Geoff and I were for a while, but we just didn't use it. Our schedules can make it a challenge, and to be honest, public scenes with strangers aren't my thing."

He nodded. He'd done scenes with people he knew, but he wasn't sure how he felt about public scenes himself. He didn't think he'd be too comfortable in a big club. "But you are a member, Doc? Did Ben enjoy it?"

Doc winked at him. "He hated it. It overwhelmed him. Too loud, too new, too much input. It was actually very enlightening."

"I bet it was. With that description, I don't think it would be Troy's scene either." And if it wasn't something Troy would like, he didn't think he needed to check it out, TNG night or otherwise.

"Troy went once. He won't go back. He decided he was better off at the gay bar for a pick up." Carter sounded so sure.

"I told him I'd take him dancing. That'll be enough of a club outing for us, I think." He sipped his beer, every bit as confident as Carter. He'd never been a good partier. He went, but he hadn't found it as fun as most of his friends.

"Oh, that sounds fun. Maybe once Krissy gets more used to his prosthetics we can both take our boys." Matt stared Kris down, expression firm, sure.

"We'd love that. The more the merrier." He smiled at Kris, gave the boy a wink. "Troy has a few weeks to go I think before he can do anything that aerobic. There's time."

He glanced toward the sliding doors to the house, wondering suddenly how the boys were doing with the food, and they appeared as if the thought had summoned them.

Doc's eyes locked right onto Ben, who had his hands full. "Here comes trouble."

That was adorable. The connection between those two was fierce.

Troy was carrying a huge tray of nachos, his boy struggling a little bit. He started to say something, but Kris rolled up.

"Hey, buddy. Balance that thing on my lap and roll me to the table?"

He glanced at Matt, and Matt winked at him. These guys were good. Kris, in particular, which made sense given the boy's own circumstances. Kris got it.

"Oh, man. I can smell those from here." Troy didn't miss a beat, just rolled Kris and the nachos over and set them out. Ben had plates and napkins, and Travis came over to see if anyone needed more beer.

"Would you like a plate in there, Master?" Troy asked.

"Is that Kosher, Carter? Food in your tub? Or should we climb out?" Every Dom he knew had rules. About all kinds of things. It came with the territory, so it was always better to ask.

"Nachos are a bit of a challenge. Let's hop out and be around the fire." Carter met Geoff's eyes. "Cushions, baby."

"Yes, Sir."

Geoff went to the seating area and pulled out soft, cozy cushions for the subs. Carter leaned forward. "Matt? Saul? What do you want for your boys?"

His boy had been comfortable on cushions and yoga mats for a while now. "Troy should be fine with a cushion, thank you. If Kris needs something special, Matt, just ask Troy to grab it for you." He climbed out of the tub, reaching for one of the fluffy towels Carter had in a stack on the edge of the tub.

"We need to make sure he has a place to rest his back." Matt hopped up, grabbed a towel. "It'll keep him from killing his abs."

"Why don't you two take the deck sofa?" They could drag it a little closer. Any old chair would work for him, and Travis and Ben were already moving some around.

In all the shuffling, he found himself standing behind

Troy and he reached for his boy, slipping an arm around Troy's waist. "All good?"

"Oh, you're cold and hot all at once. I'm happy, Master. It all smells good, hmm?"

"It does." He was glad for the contact though, the check-in. "Let's sit. Just be comfortable." He picked the closest chair and held an arm out in case Troy needed some support getting down.

Troy took the offer, although Saul didn't think his boy needed it. Still so damn graceful.

"Good boy." He really wanted to ask what had happened at the Sanctuary that Troy had had such a reaction to, but he decided asking in front of the group wasn't really fair. He was going to ask though, he needed to make sure he understood. "Oh. I forgot food. Don't get up again, boy. I can get it."

"Thank you, Master."

"I'm up, Master Saul. Would you like me to get you a big plate to share?" God, Little Ben was adorable and totally in hard-core hero worship with Troy.

He smiled at Ben, rewarding the boy's good instincts. "You do your Master proud, boy. Thank you. I would like that." He liked the idea of his boy as a role model, he thought maybe it would be good for Troy.

Saul sat and stroked Troy's scalp, those curls soft. Everyone was getting settled with food, towels, fresh beers, and he took the time before Ben brought the plate over just to let his boy know he was there.

"Oh, Matt! Emma should be in touch in a couple of days about Kris' bike. She got in the last couple of parts she was waiting for on Friday and it's just about assembled. It looks great."

"No shit? We're excited. If your boy rides, Krissy is interested in riding together."

"Troy used to ride some and wants to pick it up again. I'm working on a bike for him too. When it's done, let's do it." Kris was going to need to start slow, and when Emma handed over the bike, he and Troy had talked about giving them a block of sessions with a trainer so Kris would learn to use it safely, and Matt could learn how to assist.

Ben handed him a plate and he thanked the boy, then lowered it so Troy could help himself.

"Thank you, Sir," Troy took a chip, gathered up a perfect bite, and handed it to him.

That just made him smile. "You're spoiling me." It was the perfect bite, too. Just spicy enough, crunchy and cheesy. "Mmm."

"It's my pleasure, Sir." Troy nibbled on a bite but was focused mainly on him.

He looked over at Carter and Geoff, who had gotten comfortable. It was so obvious how long they'd been together in the way they sat, their body language, and all the little touches. He rewarded Troy with more touch of his own, tugging the tiny curls on his boy's nape.

Troy ducked his head, giving him more access. That easy motion felt like heaven, like an expression of honor.

Doc was watching them, but he wasn't sure why until the Dom asked Carter about the diner. "Still managing all right without your head cook, Carter?"

"Managing, but we miss him. He's irreplaceable. No one makes French toast like him."

Troy sighed so softly that no one but Saul would have heard it.

"Well, I still get it every weekend." He couldn't help but

grin, and he gave Troy's shoulder a squeeze. "This morning they were shaped like dinosaurs."

"Okay, when are you coming back then? You want to start tomorrow? Wednesday?"

Troy shook his head. "Not tomorrow, Sir."

He sensed the stress building, could see it in the set of Troy's shoulders.

He could take this on for his boy. He didn't want to be an ass to their friend, but he didn't want Troy to feel that pressure either. "He's not ready, Carter. Troy is doing great, but we're working on stamina and strength still. You'll be the first to know if I'm ready to allow him to go back to the diner."

Saul wasn't sure what felt better—the shock and respect in the other Doms' eyes, or the way Troy immediately relaxed under his hand.

Troy's reaction mattered more to him, though. Suddenly that need to be accepted, his desire to make a good impression just disappeared as he realized that none of that actually mattered. What mattered was his boy.

"These nachos are so good." He took another bite and swallowed it down with the last sip of his beer.

Troy eased himself up. "Another beer, Master?"

"Thank you, boy. Just a Diet Coke, please." Saul kept his eyes on his boy, watched him head inside.

The guys were subdued for a minute before Doc turned to him. "Nicely done. We all may take a little training where Troy is concerned. He's been unattached for a long time, and we're used to that."

He smiled at Doc. He knew, and Troy too, that everyone meant well. "You're all his family. I'm just the arrogant date he brought home for dinner." He laughed, his grin growing wider.

"You're the one he chose after twenty years, Sir." Kris' voice was soft, but firm.

That sobered him up a little and he nodded to Kris. "I'm very lucky." Lucky and in love. "Once you almost lose that you don't take it for granted even for a second. Your Master knows what I mean." He looked at Carter. "I'm sorry, man. But I don't think Troy will be coming back to the diner. I hope you understand."

Geoff and Carter were totally stunned.

"Ever?"

"You told me he was fine!" Geoff's voice was shrill, sharp. "He told me it was going to be fine! Goddamn it!"

"Boy!"

"Geoff? Honey, what's wrong?" Troy stood there, pale as milk.

"You said you were fine!"

"I am!" Troy stared at him, wide-eyed. "Master?"

"He is going to be fine, Geoff. We talked about this, remember? Yoga?" Saul held out a hand to Troy. They'd been pretty stoned, maybe Geoff had forgotten. "I'm trying to convince Troy to get his teaching certificate. He's been talking about opening a studio."

"I thought that was a five-year or ten-year plan deal."

"I'm healthier now than I was a year ago, y'all. Recovering, sure, but healthier." Troy came back to him, handed him his Coke.

"Well, we're negotiating." He smiled at his boy. "But Troy has a talent, and a passion, and I'd like to see him use it."

"I think that would be a fascinating idea," Matt said. "Seriously, you've got all the skills you need."

Saul glanced at Carter again, who hadn't said a word yet. "You understand, right?" It would be hard for Troy to do if he thought he was disappointing Carter.

"I understand it, but I hate it. You're supposed to be in the kitchen working with me forever, kiddo."

Troy looked to him, then to Carter. "Master Carter, let's talk tomorrow? Please?"

"We'll talk tomorrow." Carter nodded. "Today we're relaxing."

Saul nodded too, and stroked his fingers through Troy's hair. He didn't regret getting the conversation started, but he respected Troy's wish to finish it later. "I'm sorry if I worried you, Geoff."

"Thank you, Sir. I-I just freaked."

Carter had Geoff, was holding him close. "Obviously we need to have a long talk."

"Our place, tomorrow night? We'll make dinner and sit outside, it'll be nice." And they could talk as friends, not as Doms and subs.

"That sounds good, man. We're in." Carter nodded to Saul, Geoff wrapped in his arms.

He smiled at Troy, and then shifted down into the cushions. "Hey, there. Breathe." He hooked a finger under Troy's chin and took a kiss, offering Troy his calm confidence.

"Master." That was a prayer, a mantra, and Troy eased in his arms.

"Good boy." He got settled, arms around his boy, fingers tucking under Troy's shirt. He looked up first at Carter, then to Doc and Matt. "He needs to work. Even though we've been pretty creative, we've had a hard time with headspace, with grounding. We're fine... and also not, you know?"

They all—to a man—nodded, but it was Matt who spoke.

"I found the most challenging part was knowing when and how hard to push, to be honest." Matt reached out and took Kris' hand. "And there were times when I had to focus on my emotions to be able to relax and give him what he needed."

Saul had been trying pretty hard to understand his emotions. He wasn't burying them or denying they existed, they just swung from one thing to another and he never quite got a handle on what he was feeling. "The emotions are hard to pin down. I know that doesn't help."

It really helped to hear Matt say that though. When and how hard to push was an issue, and he'd been second-guessing himself, questioning his own judgment.

"That's always the thing, isn't it?" David chuckled, and the sound was wry. "I have a terrible trouble with my temper, as I know it, but sometimes swallowing it isn't the best answer, you know?"

"Yeah. It'll come out one way or another, right? If you don't talk, it might come out your arm instead. Or cloud your judgment." He'd been there. Hard stop safe words were no fun if you didn't know you were riding a line.

"Exactly. If you're going to push your boy over an edge, your responsibility is huge. Hell, if we expect them to hand us their bodies, their souls, we have to deserve that trust."

He slid his fingers over Troy's scar. "I try not to expect it. I try to earn it, you know? Make that ask every time, treat the acceptance like a gift. Elevate the scene."

"I like that," Doc said. "I like the way you come at that, Saul."

Oh, that praise felt good.

"Thank you. It works well for us. I like to remind my boy that a scene is about us, not just me."

No bag of rocks.

He smiled at Doc. "I'm guessing your boy needs a slightly different approach."

"My boy and I are learning about trust still, and about how to find our balance."

It would be easy to assume that was because Ben was young, but he knew better than most around the fire right now that age was only a small piece, if it meant anything at all. It was far more likely to be Ben's background and old habits getting in the way.

"That's good work." He glanced at Ben. "That high when your trust is validated is... wow. Really important work."

He could feel Troy's heart beating, strong and steady under his hand.

"It is. It's a gift, and I respect that." Doc smiled, and Ben beamed at his Master.

He liked the way Ben looked at Doc, whatever the boy had in his past, that was the appearance of a sub who felt safe.

"What about you, David? How are things with you and Travis?" David and Travis had an interesting dynamic. They seemed perfectly happy to him, they were just... quieter.

"Smooth sailing, don't you think, pet?"

"Yes, Sir." Travis was on his way back to David with a beer, handed it to his Master and kissed the side of David's neck. "For now," he teased, mischief in his voice.

"Don't you make me put you over my knee now." They both laughed together, the sound harmonious, happy, and healthy.

"Oh, it's like that, is it?" He glanced at Troy. "Don't get any ideas, practical joker." Actually, Troy and Geoff hadn't been in much trouble at all since... well, since the first time Troy brought him to a gathering. Was that good or bad?

He got the sense that Troy had been rotten in the past—playful and teasing—and his boy was Zen, as a rule. Troy needed Zen. Crazy, stressful hours as a line cook could

380 | JODI PAYNE & BA TORTUGA

really take it out of a guy. Not that he had a strong opinion on the subject.

His boy was calm but not really Zen right now though, and although he loved the feel of all that warm, smooth skin under his fingers, he was jonesing to mark it up.

He wanted to know what his marks looked like with the ink. He wanted to turn that sweet, bare ass colors.

As if his boy could hear his thoughts, Troy nuzzled into his neck with a barely-there moan.

"Got you," he whispered. Done deal, then. They had safe words for a reason.

He put his beer down and braced himself on one arm so his boy could lean on him, feeling that little promise hum like electricity between them.

Yeah. It was time.

34

The world was a better place with coffee, no lie.

Troy sat in his recliner, wrapped in a huge blanket, and watched the sun come up. Damn, that was pretty. The trees that would turn had started making colors, the promise of fall in the air.

He grinned at himself. Last night's gathering had felt amazing, and he was still buzzing happily from his Master's touch, the connection between them. From belonging.

Saul's playfully stern voice startled him from the top of the staircase, echoing against the ceiling. "Hm. Strangest thing... the bed is cold and my boy has coffee, but I don't. Does any of that sound right to you?"

He chuckled softly, his grin growing into a smile as he rolled up to pad to the kitchen. Oh, chilly. "Good morning, Master. I love you."

"I love you too, boy." Saul came down the stairs, stopping before making it into the kitchen. "Oh, look at that sky."

"It's gorgeous, isn't it?" He started Saul's coffee before heading to get a hug. He should have put clothes on, but he had his blanket.

Saul had pulled on a pair of sweatpants that looked like they could unravel any minute. "Beautiful. Mm. This view is inspiring too." Saul pulled him right in and surrounded him with long arms. "Good morning."

"Good morning, Master." He loved the way Saul smelled, fresh out of bed. It was pure male.

"I hope you got a good night's sleep, boy. We're going to have our coffee and a little talk, and then I hope to get right to work."

"I did. I was warm and happy. Last night felt good." A little talk. Huh. Troy found himself curious, but not worried, and that felt so good. "Let me fix your coffee. Do you want breakfast, Sir?"

"I don't think so, thank you. The coffee will be enough." Saul let him go and took a seat at one end of the couch, leaving plenty of room for him.

"Yes, Sir." He doctored Saul's coffee and handed it over before grabbing his own cup and his blanket. He wrapped the covers around him and settled in close.

"Last night was great." Saul blew across the top of the mug and then took a sip. "Good company, good conversation."

"Yes, Sir. It was..." It seemed ridiculous to say it was magical or a dream, but it was. He'd craved having a true partner, someone to share his life with. "...lovely."

"I felt good there, too. Respected, supported. Close to you." His Master hooked an arm around him. "We'll get things out in the open with Carter and Geoff later, and we'll all feel better, right?"

"I hope so. I don't think I'm ready to go back. I don't know if I can make our bills teaching yoga, either. But I know I need more time."

"We'll talk money and figure it out. I do okay. I think we

might be able to make it work. Maybe you can do part-time or something for a while. I'd like to keep the conversation with them about your health and your mental state though. Okay?"

"Yes, Sir. The rest is for us to talk over, in private." He was comfortable with that. Carter and Geoff were good friends, but he and Saul needed to make their life decisions together.

"Good. So. You remember what Matt said last night about knowing when and how far to push? I'd like to push today. I'd like to see what's reasonable. I don't think we even have a benchmark starting point right now, you know? So I want you to tell me how you feel about that, and whether you think you're up to some real work."

How did he feel? It took a moment to unpack it, to listen to his soul. "I'm excited, hopeful, a little worried that I'll fail you." He chuckled softly. "Which is the paradox of being a sub, isn't it? You worry about failing when you know this shouldn't be a fail situation."

Saul rubbed a reassuring hand over his back. "It's not. But I understand worry, I hear you. There may be a time when I do ask you for something you're going to have to work hard for. Not today though. Today I want to take steps together, communicate, see where we can go. I think 'hopeful' is an interesting choice of words. What are you hoping for?"

"That we find something new together, something special. I hope that this brings us closer together." Troy met his Sir's gaze and smiled, feeling a sweet anticipation buzzing through his veins. "I hope we both get what we need."

Saul looked right into his eyes, totally open to him. "Mmm. I hope so too, boy." He got a kiss, just a light one, only enough to leave him wishing for more. "Are you leaving the mechanics to me? Do you have any thoughts? Something you feel like you need? Something you'd like?"

God, it had been so long. He had good memories and bad, but he wasn't sure what had been changed by time.

"I'd like to wear your marks. I'd like to see what makes you feel strong."

"Thank you, boy. Marks are on my mind too." Saul sipped his coffee. "When we worked with the flogger before I tried not to, but I'd like something I can see this time. Something that will stand out on top of your ink if you can handle that. That will probably be pretty intense."

His Master caught his eyes again. "You know what I want. If you say that you're ready for that and then it turns out you're not, I need to know that you'll use your words even though you might feel like you're disappointing me. Can you promise me that?"

"Yes, Sir." Saul had promised him that no one was keeping score, and Troy had to believe him. "It will be hard, but you have my word."

"Good boy, Thank you. I can't promise you won't need those words." Saul put down the coffee and pushed a hand into his blanket. "It's warmer upstairs, but if you think you'll be chilly you can start a fire."

"Oh, that's tempting, but I'll wait for an evening scene when it'll be so pretty." He could lose himself in the dance of the flames.

"Ooh. I like that idea. I'll just have to keep you warm." Saul's fingers grazed over his nipple, circled it, rolled it, pressed it against his chest.

He blinked, his body waking up, heating, and his heart rate quickened. "You're good at that, Master. Warming me up."

"And we haven't even started yet." Those fingers moved to his sternum and flattened out against his chest. "Feel that heart pounding."

"Yeah…" He looked down, then blinked back up at Saul. "Master, it doesn't hurt. I mean, at all."

Saul nodded, smiling at him. "Stronger than before, right? That's what they said." They shared that moment, eyes on one another until his Master sighed and kissed him. "Breathe, now. Focus, hm? Calm."

He inhaled deeply, then blew out, the action familiar and comforting, so he did it again. He found calm before focus, but he managed them both.

"Good boy." Saul stood and offered a hand. "Leave the blanket."

"Yes, Master." He took the help offered and stood, half-hard, eager, ready for this.

They went upstairs, Saul pulling him along. His Master placed him in the middle of the room. "This is exciting. It should be. But my focus is on you, boy. On your needs. And yours should be on mine."

"Yes, Sir. Always." That was the easiest part—listening to Saul's need.

"Hands flat on the window." Saul gave the order and then reached for the toolbox and dug through it.

He did as Saul asked, smiling as he thought of the handprints he'd leave. Reminders. Marks.

"Legs a little wider, please." But Sir didn't wait for him to move. The cool touch of a riding crop tapped his thigh, encouraging him, the leather warming quickly against his skin.

"Yes, Master." He took a deep breath, in and out. "As you wish."

"Better." Saul started tapping him gently with the wide,

flat end of the crop across his shoulders, hips, thighs, arm, calves, ass. A light but constant touch that seemed random until he realized his Master was choosing the exact same spots, over and over again. "Give me your words, boy."

"Red and yellow, Sir." Christ, his voice was husky, like he'd been well-fucked.

"That's what I remembered. Red and yellow. But that's not all I want to hear you say. Talk if you want to. Speak respectfully, but freely. This session is to help us figure out what does and doesn't work for you. For us." The tapping stopped and Saul stepped close to his back, hands resting on his hips. "I want to know if you love something. And you'll be sure to tell me if you want more of something too."

God, those hands. So warm that he could feel every finger, every single finger pressing against his skin. His lips parted, and his abs rolled with the sensation. He made this sound—part "oh" and part "fuck yes" but mostly "please"— that tore out of him.

Saul laughed softly. "Oh, I know, boy. You need this, right? Down deep. It's been too long." Saul placed a kiss between his shoulders, stepped back, and drew the crop up the inside of one thigh as high as it could easily go. "Me too."

The next set of taps were to his sac and grazed his piercings.

There wasn't pain, but God the vulnerability, the wild rush so much like riding a rollercoaster—there was the spark of fear, the adrenaline high, but he knew he was safe with his Master.

The crop slipped away, and without warning he got a smack to each ass cheek, louder than the little bite would have suggested.

"I've barely touched you, but I can see the blush rising

up your neck. Lovely." The next thing Troy felt were the wide falls of a heavy flogger landing with a thud on his ass.

He hadn't even noticed when his Master had switched tools, and the sting he'd anticipated wasn't there, so the heavier blow sank deeper than he'd expected. Oh, he felt that.

His Master must have sensed something. "I don't usually give a warning unless I expect what's happening next to hurt. I'd have to try hard to make this one painful, it's pure sensory." The heavy falls battered his thighs, their weight and the strength of Saul's arm threatening to buckle his knees. "Oh, yeah. And it gives a sub something to work against. A challenge."

"Yes." He was ready to work, to make Saul proud. "I feel that. So deep." The crop floated above his skin, the flogger got under it. Together they fascinated him.

Saul kept after him with the flogger, the blows shoving him forward so he was forced to push back, to lean into them. "That's it. I like how you move, boy. I could cuff you if I wanted to, shackle your feet, but those things serve to force a submission, and I want your choices. I want to see you choose not to walk away or put your hands down. I want to be the answer to the question of whether you want to be standing here."

"Listen to you." His cock jerked at Saul's words, but they served their purpose. He would stay where he'd been put, because it was his Master's will.

"Surprised? I like restraints just fine, as you know. But right now, I want it all to come from you." There was a short, quiet moment, and then Saul called out, "Next flogger's gonna sting."

He heard a couple of swoops but nothing touched him. In the silence that followed his Master took a deep breath.

"Left to right, shoulders first, then your ass. Tell me when you're ready."

Shoulders then ass. He imagined the way it would feel, the snap, the burn, the rush of blood to the surface. God. "I'm ready, Master."

"Steady." Saul didn't give him a second to think. Four biting blows fell just as his Master said they would, without a breath in between.

Jesus that strength! Fire hit him for a second before it disappeared into ice. The heat crept back in trickles and tingles, and by then Saul was laying down another set.

He knew the third set was lighter, but the warm leather that scraped his skin might as well have been sandpaper. He wetted his lips, willing his damp palms not to slide along the glass. God, he was beginning to shake like he'd taken earthquake pills.

"Boy." Sir's voice cut through his thoughts. "Get out of your head. Talk. Tell me how you feel."

"Burns. I feel like I'm falling, like I'm going to slide, Master. Not bad. I don't feel bad." He didn't want to be misunderstood in his amazing confusion.

"Lower your arms." Saul moved to him, slipped into the narrow space between him and the window. "Kneel. Lean on me if you need to."

Troy let his knee bend, trusting his Master to steady him, to ease his way to the floor, and of course, Saul had him, all the way down.

"There. Good boy. Sliding didn't sound safe." His Master knelt as well and kissed him as a hot hand wrapped tightly around his cock.

"Master." Oh he hadn't even known he was hard. "You were right." He *had* been trapped in his own head.

Saul smiled at him and let him go. "Breathe, and then tell me again how you feel."

"I feel—" *Breathe. Breathe, Troy. In and out.* "I feel loose. I feel you. I'm so fucking proud of us and turned on." He chuckled, the sound bubbling out of him. "And I'm really happy."

He got another kiss and then Sir stood. "You wanted to know what makes me feel strong? It's this. Making you feel like you do right now. Looking at my marks on your body."

"Can you see them?" Oh, that pleased him, sort of unreasonably, enough that his cock jerked, clear drops sliding from the tip.

"I can." Sir moved around behind him, and traced a finger across his shoulders, lighting his skin on fire. "There's one right here. And another over here. They're beautiful."

"Oh fuck." He jerked, his eyes rolling back in his head, a jumble of emotions flooding him. He didn't try to fight it. He let them run through, and then he let them go.

"Good? You like that. That's a reward for good work, boy." Saul stroked his cheek with the handle of a flogger. "And I'm glad we paused here. But I promised you I would push you, and it's time. Take a breath."

Saul stepped away, and the sound of the flogger swooping through the air behind him changed the energy between them completely. "Tell me when you're ready."

"I'm good where I am, Master?"

"Just fine for now. If you're uncomfortable on your knees call out yellow and we'll change it. But I don't want you losing your balance, this is safer."

"Yes, Sir." Tall kneeling was familiar, comfortable, and a position he could hold.

He'd never tried to do this with a flogger, he admitted.

Saul rested both hands on the top of his shoulders, the gesture reassuring, steadying. "Ready?"

"Yes, Master. Ready." He engaged his abs, his quads, and braced to accept his Sir's will.

"Good boy." His Master's flogger came up from below and caught his ass, then the falls continued upward, gliding across his back and over the marks on the opposite shoulder.

He spread his thighs to make room for his heavy, aching balls. Every motion of the falls made lightning spread across his skin, and he caught himself gasping, groaning, unable to stop his sounds.

The blows continued making an "X" across his body until he lost count, lost himself in the repetition as the sting and the burn intensified.

"Gorgeous boy." His Master's voice seemed distant until the flogger cut between his thighs and licked at his balls.

His eyes went wide and he barked out a sharp scream, his orgasm shocking, stealing his breath as ropes of seed splashed on the window.

"Oh, very nice, boy. I'll take that as a compliment." His Master kept going, the falls of the flogger lapping at his piercings and flicking his sac. "And you're welcome."

"Th-thank you, Sir. Master. Oh sweet fuck." The pleasure went on and on, making him dizzy. "Master."

"My boy." He knew his Master was pleased, he heard the low rumble in Saul's voice. "I need your shoulders. Try this for me. Bend one knee up, a nice wide stance, and brace both hands on that knee. Let me know if you feel steady."

He eased into a modified *utthita ashwa sanchalansana*, crescent pose, stretching his arms high before settling them on his knee. "Yes, Sir. Steady."

Steady. Happy. Settled. Present.

"Beautiful. Yellow and red, remember. And I'd much prefer to hear yellow before red." His Master went to work, the flogger falling in quick, short, stinging blows in a figure eight pattern on his shoulders; Down on the right, up on the left, and then the same thing reversed.

Troy swore he could feel every single hair on his body— from his head to his thighs. He panted, his muscles straining, and he knew he was going to have to change legs. "Master, yellow. I need to switch legs, please."

"Good boy. Go ahead."

As he moved he caught Saul pacing the room behind him shaking an arm out. "Your range is impressive. That's what I get for taking on a bull rider."

"You're strong, Sir. I can feel everything." He groaned as he stretched up this time, the burn deep, his muscles heavy. He'd never felt so in his own skin, so present.

"I am. And you're still not contemplating stopping me yet." His Master crouched in front of him, tugged on his nipple hardware and kissed him. "I'm going to have to switch it up though, boy, I don't want to damage your shoulders. They're striped to hell. You're the hottest thing I've ever seen. Ever."

Troy wanted to answer, to tell Saul he was good, but that kiss, the sweet tug in his nipples just made him stupid. "Master."

"My love." Saul smiled at him. "Bed. Surely there's a pose in your practice that will stick that lovely ass in the air for me?"

"Dozens, Sir. I need you." He smiled back, this wild joy bubbling up inside him. This wasn't what he'd found with Geoff or with Arnie. It burned, and tomorrow it would hurt, but the pain part was a fraction of the whole.

"Mmm. Don't want to wait another day. It's been long

enough. You've got me so hard I ache, boy." Saul helped him to his feet. "Take it slow."

"I'm buzzed, Master." Saul said Troy should talk, so he babbled as he moved, sharing as best he could the way he felt home, how he was soaring.

"Gorgeous boy." His Master got him settled on the bed, kissed him, helped him get comfortable. Then Saul tossed the sweats aside, showing him a heavy, hungry erection.

His words dried up like someone had turned off a faucet, and his lips parted.

"You want this? Come have a taste, boy." Saul cupped a hand under his chin. "Come on."

A whimper passed his lips. He more than wanted. Right this second, his name was need.

He reached out with his tongue, gathering a bitter salt that made him shiver, but only long enough to follow his Master's lead and take Saul in deep.

"Yeah. Fuck, that's good." Saul's fingers slid along his arm and hovered over his shoulder, almost but not quite touching his aching skin. "You look amazing."

He hummed in thanks, using the sound to vibrate Saul's cock, all the way in.

His Master's moan was long and appreciative. "Jesus, don't make me come, boy. I want to fuck you. We need that."

Troy's spine arched at Saul's words, and his suction increased, his desire and agreement making him wild.

"Boy." Saul touched him, a hot finger putting searing pressure on his back, drawing a line diagonally down his shoulder blade.

He stared up, eyes snapping to Saul's, even as Sir's prick popped out of his lips. "Master."

He got a wicked grin. "Show me that ass."

Troy spread his thighs, pushed his ass back, and offered himself totally, both sets of cheeks on fire.

"Damn, boy. That's hot as fuck." Saul's fingers spread him without warning, tongue teasing sensitive skin.

Troy's thoughts shattered, the world tightening down to the only thing that mattered—his Master.

There was cold lube and slick fingers, a condom wrapper landed on the bed, but nothing really registered until Sir's cock breached him, stretched him slowly, a needy groan filling his ears. "Damn, boy. Tight."

"Full." He braced himself against the mattress. *Their* mattress.

"That's right." They started to move together, Saul's hips thrusting forward as he rocked back. "Everywhere now. All over you. Inside you. So good."

"Yes, Sir. Fuck, you're my everything. Need you." He couldn't seem to shut up, but he needed Saul to understand where he was, soul deep.

"Mine." Saul held his hips in strong fingers and took him hard, hips slapping into his stinging cheeks, relentless until they were both panting, their sounds filling the room.

He added his strength to Saul's, sweat pouring from him as he fought for Saul's pleasure. It wasn't long until his Master was shaking, hips stuttering, so ready.

"Fuck, boy." Saul's voice sounded gone, shattered. "Gonna..." That heavy prick jerked and pulsed inside him as Saul shot. "Love you."

"Love." He eased himself onto the bed, his muscles and skin demanding relief.

Saul rolled and flopped on the bed bedside him, breath coming in rough pants. "Aftercare in a minute. I just need to remember how to stand up."

"Mmm..." That was close enough to agreement, right?

Saul found his hand and tangled their fingers. "How do you feel?"

"Loved." He sank deeper into the covers. "Like I could glow in the dark."

Saul laughed gently and pressed their foreheads together. "Wait until you see your back. You might actually be glowing."

Troy could believe it. He'd been stupid with sensation. Now the reality of what they'd accomplished was written on him.

"I want you to rest. Breathe. Sleep if you can. I'm going to tend to my marks. I have something that will calm the burn and numb the sting enough that you should be able to relax." Saul kissed his cheek and he had to grin at the groan as his Master hauled himself out of bed. "I'm enjoying the tired ache in my arm, boy. Well done."

"Thank you, Master." He blinked over, the aftershocks beginning to rock him, move through him.

Saul put a bottle of water in his fingers and covered his legs with the comforter. "If you start feeling cold let me know and I'll turn the heat on. Don't let yourself get chilly, there's no hot showers for you today, and no blankets." Saul chuckled. "Possibly no clothing either. Socks, maybe. And a little hat."

"Carter and Geoff will be so pleased." He drank his water, the liquid splashing in his belly.

He got a happy laugh from Saul and started smoothing the salve on his backside. "I love you. Actually your ass isn't nearly as marked up as your shoulders. You could pull off loose sweats later I think. Maybe. We'll see... or they will."

"Geoff pierced my cock and has molds of it. He's seen."

"I knew he'd seen it. And other fairly intimate places." Saul ghosted a hand over one shoulder. "I'm going to do my best to keep this gentle, boy. The anesthetic works pretty fast, but it may sting at first." The salve went on thick and Saul worked carefully. "You know, I'm not sure I needed to know about the molds."

"No? It wasn't about sex. He wasn't here when I made them. He needed them to design ink that was good with my cock hard and not. I won't let him do it until he could manage it." The last bit was husky, his focus on his Master's hands.

"I was actually joking, but that's a wild idea. That cock is mine now, though, remember." His Master's tone was light, teasing, playing with him. "If anyone's going to touch it, I want a say."

"I remember. You'll be there, if anyone touches it." He'd been fairly good about not touching it himself, even.

"Mmm. Such a good boy." The calm that followed Saul's words was anything but silent. Saul was humming softly, something familiar but not precise enough for him to name, and reacting to his sounds with praise.

He floated, soaring on waves of adrenaline and endorphins. At some point, Saul touched his cheek and Troy realized he was crying. "Stupid body."

Saul leaned over and kissed the same spot. "Go with it. There's nothing as beautiful as truth."

"I love you, Master." The honorific made his breath hitch, the meaning so much deeper now than it had been.

"I know you do. You're a good boy. You're also my best friend and an incredible lover. I love to hear it, but you should know that I know." Saul put the top back on the tub of ointment and set it aside. "Man, this is crazy huge, isn't it?"

"God yes. Thank you." That was the best he had, and he offered it over.

"Well, we're agreed on that, then." Saul climbed back into bed and tucked in close. "Why don't you catch a nap? We have hours until we have to be presentable."

He moved over until he was snuggled up. "I think that sounds like a plan."

The sound of Saul's heart was steady and eased him right down into a deep, well-fucked sleep.

35

S aul got out of the shower and grabbed a towel. Troy was up and moving, carefully, but Saul didn't want to leave the boy to his own devices too long. Troy would start trying to do things he shouldn't be doing. They'd compromised, allowing Troy to make meals, but his boy had already flat out said no to any help with the stairs. So stubborn.

He'd just gotten right into the shower, so he didn't have to fight his instincts watching Troy manage it all alone. He knew Troy was happy, but he also knew his boy was hurting.

His marks, though. God, just thinking about them made his balls ache. He was flying. High as a kite. What a crazy, amazing morning.

He had more in mind for Troy today, and he couldn't imagine a more perfect setup for what he'd planned.

Sweet.

He swiped the fog off the mirror and caught himself grinning, which just made him grin even wider. The lucky bastard staring back at him had just made his sub come with a flogger. With his fucking flogger. How fucking hot was that? He'd thought that was a stunt saved for porn sites, he didn't know that actually happened for real. He was going to remember that moment with Troy for a long, long, *long* while. Maybe forever. Or at least until the next time he got to do it.

He toweled off, combed his hair, brushed his teeth and found blue jeans. He debated over shirts, finally deciding less was more and went with a gray CU T-shirt. Carter would look all put together he was sure, and who knew about Geoff. Geoff was khakis and collars one minute and cut-offs and T-shirts the next.

He pulled a long, black velvet box out and opened it, taking a second to run his fingers over the heavy silver links. He looped his index finger through the symbolic ring at the center. He was going to be grinning like this for days.

Smelling something cooking, he closed the box, stuck it into his back pocket and headed for the stairs. Troy was making more than guac. He should have known. "I'm going to beat your ass, boy."

"Hmm? Would you like a margarita, Master?"

Damn, his boy looked good. "We agreed we'd make dinner together, didn't we?" He stepped up as close as he dared with the stove going and pulled Troy into a kiss. "Naughty."

"Never. I'm good as gold." Troy opened to him, hand burning against his waist. "We could ask them to cancel."

"We could. But you want me more than you want to have this conversation. You're not getting out of it." It was time to have a good talk, figure it out. Figure Troy out, figure Geoff out... negotiate with Carter. Just move past all of this tension.

"No? There's no way?" Troy was in an amazing mood.

"No. It's important." He had to smile though, and he

combed his fingers through his boy's curls. "But we can send them home early."

"Fair enough. You have to work tomorrow."

"I do. I think Ben is coming over."

"He doesn't have to. I'm going to repaint the guest room, though, so maybe he'll help." Troy kissed his nose. "Let me stir the onions."

'He doesn't have to' was code, Troy knew he shouldn't be alone right now, but Saul pretended he didn't know that. "It's good for the boy. He looks up to you. I'm sure he'd be happy to... help." *Damn*. "You look incredible."

"I feel incredible. I've never had a scene like that. Ever."

His chest grew tight knowing that. Mostly because it was amazing to hear and made him proud of himself and his boy. But part of him ached for Troy, who deserved to have so much more so long ago.

Saul knew he could make up for lost time though. He wanted to give Troy everything. And that was going to start today.

"I've had some good scenes, but I haven't had one that made me feel the way you did. The way I do. Light. High."

"Good. I need your satisfaction like I need air." Troy sliced up the steak, his words spoken without guile, worry, just like it was a known truth. "Is dark blue okay for the guest room?"

"It's your—" He stopped himself. Whoa. No. "Sorry. Dark blue sounds fine."

"Yeah?" Oh, that smile made him a little dizzy. "Cool. It will be calming, I think."

Calming was good. And that reminded him. "You know, since Ben is going to be here anyway, I think you guys should take your truck and hit the hardware store. Will you let him drive?"

"The hardware store? Totally. Do you need anything?"

"Yeah." This was going to be fun. "I need you to trick out the bed with some tie downs, and we need something you can brace yourself on when I'm flogging you that isn't glass. What do you think? Chains from the ceiling? A bar?"

Troy's tilted his head like a puppy that had heard a whistle. "A bar, hmm... I can try. You want pretty sturdy?"

Oh, such a naughty boy. "Yeah, sturdy." He put some gravel in his voice. "I can do so much more if you're standing and properly braced. And it will need to hold your weight at least for a minute or so."

"You have plans, Master?" Troy's prick began to fill, pushing at his sweats. Oh, that was lovely.

"I do, I think. I'm also open to requests, suggestions..." He leaned in and traced Troy's ear with his tongue.

This was the moment.

"Kneel, boy."

Troy hummed softly, sliding down his body to kneel in front of him, right there in the kitchen.

The kitchen.

He almost laughed at how perfect it was. He might have, but Troy was trying to make him groan instead.

"I think if I'd been looking, I wouldn't have found you, because everything about you, about us together, has been unexpected. I love you, Troy. You always give me everything. Your body, your trust, your obedience... I'm always stunned by you. Awed by you. I didn't understand the full potential of living this lifestyle until you."

Troy blinked up at him, eyes shimmering as his boy reached for him. "Thank you."

"So, before the guys get here, and before we get distracted from the amazing high we're on, I wanted to..." Shit, he was suddenly so nervous his mouth went dry. He swallowed, and he took a step back so he could see his boy better. And to keep Troy's hands off him for another minute so he could think.

He pulled the box from his pocket and held it out to Troy. "I want you to wear my collar."

"Master?" Troy's eyes went wide, and his boy's butt slid to the floor. "Oh."

He laughed softly and sat right down with Troy. "Boy?"

"Yes, Sir." It wasn't a question, not at all.

He opened the box and showed it to Troy, then pulled the weighty collar out and put it in his boy's fingers. "What do you think?"

Troy turned it over in his hands, first staring at the collar then staring at him in awe. "It's beautiful. It's... It's the most perfect. Put it on me, Sir? Please?"

"Oh." Right. Put it on. He should be way more together than this, but he was so excited. "I can do that."

He took the collar and held it to Troy's neck, fastened the clasp, which closed down with a finger screw, and let it go. It lay against Troy's collarbone and he smiled, hooking his finger through the ring again.

He wasn't nervous anymore. He was proud. "It looks great."

"Does it? It's heavy." Troy reached for it, his lips parting. It was fascinating to watch Troy's fingers explore each link. "It's amazing."

"Come see." He stood up and helped Troy carefully to his feet to lead his boy to a mirror. "Sore, huh?"

"Burning. It is amazing. I feel like I'm here. Does that make sense? I'm here, and I'm yours."

"I think I know what you mean. Present. In the moment? And most definitely mine." He let that thought straighten his shoulders and steered Troy over to a mirror that hung in the hall. "Mine."

"Oh…" Nothing would ever feel as good as the look of pure bliss on his boy's face. Nothing ever could.

"I love you," he whispered and kissed his boy's cheek.

"I love you, Master. Thank you for this." Troy leaned back against him, the stripes burning between them. "God."

"Good boy. Breathe, then turn around and kiss me."

"My pleasure, Master." Troy inhaled, the breath moving them together. That earned him a gasp, and Troy spun, eyes alight. "Wicked man."

Then his boy kissed him, pressing right into his arms.

He fumbled for a second, partly off-balance by the heat in Troy's kiss, but mostly because he didn't know where to rest his hands that wouldn't hurt the boy. He settled on Troy's hips, pulling Troy as close as he could.

He'd never been called "wicked" before, and he liked it.

Troy was excited, hard, which blew his mind. Troy went on about his age, but was already hot to trot again.

He was just thinking maybe he'd let Troy take him into that amazing mouth when there was a rapping at the door.

"Mmm. God. Was that the door?"

"Mmm… I doubt it." Troy sounded well-loved, well-fucked, and well-marked. "I think it was the wind."

He slid his hand along the ridge in Troy's sweatpants and whispered, "Don't burn dinner, boy."

"Jesus…" Troy stirred, but not before he bucked into Saul's hand, driving into his touch.

"Rain check." Saul laughed, and the knock came again. "Yep, that was the door." He stepped away, breathing and willing himself back in control as he headed through the living room to Carter and Geoff.

"Hey, you guys. Welcome. Come on in." *Come see my boy's new collar.*

"We brought apple pie." Geoff grinned at him, holding out a bakery box. "Smells delicious in here."

"Oh, I love pie. Thank you." He took the box, gave Geoff a hug and shook Carter's hand. "A naughty boy I know was supposed to make guac and instead, started dinner. I don't even know what he's making."

"Smells like fajitas to me. I'll take over in there, so he can rest, yeah?" Carter winked at him, even as Geoff squealed from the kitchen.

"Oh my God! Look at you. Lucky bastard. And—is that a *collar*!"

He glanced at Carter, willing himself not to blush. "We had a busy morning."

"Fuckin' A, man. Congratulations." Carter clapped him on the shoulder. "We'll have to have the boys compare stripes, and I can't wait to see his collar."

He knew he looked at little smug, he couldn't help it. "Geoff's feeling better? I'd love to see."

"I'll have him show off. Let me help in the kitchen, yeah?" Carter's question was indicative of respect, and he appreciated it.

"Be my guest, if he lets you." He let Carter pass by and followed along with the pie. "Smells good in here, boy."

"Thank you, Master. Carter. How's it going?"

"I'm well, thank you. Smells like fajitas. Put me to work so you and Geoff can visit. He's missed you."

Troy glanced at Saul, and he nodded. "Are you sure?"

Carter rolled his eyes and then winked. "Totally. Go."

Geoff took Troy's arm and they left the kitchen, Geoff's voice trailing off as they headed for the living room. "Come on, honey. We need to catch up. Where's your mat? That'll be easier than a chair, don't you think? God it's so pretty. It glows against your skin."

He chuckled and set the pie down on the counter. "It's like a play date." He started to show Carter around the kitchen but realized quickly that Carter was already quite at home.

"They are close as brothers, those two. I'm grateful that they have each other." Carter's words were questioning what he thought, it was obvious.

He knew Carter was getting at something specific, though he couldn't pin it down. He leaned against the counter and nodded. "You're both Troy's family. Geoff and I had a good talk a couple of weeks ago. I know how much he cares."

"Excellent. We'd like to be part of your family too."

Saul could see who'd taught Troy to cook, how he'd learned the efficient motions, the speed.

"I don't know what I would have done without you guys these last few weeks. I'm a little overwhelmed honestly. I've just never... and I felt completely at home last night. I just have to get used to it. I haven't had anything like this before."

Jesus, he was babbling.

"I owe you. I was out of line the morning Troy called in. I disparaged you and him, and I have to be honest, I had to think about why."

Whoa. Okay this was serious shit Carter was talking about. He reached out impulsively and gripped Carter's shoulder. "Hey. The doc said it was going to happen. If not that day than another one. It was just a matter of time, he said." Was he supposed to ask why? Was Carter thinking out loud?

"I know, but I would owe you an apology regardless. We

were used to being Troy's whole world, I was having a shitty week, and everything came to a head. I vote we don't do that again, yeah?"

"Yeah. We better drink to that. Beer?" He went to the fridge, pulled out a couple, and handed one to Carter. "To family."

"To family." Carter grinned at him, eyes twinkling. "So, dinner or admiring our work first?"

Okay. Cool. He handled that like an adult, and Carter looked relieved. All better. Go him.

"Well, that depends. Is Geoff itching to show off? I would love to see your work, man. And you could let me know what you think of Troy's." It wasn't a pissing contest at all. He thought maybe he could learn something.

"Are you kidding? My boy loves to be watched. He's an exhibitionist and a half."

"All right, set dinner on simmer and we'll let the boys show off." He'd never done this either. He'd never had a friend that was a Dom. Acquaintances, people he knew through the subs he'd worked with, but not friends that really got him. Carter got him. Maybe even in a way Troy couldn't quite.

"Sounds good." Carter set everything up to stay warm, and they headed to the front room. Troy sat cross-legged on his mat, Geoff curled on the couch, and they were chatting.

"Did we come back too soon?" He went to Troy, reaching out and running fingers through red curls. The collar—*his* collar—was right there, resting on his boy's throat.

"No, Sir. We were just talking. Sharing war stories, so to speak." Troy sparkled—simply fucking sparkled.

He wanted to tell Troy that using his name was okay, that they were just being themselves tonight and having dinner with friends, except just as that was about to come out of his mouth, it hit him.

They were just being themselves.

This was who they were, all the time. Troy was just as likely to call him 'Saul' in the next breath as his boy was to say 'Sir'.

Huh.

And he apparently could use both 'Troy' and 'his boy' in the same thought without issue too.

This was the twenty-four-seven lifestyle that other people talked about. Or their version, anyway. He wasn't thinking about Troy as a sub who also happened to be a lover. Or friends with bennies. Troy was all of it, everything, there was no way to separate one from the other anymore.

Man, now he totally understood how difficult it had to have been for both Carter and Geoff to let Troy move on. How hard it might still be. It wasn't the same relationship, but Troy had become part of their twenty-four-seven. Same friendship, entirely different dynamic.

"Were you talking about your stripes? Did you get a good look, Geoff?" He wasn't going to pretend he wasn't proud, he thought he'd done well. He thought Troy looked amazing.

"They're stunning. Somehow, they work with the ink, and I've never—never—seen him glow like this. And the collar..." Geoff beamed at him. "You're amazing."

"I told you." Troy waggled his eyebrows. "He's got it down right."

Okay, that time he did blush. A little. He tipped Troy's face up and kissed his boy to cover it. "Thank you, boy. It seems to be enough for us, at least." When he glanced up again, Geoff and Carter were holding hands. "You have something to show off, don't you, Geoff?"

"Master?"

"Go on, boy. Show them."

Geoff stood and stripped off his shirt, showing a black and white back piece with five dark red stripes, the cane work accentuating his tattoo.

Saul straightened up slowly, drawn to the art of it at first and the cane work second. "Oh, wow." He stepped closer, wanting to examine the welts from the cane, which were already healing. They must have worked late last night. That would make sense, poor Geoff had been a bit of wreck.

"Carter, this is gorgeous." He admired the evenness of the stripes, the uniformity of length and color. He liked the cane but hadn't ever used one on a sub's back. He'd done some decent work on Deitz's ass a couple of times, but nothing as skilled as this.

"Thank you. I want to work with the art, always, and he needed something to remember for a few days."

"Geoff, you're beautiful. Thank you for sharing that with us." He looked at Carter. "I hear you. I think maybe there's a deeper conversation there we should all have after dinner. I hope no one minds if Troy leaves his shirt off at the table, I can't ask him to cover up just yet, the stripes are too fresh."

"Of course. No one minds seeing Troy's ink. Boy, you can leave yours off as well."

"Yes, Master."

He gave Carter a nod. "Will you show me your technique some time? I've only ever tried the cane on large muscle groups because across the back has a risky feel to me. At least at my skill level."

"Of course. I've got a lovely collection of tools downstairs and a dummy to practice on. I put layers of newsprint on to judge my arm."

"Oh." He tried not to drool. Or be too jealous. "I'd love a place to work out. That's amazing."

"Just give me a call. We'll have a go at the cane, see how you like it." Carter headed for the kitchen with Troy, both of them working in unison to get the food out.

He loved the little back patio with the lights all around it, and it was fun to be entertaining, he hadn't done hardly any of it because he really didn't have anywhere to entertain until now. He led Geoff outside, making sure the boy had his Master's beer. "God, look at all of this. Those two are good together."

"They've been working for a long time. Carter's going to miss him. They've spent more time together than Carter and I have."

He nodded slowly. "I'm not sure Troy's ready to leave the diner, he's worried. Plus, I don't think he disliked it. He was just burning out. I'm wondering if he'd not going to propose some kind of compromise. I guess we'll see. It's his decision, as much as I'd like it to be mine."

He hoped that Troy was starting to see that he'd been in a twenty-year holding pattern. The diner was a dead end. His friend's dead end, but still a go-nowhere job.

They all settled at the table, Troy serving him, then Carter, then Geoff.

He watched Troy, more curious than concerned, but he still filed that away for later. No one had asked the boy to serve everyone, he hadn't even expected to be served himself. But he was still learning Troy's needs, and many of his boy's habits too, and this was something he didn't quite understand yet.

Troy smiled at him, and the expression was so satisfied, peaceful. "It smells good. It feels like forever since I cooked for you."

"It's been a little while, but everything is shaking out now. We'll get back to normal. Better than normal even, right?" He smiled back so his boy would know he was pleased. "Make yourself a plate and sit."

"Yes, Sir." Troy settled with his plate, and they all spent quite a few minutes doing nothing but eating. The tacos were delicious, spicy and rich, and the guacamole made Saul a happy man.

"So are we all going to talk, Carter?" Geoff asked. "I hate waiting."

Carter rolled his eyes dramatically. "Brat."

"Yep!"

"Why don't you start, Geoff?" Saul picked up his beer. "I think I have an idea what Carter needs, and I'm starting to understand what Troy needs. But you I am less sure about."

"Me?" Geoff was totally shocked, almost comically so. "I don't know what you mean."

Troy blinked over, lips twitching. "Are you sure?"

He glanced meaningfully at Carter. "I think this is where this conversation needs to start. Am I wrong?"

"No. It may be uncomfortable, but Saul is right. We're family." Carter took Geoff's hand. "This is a safe place, yes?"

"It's safe, Geoff. We want to listen. I want to. Your friendship, your support is important to Troy. Essential, even. I absolutely recognize that. And we are family now. You've been a good friend to me too." He was determined to hear Geoff, not just listen. There was something he didn't understand, and nothing was going to be really right until they talked this out.

"I'll always be Troy's friend. Always." Geoff seemed a little panicky around the edges. "And yours, Saul."

"Of course you will." He held Geoff's eyes for a long minute trying to decide what he should say, and how to say it. "What do you need from us, Geoff? From me? Just ask."

"I just want—" Geoff reached for his Master's hand, and Carter immediately took it. "I was Troy's stand-in for a long time. I don't want to lose our connection, you know?"

Saul took Troy's hand and pulled it into his lap, knowing this was important for Troy to hear too. "Twenty years is too long to be considered a stand-in. I mean, I know I'm the baby in the room here, but I don't see it that way at all. You and Carter together saw to Troy's needs in different ways, and I know he's grateful for that. I was touchy about the ink at first, I own that. But your connection with Troy doesn't at its core interfere with mine. What can I do to help?"

"You weren't a stand-in. You're my best friend. I never thought you were... Geoff, honey, do you feel like I was using you?" Troy's eyes were wide as saucers.

Saul squeezed Troy's hand, glancing between the boys. Damn. He had no idea how to help with that, he was just going to have to let them hash that out. He looked at Carter again, who was calmly holding Geoff's hand but keeping quiet and decided it might be time for him to do the same.

"Shit. We were using each other. That's why we're friends. You let me have total control. You trusted me with your skin. It was a fucking gift."

"Boy, no cursing." Carter sounded like he'd said that a million and a half times.

"Goddamn it!"

"That's another one."

"That's not why you're friends. You were friends first." He hid his grin. "Looks like your boy is a bit of a switch, Carter. He's jonesing for control."

"Tell me something I didn't know." Carter didn't even try

not to smile. "I don't suppose you'll lend your boy to mine once a month?"

Well that explained a lot, didn't it? Geoff's restlessness, Troy's desire to serve everyone, and now he could remember a handful of other moments over the last few weeks that made more sense. "I think we can work that out, as long as Troy agrees, and I'm consulted on any permanent marks."

Which meant everything, right? Geoff was all about ink. They were all going to be permanent.

"You're Troy's Dom. I wouldn't ever overstep." Geoff stopped, stared at Carter. "You knew?"

Carter laughed. "It's my job to know, boy. Did you really think I stopped coming to your sessions because Troy was cursing? I saw what was happening. You didn't need another Dom in the room."

Saul leaned back in his chair and sipped his beer. "Huh. Now I get it." That's why the ink made him uneasy, why he'd wanted to keep Troy away.

Troy sat, so quiet, preternaturally still. Then he stood and began clearing dishes.

He watched Troy move. There was no hiding the discomfort in his boy's shoulders and he guessed that whatever was on Troy's mind wasn't for company. "Excuse me." Saul glanced at Geoff and Carter, and then gathered up dishes before following Troy into the kitchen. Once they were there, he stepped between his boy and the door, not letting Troy leave the room. "Talk, boy."

Troy stared at him for a long second. "I haven't... I haven't ever been unfaithful to you."

"Un—what?" He reached for Troy. "I know. Why would you say that?"

"I just... I love Geoff and Carter, but you're special."

He blinked, trying to figure out what Troy was getting at. "There's all kinds of love, baby. I trust you."

"Good." Troy took a deep breath, then nodded. "I'll start the dishes and bring out the apple pie."

"Wait." He pulled his boy in close for a kiss. "Is this what you want? Once a month with Geoff?"

"I don't know how to answer that. I don't want to hurt you."

Jesus. What was Troy so afraid of? "With the truth, boy. There is no other answer. Don't make this so hard. I need to know everything or I am no use to you."

"What I have with Geoff, it's not sex. It sounds so fucking awful, to say we were giving each other what we needed, but we were, and it wasn't shitty. It was love. It could get out of hand sometimes, because we were both so into it, but..."

"What does 'out of hand' mean?"

"Sometimes, like the last time, it was too long a session, too deep, but I didn't want it to stop. I wanted to stay where I was."

"Yeah, the last time was brutal. You were a wreck. But it was something you said you needed, that you'd established with Geoff..."

He watched his boy, so unsettled and tense despite all the good their session had done them both, and decided he'd better just say what was on his mind.

"Listen, Troy. Whatever it was you had with Geoff, with Carter, you don't owe anyone an apology for that. You don't need be ashamed or worried about how I feel about it. I wasn't around. It's not my business, okay? But I'm around now, and I want you to get everything you need. If you need that time with Geoff, that headspace, it's okay. I will make sure you get it. I'm not a tattoo artist, so we have to go to Geoff for that. If you needed a bull whip or something we'd have to find someone for that too. This isn't a problem, and it isn't hurting my feelings."

He made sure he had Troy's eyes. "But it can't get like that again. Carter and I need to monitor you both. That's all. And please don't get hung up on sex. Scenes get intimate sometimes, that's the nature of the beast. It's not a betrayal of any kind."

"Shit, lover. Getting hung up on sex is how I was raised." Troy pushed into his arms, a soft sigh in the air. "I feel... spoiled. And I feel like someone told a secret."

"Yeah. You told me one, finally. Thank you." He gave Troy a squeeze. "I'll send Geoff in to help with the dishes, and then you can bring out the pie when you're ready. Okay?" That would give the boys a minute to talk and he and Carter a minute to put their heads together. He let Troy go after one more gentle kiss. "I love you. Bring ice cream with the pie."

"Yes, Sir. I love you." Troy shot him a smile and turned toward the kitchen. His boy looked more relaxed, easier in his skin. Hopefully, Troy would feel even better after a chance to connect with Geoff.

"All good out here? Carter, can I borrow your boy to help Troy with the dishes?" He grabbed his beer off the table as he sat down. "And then we'll have some of that pie."

"Of course you can." Carter tweaked one of Geoff's nipples. "Go help. Troy will need you now."

He winked at Geoff and said thank you as the boy took off for the kitchen, sipped his beer, and set it down on the table with a sigh. "Okay then."

"I assume yours had a flutter like mine?" Carter seemed relaxed, unconcerned.

"Is that what you call it?" He grinned at Carter. "What did Geoff tell you about their last ink session?"

Carter tilted his head and hummed, lips pursing. "That you were coming to stay with Troy. That it was long—too long, in my estimation. Geoff's hands were destroyed."

He nodded. "Troy was a wreck. Emotionally, physically drained. We have to supervise them. Or at least set a limit for each session and consequences for going beyond our limitations."

"Fair enough. It may be an interesting exercise, watching together." Carter's smile was the slightest bit wicked. "He's a master at what he does. I'd love to know how it changes since we've acknowledged certain truths."

"Oh. I don't know. I didn't think about that. I guess it might be a little... intense, huh?"

"You'll have to speak to your boy about allowing me to watch. Also, no one can judge his stamina like you, hmm? Until we understand how his heart responds, I'd be more comfortable with a failsafe."

"I'll be there. No worries." He looked at Carter. "Troy might need my reassurance anyway. He's worried about what I think is really going on."

"That doesn't surprise me."

"No? I think my relationship experience might be a little broader than his. I have this feeling he'd be shocked by how open I am."

"Has he ever told you about Arnie?" Carter leaned back, checking the door as he did. "Arn was my best friend in school. Good man, but damn, he had some off ideas about how to be a Dom."

"Troy has said a couple of things. Geoff told me a couple of things, but no. We've never really had a conversation about him. And that's my fault because after I found out how he died and everything, and how devastated Troy had been, I told Troy we should hold off on talking about him. I was intimidated I guess, I didn't want to feel like I had to live up to a shadow so tall." This was Carter's best friend, he wasn't going to insult Carter with his feelings about Arnie as a Dom.

"He was a possessive asshole who almost ruined one of our own." Carter didn't sound angry, not really, more... resigned. "He was terrified that he'd be discovered, that he'd be outed, so he kept Troy controlled, frightened, off-balance."

He nodded. He understood that being gay and in rodeo just wasn't a thing back then. Maybe not even now. But... "That bag of rocks. How do you live like that?"

How do you let your friend do that to someone?

"I don't know." Carter must have seen his disbelieving expression and shrugged. "You have to remember, this was before cell phones were a thing, before anyone I knew had emails. I got postcards, a call once a year on my birthday. I never met Troy before Arnie was gone."

"Oh." *Whoa.* "Yeah, I see what you're saying." Damn. "Why..." He looked past Carter to the patio doors to make sure they were still alone. "Why did Troy allow it?"

"My guess? Part youth, part stupidity, but mostly he'd been taught what he wanted was going to send him to hell and this charismatic cowboy offered to give him a place to belong."

"Hm." He got it. He didn't know what to say about it, he didn't grow up being told to hate who he was. Plenty of people had, he knew that, but he hadn't seen it that often himself. "Has he... I guess you guys haven't ever had that conversation. Do you think he's past it?"

"Past Arnie or past his psycho father?" Carter snorted. "Not that the answer would be different either way. Twenty years is a long time to figure out what you know to be right."

416 PIJODI PAYNE & BA TORTUGA

"I hope so. He deserves better. He's so... loveable." He scraped at the label on his beer bottle with his thumbnail. "I want him to be happy."

"Good. So do I. I vote we're all happy. Happy, busy, and well-satisfied." Carter clinked their beers together. "On to happier shit. Are you stoked about watching the boys work together?"

Yeah, that was enough hindsight. "I'm not sure if stoked is the right word. I'm... intrigued? Curious. A little turned-on."

"Yeah. I fought it before, because it didn't feel appropriate."

"Well, I guess this is a whole new game, huh?" He grinned at Carter. "Should be fun."

"Yeah." There was a long pause, a heavy sigh. "He's not coming back to work, is he?"

Saul shrugged. "He's been cleared to work, but he can't be on his feet for long, he can't lift anything heavy yet, he's not supposed to be under stress. He's getting better, he'll be a hundred percent soon, honestly. It's his decision but if it were up to me, I'd want him to find something he loves. Not just a job."

"It's not just a job, is it? He's been with me forever." Carter shook his head and put the beer bottle on the table. "Maybe he'd be interested in working part-time in the office —inventory, scheduling, ordering."

"He might. I know he's worried about whether he can afford to teach, he might take you up on that." That was something Troy could start right away too, and it would be good for the boy to get out of the house. "But Carter, I think in his mind he's been working for you all this time, not with you, no matter what your intention was. You've been his boss, at work. His superior. His Dom in effect."

Work was one area he didn't know much about his boy, one area he'd tried to keep his fingers—and his opinions—to himself until the day Troy got sick. Would Troy appreciate that change in status, if it was made clear to him?

"A Dom at work, a Dom at home, his best friend taking on that role from time to time, that seems overwhelming to me, but..."

Carter shrugged. "I'm not a Dom part-time, I suppose. I can back off."

"You're not a bitch about it. You're a boss." Troy came out with Geoff, pie in hand. "When did everything get complicated?"

Actually, he'd been thinking that having a Dom at work wasn't such a bad idea. He winked at Troy. "About the time your triad became a quad." He wasn't trying to be shocking; it really wasn't a difficult leap in logic.

There was a silence, then Geoff popped off with, "Two and two is four. Two and two is four."

"Wait." Saul snorted and leaned back in his chair. "Did you really go twenty years without looking at what was going on?"

"No." That was Carter, and Geoff shrugged, blushing a sweet rose.

"Okay, Carter and I talked about it."

He glanced at Troy. "You're quiet, boy."

"I am." Troy had put together four plates—two with pie and ice cream, one with just pie, and one with a scoop of ice cream. Saul and Carter got the full deal, Geoff was handed the pie.

"You're upset with me. But I didn't say that to make fun of anyone. Relationships can be complicated, fluid. Yours with Carter and Geoff... when I stepped into the middle of that it complicated everything. It changed all of you. It changed me. I think it's difficult to talk about us without also acknowledging that at this point there is also a we." He tilted his head at Carter. "I'll accept that I'm off base if you disagree but... I doubt you do."

"No. We're a family, the four of us. It's about time we talked." Carter looked at Troy, so serious. "And you don't get to shut down and stress yourself out. You've got three men who love you dearly."

Saul stood, moved to Troy, and rested his hands heavily on his boy's shoulders. Making sure Troy felt their weight. "Boy. Listen to me. Pay attention to those stripes on your back. You're mine. My boy. I'm your Master. Clear? What Carter and I are talking about isn't about changing that, or asking more of you. It's about understanding everything else we have. Everything else we are."

"I must look like the world's oldest idiot to you." Troy sighed softly. "To all y'all."

"Not at all." Saul pulled his chair closer so he could keep hold of Troy's hand. "Serving comes so naturally to you I'm not surprised all this talk is stressing you out." Troy just wanted to get on with it.

"You're not an idiot, honey." Geoff took Troy's other hand. "You're amazing."

"Shut up."

Geoff's eyes twinkled. "Don't you mean shut up, Sir?"

Troy let go of Saul's hand and covered the twitch of his lips with his middle finger.

That got laughs from everyone. Saul scooped up a bite of his pie. "That's reserved for one day a month. Otherwise he's the same sort of naughty submissive that you are. Except, apparently, when serving dinner." He winked at Carter. "Did you notice he even knows how we like our pie? You'd think he'd been serving you forever."

"He has." Carter nodded to Troy. "I want to talk to you about the diner. I want you to come home. You don't have to cook. We can discuss other arrangements, but I want you to come home."

"Carter was talking about maybe working in the office part-time. You could even start that right away because you wouldn't be on your feet." Carter's offer made sense and Saul felt like Troy needed to feel included again. Productive. Capable. Troy needed all of that before he could pursue the things that spoke more to his heart.

"No more five in the morning start times? I'm used to sleeping in with Saul."

"Oh, the negotiations have begun. My favorite part!" Geoff clapped his hands like a little boy at his birthday party.

"Oh, Troy's lover would appreciate that, Carter." Not that he slept past seven most mornings, but that was sleeping in when you were used to getting up at four.

"Eight thirty to three, three days a week," Carter offered. "On salary."

"Wednesday through Friday?" Troy countered.

"Works for me."

"Good. What salary?"

Carter met Troy's eyes. "I want you to be part-owner of the cafe."

Whoa. Okay, that he hadn't expected. He glanced at Geoff, trying to figure out if this was an in-the-moment thing, or if Geoff had known it was coming.

Geoff nodded to Troy. "Carter's been hatching a plan, honey. He wants time too. You can both work together toward something... great."

Damn, had he hit the nail on the head with this quad thing or what? Geoff and Carter both arrived tonight intending to dangle carrots to keep Troy close. Still, the diner wasn't a yoga studio. He took Troy's hand again and decided he'd better keep his mouth shut. The fact was he had everything he wanted.

"I—We'll have to talk about it, but I'm interested. I need to do a lot of work before I can start thinking about training for my teacher hours." Troy sounded more sure than Saul had heard him in weeks.

"That's a yes, though right?" Geoff looked at Carter. "That was a yes."

"It'll be a short talk. This pie is really good," Saul said with his mouth full.

"Of course it is," Geoff said. "I didn't make it. The pros did."

"Troy's is better though. You might have to let him do your desserts too." He gave Troy a sideways grin and a wink.

Troy rolled his eyes dramatically, shook his head like he was wagging an invisible beard. "Go back to work, don't go back, go back and do more. Make up your mind, man."

As if he didn't know Troy wanted to accept Carter's offer. "Right. We're going to talk it over. I'm just trying to sweeten the deal." Oh, good one. He sat up. "Pun intended."

They all groaned. All of them.

"That was wonderful," Carter started, but Geoff just shook his head.

"Awful, he meant."

He ran a hand over Troy's thigh, suddenly so ready to send everyone home so they could pick up where they left off before their company arrived. "You're the tie-breaker, lover. Yay or nay?"

"I'm always on your side. Always."

36

Troy was nervous, which was stupid as fuck. Carter had been his friend for twenty some odd years, had seen him at his worst, and had been his boss for a damn long time. Troy trusted the man with his life.

Still, last night had rocked him a little, shed light on things that he wasn't sure he'd been ready to look on. Still, the horse had bolted, no putting him back in the box now.

He smoothed his good button-down and headed in, feeling like a newborn foal.

The diner was busy with breakfast shift well under way. It smelled about the same as ever, sounded the same. He was greeted by everyone with cheers and hugs and warm smiles, so that by the time he made it to the office it was well past eight-thirty.

Carter was leaning on the desk and glanced up as he came in. He got a once over and then Carter smiled, levered off the desk, and pulled him into a hug. "Glad you're here. Take a deep breath, you look like you're going to pass out."

"I feel like it." He hugged Carter back, letting it bring him to rights. "It's been a strange few months, hasn't it?"

"It's been quite the ride. Have a seat. Coke?" Carter tugged a chair out for him and opened the mini-fridge.

"Please. Dr Pepper if you have it. It looks busy in there. How are the new cooks doing?" *Are we okay? I don't know what to do, not exactly.*

"Butch caught on quick, he has some experience from another diner outside of town, he's a team player, he does everything right." The words were complimentary, but the energy behind them wasn't nearly as enthusiastic. "He's... fine." Carter handed him a Dr Pepper and leaned on the desk again. "I've missed you around here. I've missed you... period."

"I missed you too. Life is weird without my daily dose of you." It seemed like saying those words was a different now, bigger, heavier.

"It took the possibility of not having you around here again to make me understand... it's not even the cooking. It's you. And I haven't had a chance to tell you. Not really."

"It's a little weird, isn't it?" He smiled at Carter, who smiled back at him. "More wonderful than weird."

"We spent a lot of years just knowing something in here..." Carter tapped the center of a broad chest. "What's wonderful is that your lover made it seem like it's as normal as breathing. I'm not sure I feel that way yet, not entirely, but how lucky are we that you found him? Of all people?"

"He's special." And honestly, Carter had found Saul and brought Saul here to meet him, so... "So what do you think? Seriously. I want to come back, but with a purpose, you know?"

"I told you what I thought last night. I want to know what you think."

"I think that I'm in. I can't invest, though. I mean, you know that, right?" Not if he was going down to half time.

"Actually, you can, if you don't mind pumping about half your pension back into the business."

"I—" *God. Breathe. Breathe, Troy. You can do this.* "I— Would you think less of me if I told you I was a little scared? I'm in, just a little wigged."

"No. You're buying half a business. That's not a light decision." Carter pulled up a chair and sat closer. "How about this. You work here with me for six months as if you've bought in. If it works out, we draw up something legal. If it doesn't, no harm no foul."

"No. No, I want to do it right. I've been thinking about it all night." He had already pulled the trigger in his heart; his mind was just slower.

Carter's mouth twitched into a smile. "Yeah? You sure?"

"I am. I'm sure. I want to do this." Troy met Carter's eyes, took a deep, deep breath. "With you."

"Thank you." Carter watched him, then took a deep breath himself. "You belong here. I know you're going to rock this, Troy. And I admit, Geoff wants me around more so this will be a good thing for everybody."

"I do belong here. This is home, right? Has been for decades."

"God, don't say decades, it makes me feel old." Carter reached out and gave his knee a squeeze, then got up. "Geoff is doing that enough these days."

"Poor old man," he teased. "You're going to be creaking and cracking around."

"Watch it, pup. I have a few years on you. And a few more on Geoff. We can't all be all *namaste* and keeping up with a jailbait lover." Carter grinned wide, eyes twinkling as he teased.

"Some of us are tough enough to deal with three men without zoning out." A heart attack, sure. Zoning, not a bit.

"I give you credit. We're not the easiest three men." Carter dug around in a drawer. "You were pretty shook up last night, how do you feel today?"

"I don't know. Worried, excited, a little buzzed, like something just woke up."

Carter nodded. "Yes. Don't you feel a little like... this might sound ridiculous, but like you're dating again? I feel like I'm looking at you and Saul, even Geoff just a little differently. Like something is new."

"Yeah. It makes me feel a little old, because Saul is so comfortable with everything. He lives in no-guilt land." It was amazing and a little unnerving, and he was trying to catch up.

"Guilt? Are you kidding? He's a twenty-five-year-old Dom who hits people—you—with floggers until they scream. And his friends do too. That's a lot of open-minded thinking." Carter laughed. "When did he get his start?"

"I don't know. I've only met one of his friends. He seems to be happy to just walk away from them." Which sounded so mean, didn't it? *Shit.* "I mean..." *Shit.*

"Oh. Well? You don't want a bunch of frat boys in your house anyway." Carter took his hand and put a key ring in it. "Your keys to the kingdom."

Whoa. This wasn't the keys to the back door so he could open. He'd had those for years. These were *all* the keys.

"Yeah?" He closed his fingers around the key ring. "Wow. No shit?"

"Of course. And do you remember the date you started working here? That's the safe combination." Carter shrugged. "See? You've always been important."

A rush of tingles hit him, flooding him from top to bottom, sending goosebumps along his arms and making his nipples hard. "Oh."

"Oh. I... sorry." Carter squeezed Troy's fingers, then cleared his throat and moved away again. "A new door opened last night, and I guess I'm anxious to see what's on the other side of it. Whatever is there has nothing to do with the diner, though. I apologize, I won't cross that line again."

"Don't apologize, please. We'll have a shitton of things to figure out. If we start with the I'm-sorrys, we're going to waste a lot of time."

Carter grinned. "Fine. I'm not sorry. You want to learn the ordering system?"

"I've been working here for twenty years, watching you. Let me order and show me what I miss?" He wasn't stupid, and he managed when Carter needed time off.

Carter raised an eyebrow at him and stepped out of his way, gesturing to the desk chair. "Be my guest."

"Thank you. I have your back, Carter. Always." And Troy could pull his weight here. He sat down, grinning up as he did. "Wow. Cushy."

"Only the best for my backside." Carter pulled out a laptop and sat in a chair on the other side of the desk. "Let me know if you have issues. I'm going to work on next week's schedule. When we're done, you can take me on a tour and tell me what you'd change if we had cash on hand. Which we do now."

"Fair enough." He wasn't intimidated. Nope. Not. Not at all. "Let's do this."

Then he'd take Saul out to lunch.

They had so much to talk about.

37

Troy headed into the bike shop, ready for a little food, a little rest, and a lot of company. He'd done some of everything, including cooking up two patty melts for Carter and Geoff, and sharing his meatloaf recipe.

Emma was at the front counter, grinning wide at the sight of him. "Look at you!"

Saul was carrying a tall box and clearly couldn't see around it. "Yeah, I know, I'm a stud."

"Not you, idiot. Your man is here."

"Huh? Oh!" Saul put the box down next to the counter, eyes lighting up. Sweaty bangs, pink cheeks. God, he looked so young like that. "Hi!"

"Hey, gorgeous. I was wondering if you would like to come to lunch." He wanted to sit with Saul, talk, tell him everything that had happened, touch base.

"Make you a deal, Emma. I take a long lunch and then you get to leave early. You in?"

"Oh. That would be awesome. I'm in."

"She has a date tonight." Saul winked at him.

Emma laughed. "No. We're not dating tonight. It's a straight up booty-call."

"Lucky woman. Congratulations." Troy high-fived with her, loving how she laughed. "I appreciate it. I just went back to work today, and I need to tell my man all about it."

"Well, get out of here. We're dead today anyway. Take your time."

"Thanks, Em." Saul kissed her cheek and then followed him out the door. "This is a nice surprise. Are we walking?"

"Is it all right? I just—" Needed to hear your voice, tell you everything, be your touchstone. "—wanted to visit you."

"It's great." Saul's hand slipped into his. "Are you okay? How was work?"

"I'm good. It was all right. Weird. Busy. Exciting. Unnerving." He held on tight.

Saul tugged his hand, slowing their pace. "Breathe, boy. Talk. I'm listening."

"I'm okay. I just— I did it. I'm part-owner. I have keys." Him. He had all the keys, and that was amazing. He wasn't just a cook in a diner. He was part of something bigger.

Saul smiled at him and leaned over as they walked to kiss him on the cheek. "Congratulations. You deserve it. It's like a promotion, about a decade late. You own a diner. Is that the unnerving part?"

"Yes? No? I— Yes." Maybe. Mostly. Partially. God.

Saul laughed, but not at him. The sound was happy, free. "It's an adventure! I'm so proud of you. It wasn't that long ago that you were perfectly happy to watch me through the pass-through window and not even say hello. And now? Look at you." Saul squeezed his hand hard. "You're in a dress shirt and you own a goddamn diner."

"Right? It was something else. I wanted to make sure Carter was absolutely ready, and he was." And they had this new energy between them, something he didn't quite know how to handle.

"What did you guys do? Divvy up responsibilities? Talk about salary? All that stuff? God, I can't wait until Emma and I buy the bike shop. I have all these ideas."

"I cooked, did orders. I'm going to stay with my current salary, but fewer hours right now." He opened the door to the restaurant. "We talked about making some changes, things I've been thinking about a lot."

"Oh. Greek. Great idea." Saul went inside and then turned back to face him. "I love that Carter is listening to those things. Good for you."

A hostess got their attention and seated them near a window. Saul opened a menu and was reading it but kept glancing up at him over the top.

Troy didn't even look. All he needed was Saul. Stupid, maybe, but they were partners. He wanted his lover's approval, his Master's support.

Saul closed the menu and took his hand again. "So? There's still something on your mind. What haven't you told me? Was everything okay between you and Carter? Was it weird?"

Thank God Saul asked. "Yes, but not in a bad way. We didn't know exactly how to interact."

There was a spark that he wasn't sure he should feel.

The server came over and Saul ordered lamb kefte and saffron rice and a big salad for them to share. His lover had an appetite and obviously wasn't having the kind of issues he was. Saul seemed completely at ease.

"I guess you have to work out how to separate your working together from all the personal stuff, huh? That doesn't seem simple, but you'll figure it out... which parts of the relationship can come to work and what has to stay home."

"Yes, and what that means. I mean, I've never thought of anything like this... thing... we're thinking about." He touched Saul's knee under the table, connecting them.

"That's the thing, baby. If it's right, you won't have to think too hard about it. You're going to know. We just have to stay honest and keep communicating. The issues happen when you don't talk."

"Listen to you. You're so calm." Troy wasn't. He felt all the butterflies. He was going to have to call Geoff and see what he felt.

"You're nervous? Why? You've known these men forever. You trust them. If you're going to torture yourself, do it with the things you want." Saul leaned over the table, grinning and lowered his voice. "Like do you want to kiss Geoff?"

"Master!" Saul did *not* just ask him that.

Saul just shook his head and leaned back in his chair. "Too soon? Sorry." His Master wasn't sorry at all.

"Do you want to kiss Carter?" Was that even a thing?

Saul looked at him thoughtfully. "I don't know. I would, I just haven't thought about whether I want to. Maybe because we haven't talked about how you'd feel about it." Saul picked up a glass of water and took a sip. "I mean, how do you feel about that possibility? About me kissing one of them. Or... more?"

"I think that, if we explore that, we should be together. All of us. I want you with me." And he wasn't going to ask whether that was okay. It was what he needed.

"Sounds perfect to me. I'm glad I asked. You can let me know if you decide you'd like to. And then I'll talk to Carter."

But if it was all on him did that mean Saul had already

decided? And if Saul and Carter decided, how would he know what Geoff really wanted? Yeah, he definitely had to call Geoff now.

"Okay. That's... fair." He would talk to Geoff, see what was what, and then talk to Saul. First, though, he needed to learn his new job, remember how to breathe.

"Hey. It doesn't ever have to happen, okay? There's no pressure here either way. You know what's there now, we can just see how it plays out. It doesn't change anything between you and me. You're mine. You're going to stay mine." Their food arrived and Saul stopped talking. Once the server was gone, his Master smiled at him. "You want me to remind you of that tonight, boy?"

He grinned right back, his cheeks going hot. "Yes, Sir. Maybe I'll show you my design for the addition to the bedroom..."

A fork came his way, a bite of lamb on the end. "I am so looking forward to that."

He opened up, the offer of the bite intimate and dear. He hummed as he ate, his eyes rolling up.

Saul cut a bite and ate it, nodding approval. "Mmm. I love this place. Thank you for inviting me to lunch, it's such a nice surprise. You're good to me."

"I love you." And that was that, wasn't it? He loved Saul.

Saul blushed a little, which wasn't common for him and kind of a score when he made it happen. "Would you like to go camping again before the weather gets chilly?"

Even if he hated the idea, he'd go. Good thing he wanted to head into the mountains before it snowed. "I think that sounds like heaven. This coming Sunday?"

Saul nodded. "Sounds great. Should we go on our own or invite Carter and Geoff?"

"Oh God, can you imagine our Geoff? Camping?" His eyes went so wide they pulled at the corners.

"Oh." Saul laughed. "Maybe not. So no, huh? Good. Just us then. You want to bring bikes? Or just your cuffs?" His Master was getting better with the straight face.

"Whatever turns you on, Master." Seriously. Whatever gave them both what they needed.

"That's a non-answer answer, boy." Saul pushed more food on him, making him eat. "You're going to need your strength tonight."

He scooped up some hummus on a bit of pita, looking at Saul from under his lashes. "Yes, Sir. I do hope so."

EPILOGUE

The last time Saul had been in Geoff's tattoo studio with Troy, it hadn't been his best moment, or theirs. He told himself there was no reason to let that stress him now, he was here helping prep his boy, Carter was having a quiet talk with his, and everything would be sane and supervised this time.

He wasn't usually sensitive like this, but there was a weird energy in the air, something a little daring, something wild. He'd never felt anything like it.

He kissed Troy's bare shoulder. "How do you feel, boy?"

"I'm so glad you're here. It's time to cover the scar." Troy had come in, turned on music, and put a soft blanket on the massage table, before he'd stripped off his shirt. It was almost as if his boy had been here once or twice.

"I needed to be here. You and Geoff need us here, I think."

The scar hadn't ever bothered him as much as it had Troy. He wasn't exactly sure why his boy was so put off by it. He knew that Troy didn't like how the ink looked there now, but it could also be more than that. It might be that it was some kind of a reminder the boy didn't want.

The session was going to be painful too, covering scars and old ink, and although he knew Troy knew that well, he found himself dreading as much as welcoming it. He wondered if his boy felt the same way.

He stayed close to Troy, close enough to feel the warmth between them, and nodded at Carter. "We're ready."

"We are too." Carter's eyes were lit up, warm, and Saul felt the excitement building between them.

Saul nodded to Carter, then hooked his fingers behind Troy's head and took a kiss, surprising himself with how possessive he felt all of a sudden. Where the hell had that come from? His chest ached with it, and when he let Troy go, he pinned his boy with a look. "I love you."

"I love you, Master. I love that you're here." Troy beamed at him.

"I'll be watching." He let go of Troy. "Okay, Geoff. He's all yours. You ready?"

Geoff nodded, and Saul could see how much the boy— no, the Dom today—how much the Dom needed this just in the way he was standing. But he didn't leave Carter's side. "Yes."

He took a breath and joined them, taking Geoff by the shoulders. "I trust you. I'm looking forward to this." It was mostly true. He was sure it would be completely true once things got started. He didn't really understand everything he was feeling right now.

"Thank you. He's... my best friend, my best work."

Saul knew it was time, because Geoff was totally focused on Troy, eyes dragging over his boy's body like he owned it.

He stepped out of Geoff's way, knowing it was okay, knowing that it would only be awkward this first time and probably not for long, but feeling like he was caught in a strange emotional tug of war anyway. He stepped in beside Carter but couldn't look over, not yet. Instead, he crossed his arms over his chest like that might contain everything and watched as Geoff approached his boy.

"It's weird huh?" Geoff asked Troy. "Just a little."

"It's just been a long time, but we know how this works." Troy took Geoff's hand, squeezed. "We've done this for so long together."

"Do you think it's weird?" Carter asked him softly.

"No. It's right. You can see that, look at them. I'm just having a little trouble swallowing that."

"If you want to, pull the plug at any time. You know that, right?" Carter focused on him.

"I don't want to. This is something Troy needs that I can't give him. It's something he needs specifically from Geoff. I just feel like I'm on the edge of a cliff and I'm ready for them to get started. I know just how Geoff is feeling."

He caught Carter's eyes. "How are you feeling?"

"Excited. It's so good, to have someone here to share this with."

Despite the odd, last minute need to lay claim to his boy that he hadn't been expecting at all, he was also excited about experiencing this with another Dom, with Carter especially. And excited about watching Geoff work too. "I'm intrigued by the idea of watching. It's kind of... voyeuristic. Kind of a turn on. I'm looking forward to the whole experience, and it is good to be sharing it." All of it. Whatever "all" meant.

Saul turned his head sharply at the buzz of Geoff's tattoo machine and tried to catch Troy's eyes for a brief second. The boy wasn't watching him, though, Troy was settled back on the table, eyes riveted on Geoff. He held his breath as Geoff bent to his work.

"You ready, honey?" Geoff smiled at Troy, and Troy smiled back.

"I am."

"Then turn up the music, and let's play." Geoff's left hand splayed out over Troy's belly; the right drawing shapes in ink and blood.

The smile Troy gave Geoff was all he needed. Everything he'd been feeling slotted into place; his possessiveness shifting smoothly into pride. He rocked back on his heels and grinned at Carter as music filled the room, masking some of the sound of the tattoo machine.

There were pauses for more ink, for Geoff to shake his hand out and wipe the blood away. His boy was in the moment, face lax, cock half-hard. He'd never seen that from this distance, and he was stunned by Troy's beauty.

He watched for a bit, admiring his boy of course, but also Geoff's focus, and then he considered Carter. He and Geoff had shared a lot of worry and emotion over Troy and he felt as if he knew Troy's closest friend pretty well. But Carter was still hard for him to read. Carter always seemed to have a poker face. He'd give a lot to find out what the Dom looked like when Geoff got him rattled. "So why did you really stop supervising them? Because this is beautiful."

"It is. I felt it was inappropriate. Troy worked for me. I couldn't see him like this. The no-cursing rule was a convenient excuse."

He glanced back at their boys and noticed a hint of sweat on each of them now. "When Troy and I had just met, and I was only beginning to understand our potential, I was ready to pull him away from you and Geoff. I thought he was being taken advantage of, even abused in some ways. If

I hadn't come to your house that first time we wouldn't be in this space. I'd have made him choose. And I'm pretty sure I'd have lost him."

Saul focused on Carter and tried to see into the man's dark eyes. "He loves you. You saved him. You belong here, seeing him just like this, being a part of what Geoff is to him. I'm grateful and it's really the only gift I have to give you." He felt young and stupid again, but it was the truth and Carter deserved it.

"Goddamn, you're amazing." Carter reached out, cupped his jaw. "We're lucky you ran into me."

He took a breath, just to let the touch settle in him and soothe the last couple of rough spots. Then he grinned at Carter. "You got a pretty sweet bike out of the deal."

"You know it. Hot as hell."

Saul was sure that Carter was about to kiss him, but Troy moaned, the sound loud, and they both turned to the boys.

Saul curled fingers around Carter's wrist and lifted his hand away, tangling their fingers instead. "Let's go see. Come on." He led Carter by the hand over to the table.

Geoff chuckled. "That was a good spot."

"Shut up."

Geoff's hand was over one nipple, as they both breathed together. Troy's eyes were closed, sweat covering him, a series of tiny triskelions outlined over the scar.

He rested a hand on Troy's hip. "Looks good so far. Are you trying to get this done in one session, boys?"

Geoff shrugged, relaxed and calm. "We'll see how far I can go."

He moved his hand down Troy's thigh. "And how do you feel, boy?"

"Sore. Buzzed. High. Is it pretty?" Troy spread for him, his boy panting.

"Beautiful. What do you think Carter? He's gorgeous, isn't he?" He let his fingers glide over Troy's cock and felt it stir under the thin fabric of the boy's sweatpants.

"It's stunning. You do beautifully together, boys."

He was half-hard himself, or maybe past that point, but he liked the little hum of arousal, the anticipation, and he decided he'd let it simmer and get out of the way. He leaned down and gave Troy a quick kiss though, and Geoff's shoulder a pat before he headed back across the room.

As he walked back, he swore he felt a warm caress, a touch brushing his ass. He looked over his shoulder, right into Carter's dancing gaze.

"I felt that." He turned, keeping just that whisper of room between them. "You wanna make out?"

Carter's answer was a hard, sure kiss.

———

Love Saul & Troy & Carter & Geoff? Download Making a Mark, Book 2 in the series, now!

If you enjoyed Breaking the Rules,
move on to Book 2 right now!

Making a Mark
The Triskelion, Book 2

When Troy and Saul became lovers, they worried about a lot of things. There was their age gap, their younger Dom-older sub relationship, and Troy's health, which was made worse by job stress. They managed all that and more with a deep commitment, and with a lot of help from Troy's longtime best friends, fellow Dom and sub couple Carter and Geoff.

In fact, Saul seems to be what all three of the other men need to see what's been there all along, and to provide the balance they need to deepen their relationship in a very meaningful way. They've already made their marks on each other's hearts. Now it's time to start living the life they've all been dreaming of.

Nothing is ever perfect or easy, though, and they all have to shift their perceptions. Geoff has to come to terms with his need for submission and desire to dominate Troy, and Carter must redefine the two most important relationships in his life. Troy struggles to understand why Geoff and Carter want this with him now, after years of watching from the outside. And Saul has to create a whole new definition of family.

Can they all break the rules again and become something more special than they can even imagine?

FIND OUT MORE
or Buy on Amazon

Interested in learning more about BA's cowboys and Jodi's gentlemen? Want free fiction and news? Join our newsletters!

What's Up with Jodi
http://bit.ly/whatsupjodi

Spurs and Shifters
https://lp.constantcontact.com/su/A9CRUzp/baandjulia

ABOUT JODI

JODI takes herself way too seriously and has been known to randomly break out in song. Her men are imperfect but genuine, stubborn but likable, often kinky, and frequently their own worst enemies. They are characters you can't help but fall in love with while they stumble along the path to their happily ever after. For those looking to get on her good side, Jodi's addictions include nonfat lattes, Malbec and tequila any way you pour it.

Website: jodipayne.net
Newsletter: http://bit.ly/whatsupjodi
All Jodi's Social Links: linktr.ee/jodipayne

Hey, y'all!

We want to thank you for giving Breaking the Rules a try and we hope you enjoyed the story. If you can spare a few minutes to post a review at the eBook website where you made your purchase, we'd very much appreciate it!

Don't forget to "like" our Facebook pages and groups to keep up with all the news--new releases, sales announcements, giveaways, sneak peeks-- and of course the rodeo pictures, coffee memes and just general fun. We'd love to have all y'all!

Yeehaw and thanks for reading!

BA & Jodi

ABOUT BA

Texan to the bone and an unrepentant Daddy's Girl, BA Tortuga spends her days with her basset hounds, getting tattooed, texting her grandbabies, and eating Mexican food. When she's not doing that, she's writing. She spends her days off watching rodeo, knitting and surfing Pinterest in the name of research. BA's personal saviors include her wife, Julia Talbot, her best friends, and coffee. Lots of coffee. Really good coffee.

Having written everything from fist-fighting rednecks to hard-core cowboys to werewolves, BA does her damnedest to tell the stories of her heart, which was raised in Northeast Texas, but has heard the call of the high desert and lives in the Sandias. With books ranging from hard-hitting GLBT romance, to fiery ménages, to the most traditional of love stories, BA refuses to be pigeon-holed by anyone but the voices in her head.

BA loves to talk to her readers and can be found at http://batortuga.com/ and her newsletter signup link is http://bit.ly/BAJulianews

AVAILABLE FROM JODI & BA

The Cowboy and the Dom Trilogy

First Rodeo, Book One

Razor's Edge, Book Two

No Ghosts, Book Three

The Soldier and the Angel, a Cowboy and Dom Novel

Sin Deep, a Cowboy and Dom Novel

East Meets Westerns

(single titles)

Wrecked

Window Dressing

Flying Blind

Special Delivery, A Wrecked Holiday Novel

Temptation Ranch

The Higher Elevation Series

Heart of a Cowboy

Land of Enchantment

Keeping Promises

Bigger Than Us

The Triskelion Series

Breaking the Rules

Making a Mark

Making the Rules

Les's Bar Series

Just Dex

Hide Bound

The Lone Star Series

Tending Tyler

Roped In

The Collaborations Series

Refraction

Syncopation

Puzzles Series

Cryptic